ALSO FROM JOE BOOKS

Disney
DESCENDANTS
Wicked World
Cinestory Comic
Volume 4

JOE BOOKS LTD

Published simultaneously in the United States and Canada by
Joe Books Ltd, 489 College Street, Toronto, ON M6G 1A5

www.joebooks.com

First Joe Books Edition: April 2017

ISBN 978-1-77275-473-5 (paperback edition)
ISBN 978-1-77275-554-1 (ebook edition)

"Better Together"
Words and Music by Jack Kugell, Hanna Jones and Matthew Wong
© 2017 Walt Disney Music Company (ASCAP), Wonderland Music
Company, Inc. (BMI) and Five Hundred South Songs (SESAC)
All Rights Reserved. Used With Permission.

Adaptation, design, lettering, layout, and editing by First Image.

Library and Archives Canada Cataloguing in Publication
information is available upon request

Printed and bound in Canada
3 5 7 9 10 8 6 4

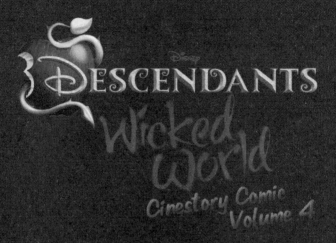

Disney

Descendants Wicked World

Cinestory Comic Volume 4

Disney Descendants Wicked World Season 2 Shorts

Written by: Scott Peterson

Director & Executive Producer: Eric Fogel

Executive Producer: Carin Davis

CHAPTER 26: EVIL AMONG US

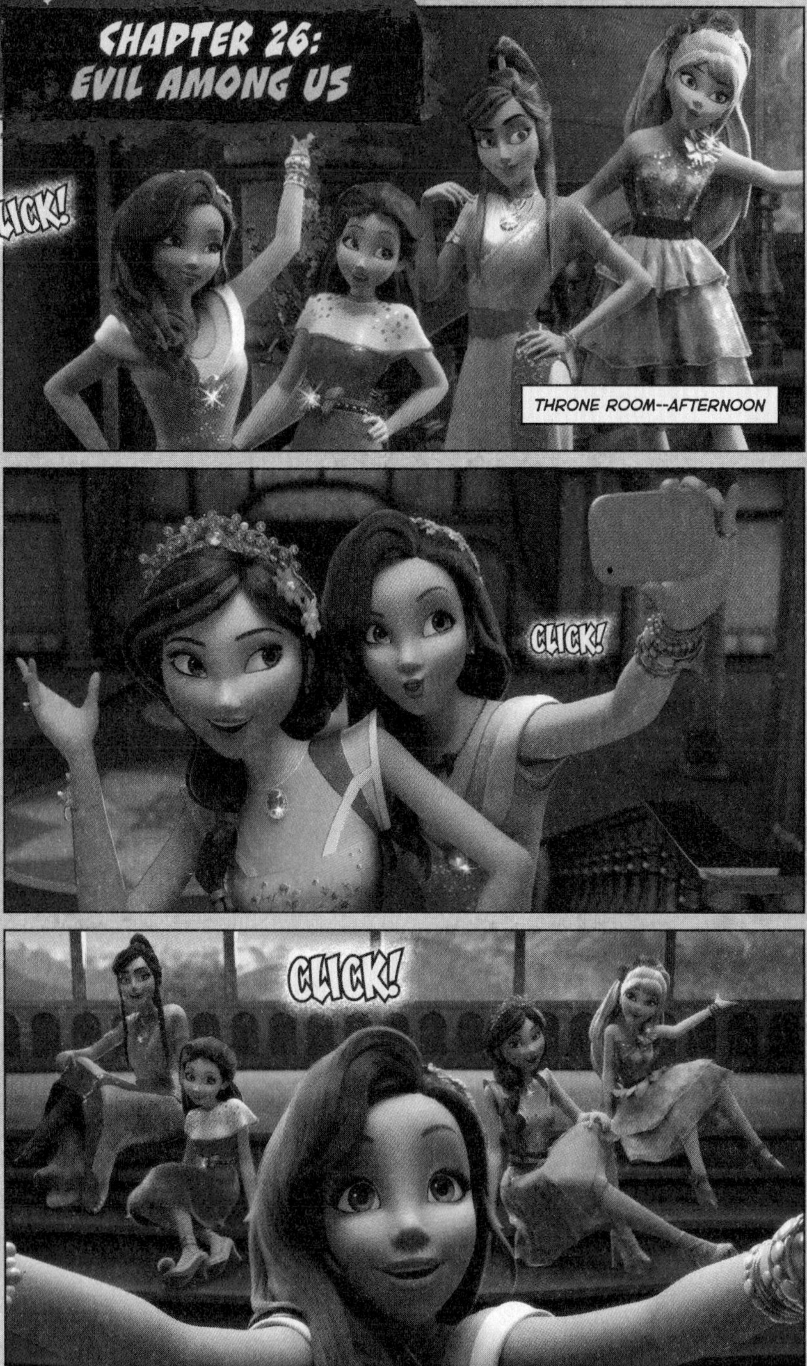
CLICK!
THRONE ROOM--AFTERNOON
CLICK!
CLICK!

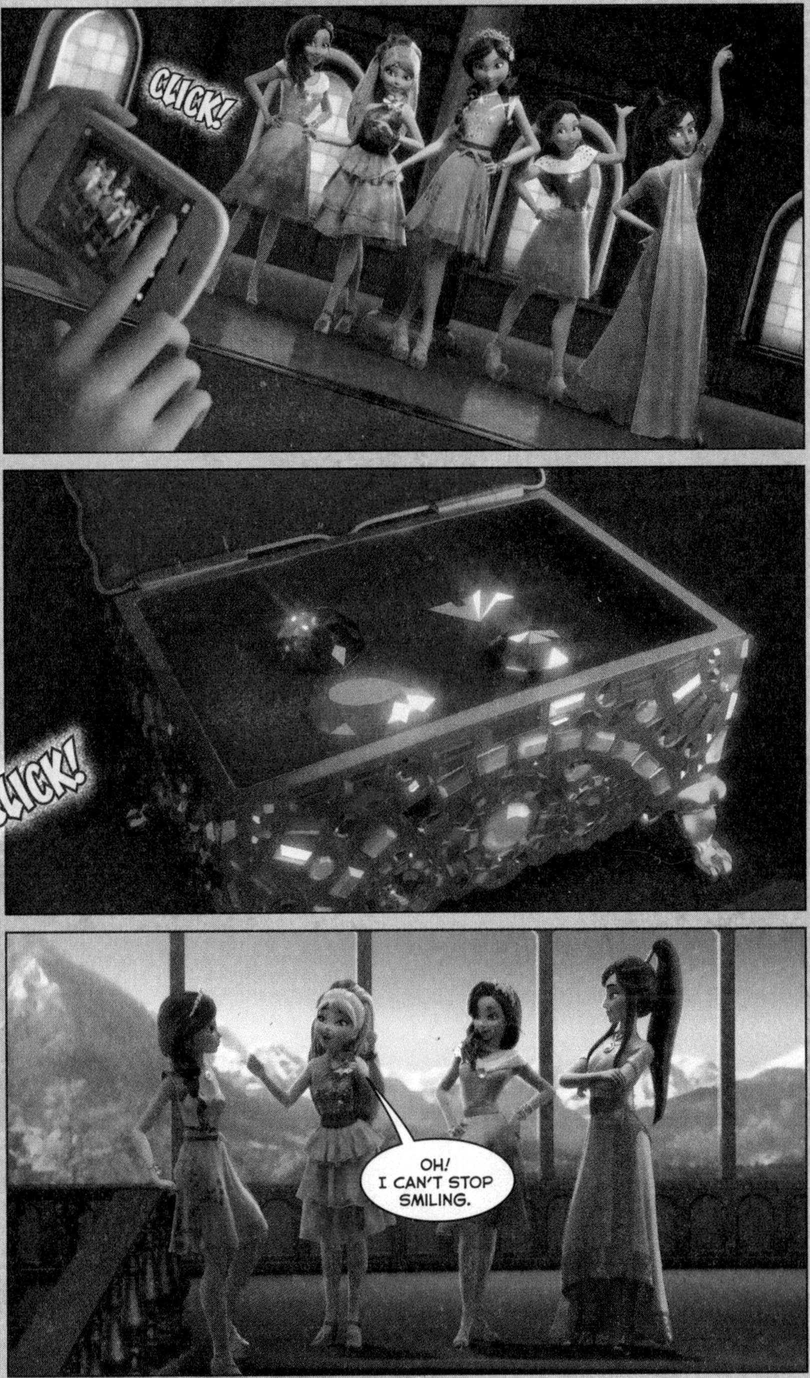
CLICK!
CLICK!
OH!
I CAN'T STOP
SMILING.

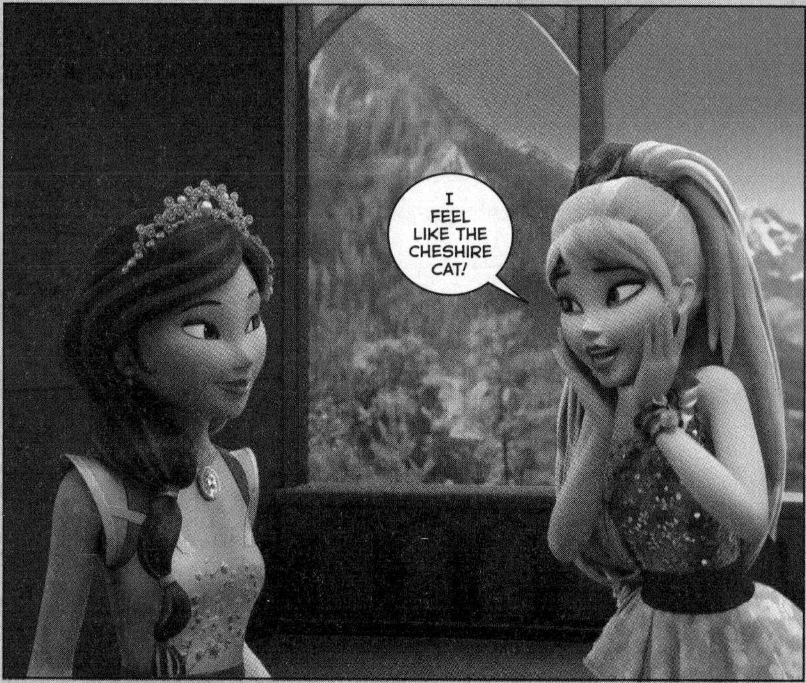
I FEEL LIKE THE CHESHIRE CAT!

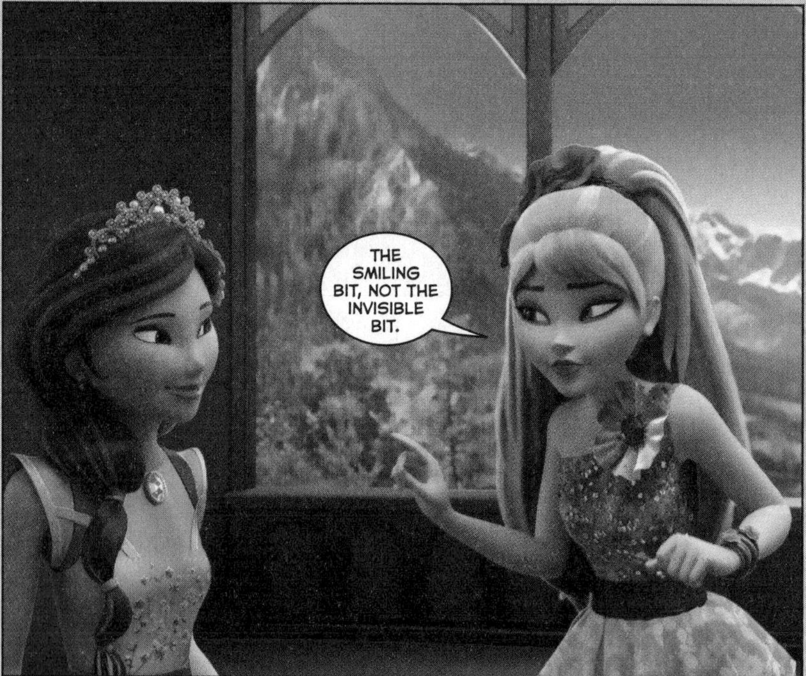
THE SMILING BIT, NOT THE INVISIBLE BIT.

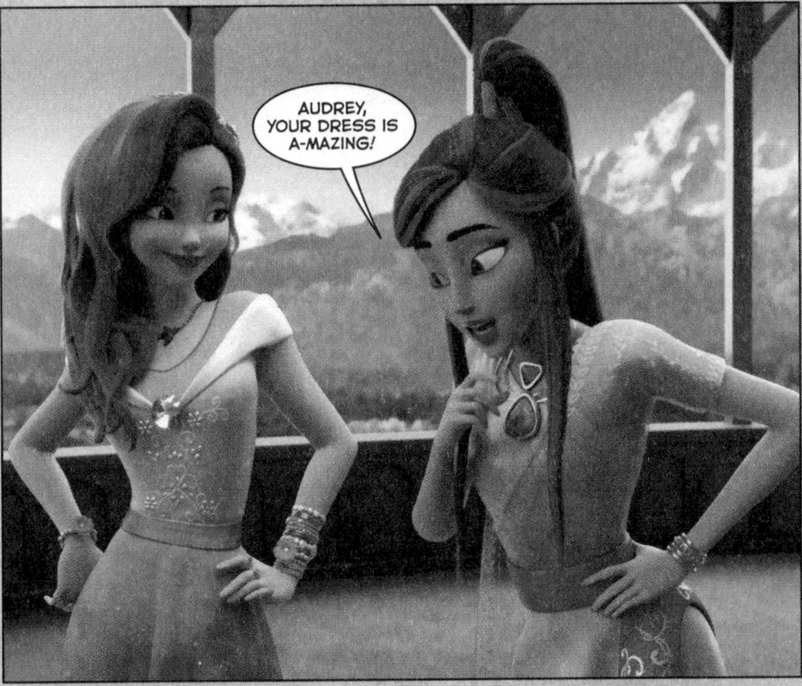
AUDREY, YOUR DRESS IS A-MAZING!

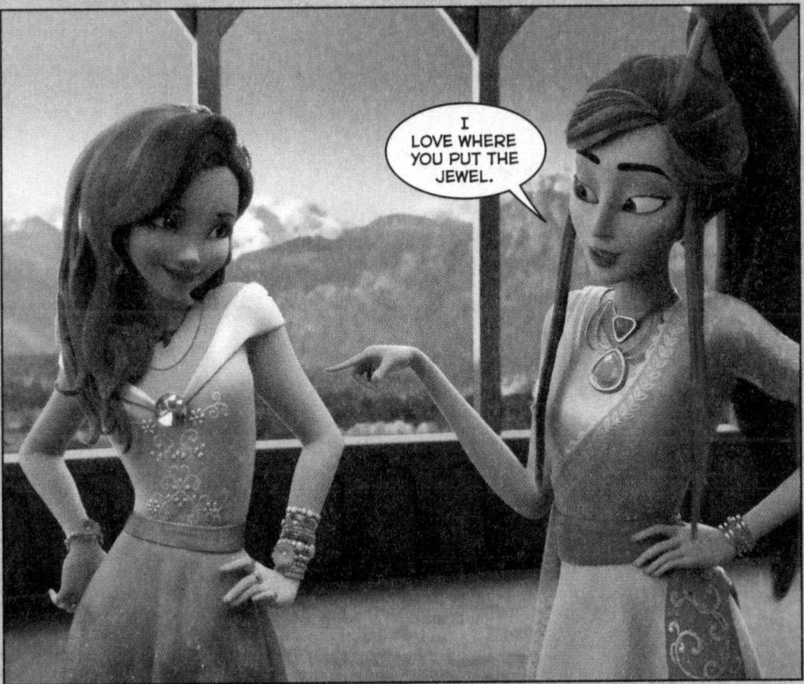
I LOVE WHERE YOU PUT THE JEWEL.

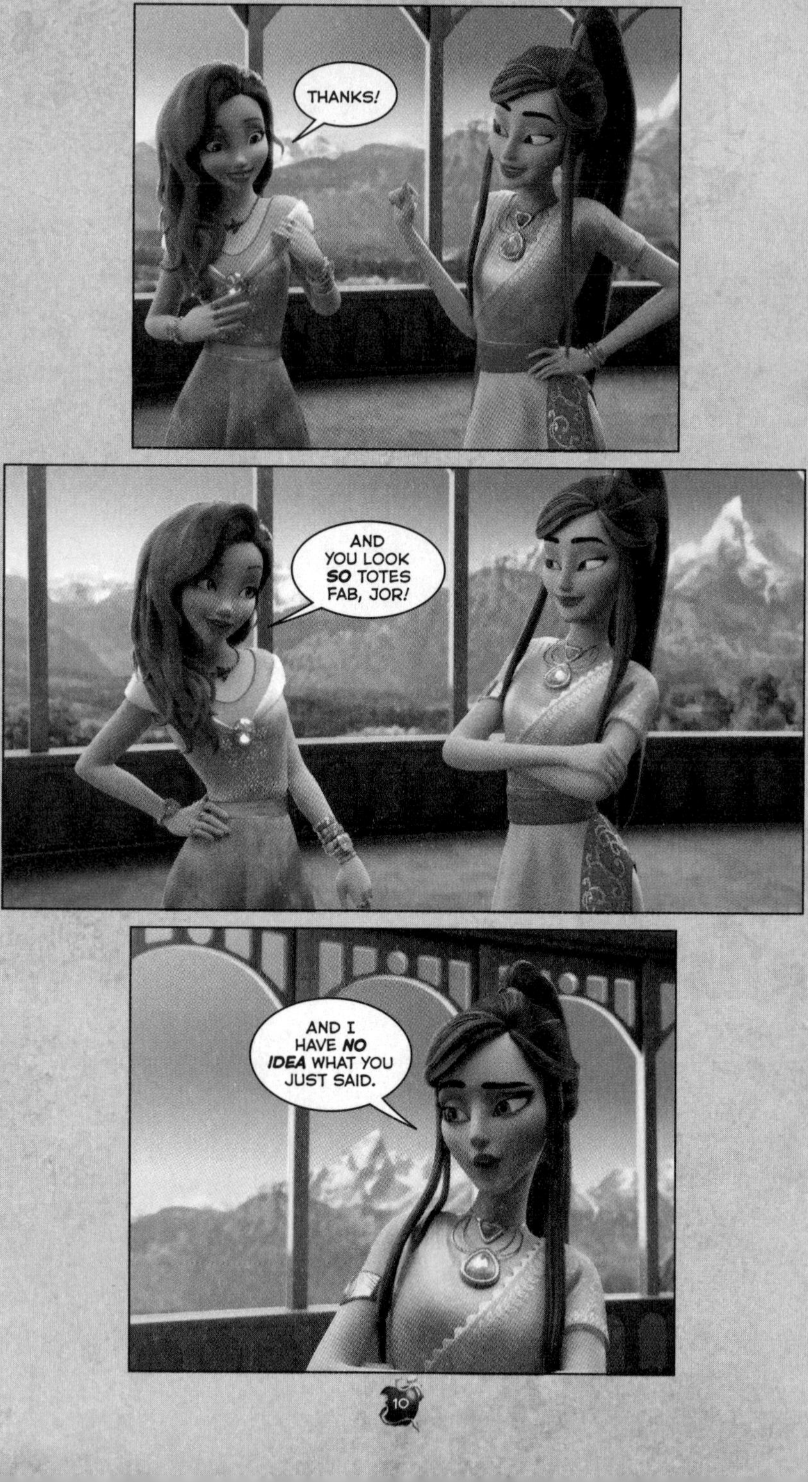
THANKS!
AND YOU LOOK **SO** TOTES FAB, JOR!
AND I HAVE ***NO IDEA*** WHAT YOU JUST SAID.

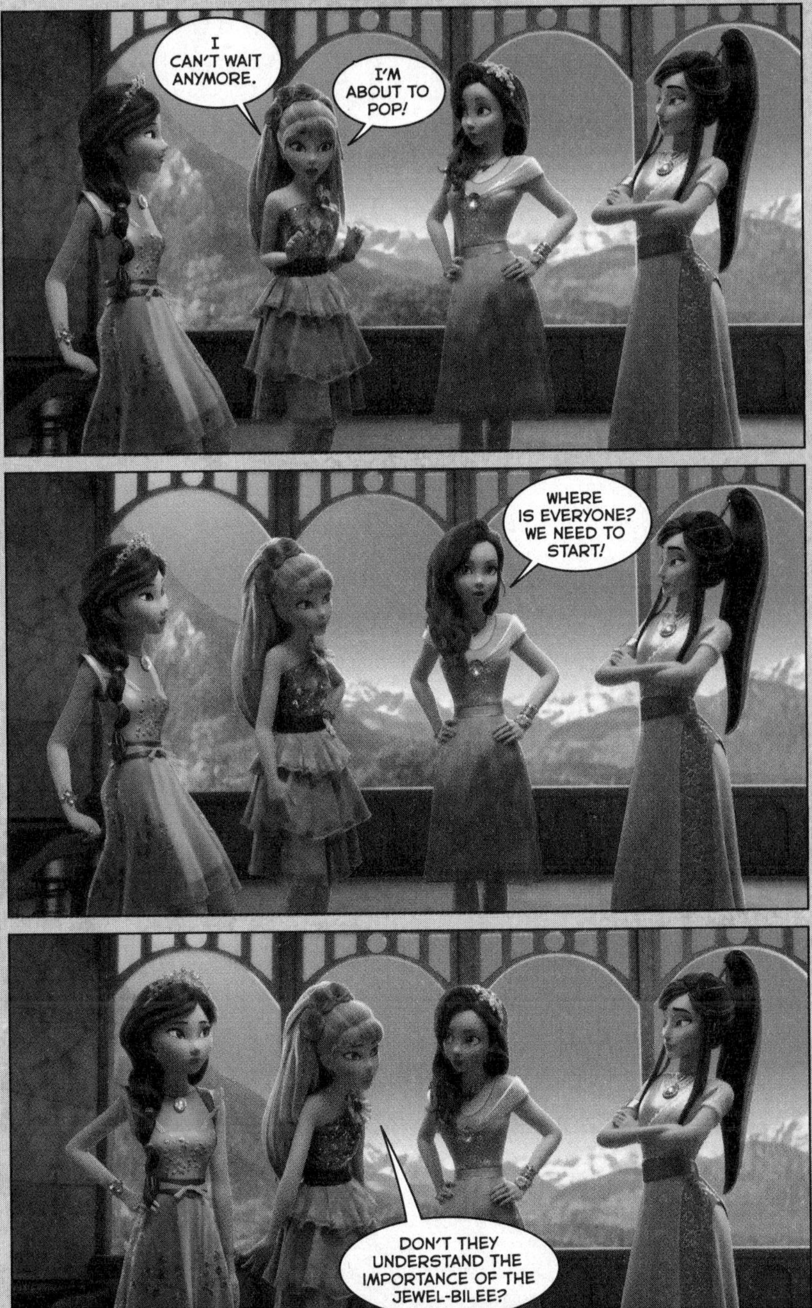
I CAN'T WAIT ANYMORE.
I'M ABOUT TO POP!
WHERE IS EVERYONE? WE NEED TO START!
DON'T THEY UNDERSTAND THE IMPORTANCE OF THE JEWEL-BILEE?

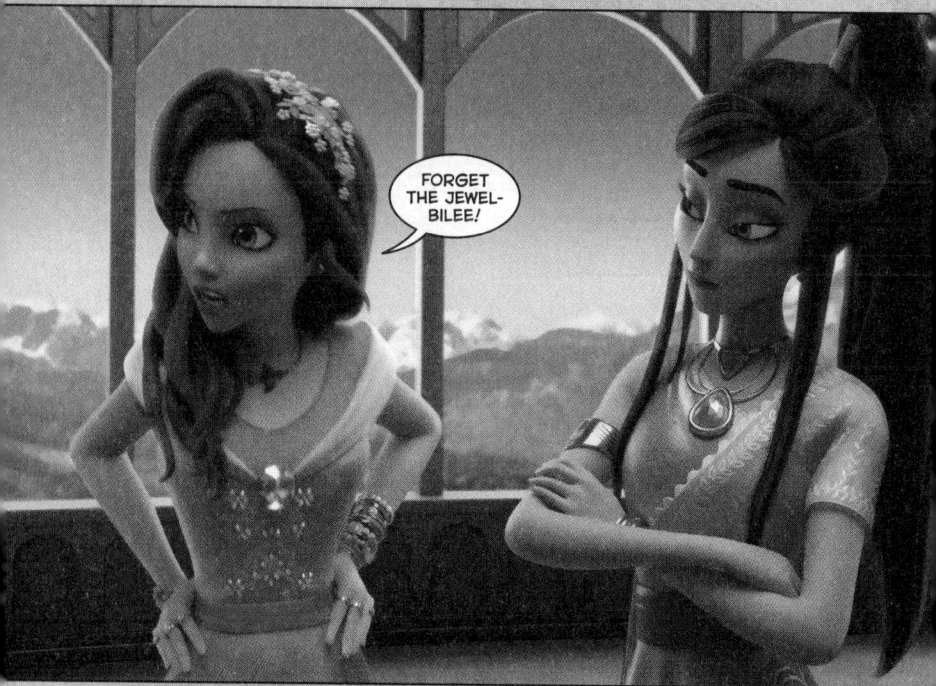
FORGET THE JEWEL-BILEE!

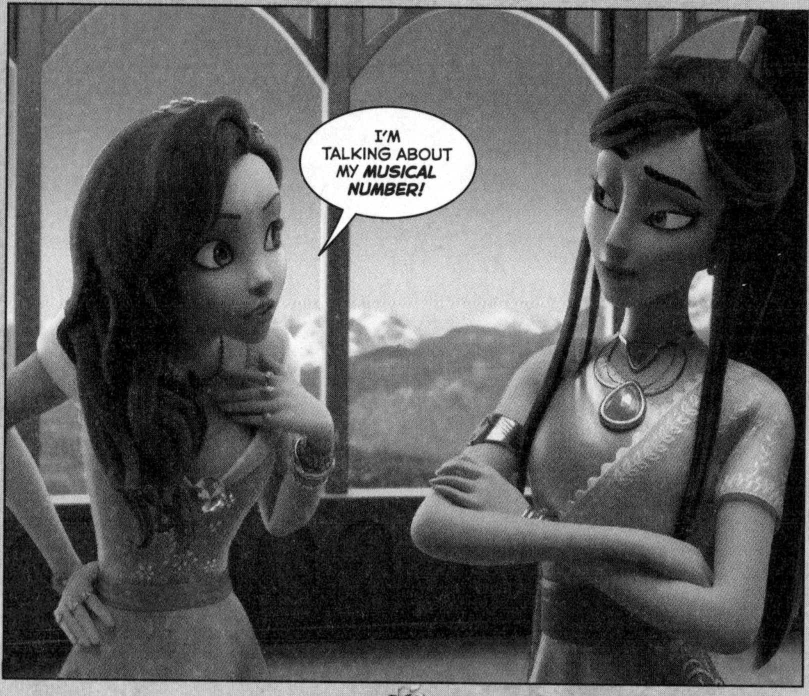
I'M TALKING ABOUT MY MUSICAL NUMBER!

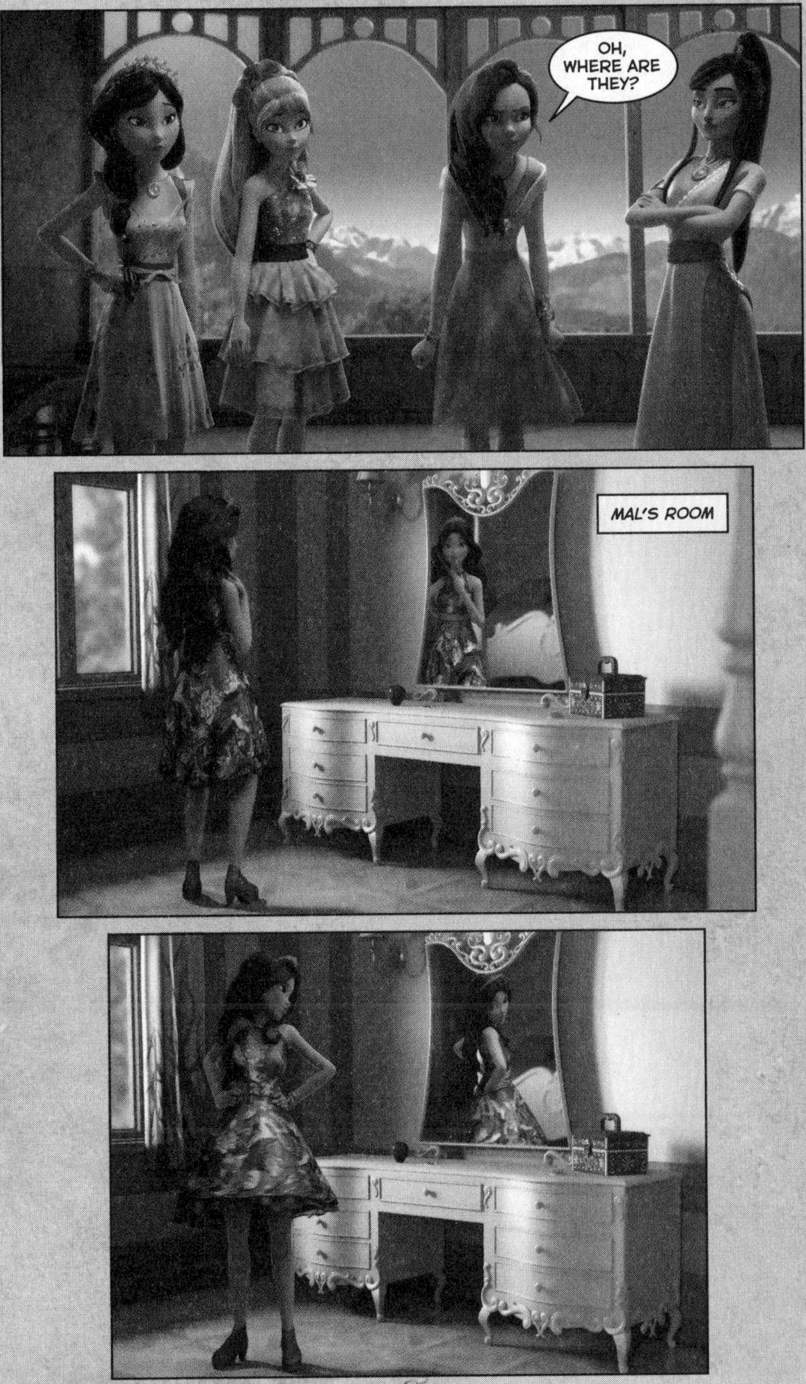
OH, WHERE ARE THEY?
MAL'S ROOM

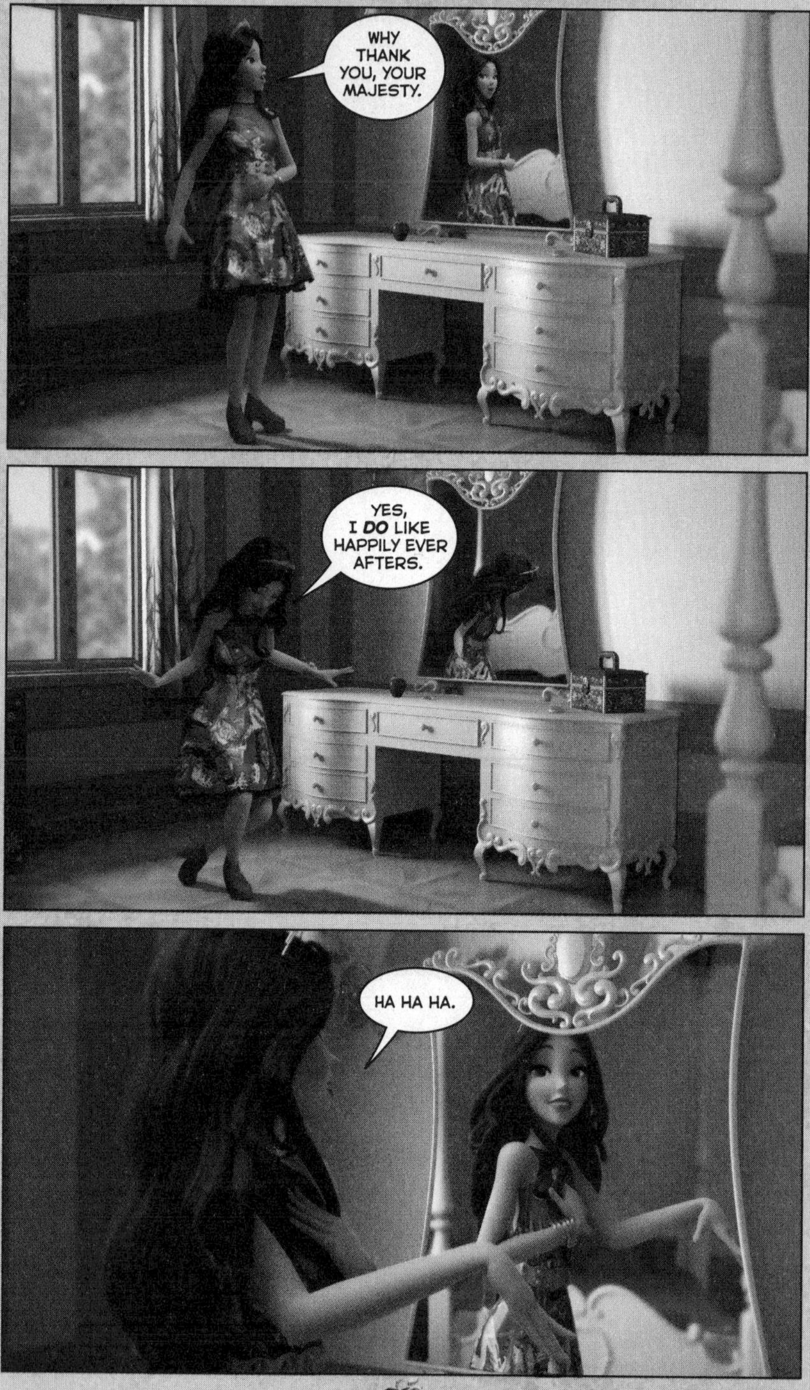
WHY THANK YOU, YOUR MAJESTY.
YES, I DO LIKE HAPPILY EVER AFTERS.
HA HA HA.

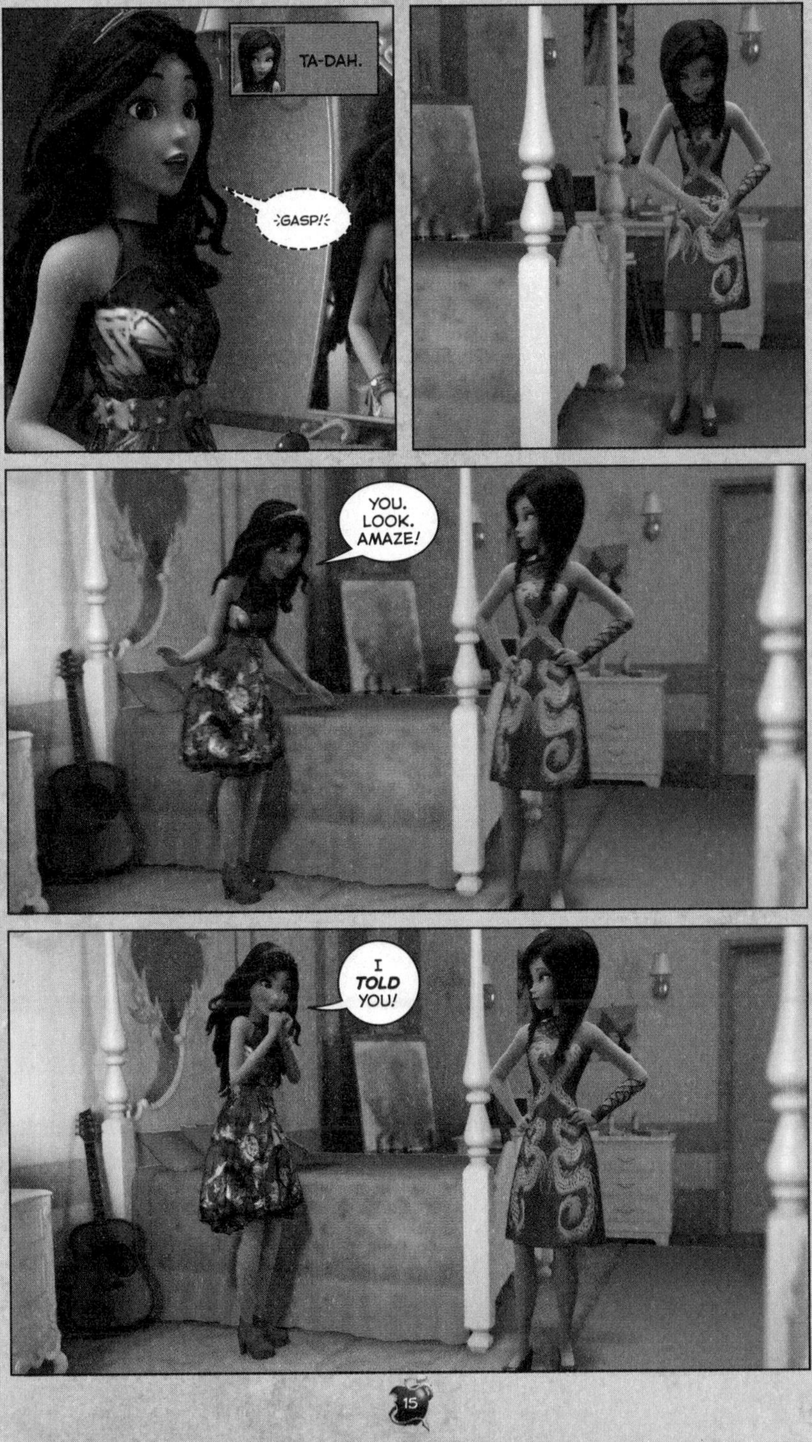
TA-DAH.
GASP!
YOU. LOOK. AMAZE!
I TOLD YOU!

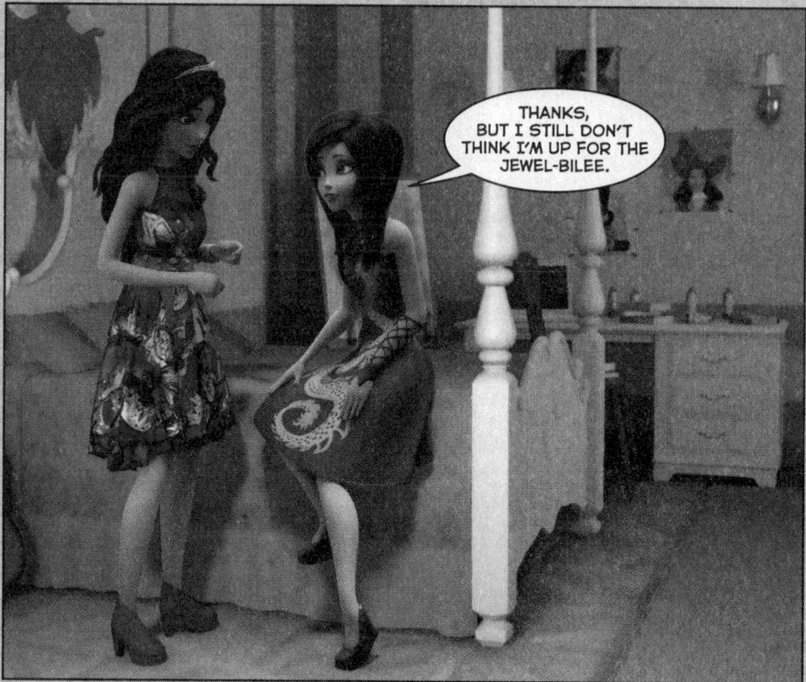
THANKS, BUT I STILL DON'T THINK I'M UP FOR THE JEWEL-BILEE.

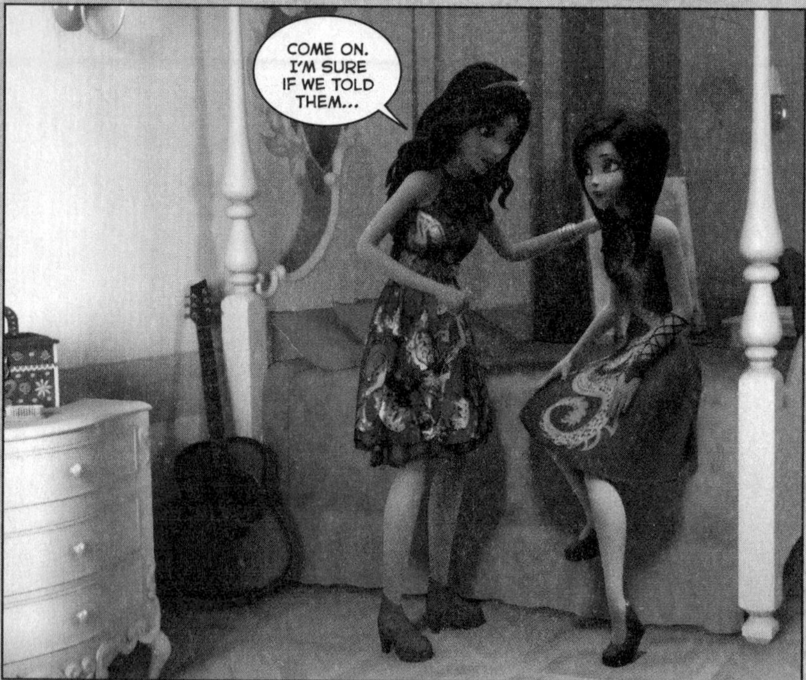
COME ON. I'M SURE IF WE TOLD THEM...

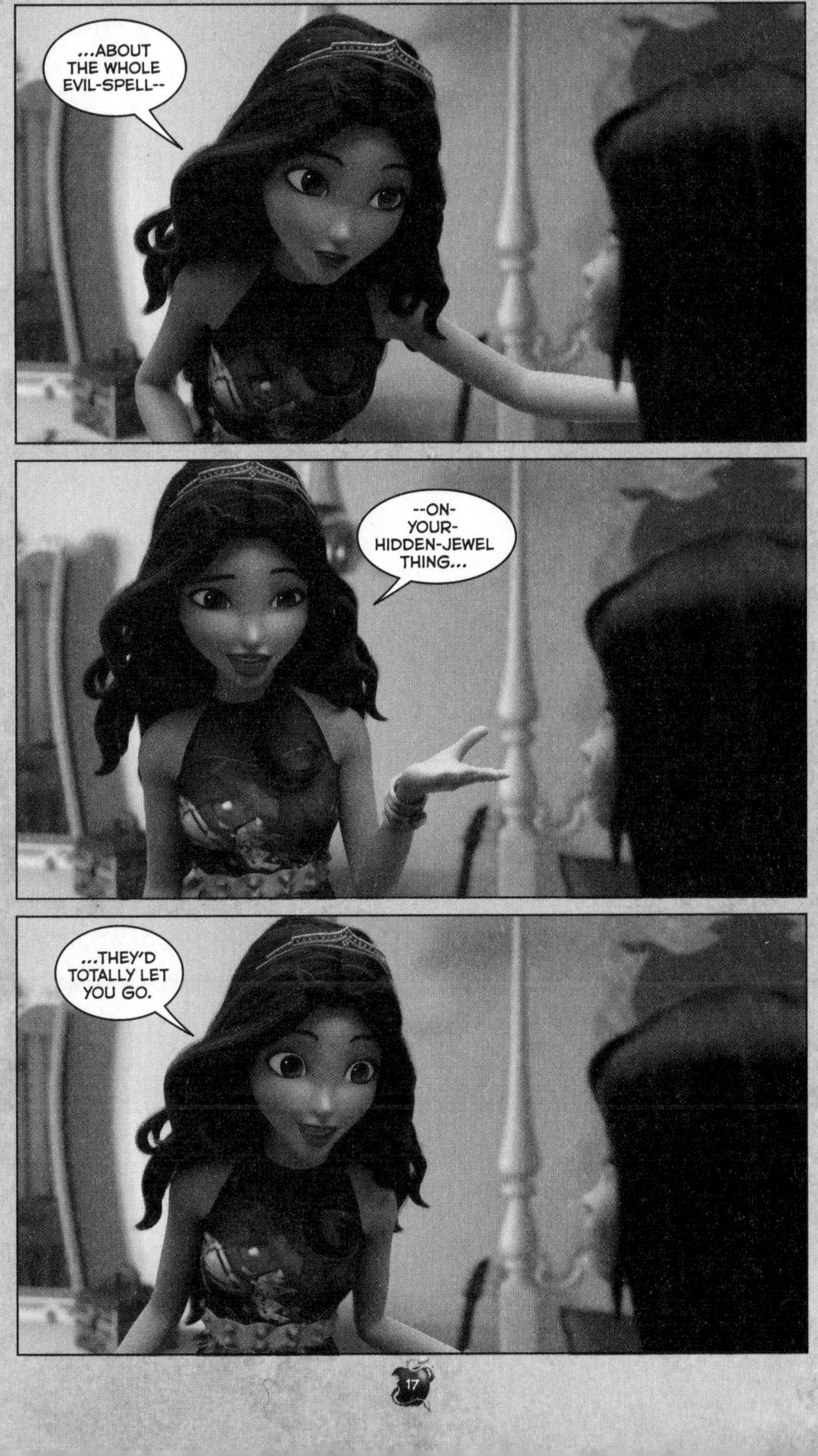
...ABOUT THE WHOLE EVIL-SPELL--
--ON-YOUR-HIDDEN-JEWEL THING...
...THEY'D TOTALLY LET YOU GO.

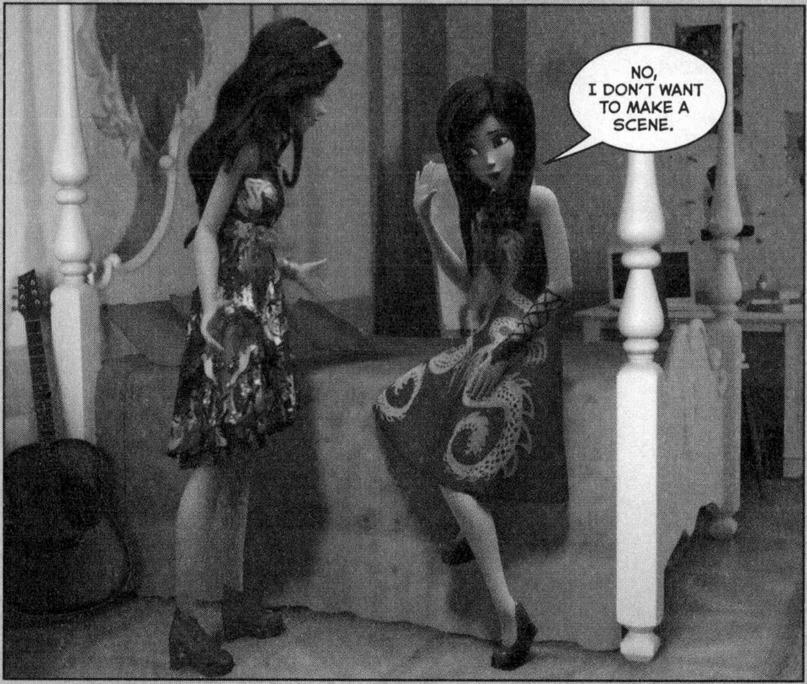
NO, I DON'T WANT TO MAKE A SCENE.

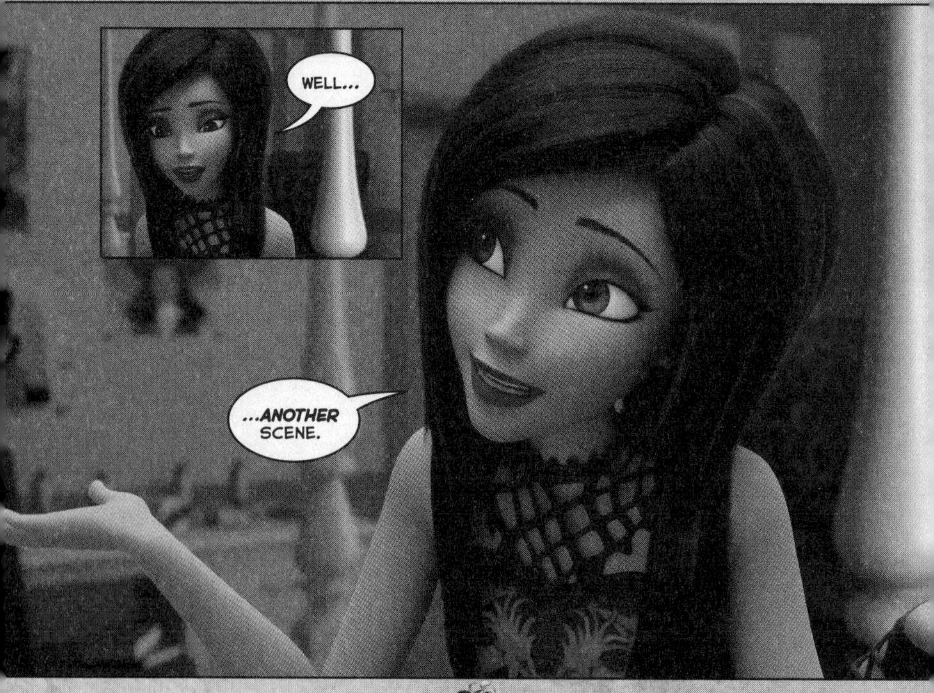
WELL...
...ANOTHER SCENE.

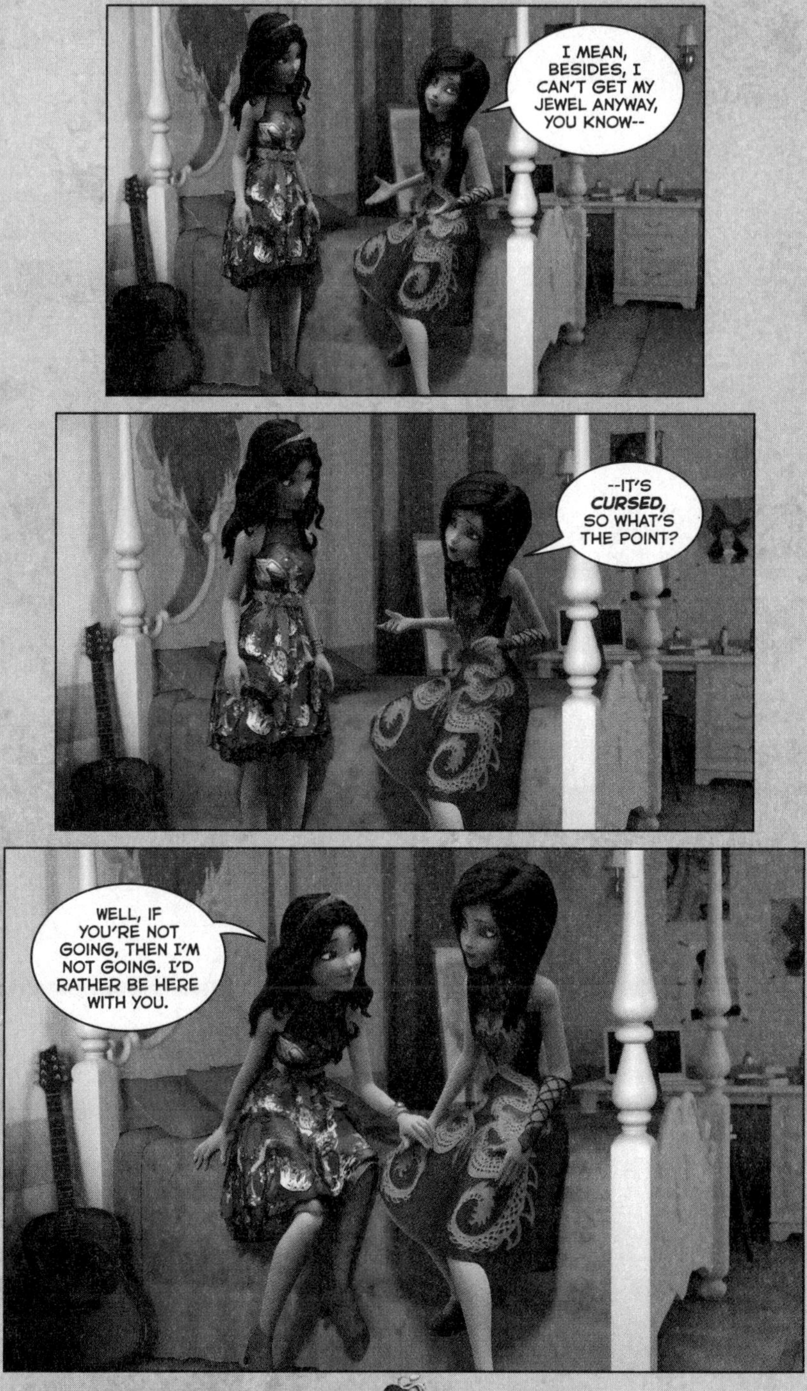
I MEAN, BESIDES, I CAN'T GET MY JEWEL ANYWAY, YOU KNOW--
--IT'S *CURSED,* SO WHAT'S THE POINT?
WELL, IF YOU'RE NOT GOING, THEN I'M NOT GOING. I'D RATHER BE HERE WITH YOU.

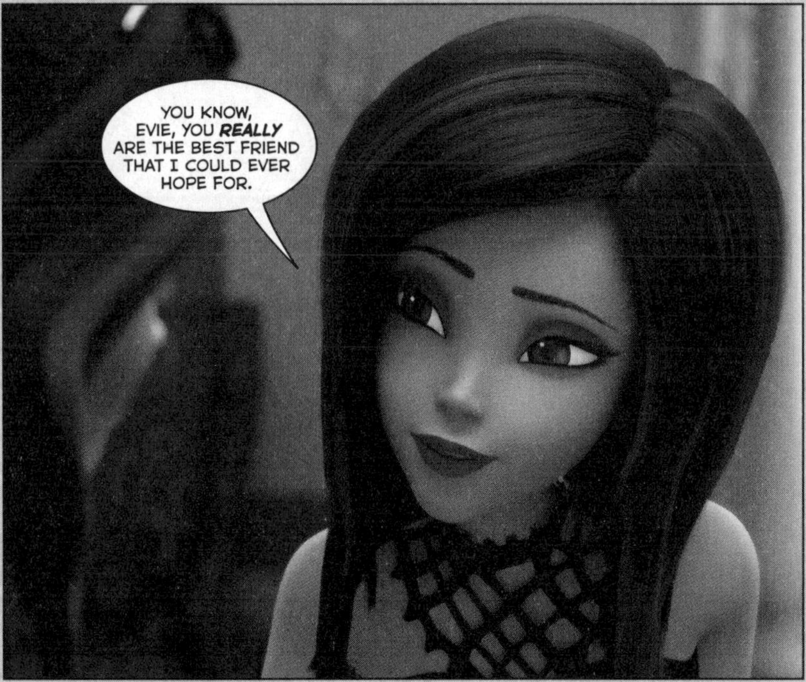
YOU KNOW, EVIE, YOU REALLY ARE THE BEST FRIEND THAT I COULD EVER HOPE FOR.

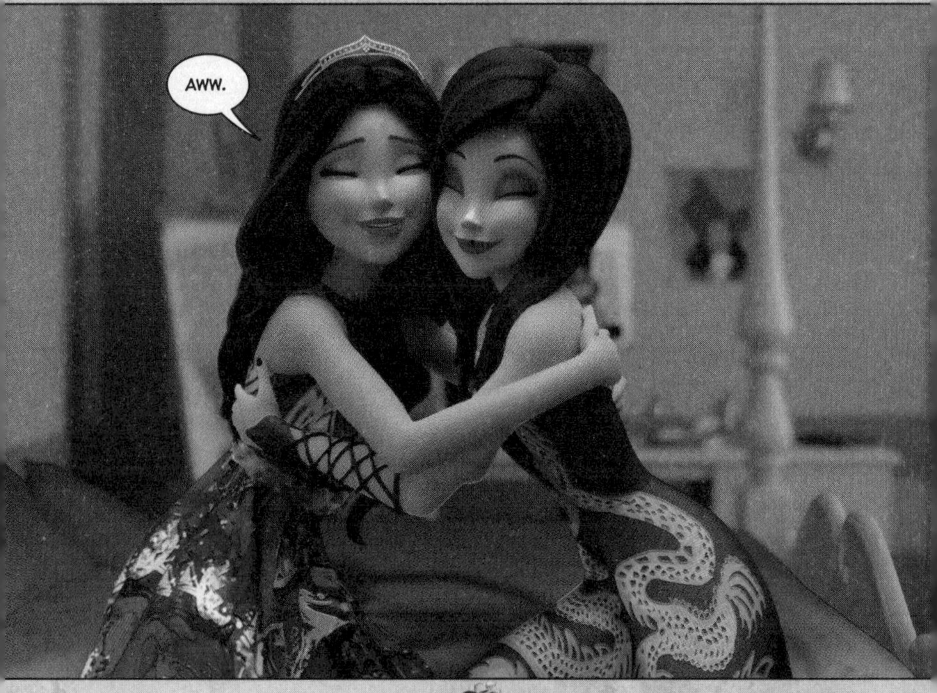
AWW.

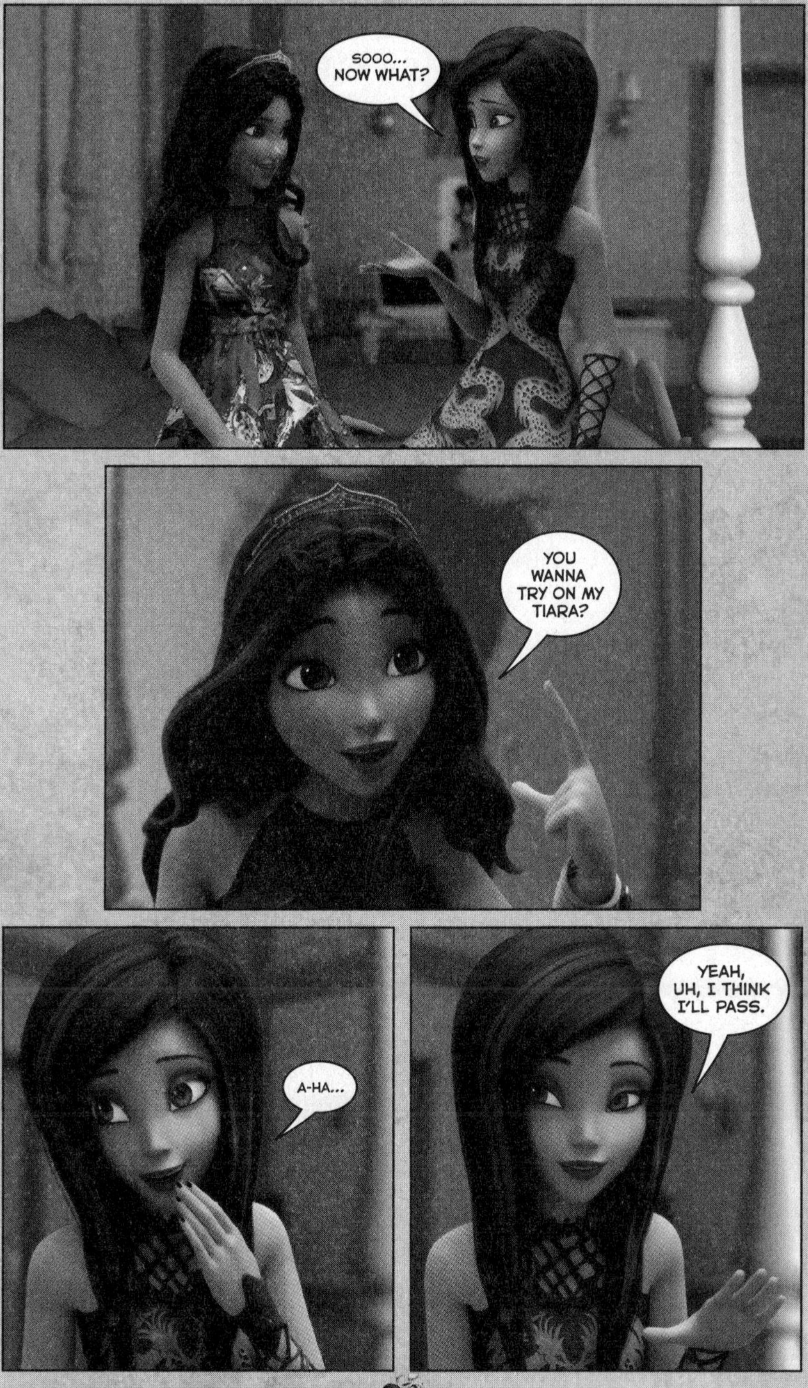
SOOO...
NOW WHAT?
YOU WANNA TRY ON MY TIARA?
A-HA...
YEAH, UH, I THINK I'LL PASS.

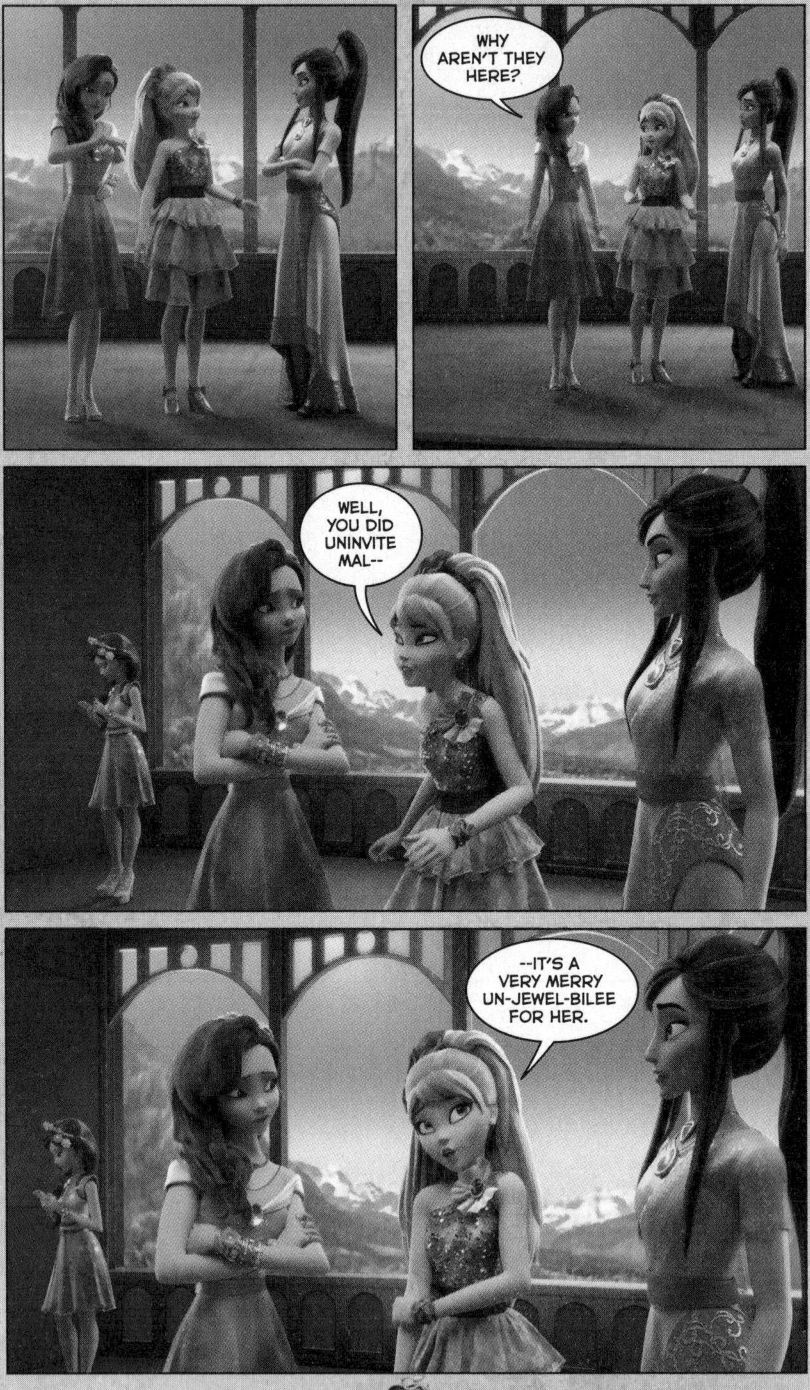
WHY AREN'T THEY HERE?
WELL, YOU DID UNINVITE MAL--
--IT'S A VERY MERRY UN-JEWEL-BILEE FOR HER.

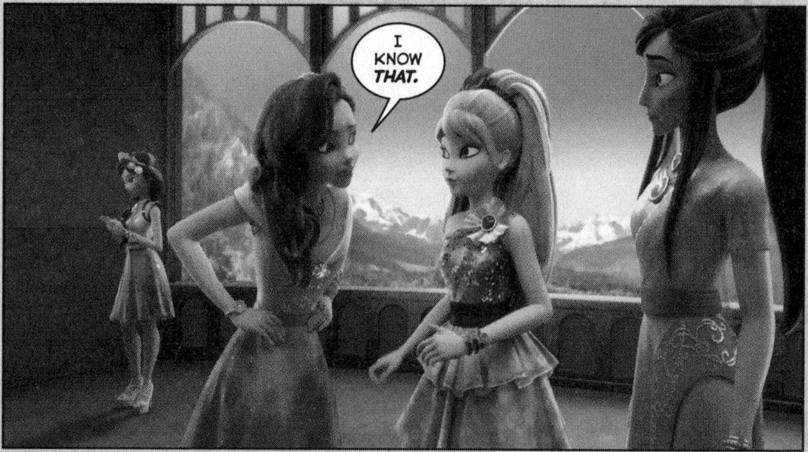
I KNOW *THAT.*

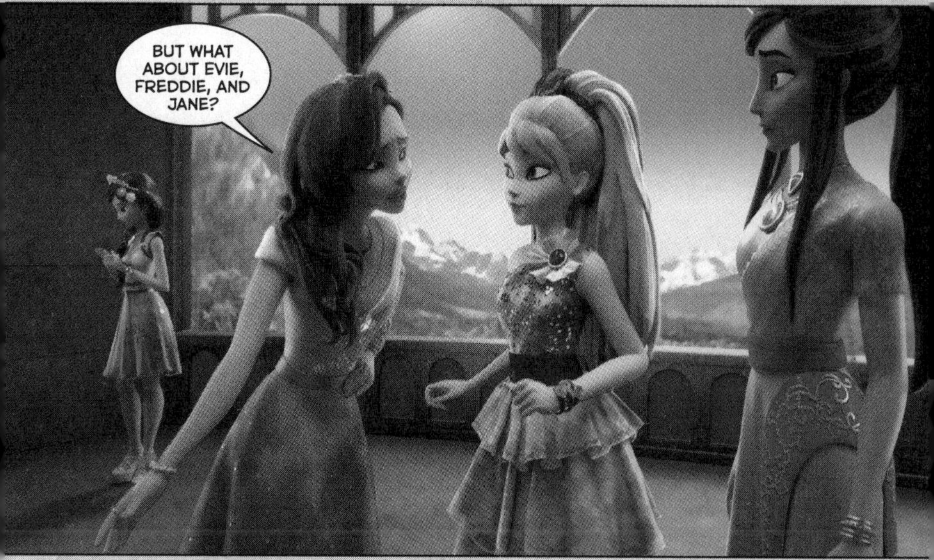
BUT WHAT ABOUT EVIE, FREDDIE, AND JANE?

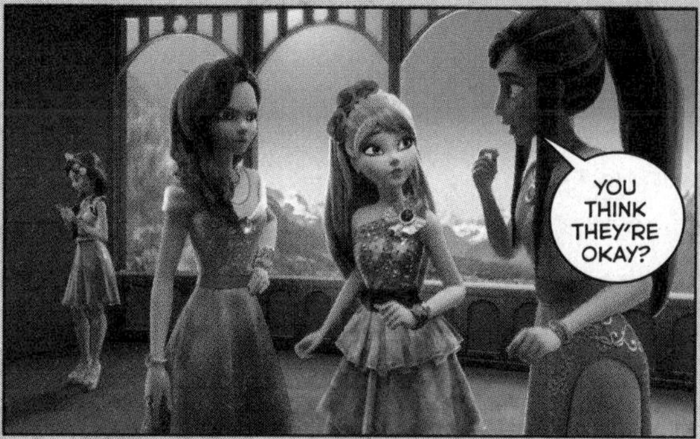
YOU THINK THEY'RE OKAY?

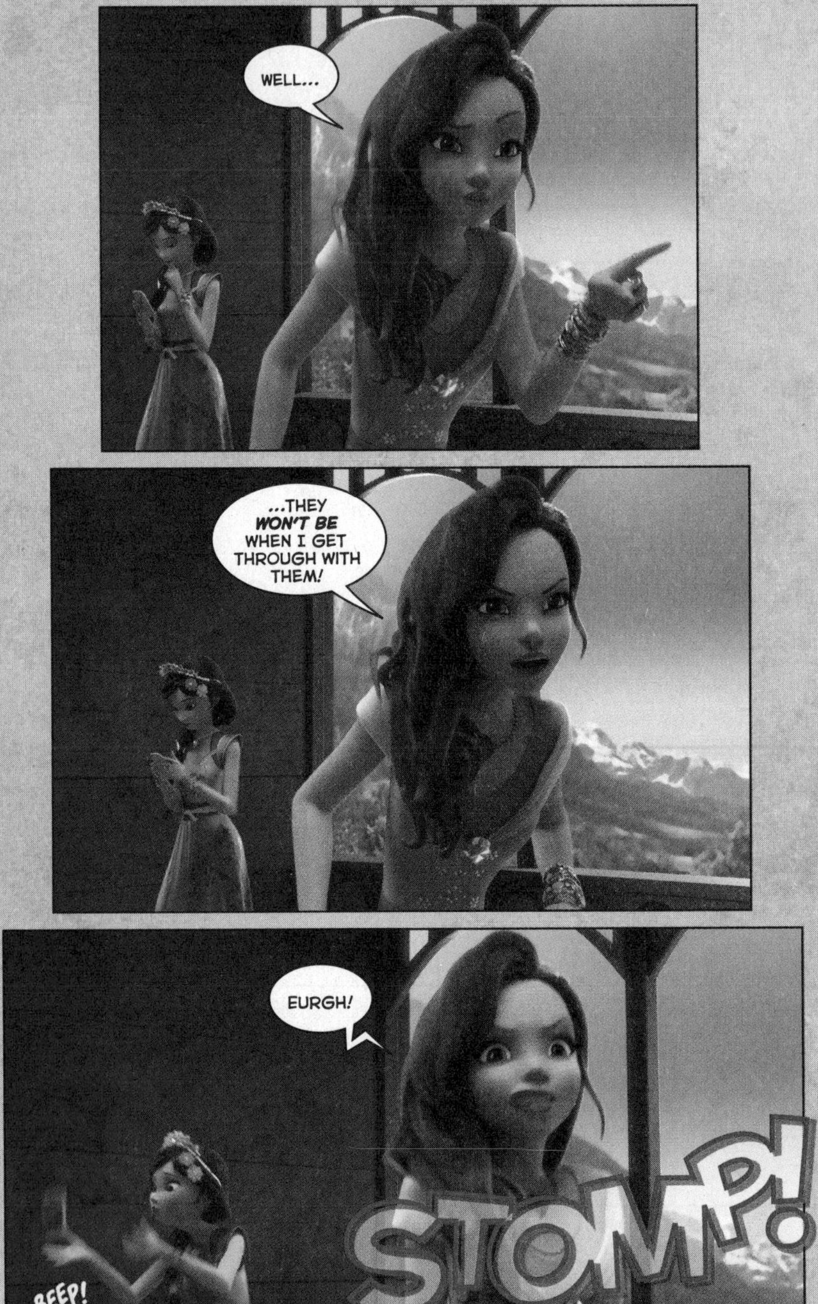
WELL...
...THEY *WON'T BE* WHEN I GET THROUGH WITH THEM!
EURGH!
STOMP!
BEEP!

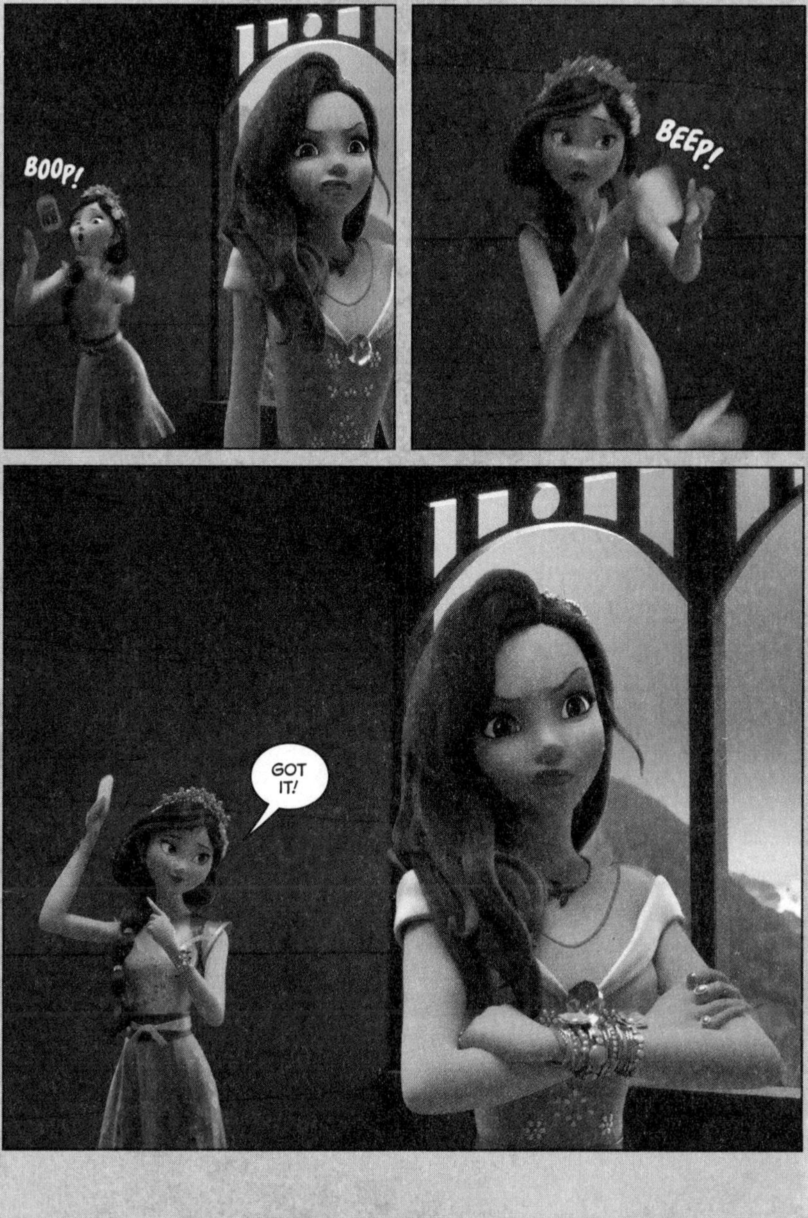
BOOP!
BEEP!
GOT IT!

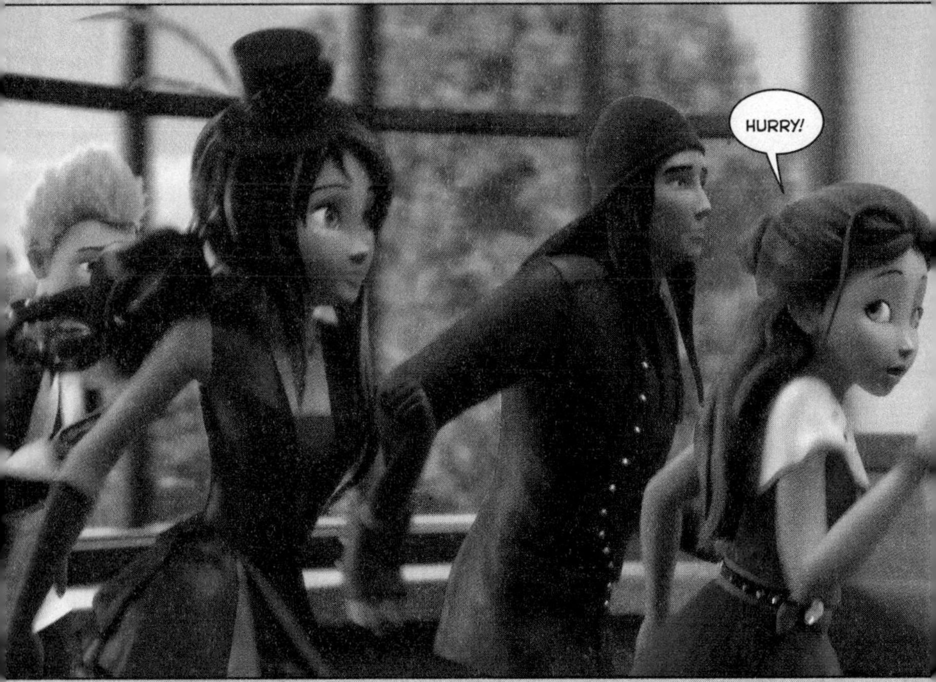
HURRY!

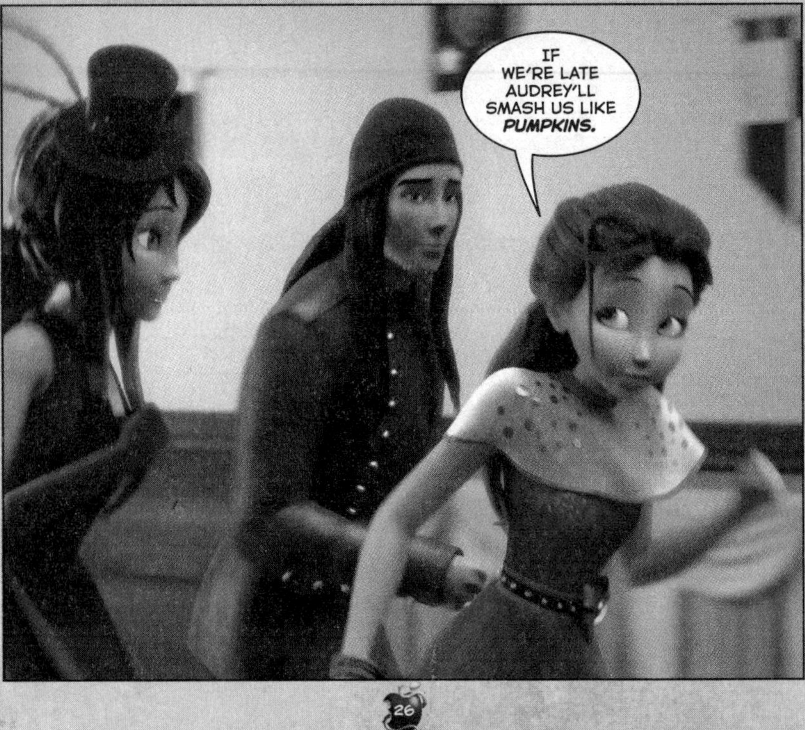
IF WE'RE LATE AUDREY'LL SMASH US LIKE *PUMPKINS.*

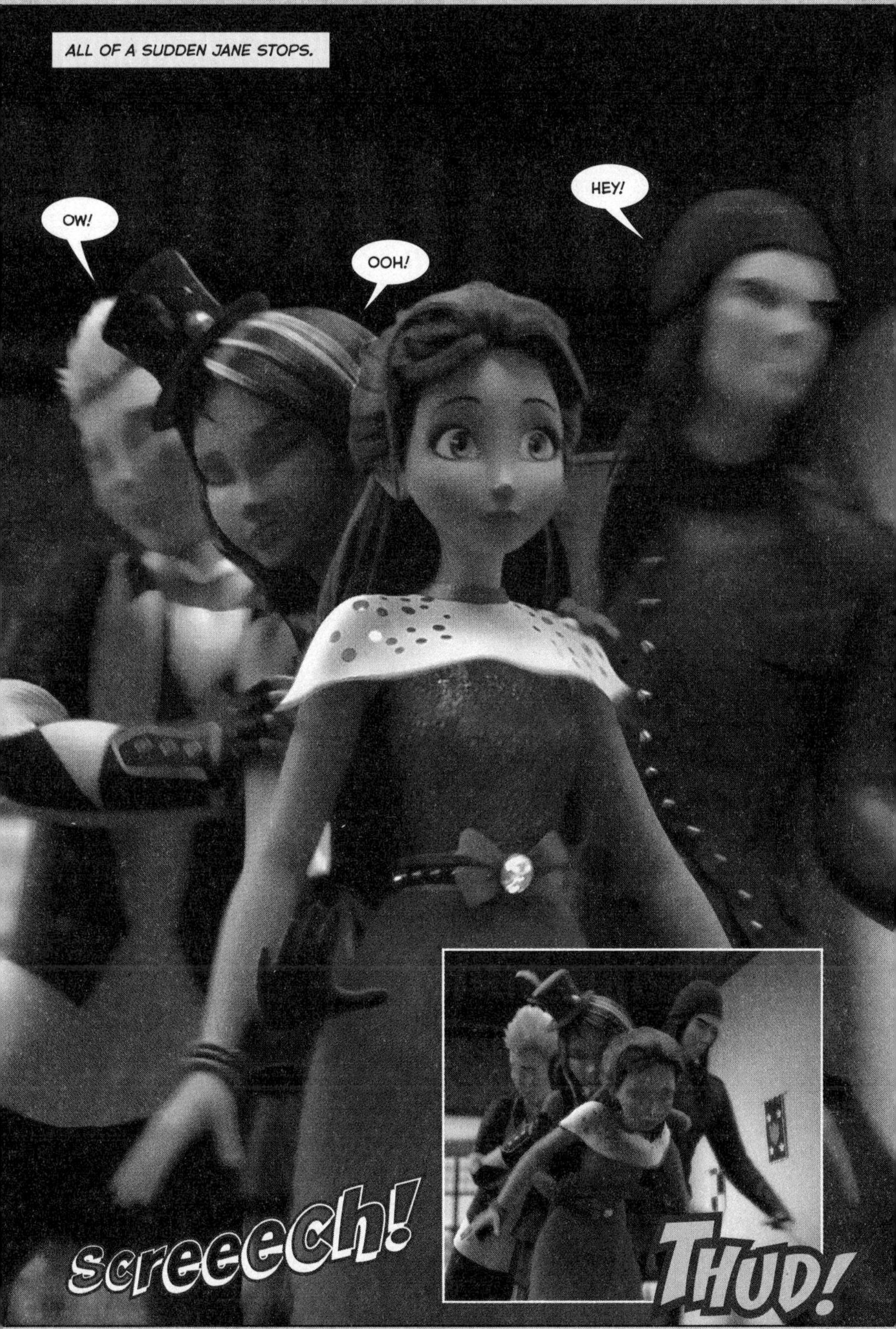
ALL OF A SUDDEN JANE STOPS.
OW!
OOH!
HEY!
SCREEECH!
THUD!

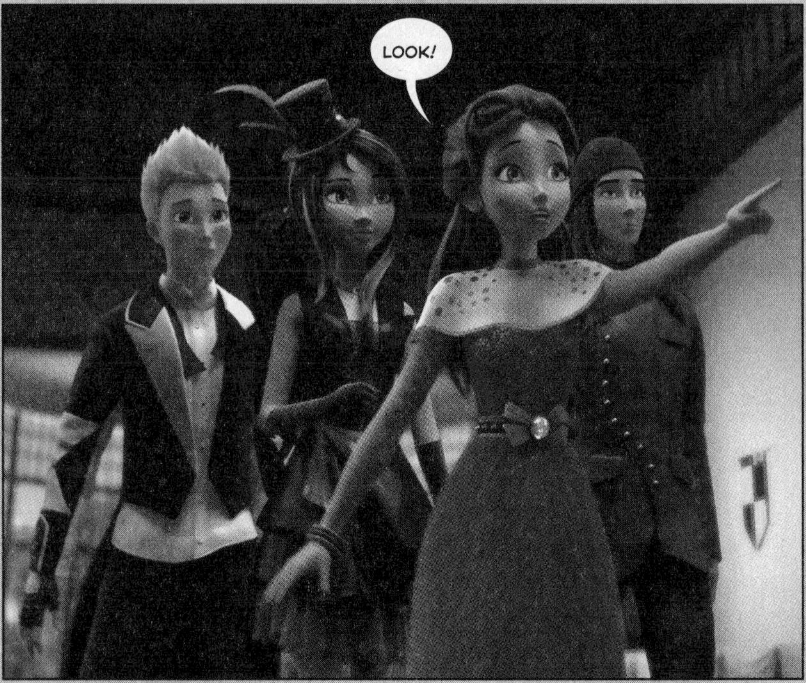
LOOK!

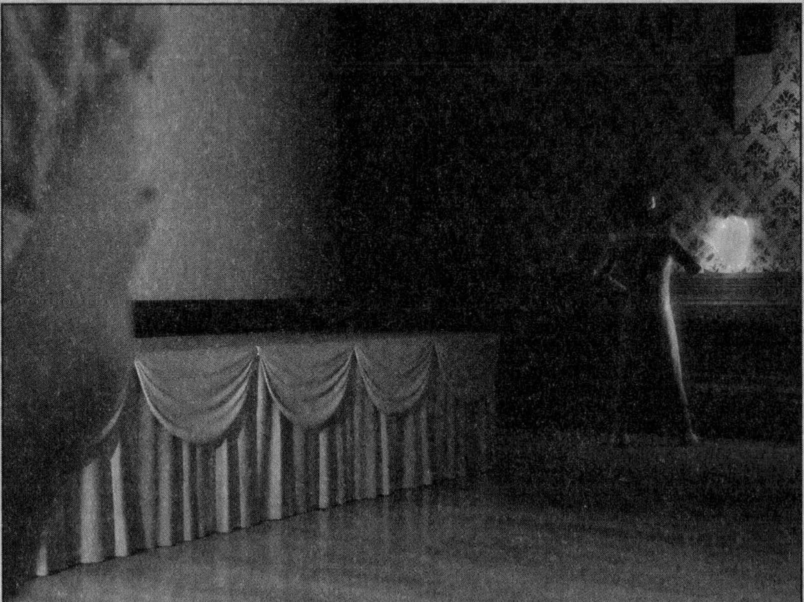

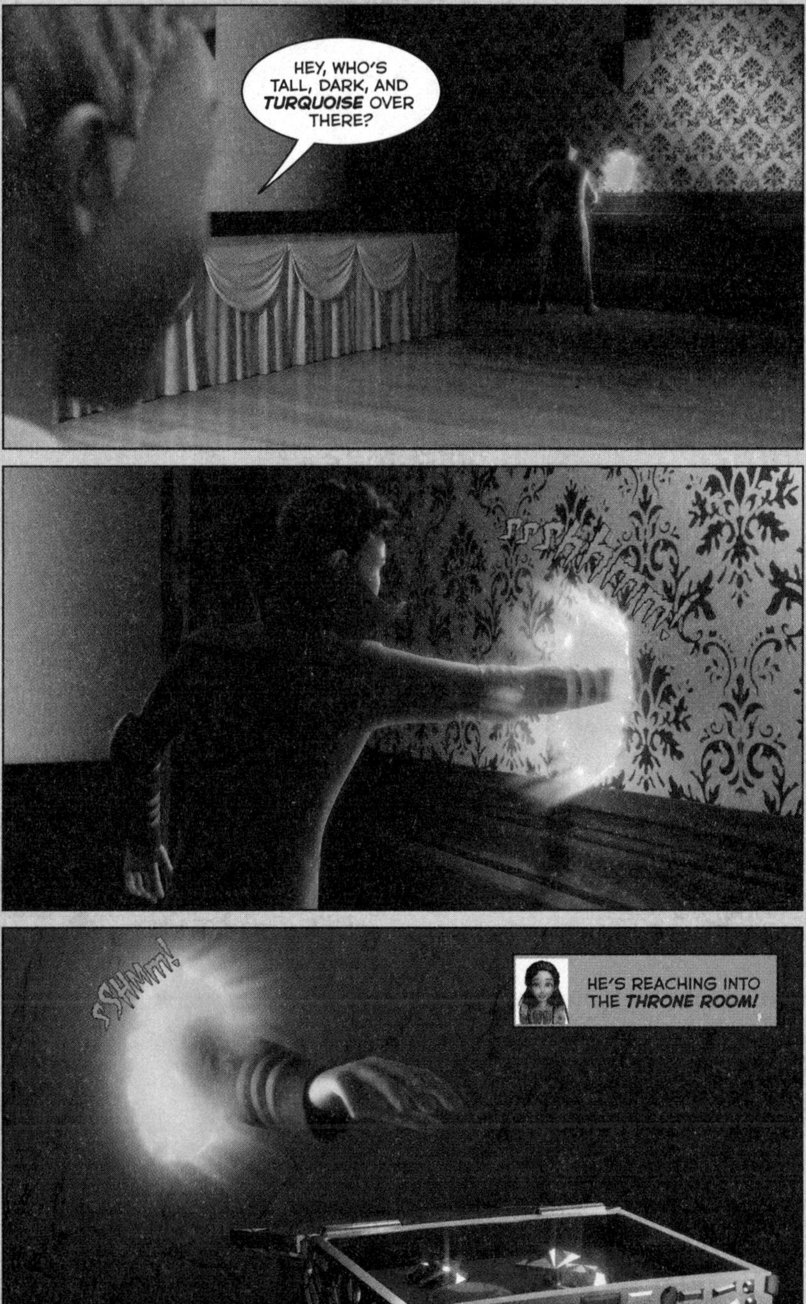
HEY, WHO'S TALL, DARK, AND *TURQUOISE* OVER THERE?
HE'S REACHING INTO THE *THRONE ROOM!*

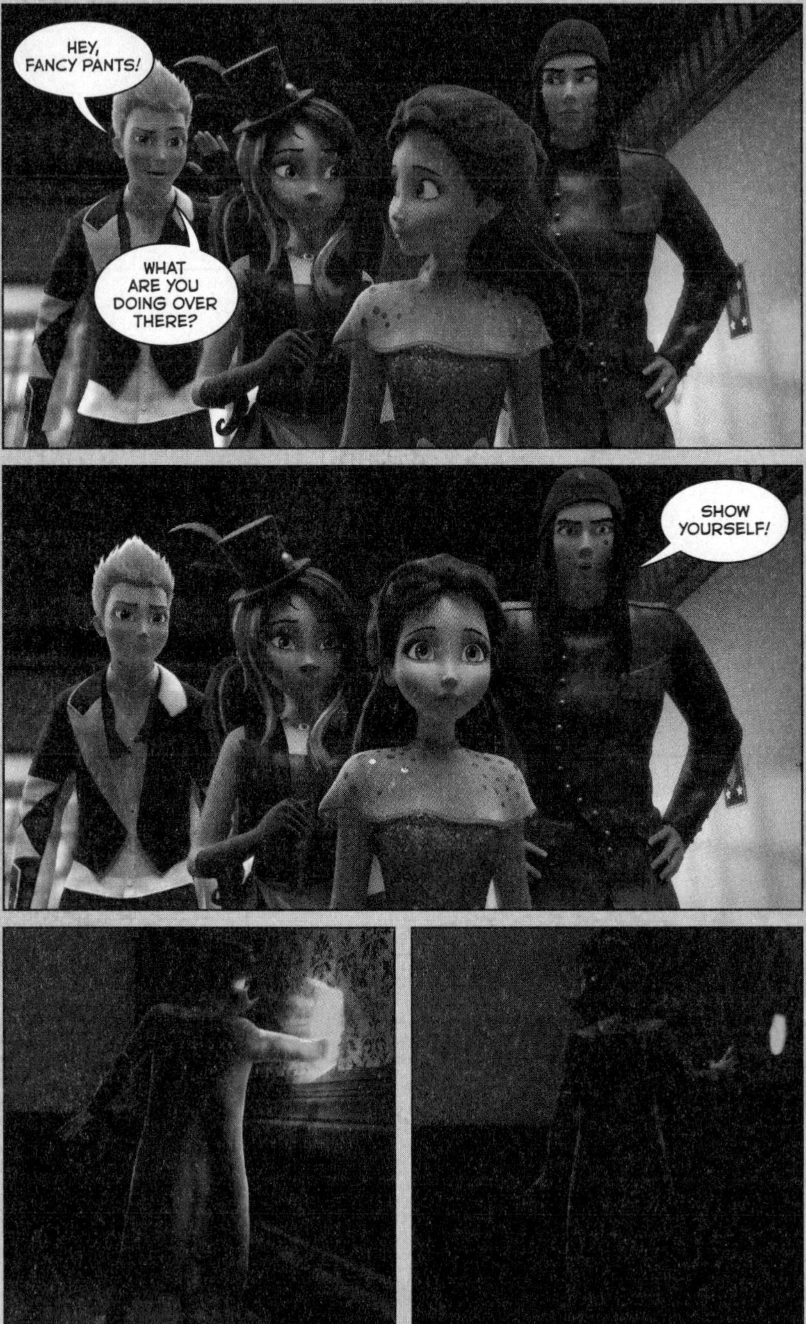
HEY, FANCY PANTS!
WHAT ARE YOU DOING OVER THERE?
SHOW YOURSELF!

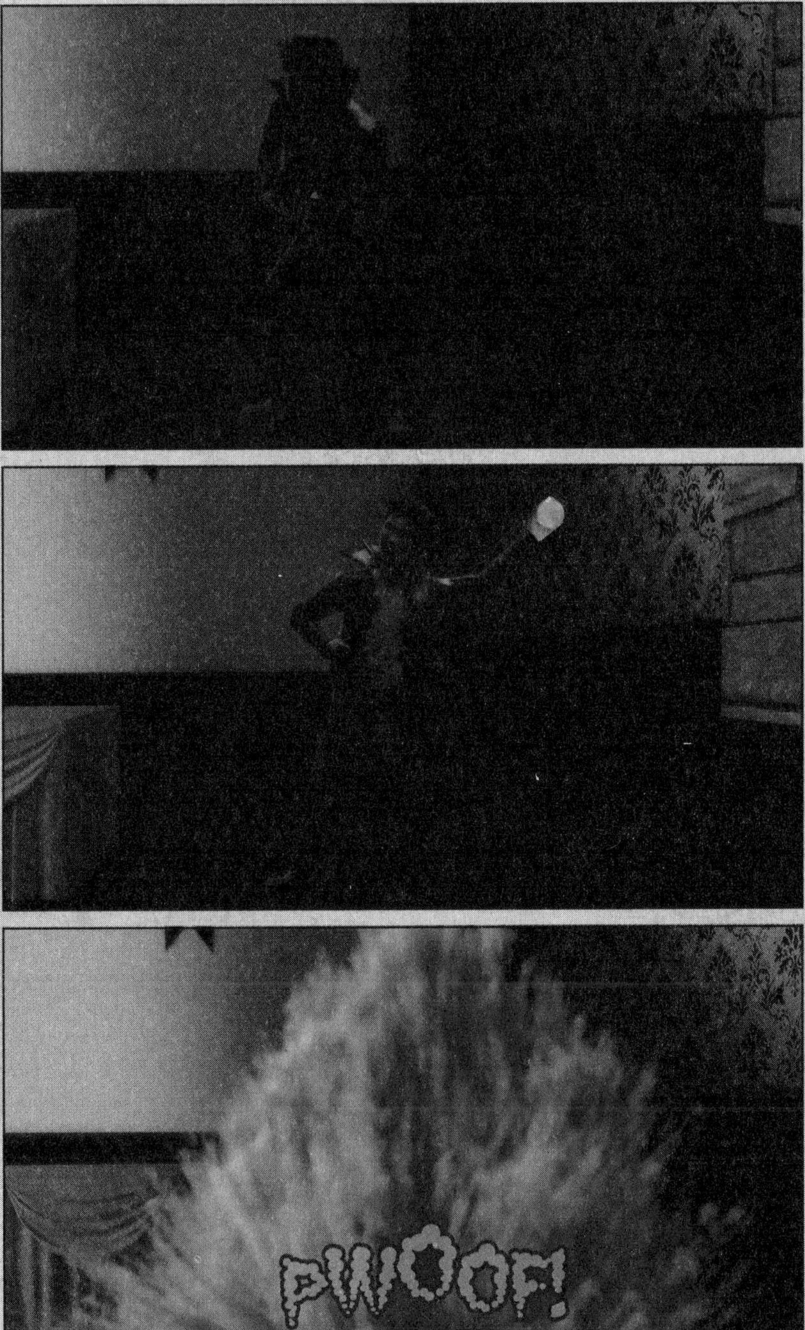
PWOOF!

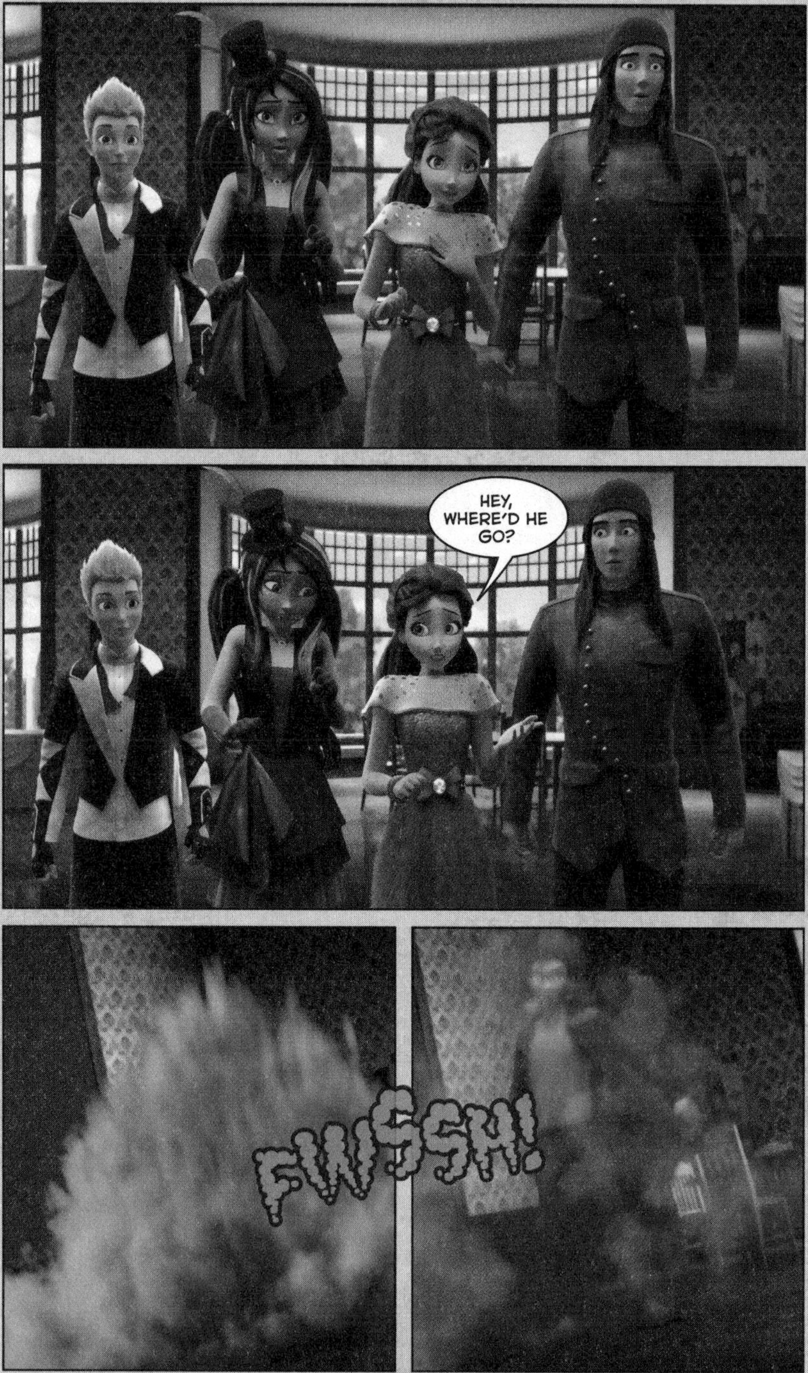
HEY, WHERE'D HE GO?
FWSSH!

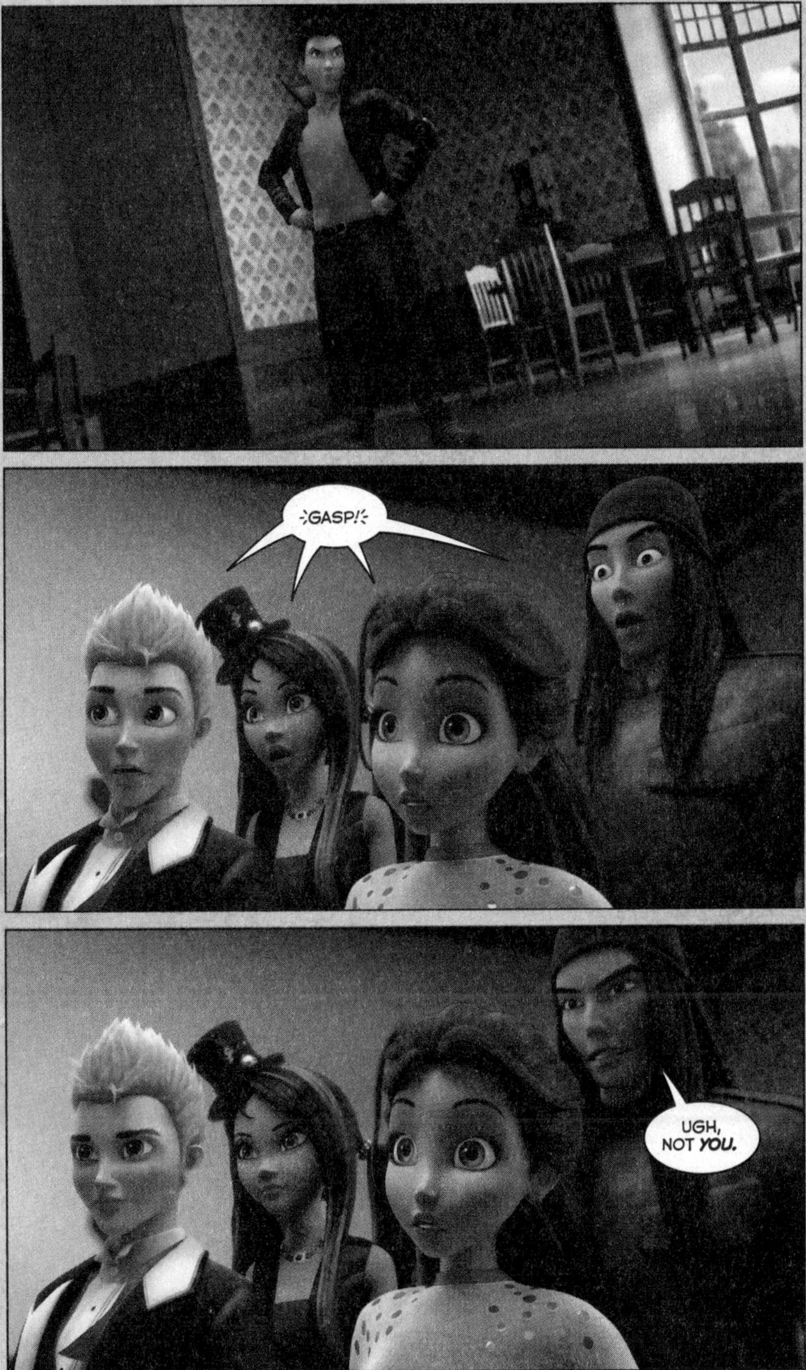
GASP!
UGH, NOT YOU.

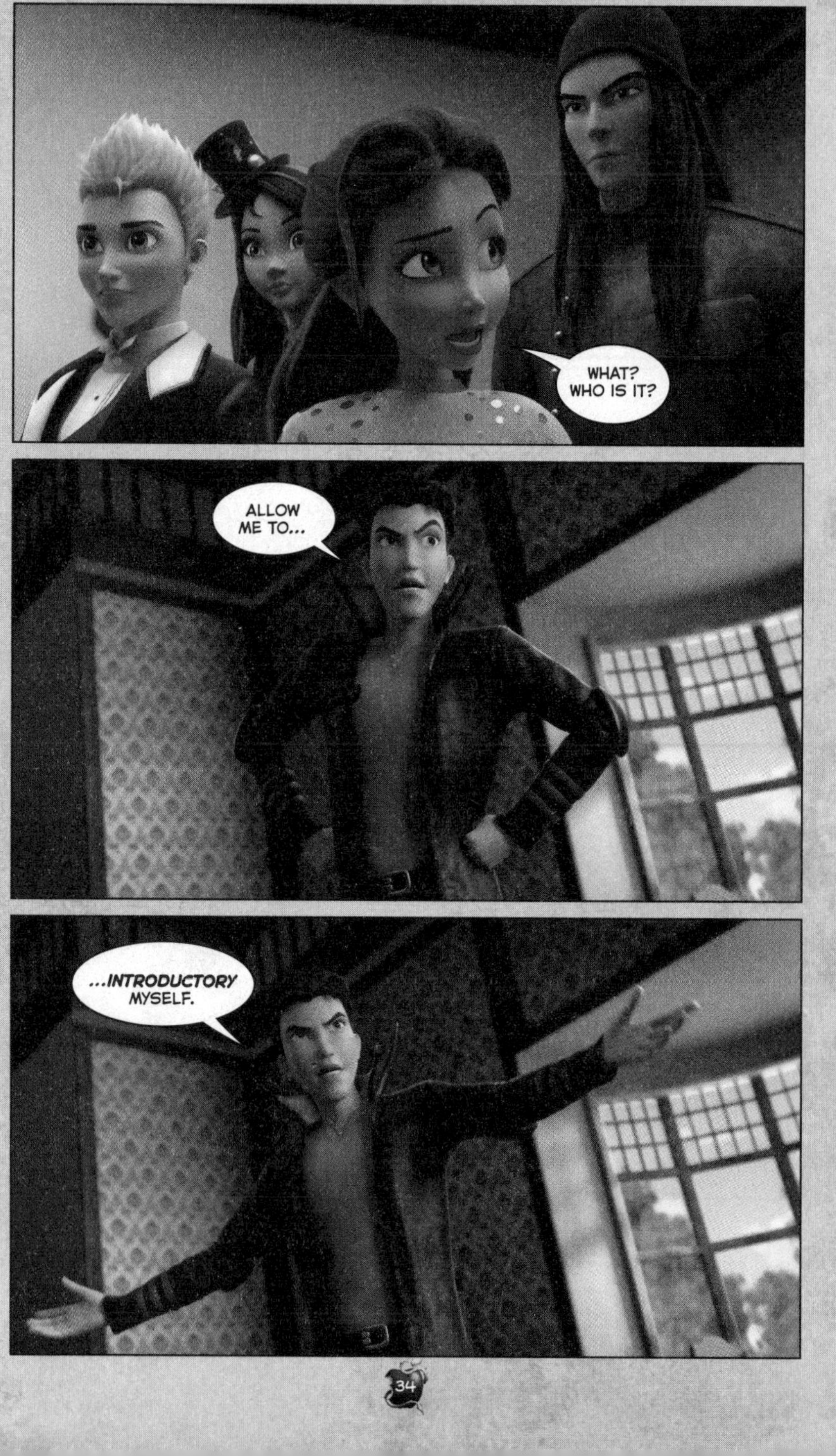
WHAT?
WHO IS IT?
ALLOW
ME TO...
...INTRODUCTORY
MYSELF.

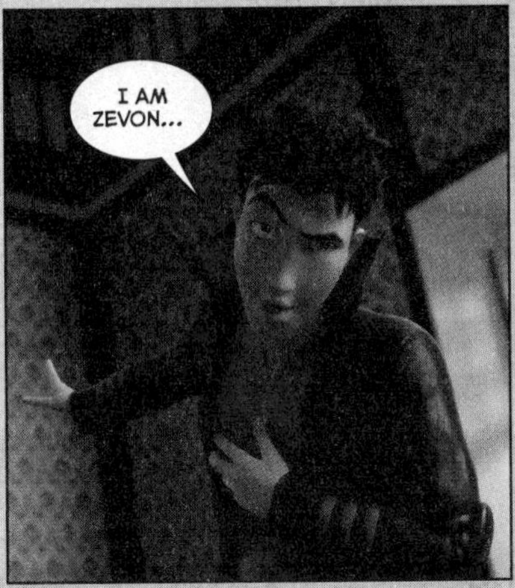
I AM ZEVON...
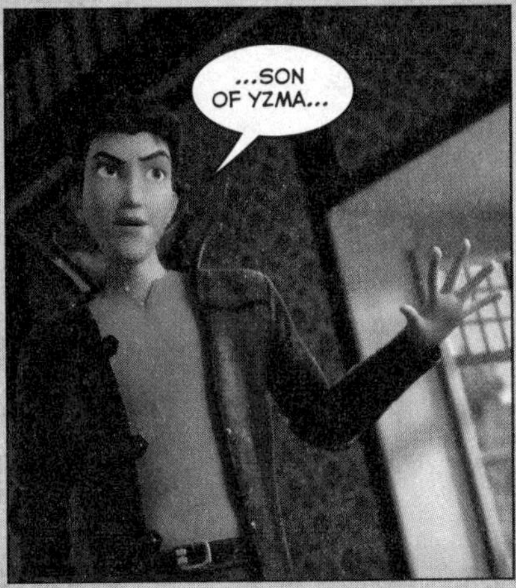
...SON OF YZMA...
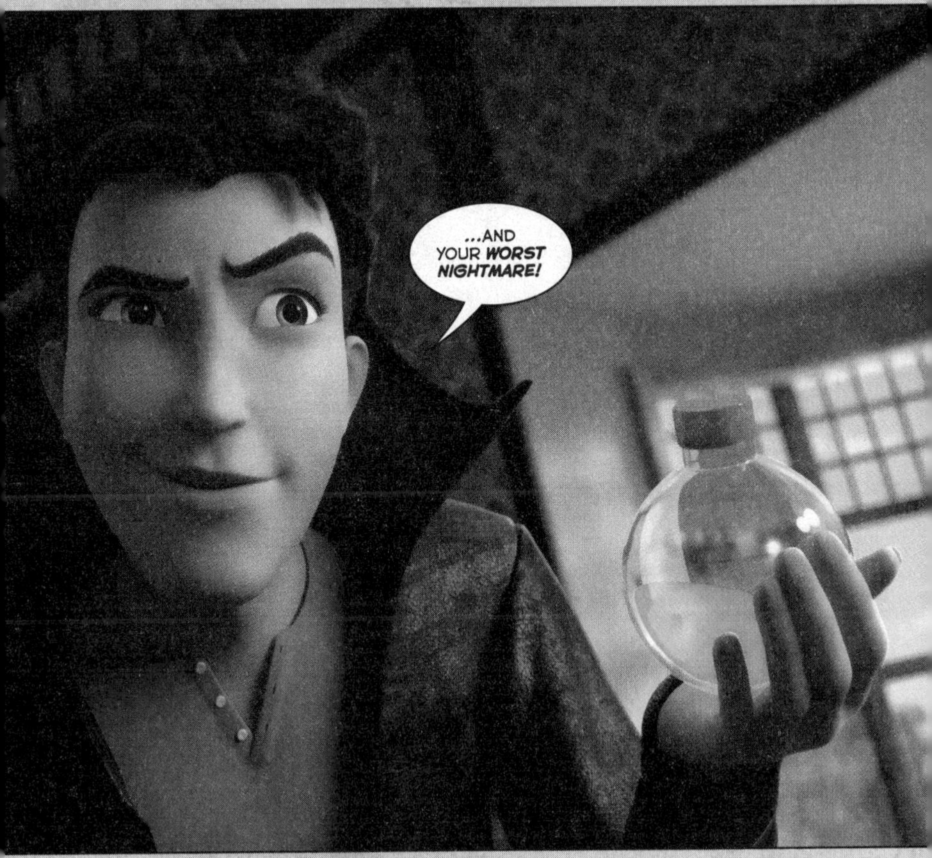
...AND YOUR **WORST NIGHTMARE!**

CHAPTER 27: OPTIONS ARE SHRINKING

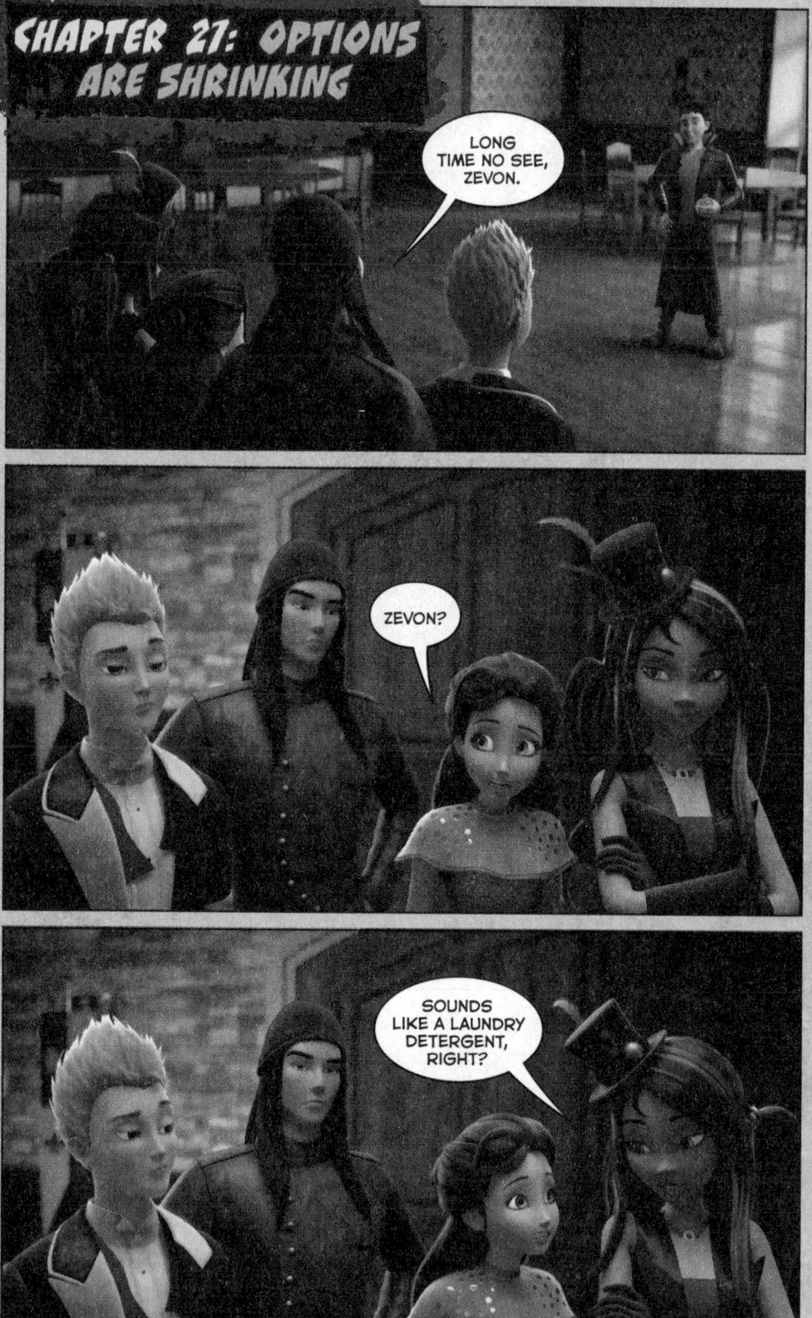
LONG TIME NO SEE, ZEVON.
ZEVON?
SOUNDS LIKE A LAUNDRY DETERGENT, RIGHT?

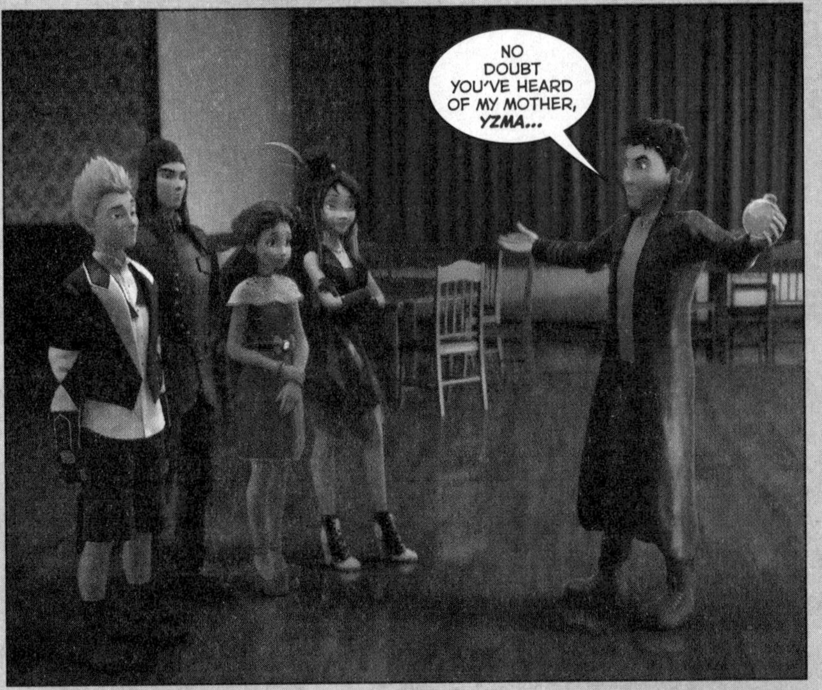
NO DOUBT YOU'VE HEARD OF MY MOTHER, ***YZMA...***

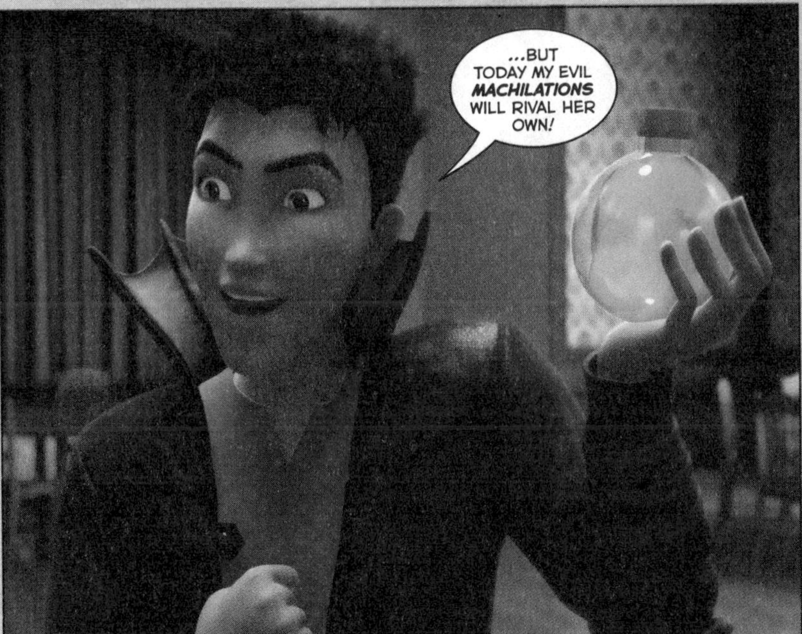
...BUT TODAY MY EVIL ***MACHILATIONS*** WILL RIVAL HER OWN!

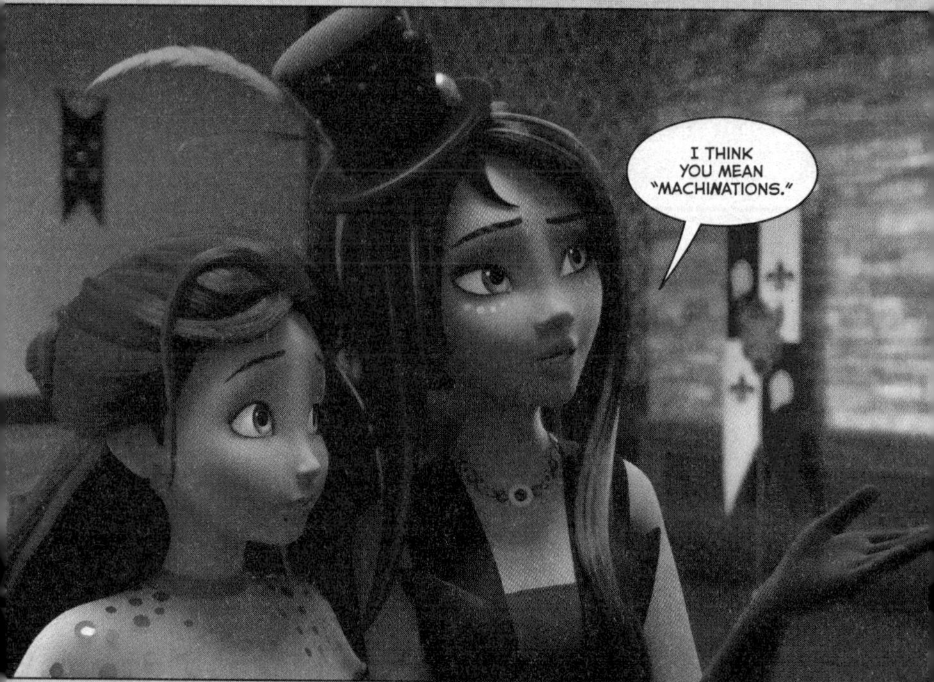
I THINK YOU MEAN "MACHINATIONS."

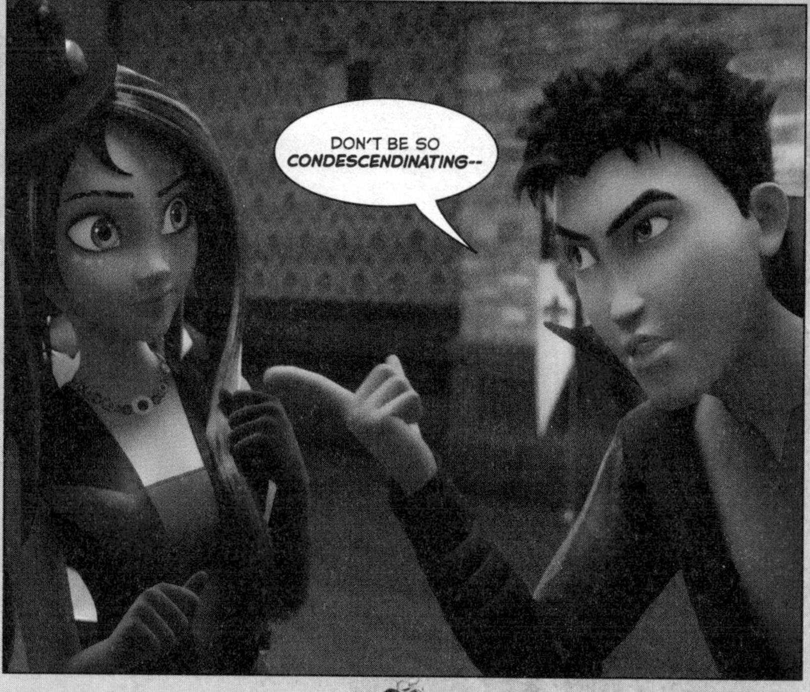
DON'T BE SO *CONDESCENDINATING--*

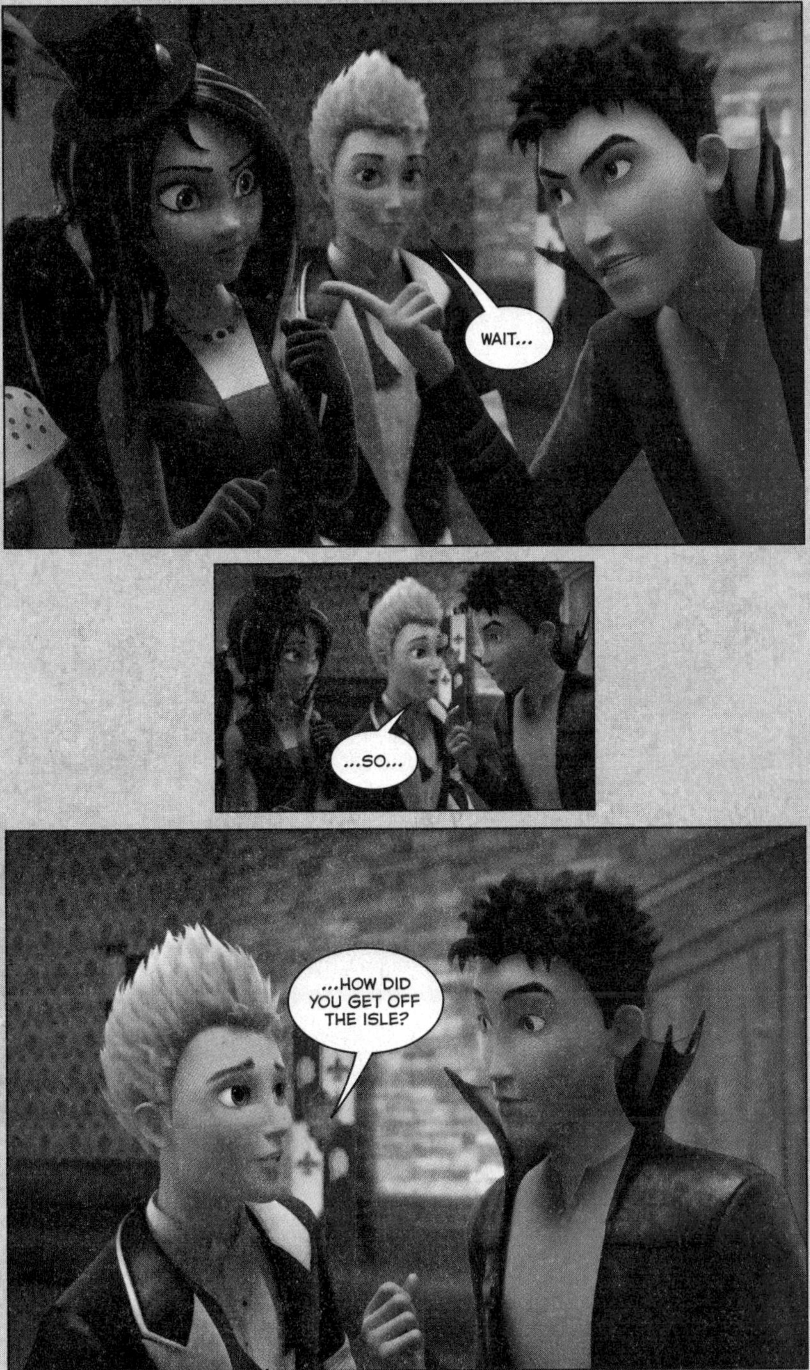
WAIT...
...SO...
...HOW DID YOU GET OFF THE ISLE?

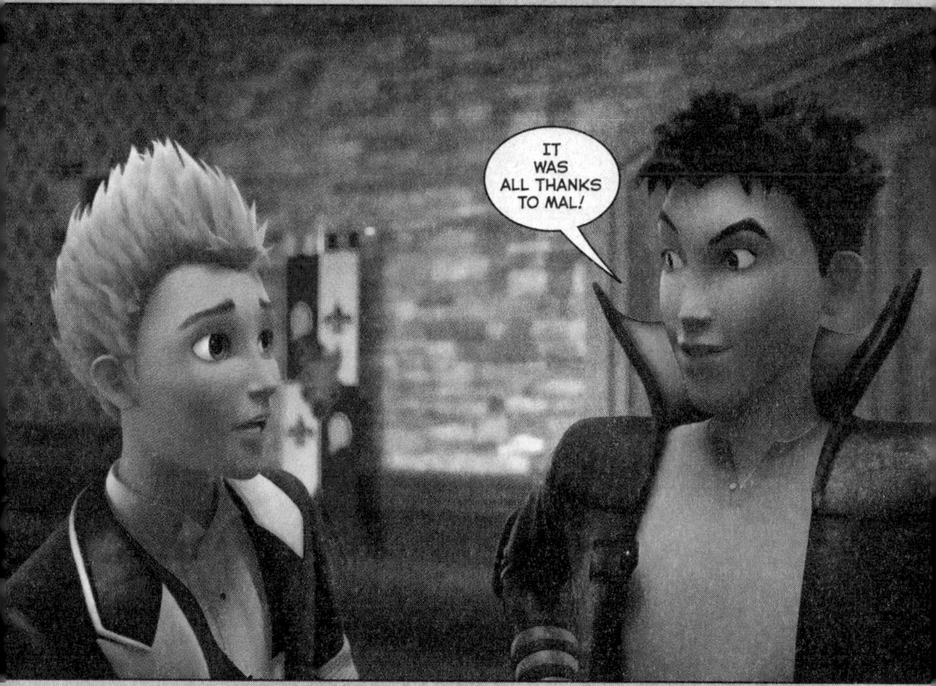
IT WAS ALL THANKS TO MAL!

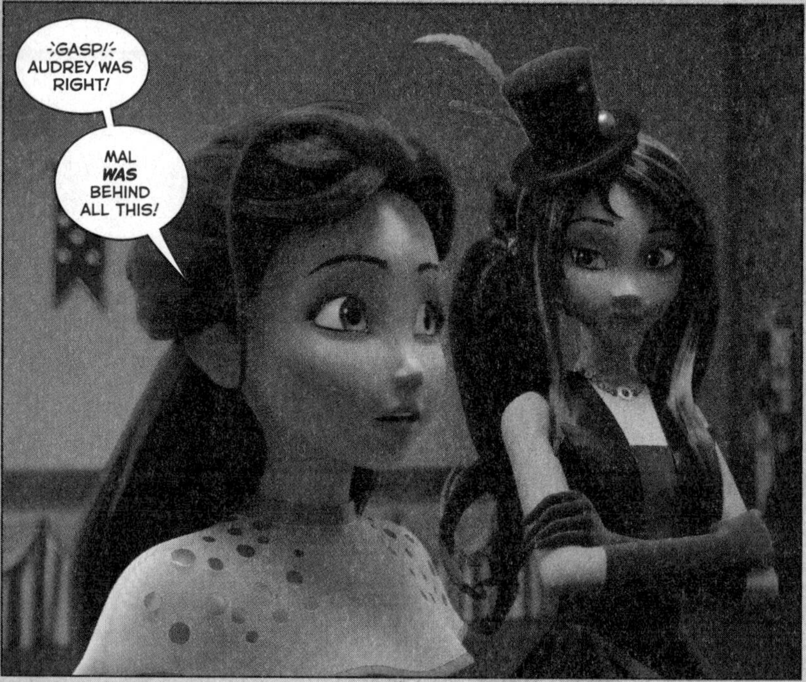
GASP! AUDREY WAS RIGHT!
MAL **WAS** BEHIND ALL THIS!

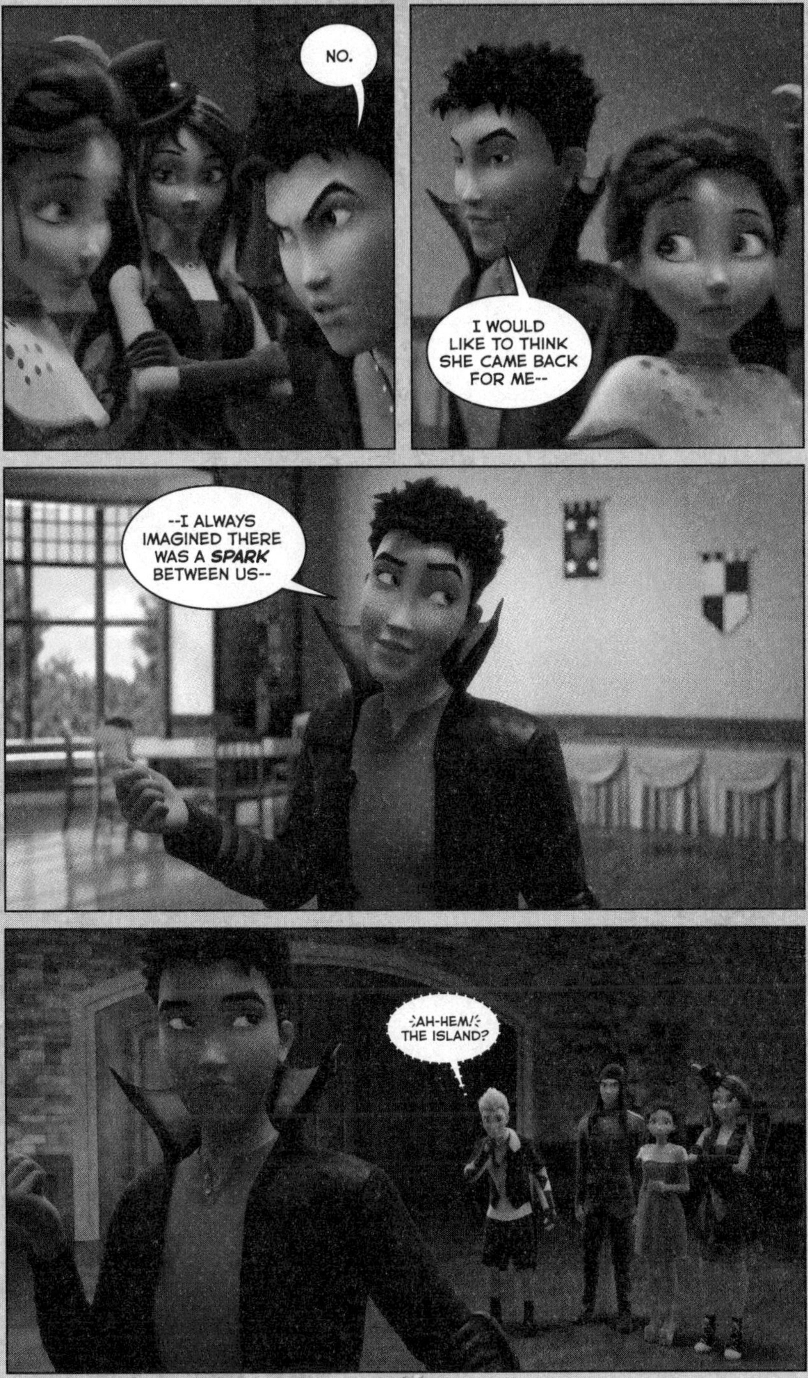
NO.
I WOULD LIKE TO THINK SHE CAME BACK FOR ME--
--I ALWAYS IMAGINED THERE WAS A SPARK BETWEEN US--
AH-HEM! THE ISLAND?

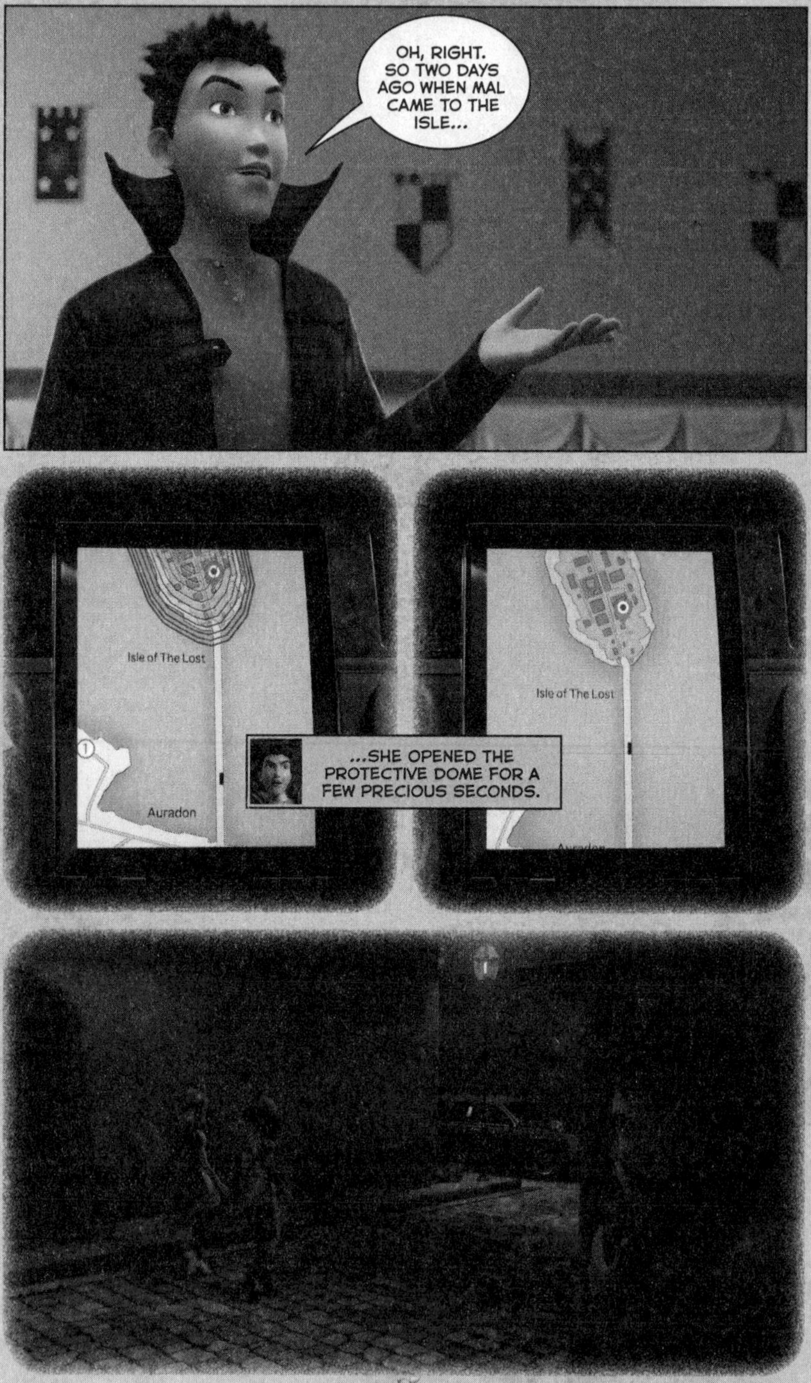
OH, RIGHT. SO TWO DAYS AGO WHEN MAL CAME TO THE ISLE...
Isle of The Lost
1
Auradon
Isle of The Lost
...SHE OPENED THE PROTECTIVE DOME FOR A FEW PRECIOUS SECONDS.

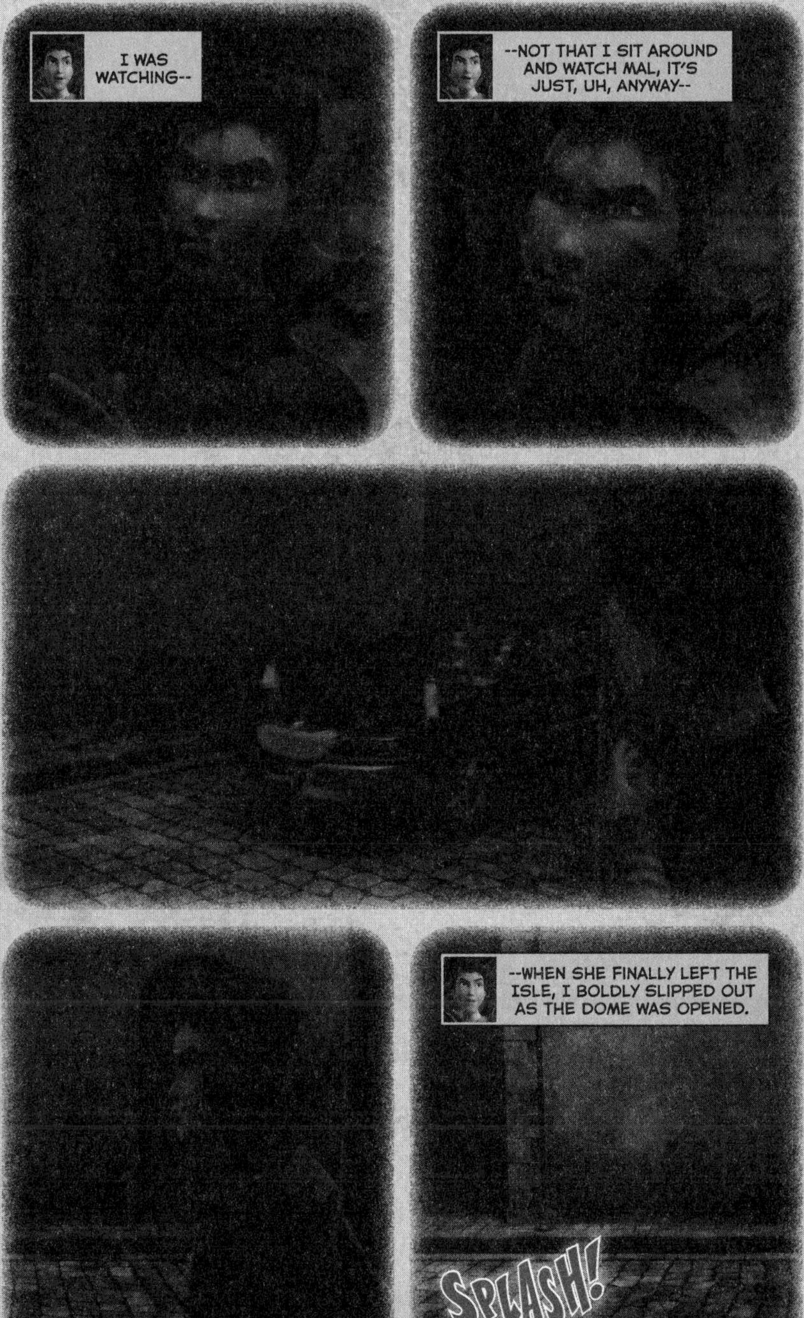
I WAS WATCHING--
--NOT THAT I SIT AROUND AND WATCH MAL, IT'S JUST, UH, ANYWAY--
--WHEN SHE FINALLY LEFT THE ISLE, I BOLDLY SLIPPED OUT AS THE DOME WAS OPENED.
SPLASH!

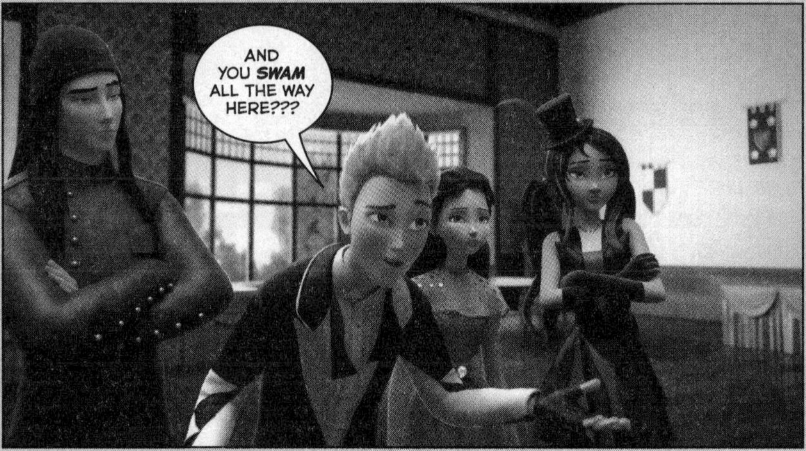
AND YOU **SWAM** ALL THE WAY HERE???

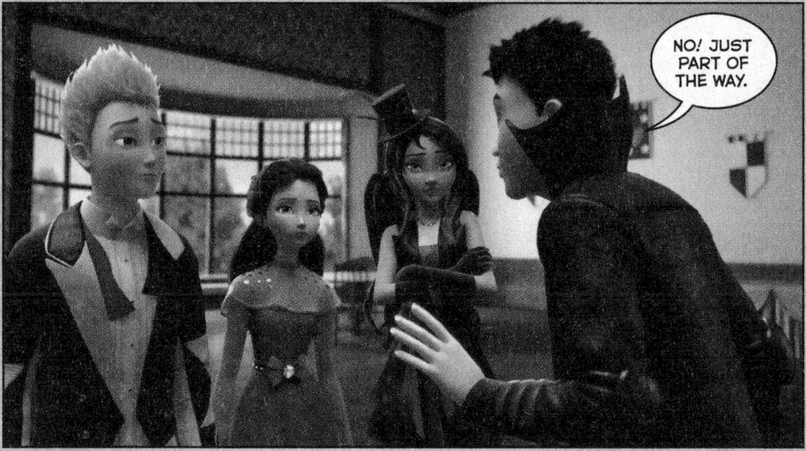
NO! JUST PART OF THE WAY.

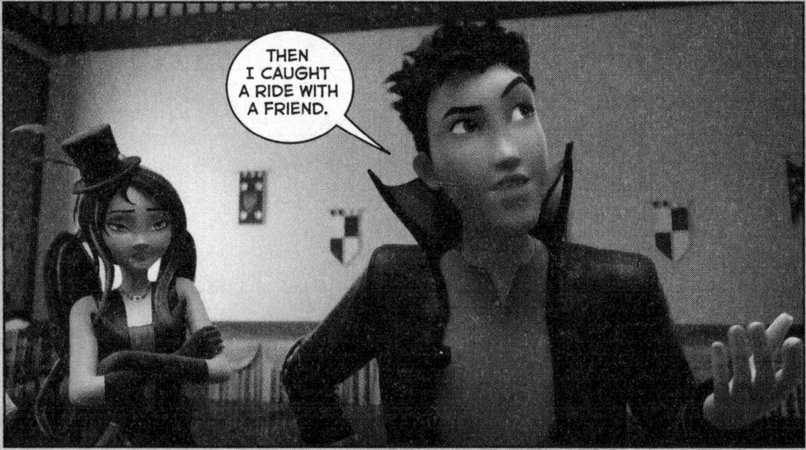
THEN I CAUGHT A RIDE WITH A FRIEND.

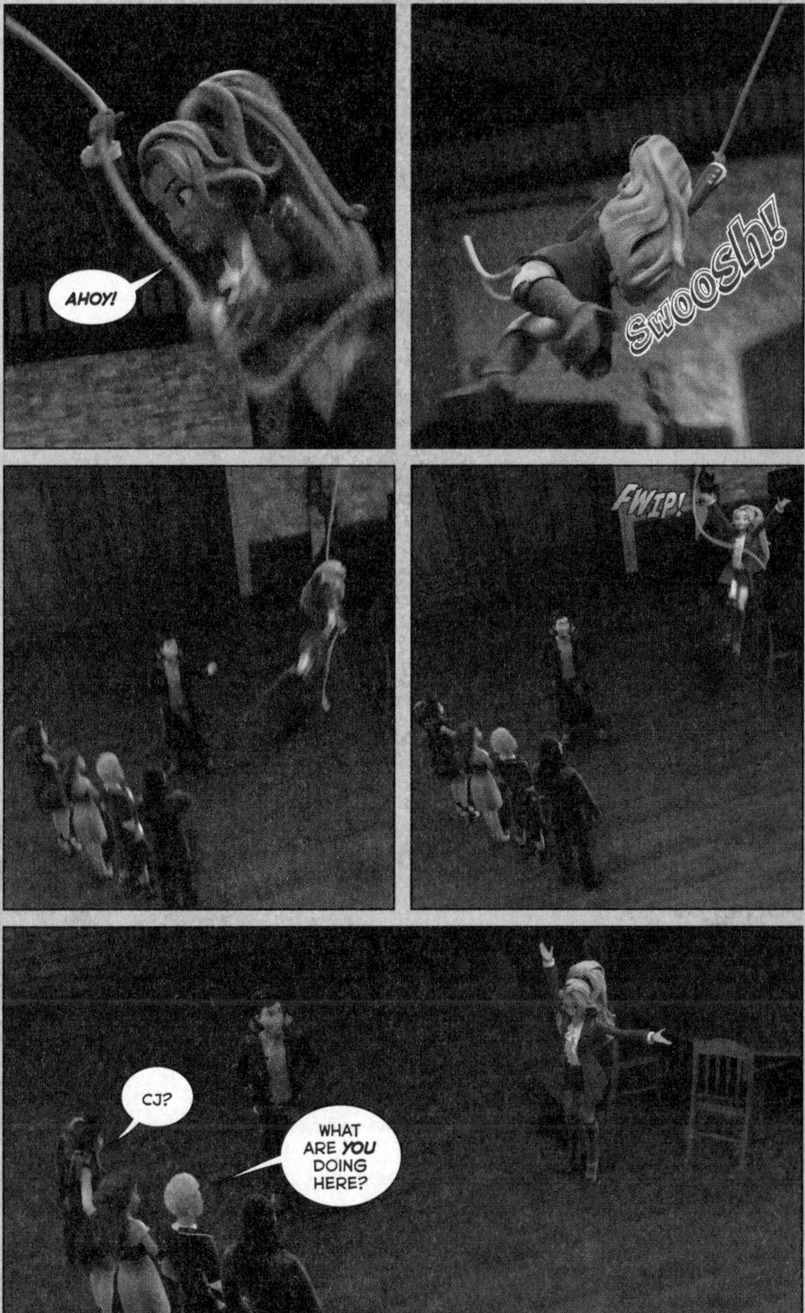
AHOY!
SWOOSH!
FWIP!
CJ?
WHAT ARE YOU DOING HERE?

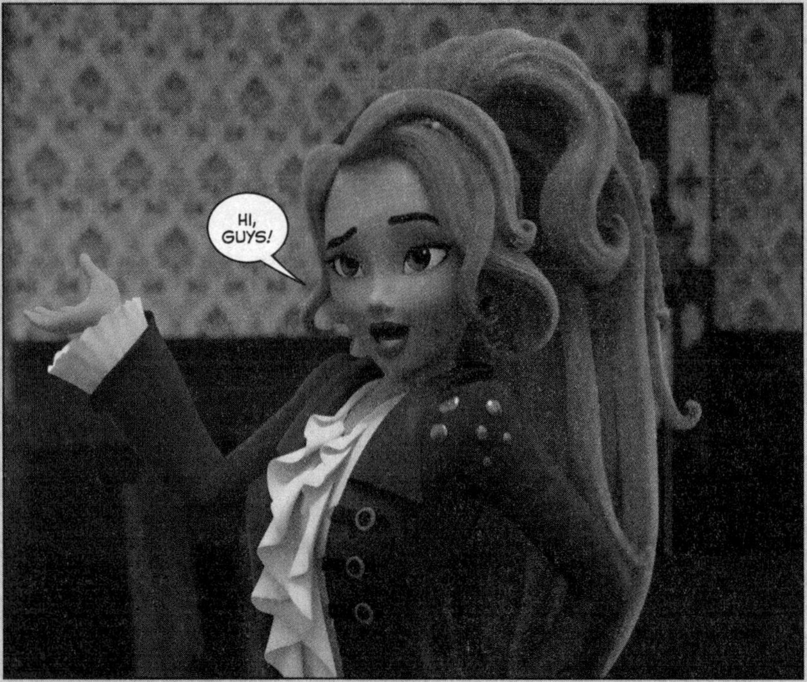
HI, GUYS!

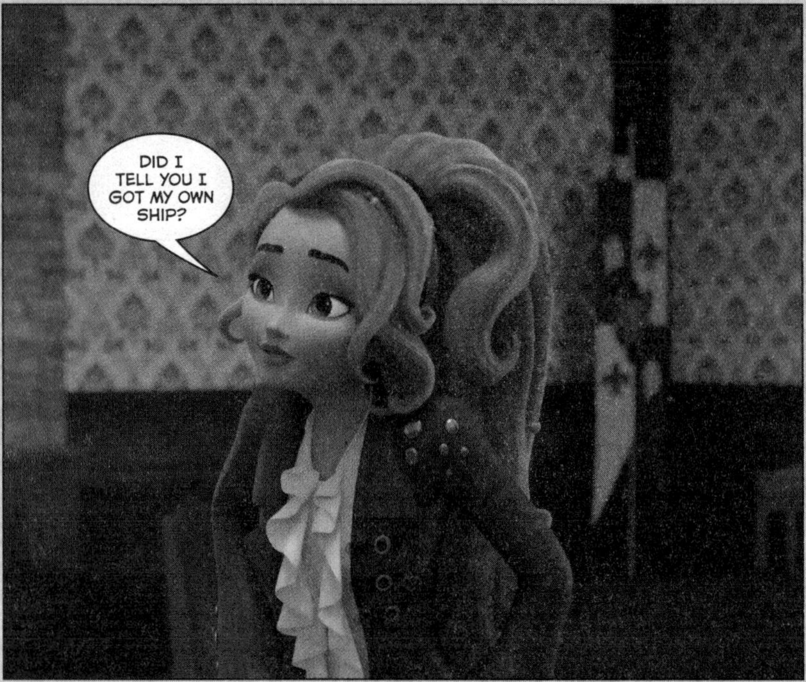
DID I TELL YOU I GOT MY OWN SHIP?

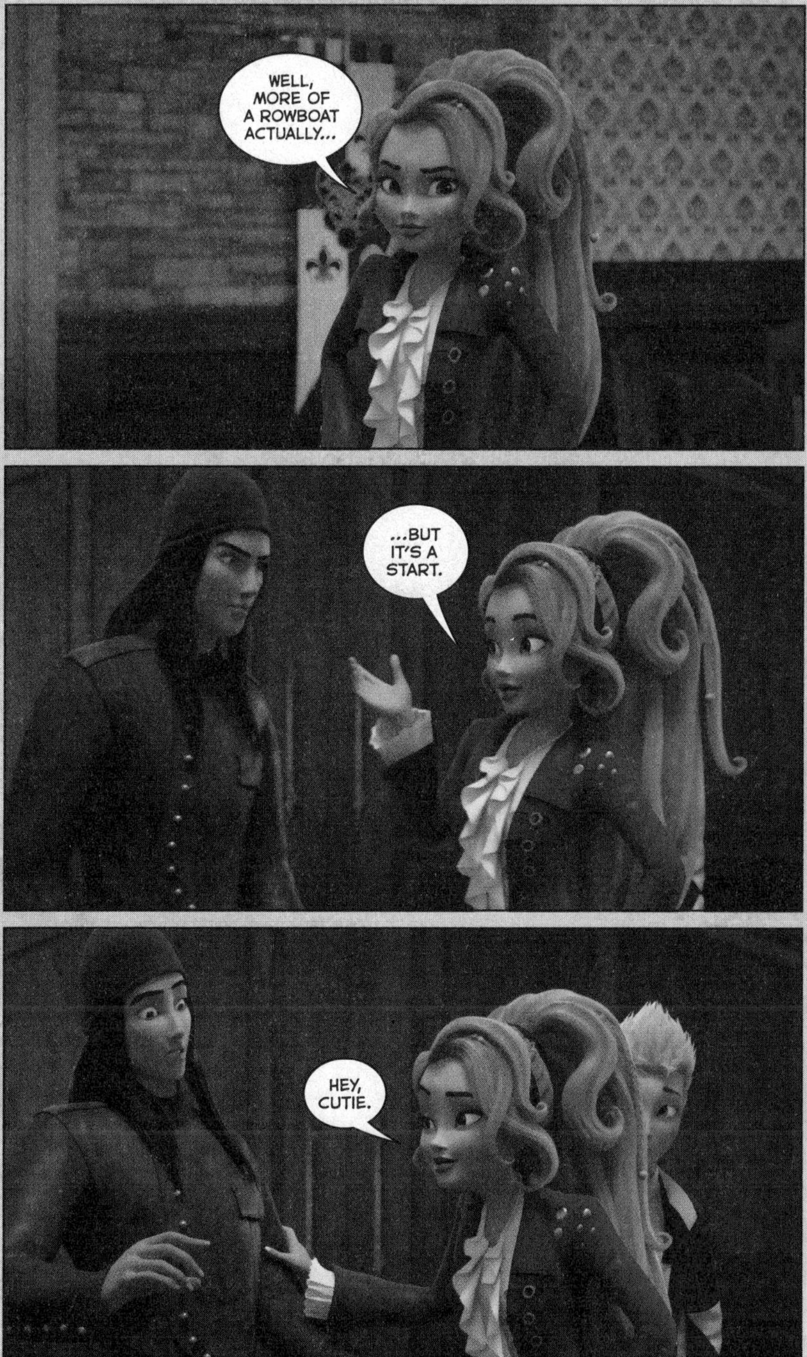
WELL, MORE OF A ROWBOAT ACTUALLY...
...BUT IT'S A START.
HEY, CUTIE.

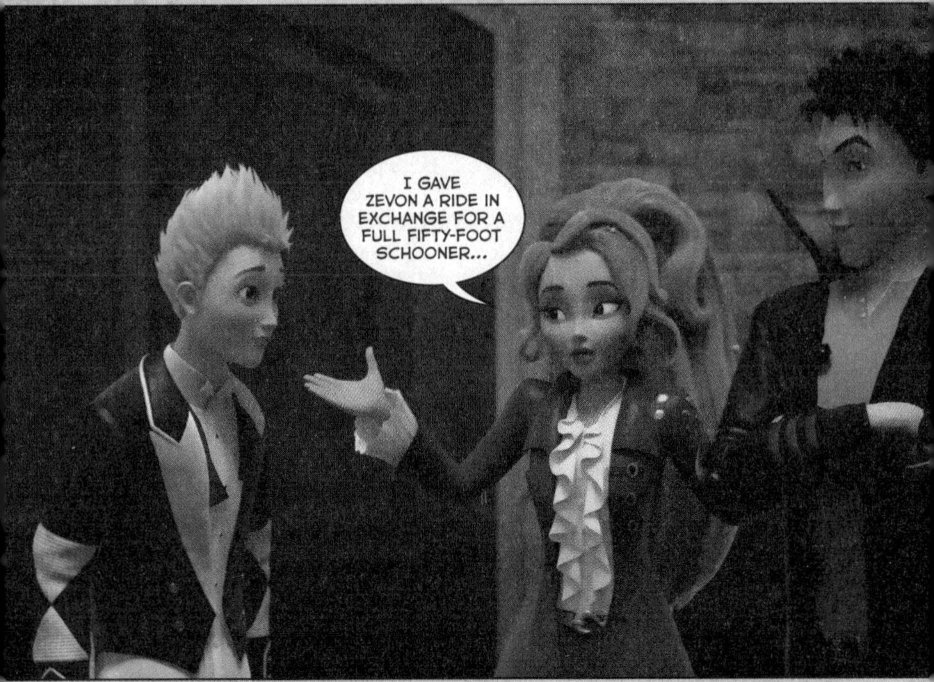
I GAVE ZEVON A RIDE IN EXCHANGE FOR A FULL FIFTY-FOOT SCHOONER...
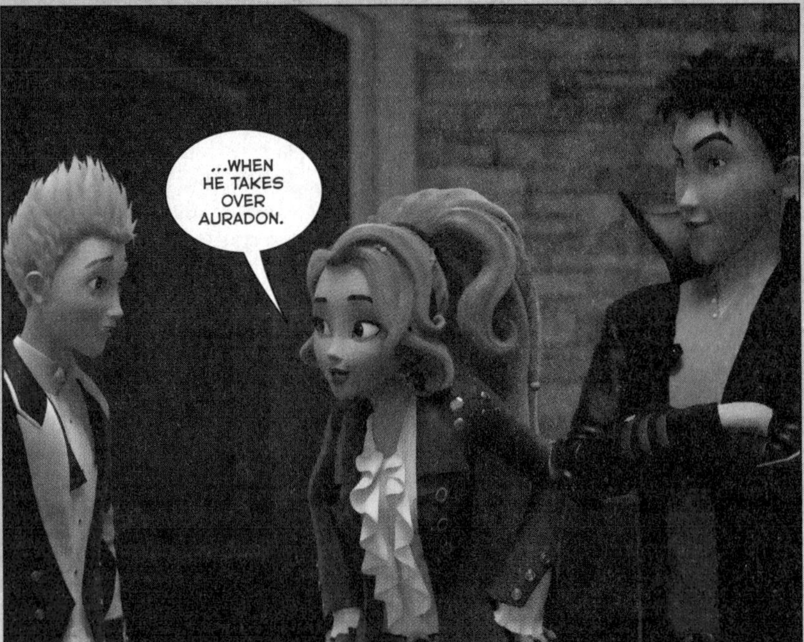
...WHEN HE TAKES OVER AURADON.

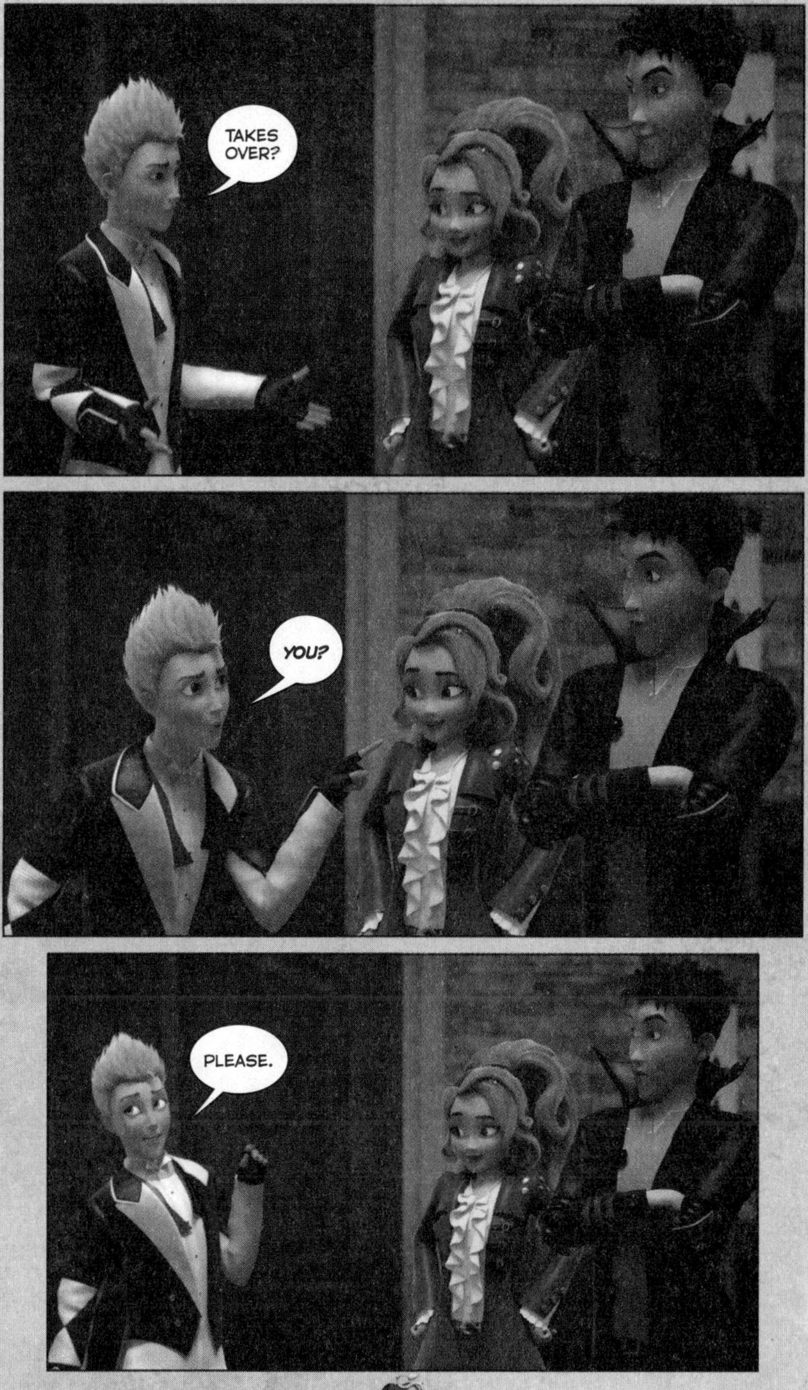
TAKES OVER?
YOU?
PLEASE.

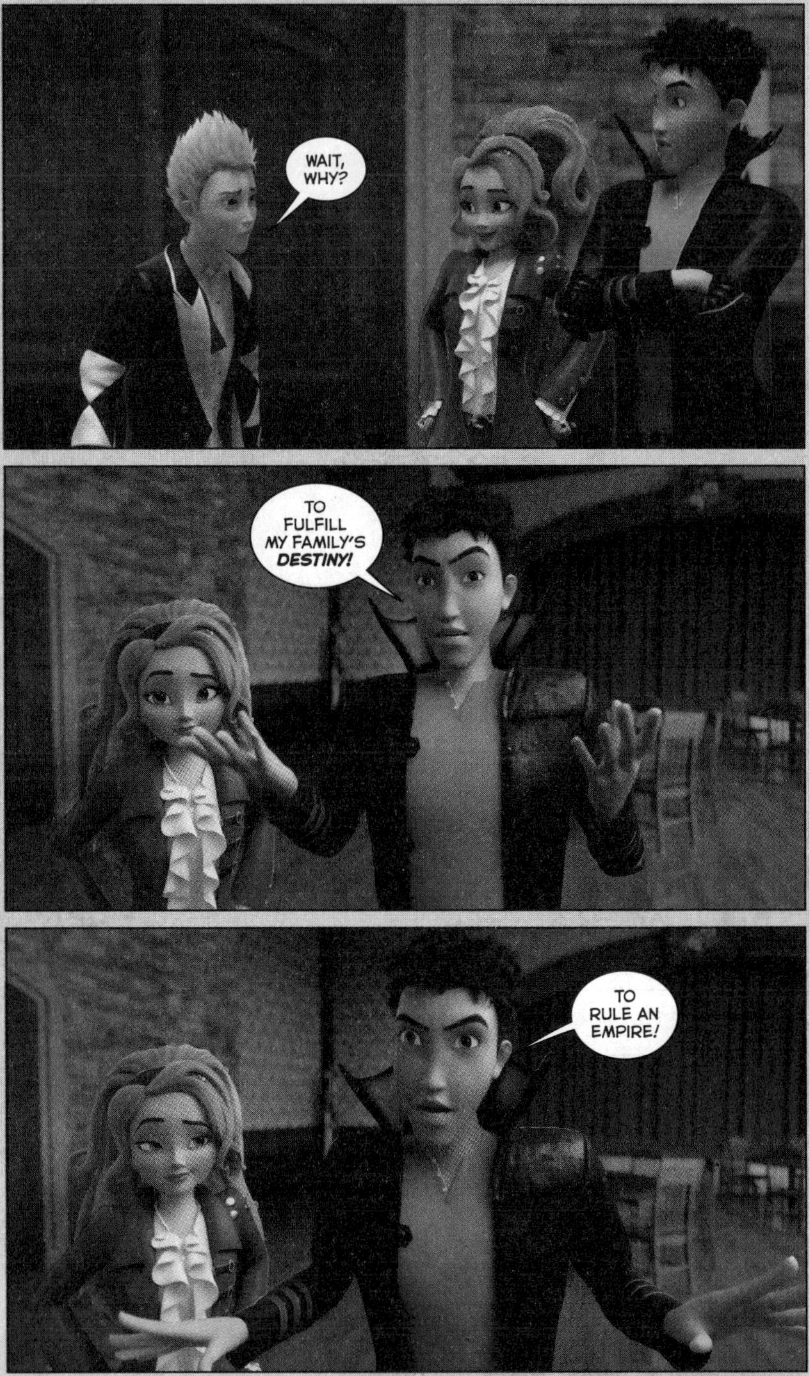
WAIT, WHY?
TO FULFILL MY FAMILY'S ***DESTINY!***
TO RULE AN EMPIRE!

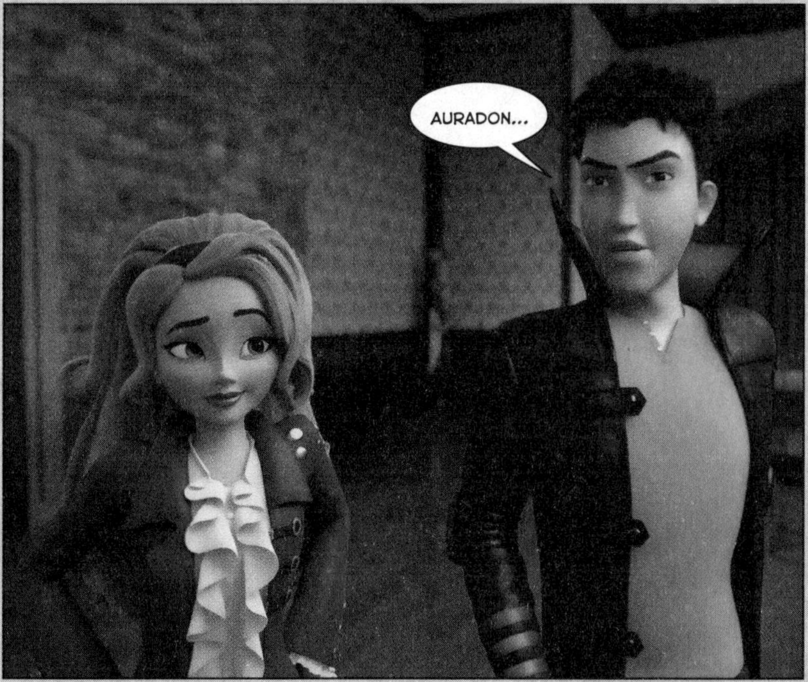
AURADON...

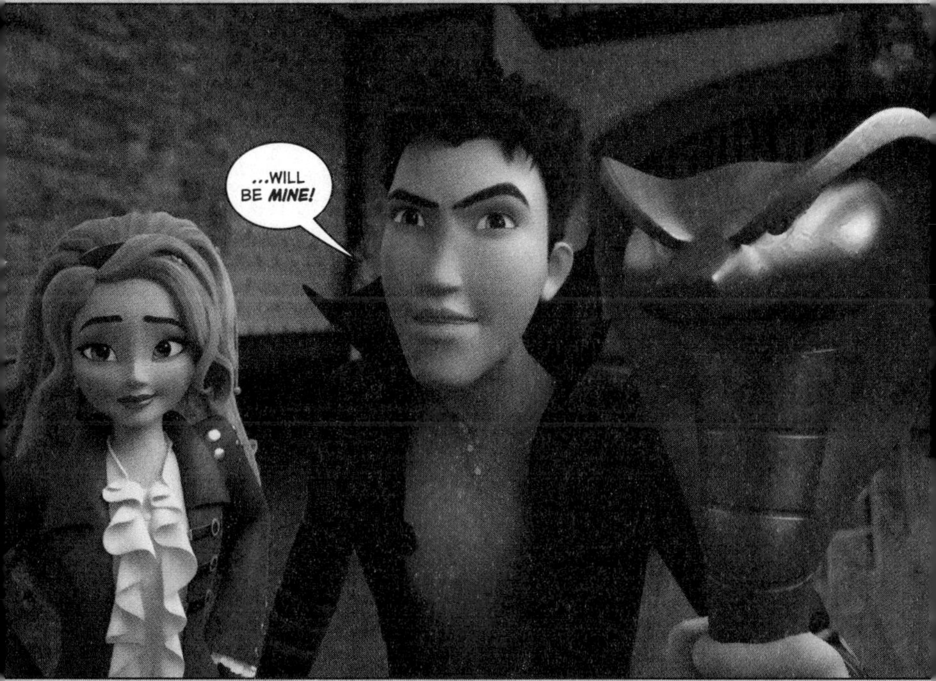
...WILL BE *MINE!*

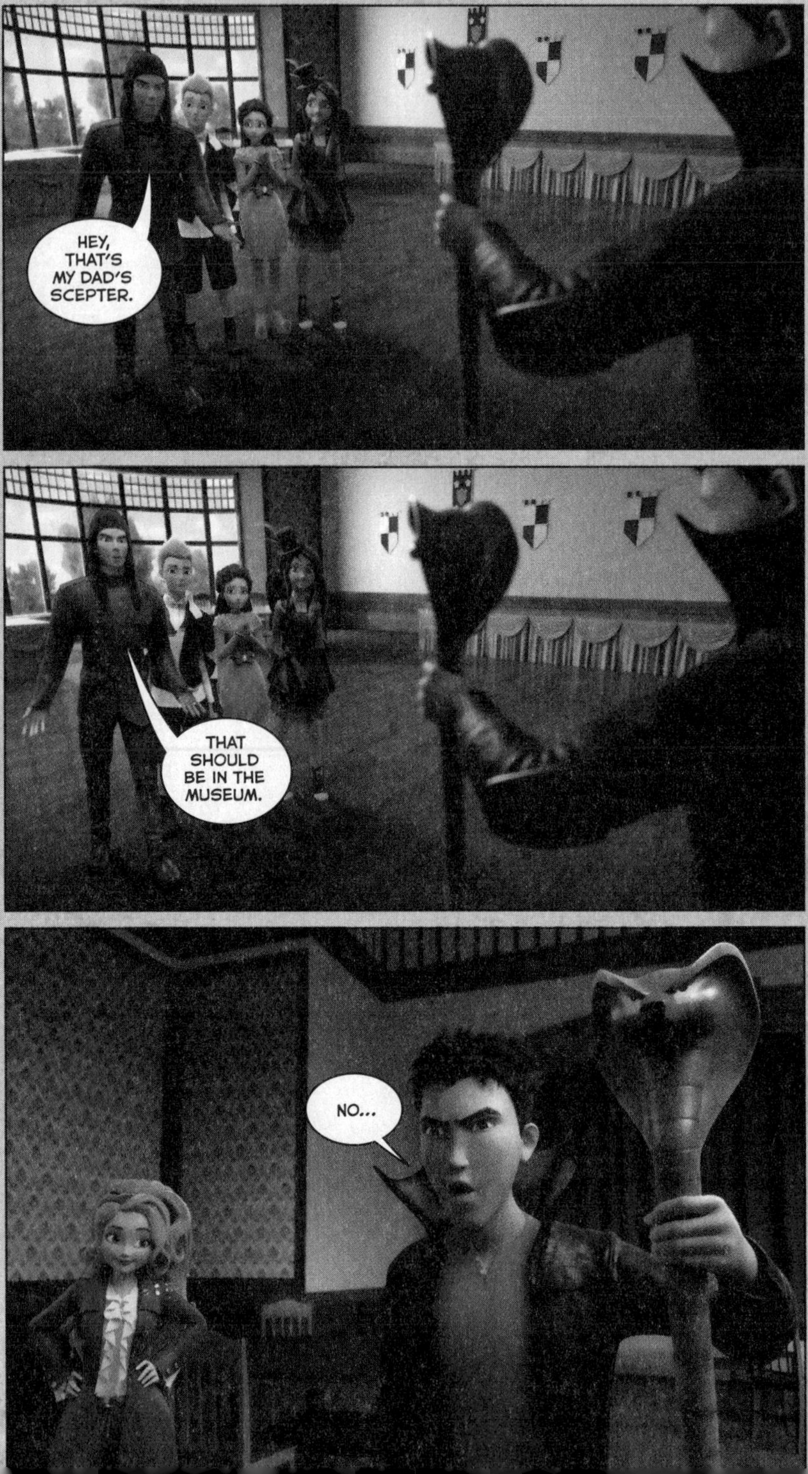
HEY, THAT'S MY DAD'S SCEPTER.
THAT SHOULD BE IN THE MUSEUM.
NO...

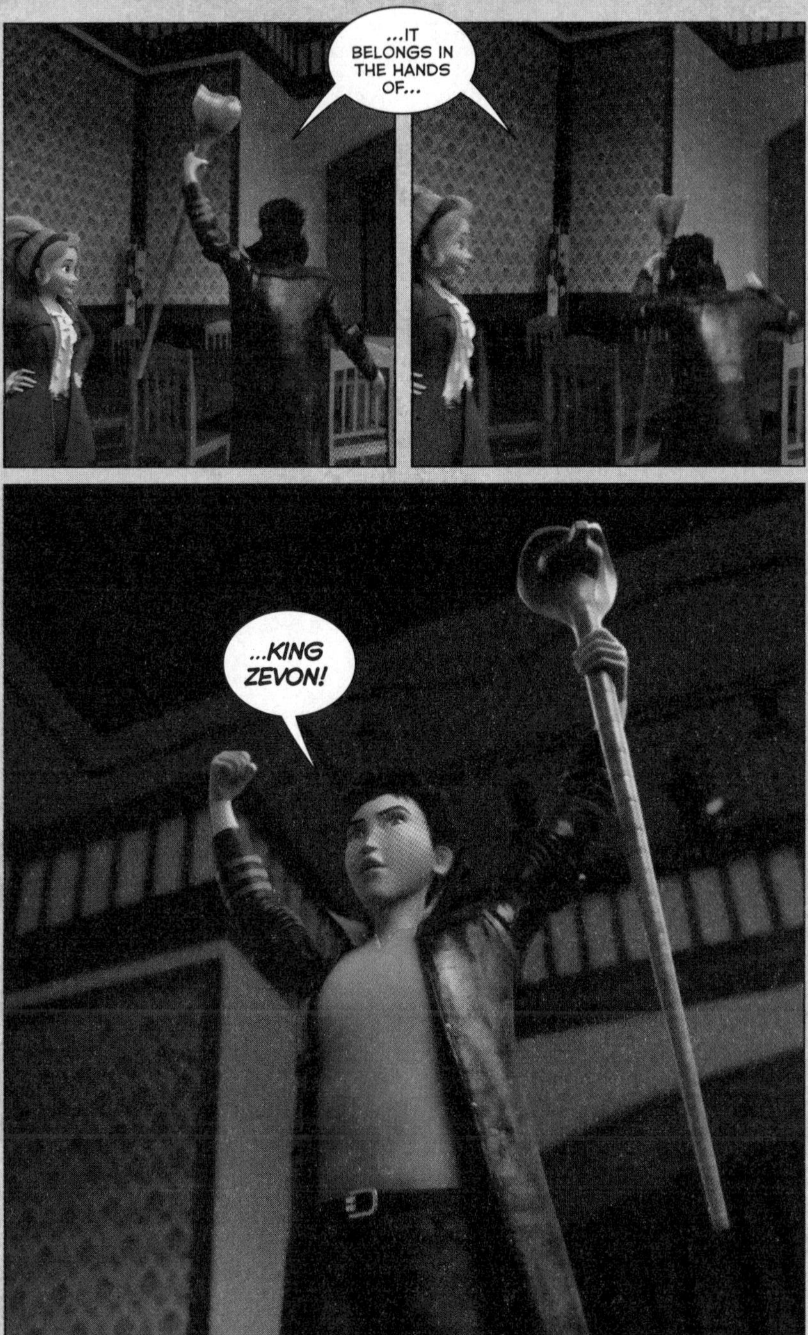
...IT BELONGS IN THE HANDS OF...
...KING ZEVON!

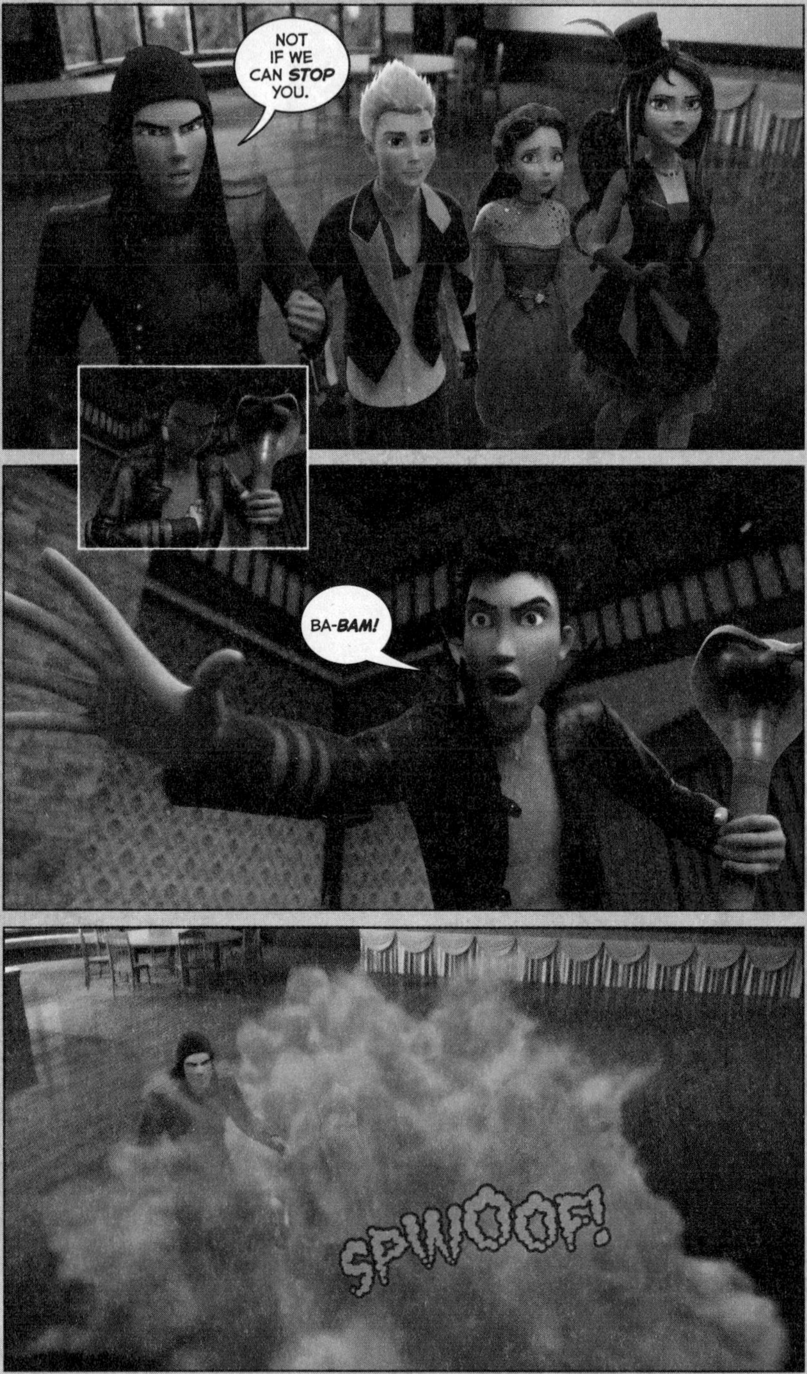
NOT IF WE CAN STOP YOU.
BA-BAM!
SPWOOF!

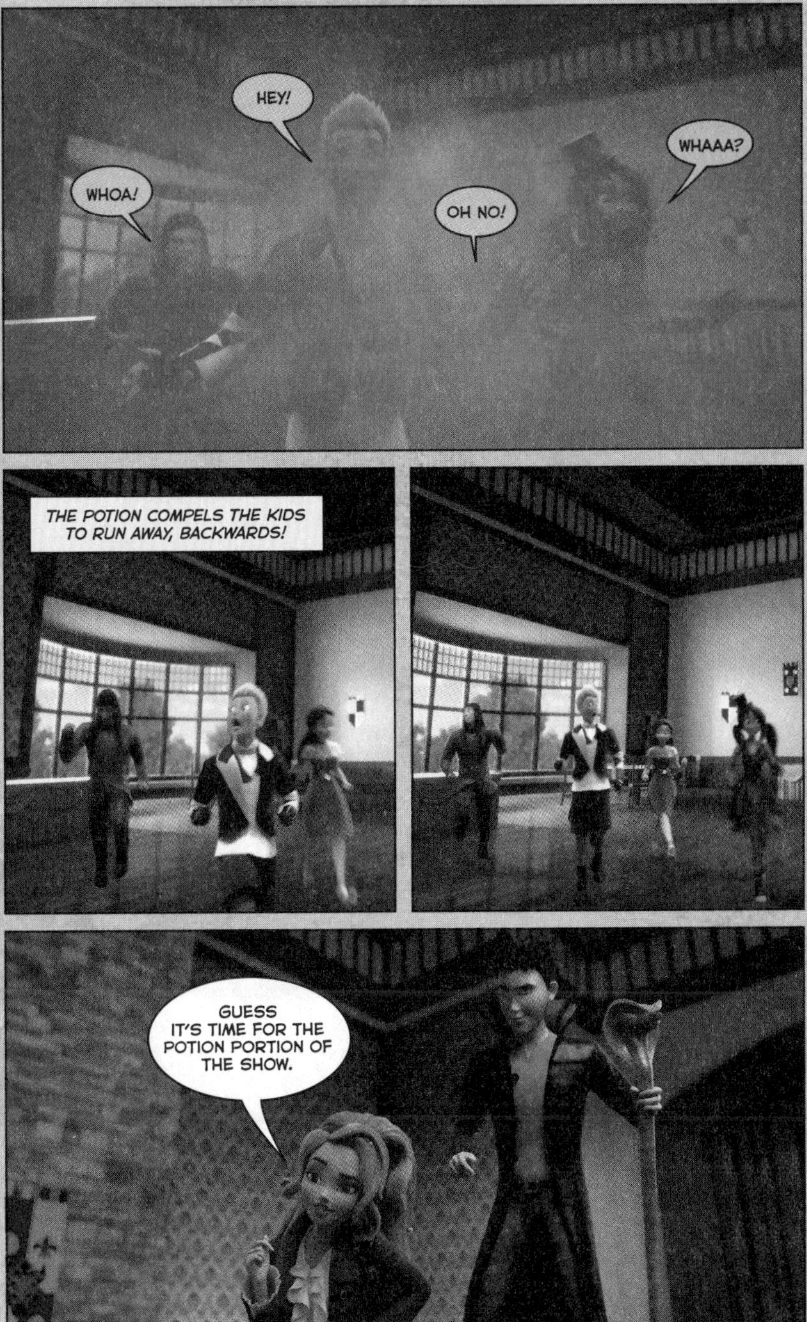
HEY!
WHOA!
OH NO!
WHAAA?
THE POTION COMPELS THE KIDS TO RUN AWAY, BACKWARDS!
GUESS IT'S TIME FOR THE POTION PORTION OF THE SHOW.

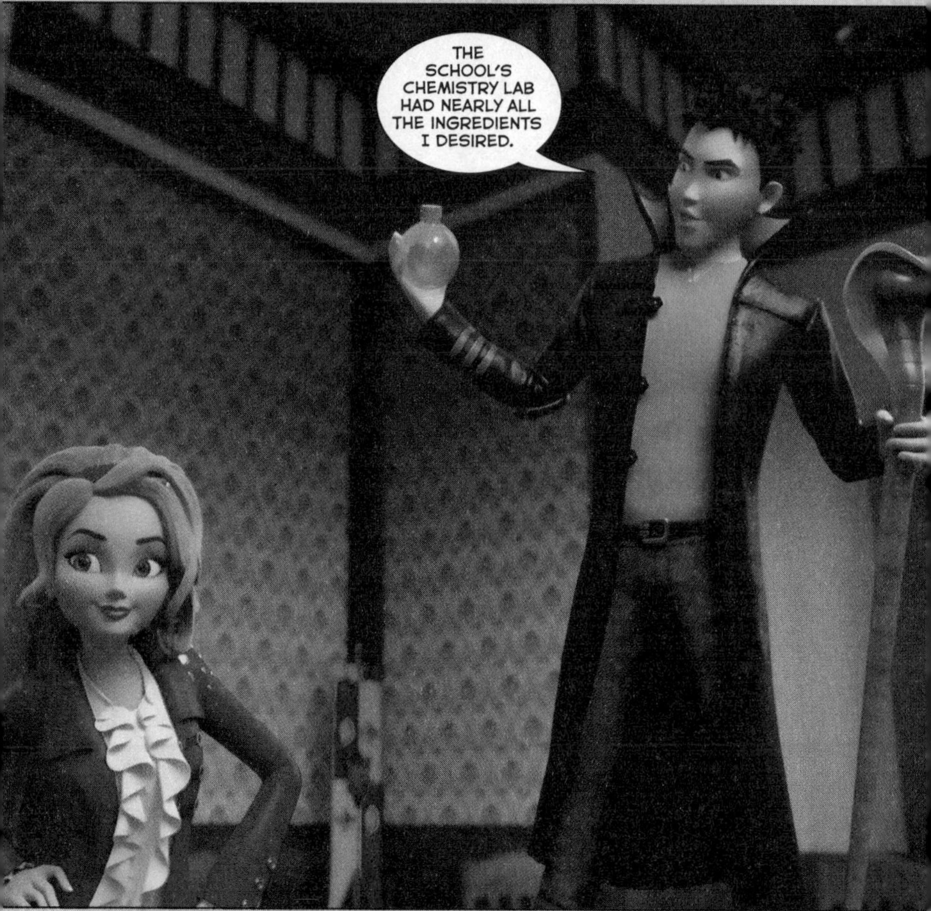
THE SCHOOL'S CHEMISTRY LAB HAD NEARLY ALL THE INGREDIENTS I DESIRED.

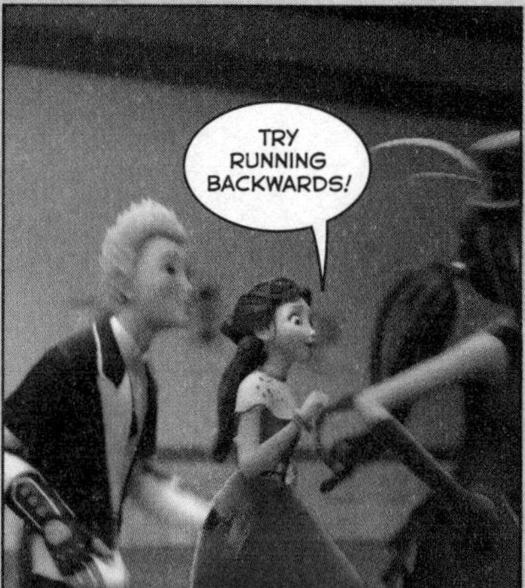
TRY RUNNING BACKWARDS!

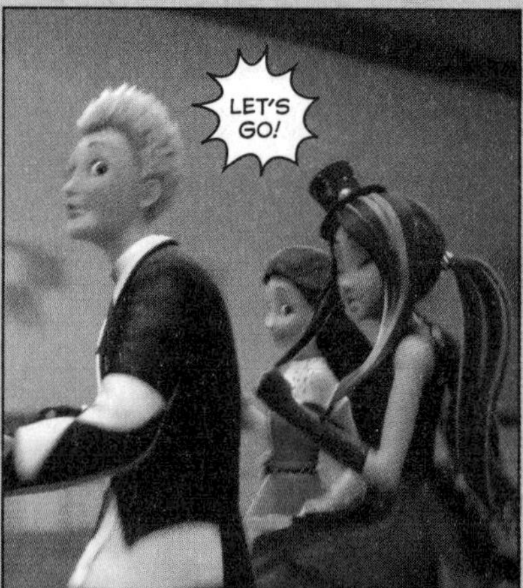
LET'S GO!

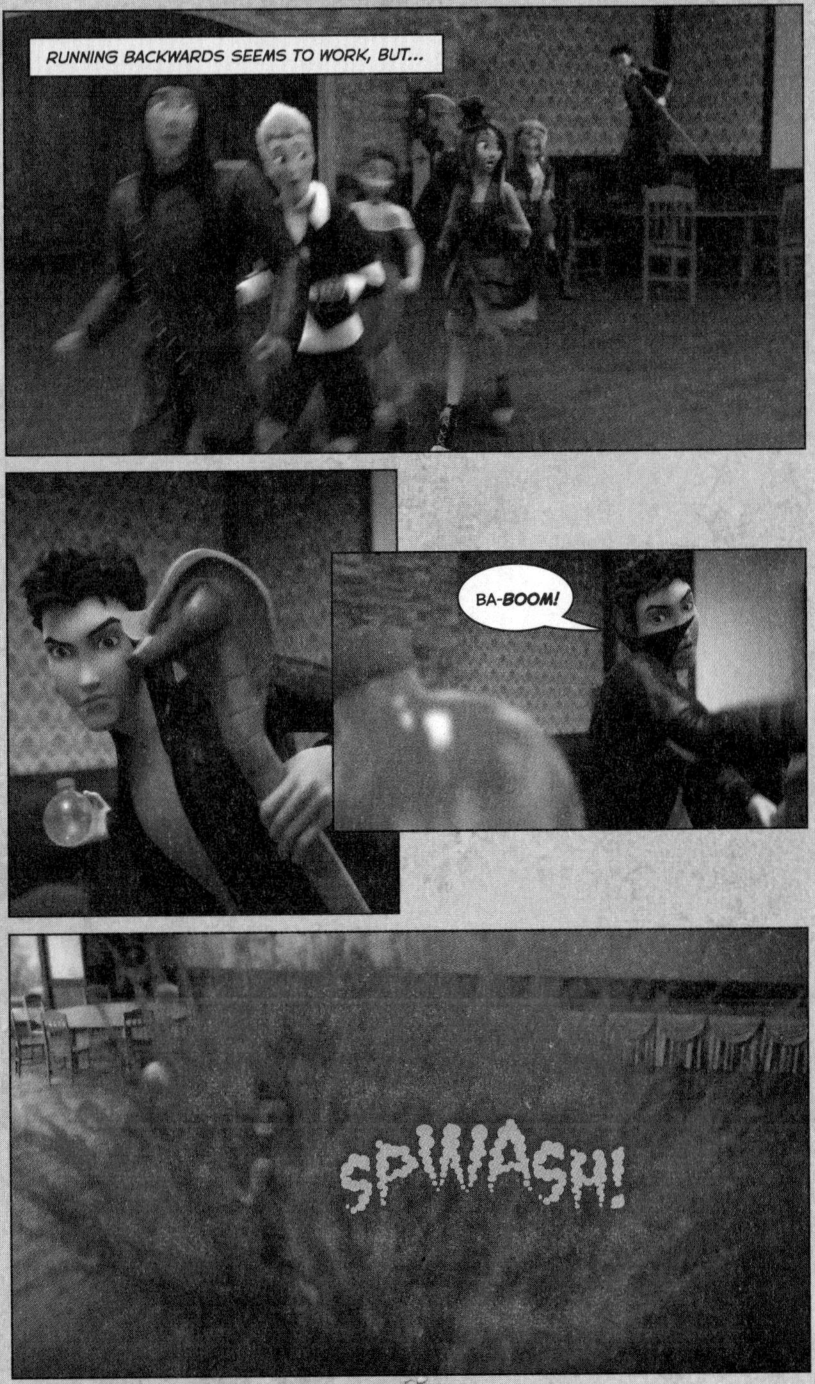
RUNNING BACKWARDS SEEMS TO WORK, BUT...
BA-BOOM!
SPWASH!

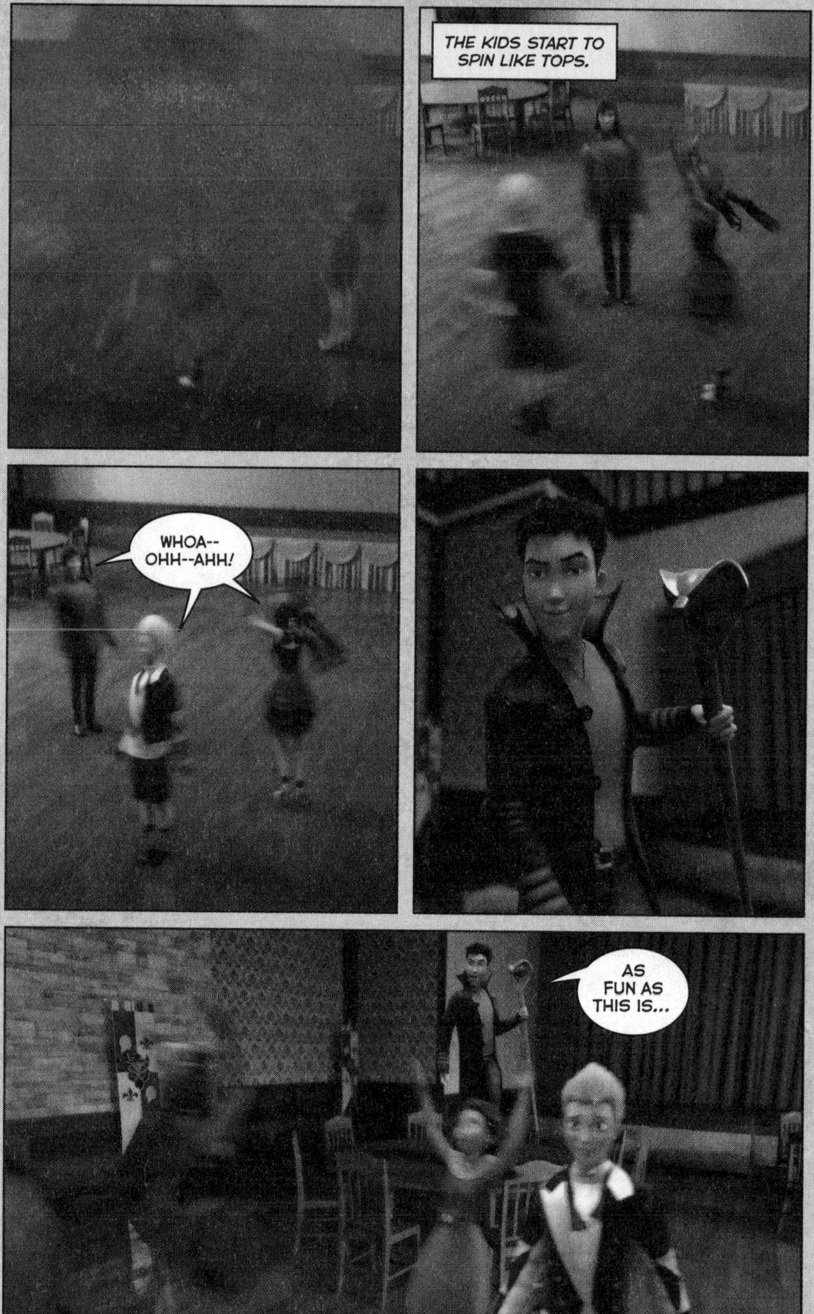
THE KIDS START TO SPIN LIKE TOPS.
WHOA-- OHH--AHH!
AS FUN AS THIS IS...

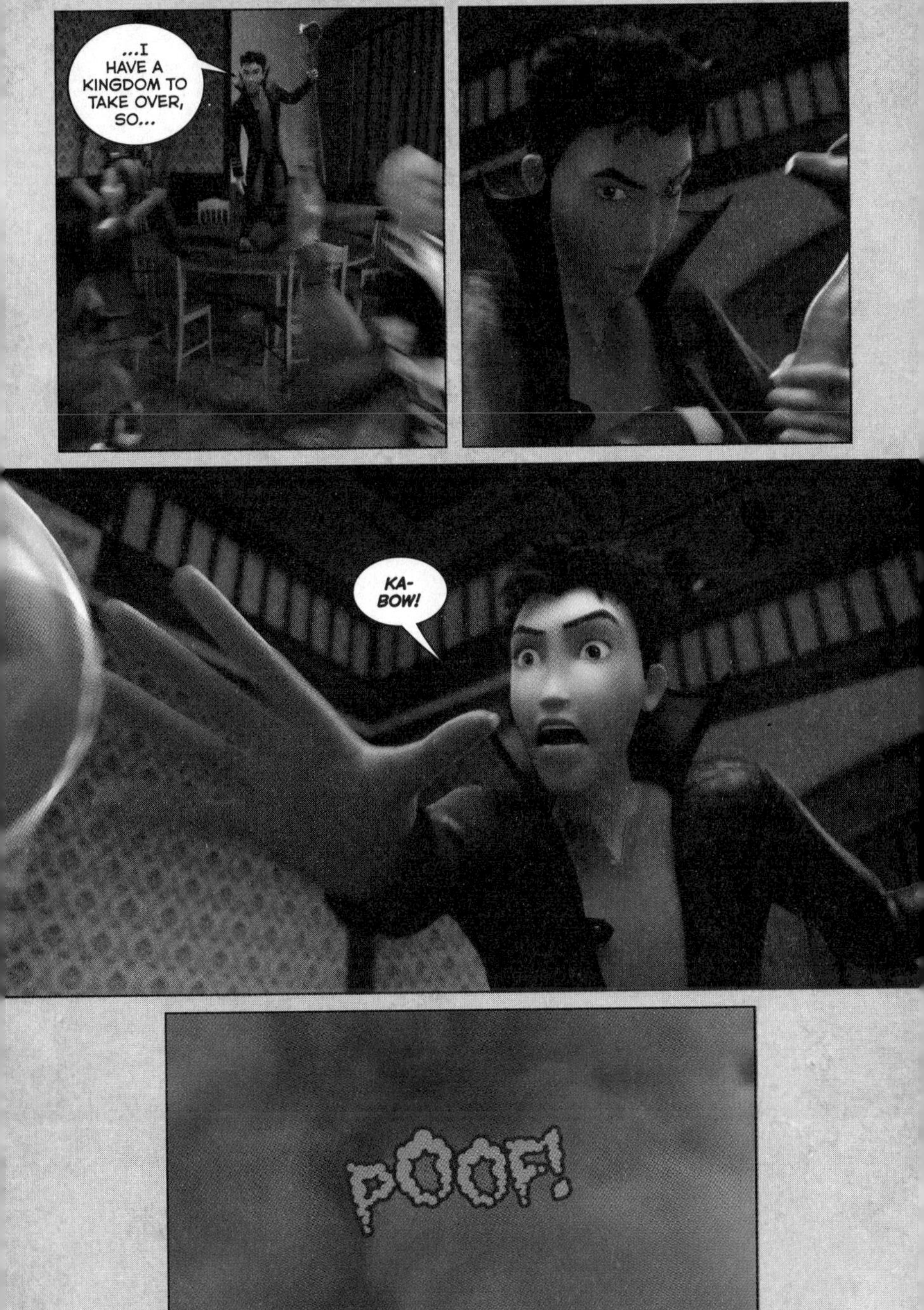
...I HAVE A KINGDOM TO TAKE OVER, SO...
KA-BOW!
POOF!

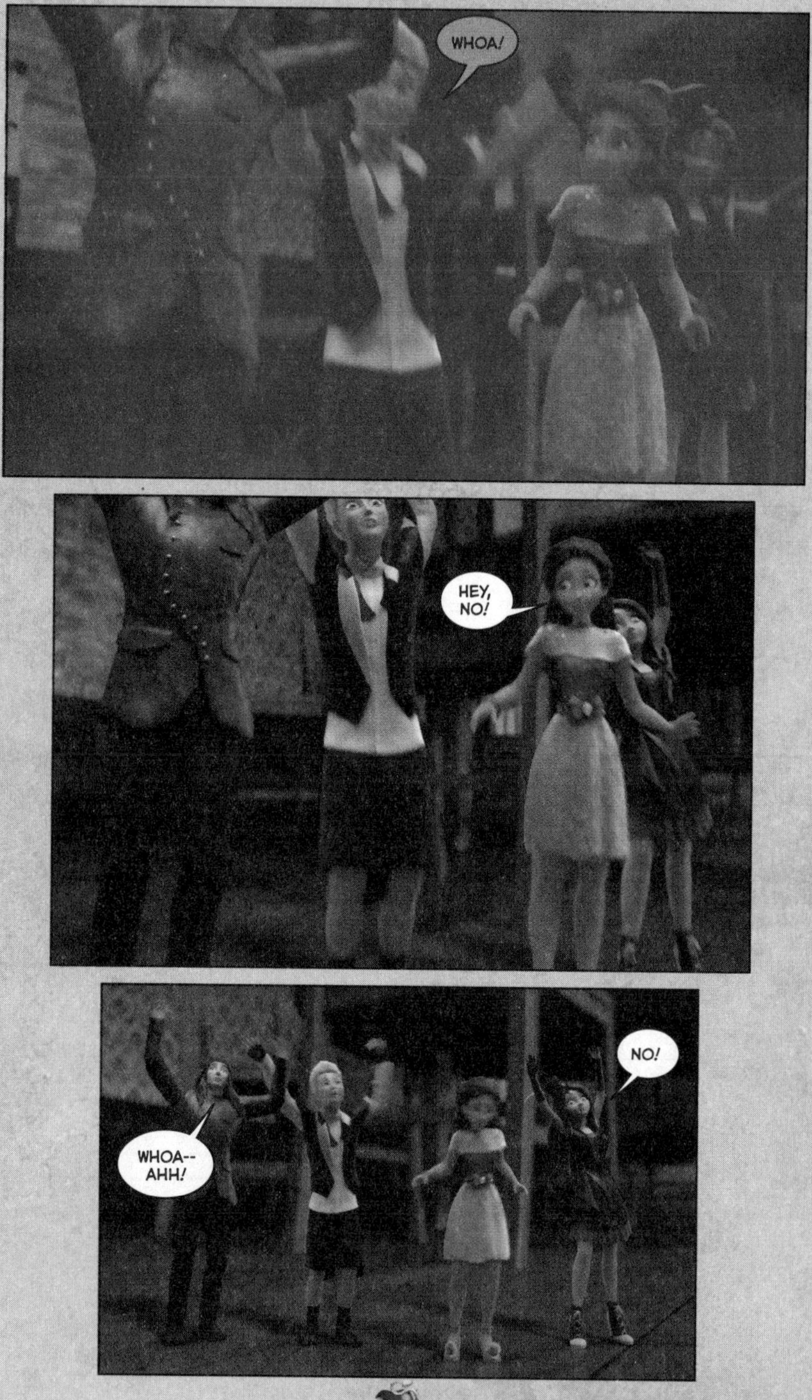
WHOA!
HEY, NO!
WHOA-- AHH!
NO!

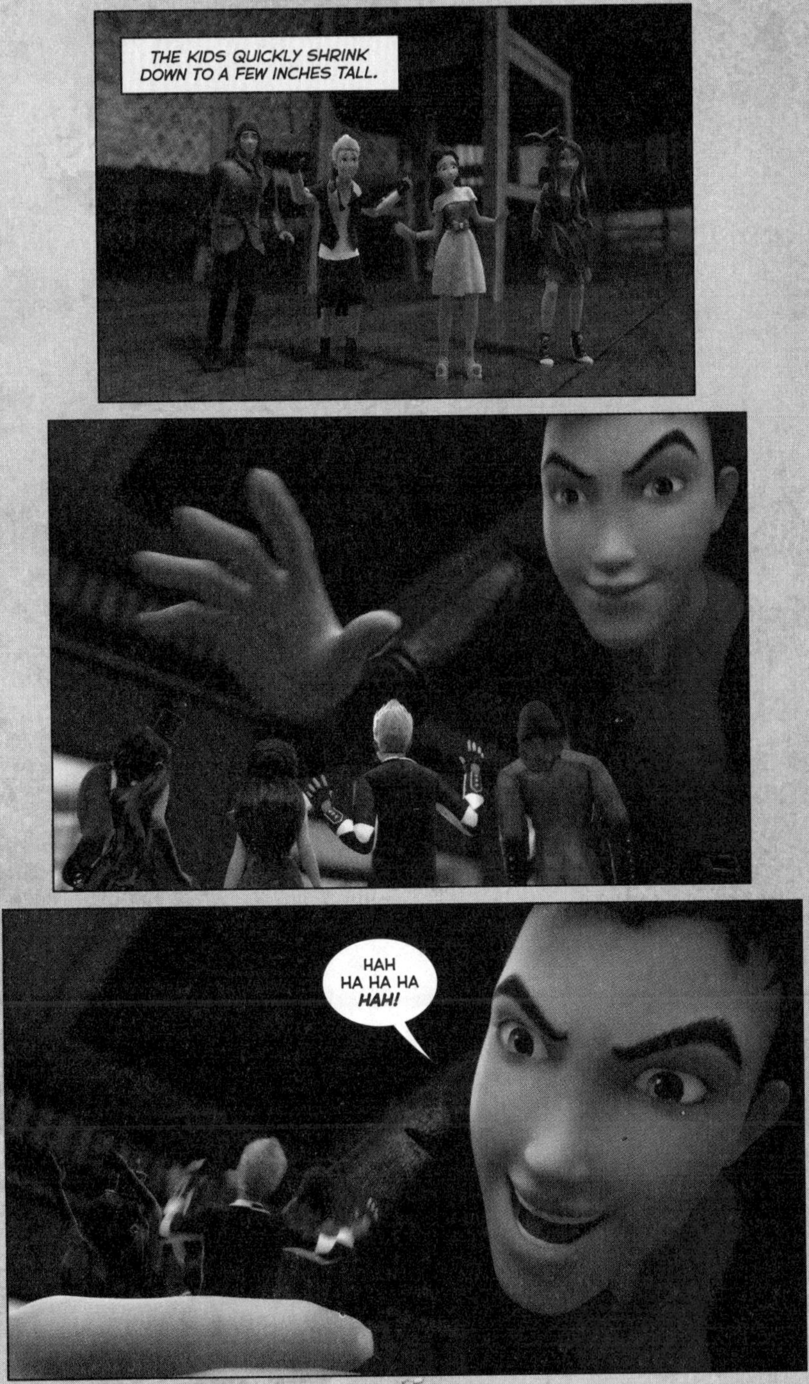
THE KIDS QUICKLY SHRINK DOWN TO A FEW INCHES TALL.
HAH HA HA HA HAH!

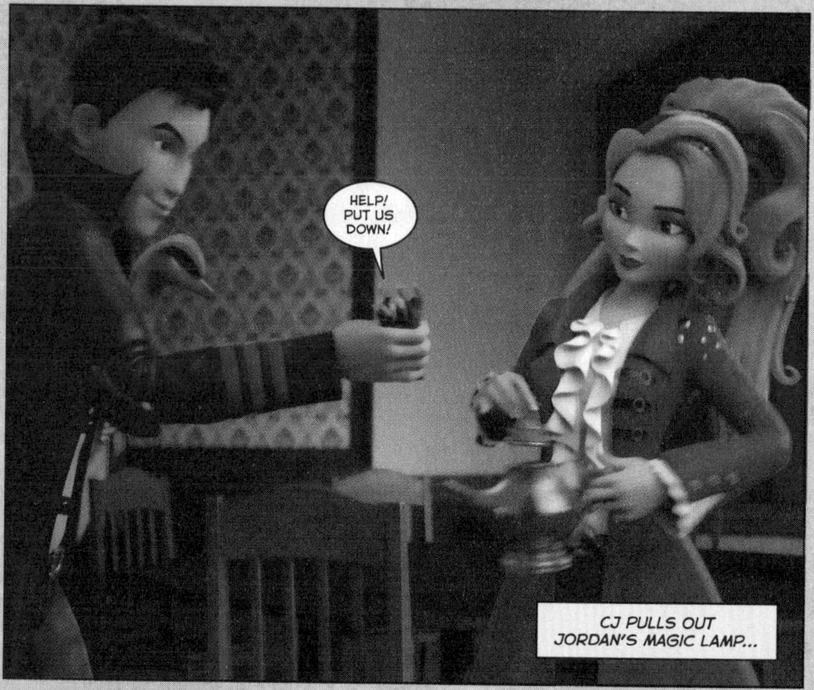
HELP! PUT US DOWN!
CJ PULLS OUT JORDAN'S MAGIC LAMP...

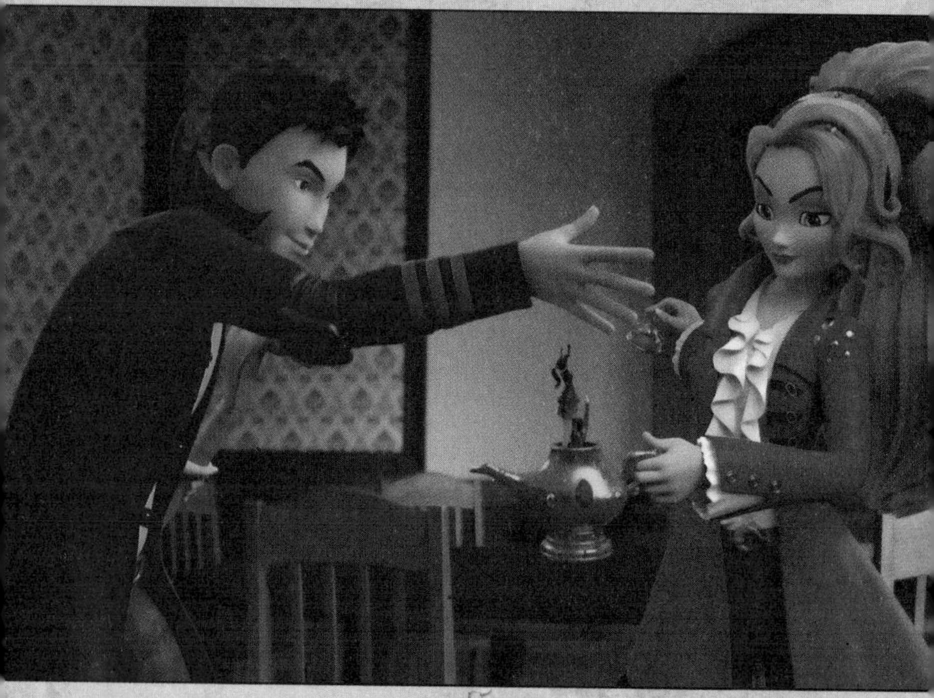

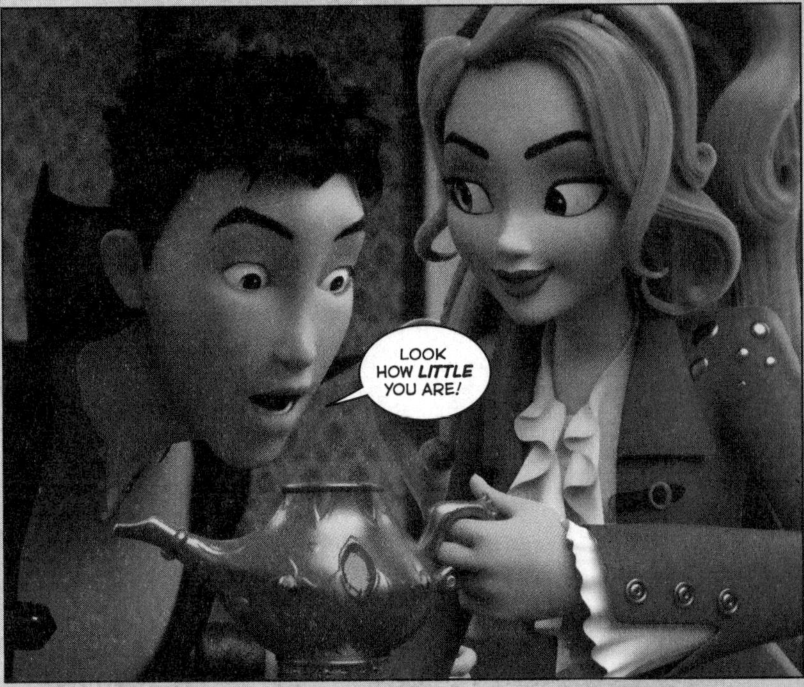
LOOK HOW *LITTLE* YOU ARE!

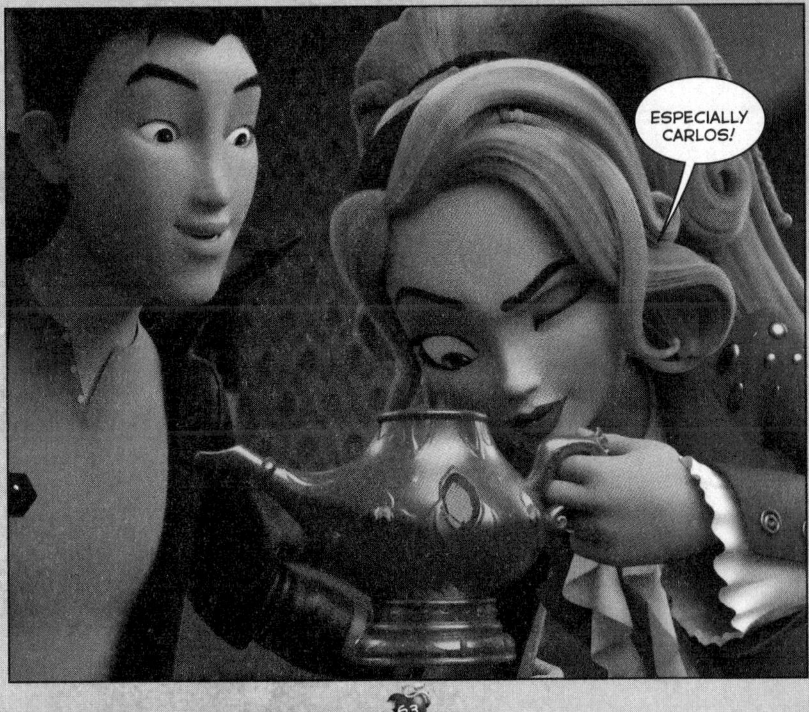
ESPECIALLY CARLOS!

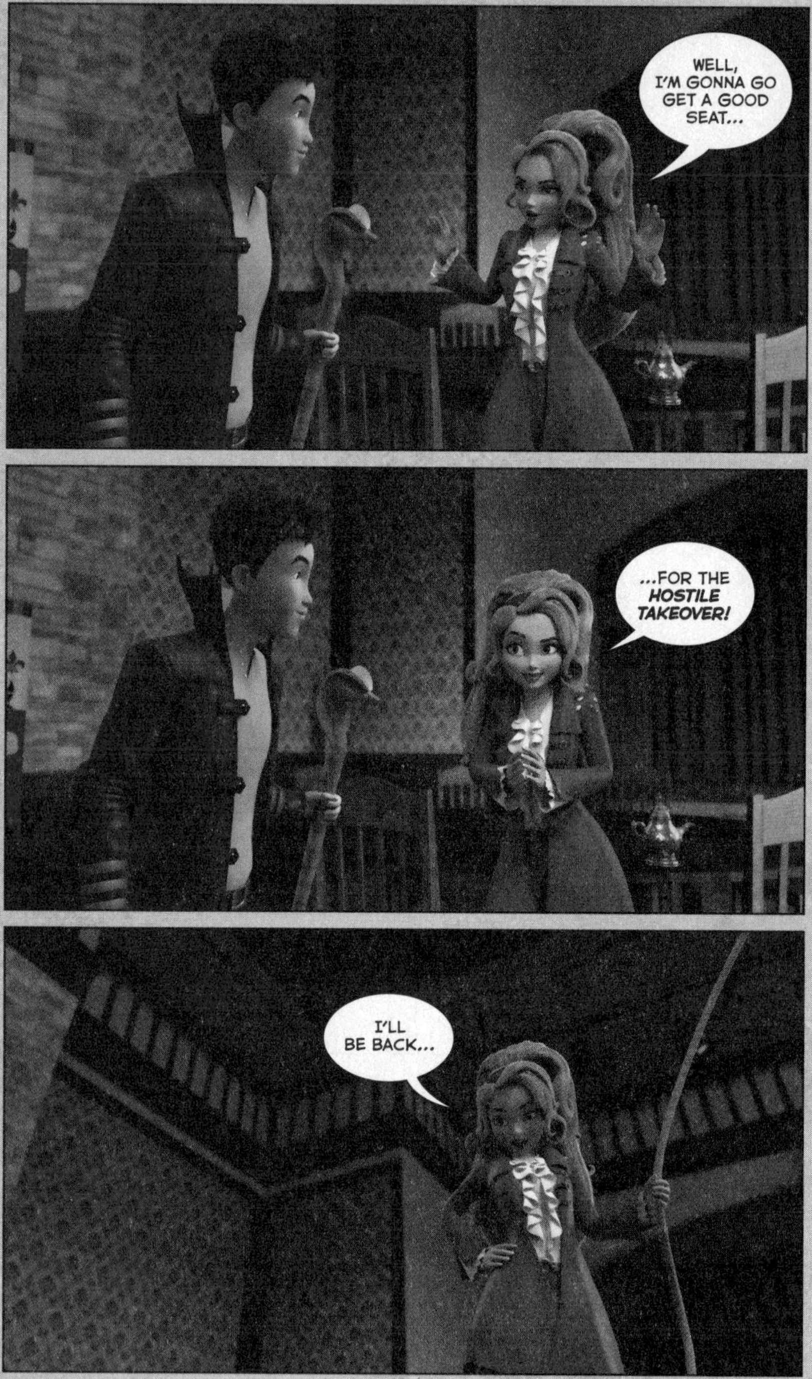
WELL, I'M GONNA GO GET A GOOD SEAT...
...FOR THE *HOSTILE TAKEOVER!*
I'LL BE BACK...

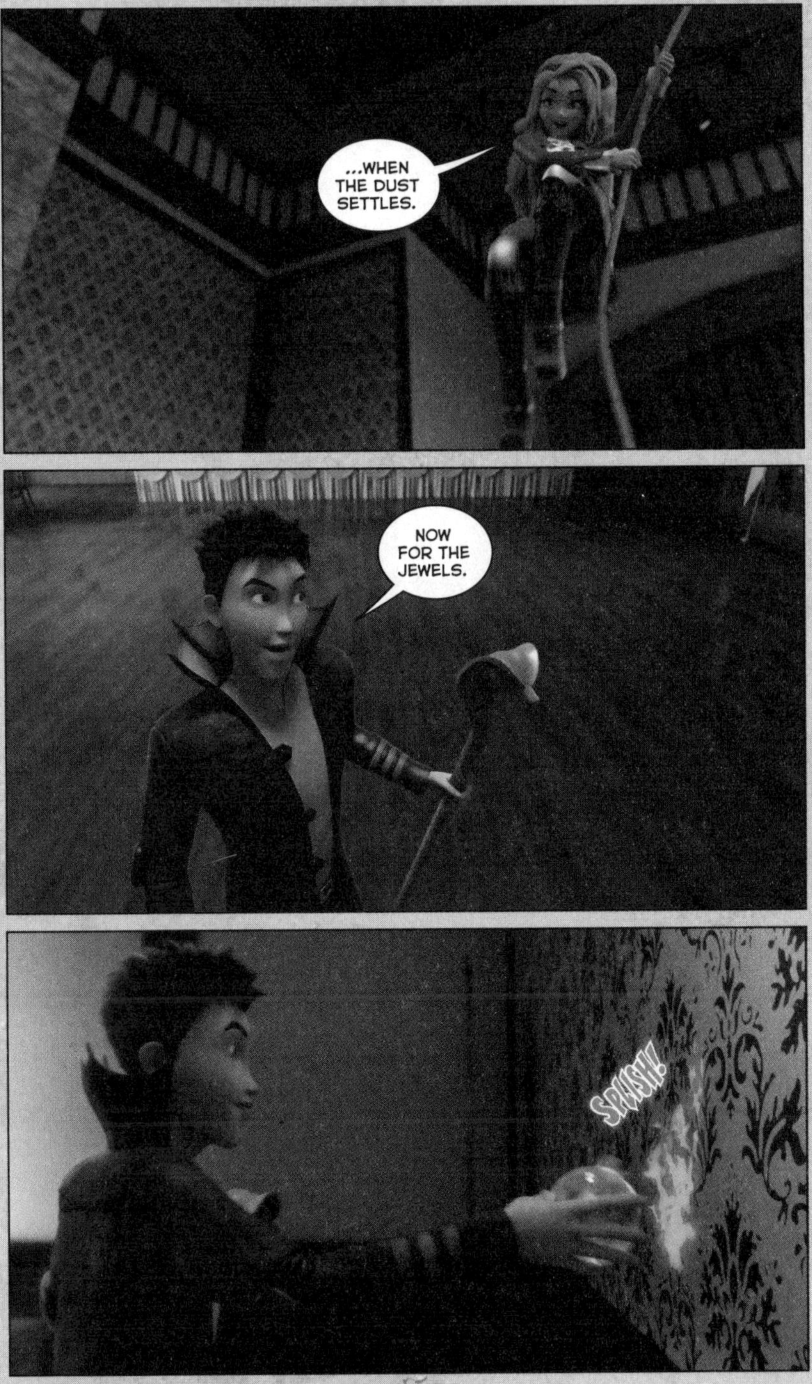
...WHEN THE DUST SETTLES.
NOW FOR THE JEWELS.
SPLISH!

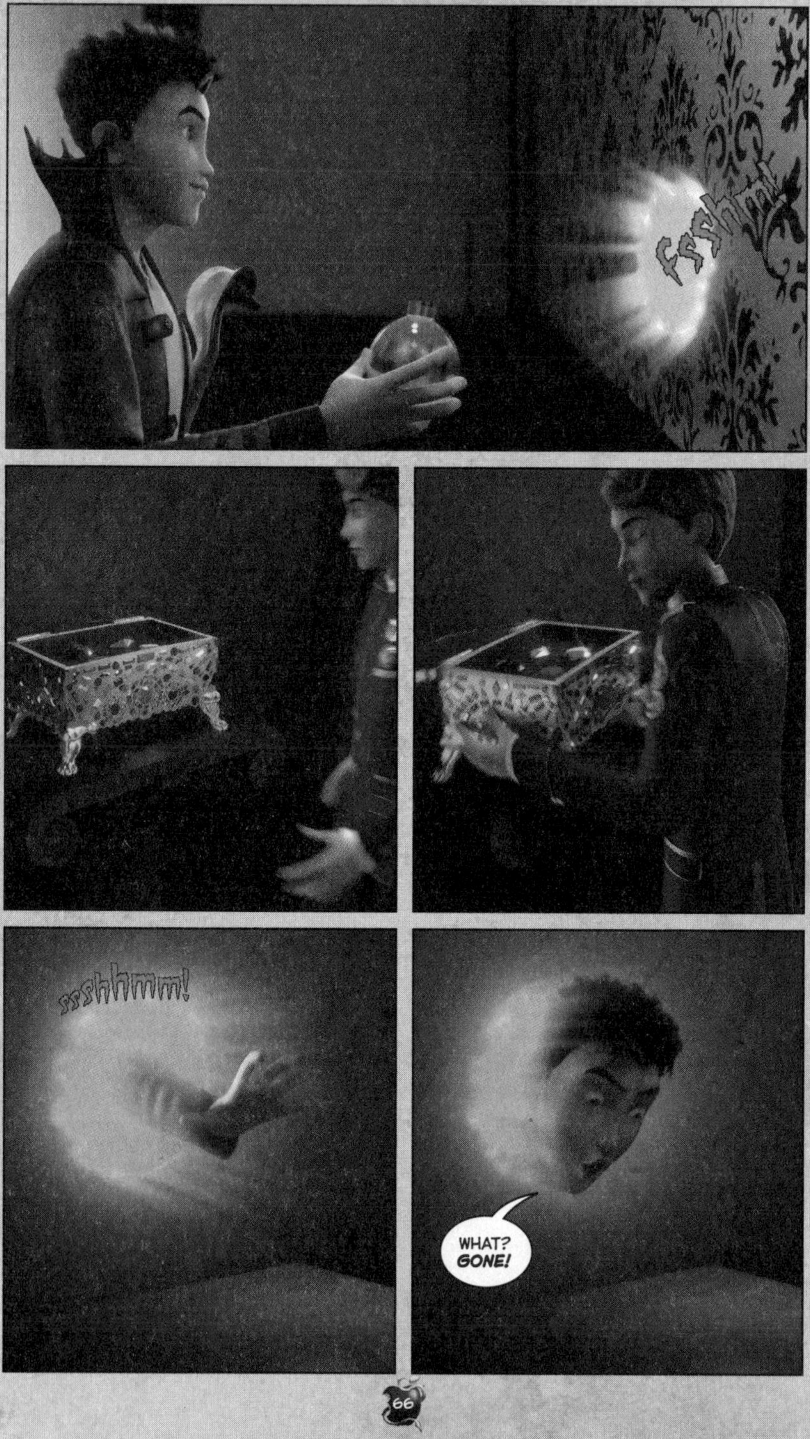
fshm!
sshhmm!
WHAT? GONE!

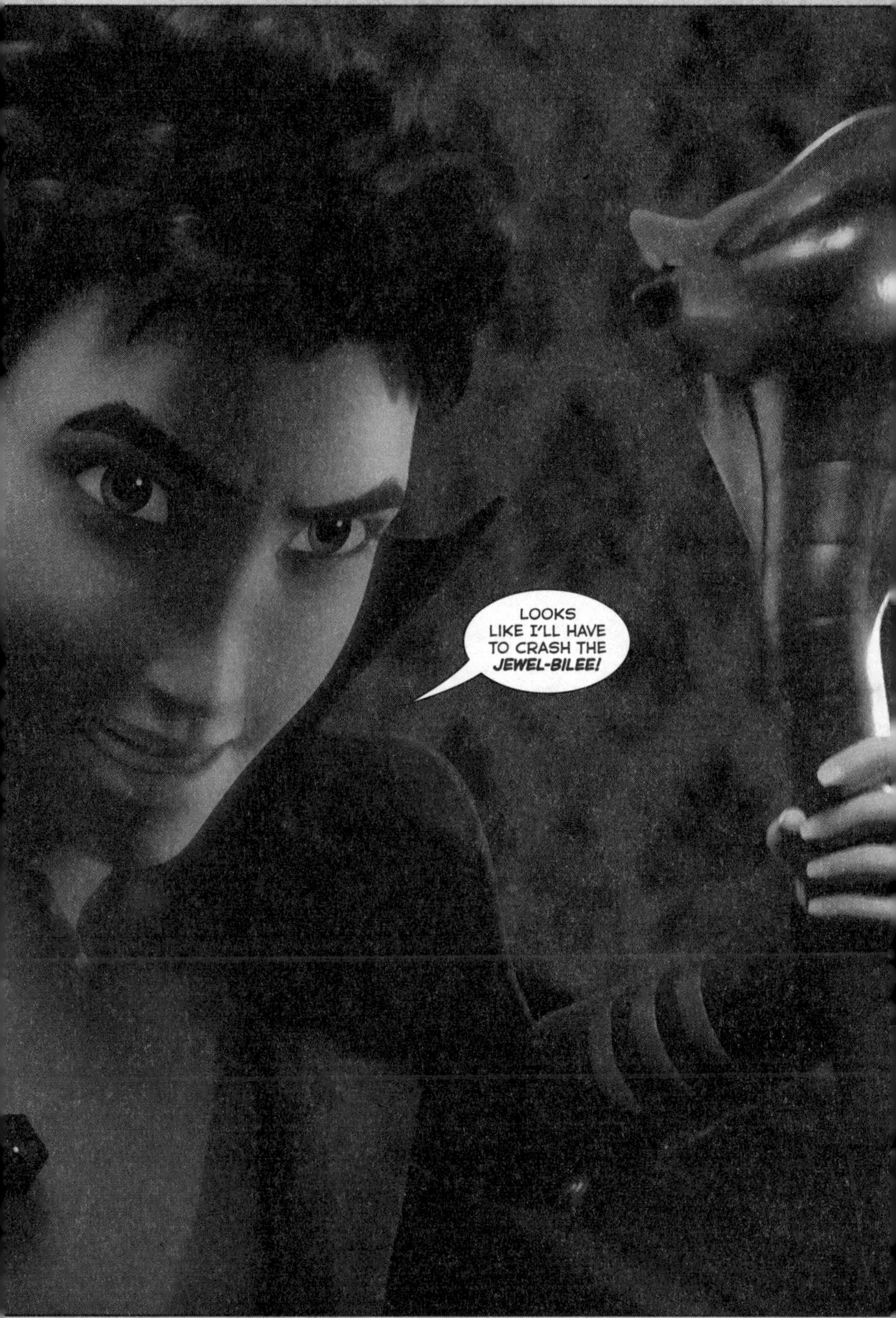
LOOKS LIKE I'LL HAVE TO CRASH THE *JEWEL-BILEE!*

CHAPTER 28: PARTY CRASHER

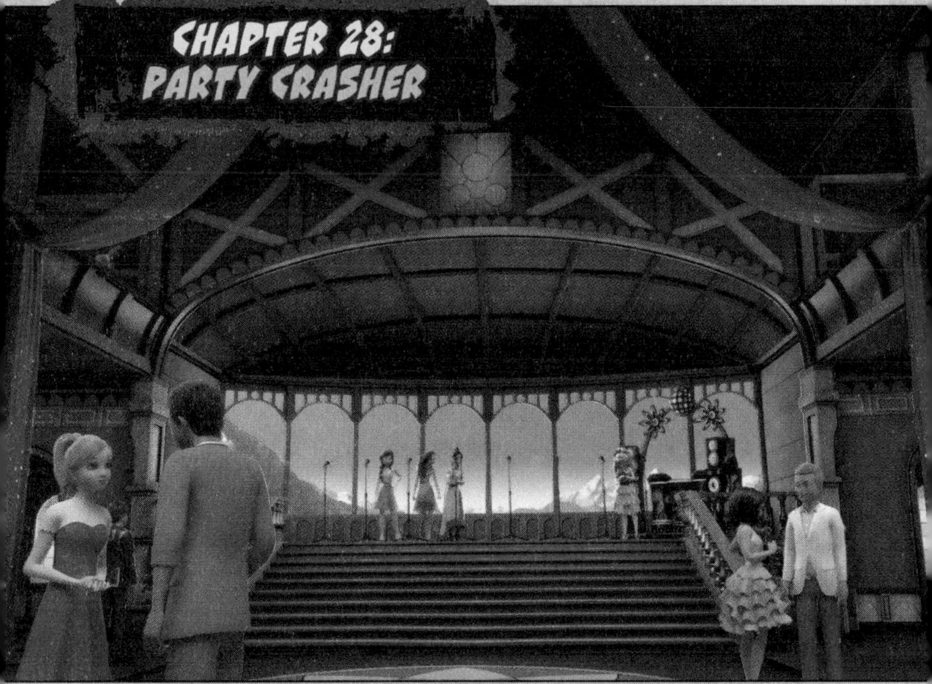

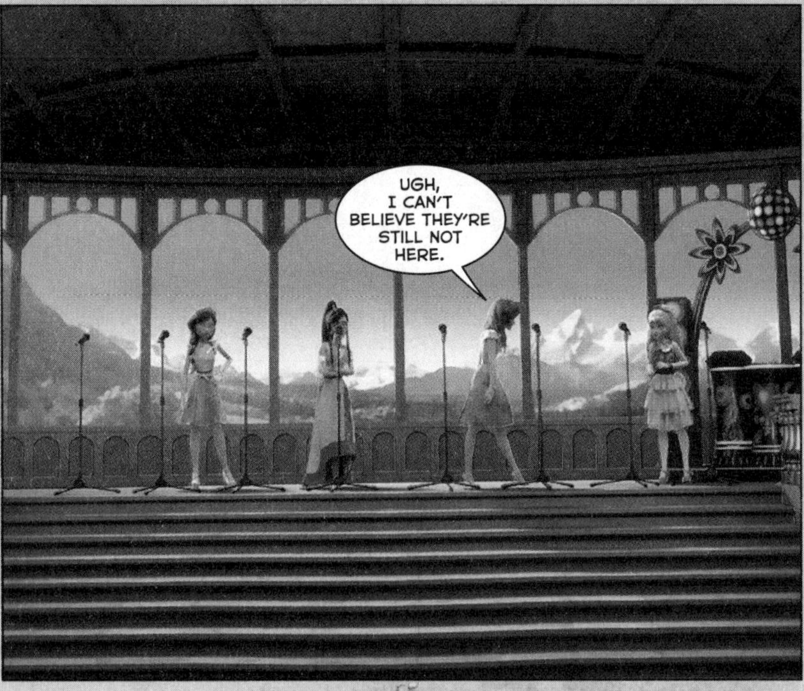
UGH, I CAN'T BELIEVE THEY'RE STILL NOT HERE.

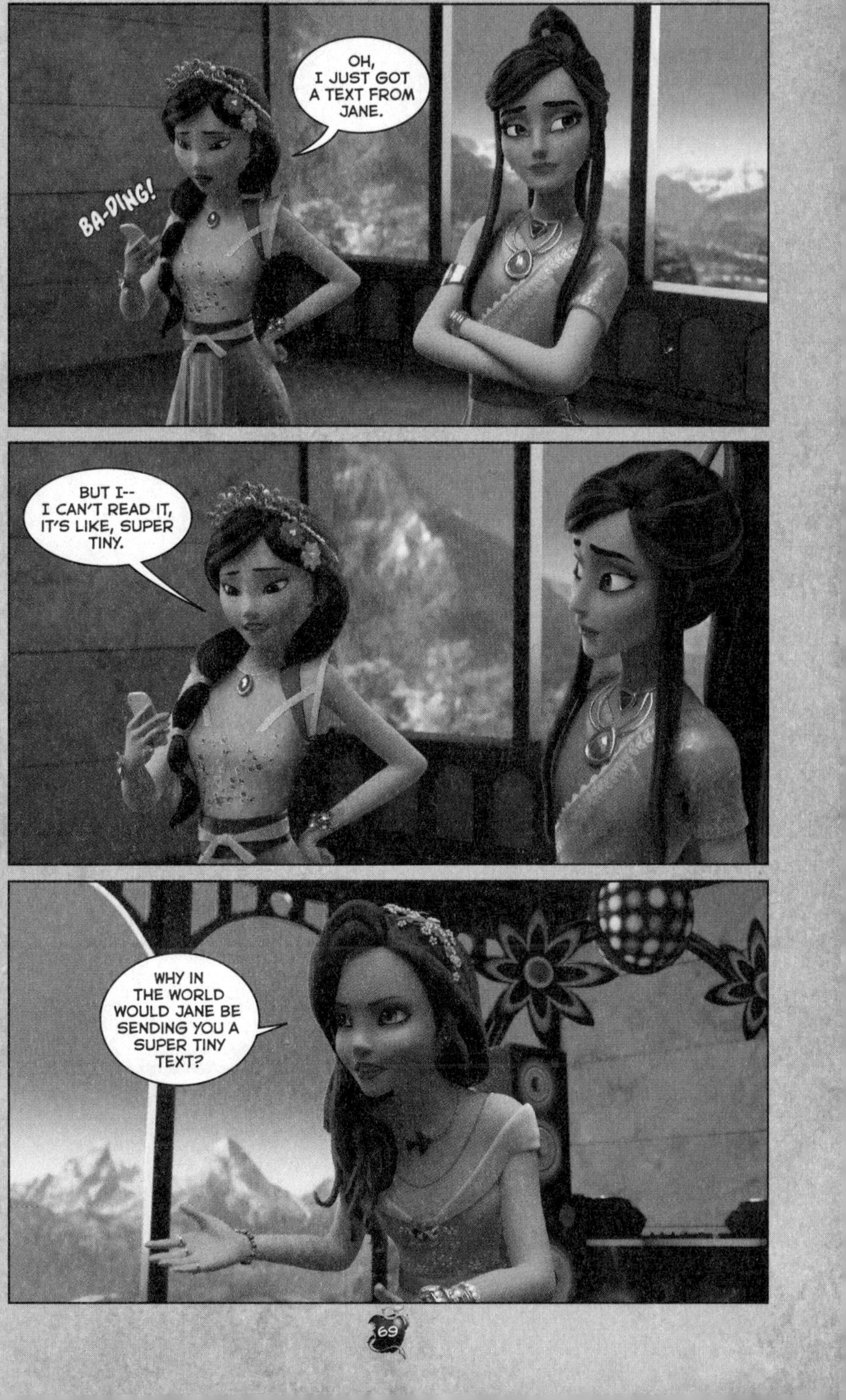
OH, I JUST GOT A TEXT FROM JANE.
BA-DING!
BUT I-- I CAN'T READ IT, IT'S LIKE, SUPER TINY.
WHY IN THE WORLD WOULD JANE BE SENDING YOU A SUPER TINY TEXT?

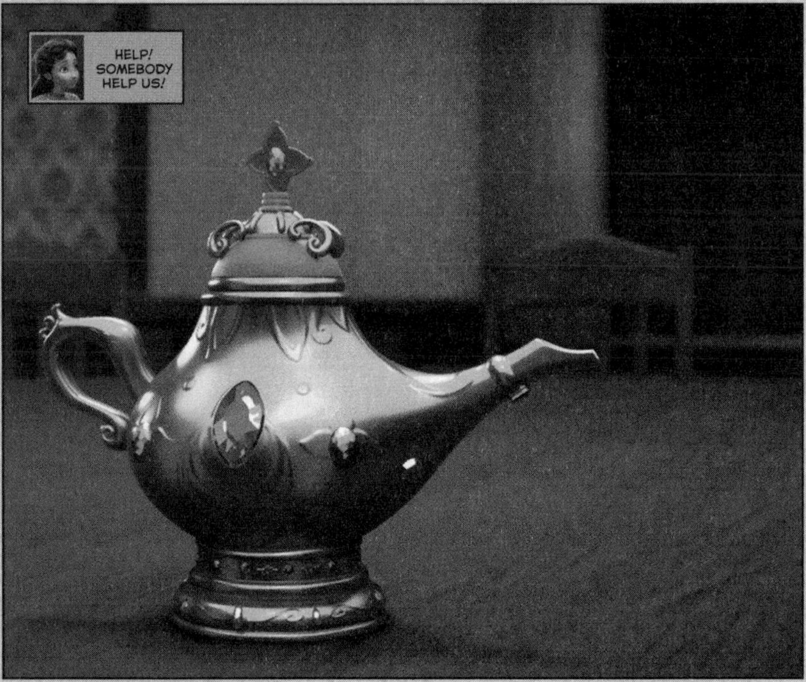
HELP! SOMEBODY HELP US!

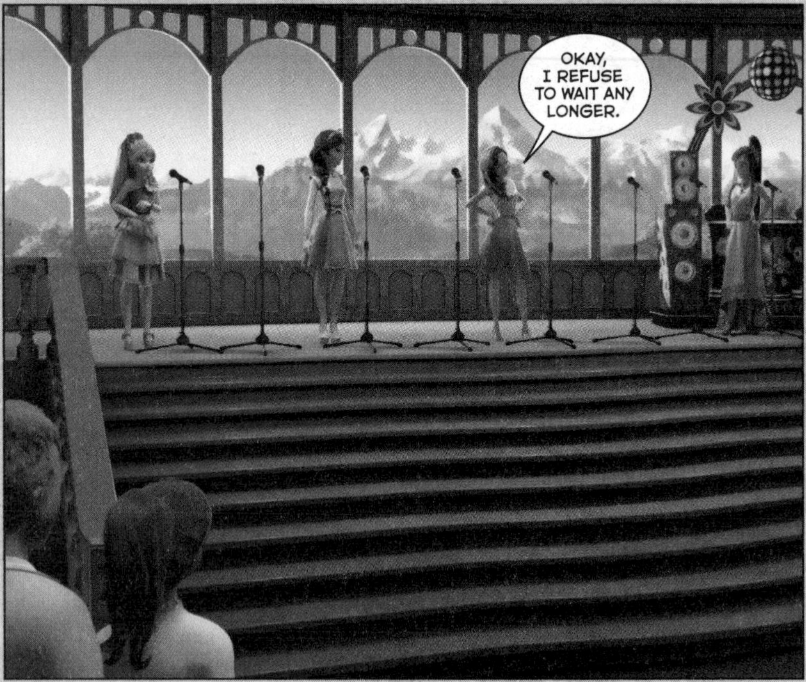
OKAY, I REFUSE TO WAIT ANY LONGER.

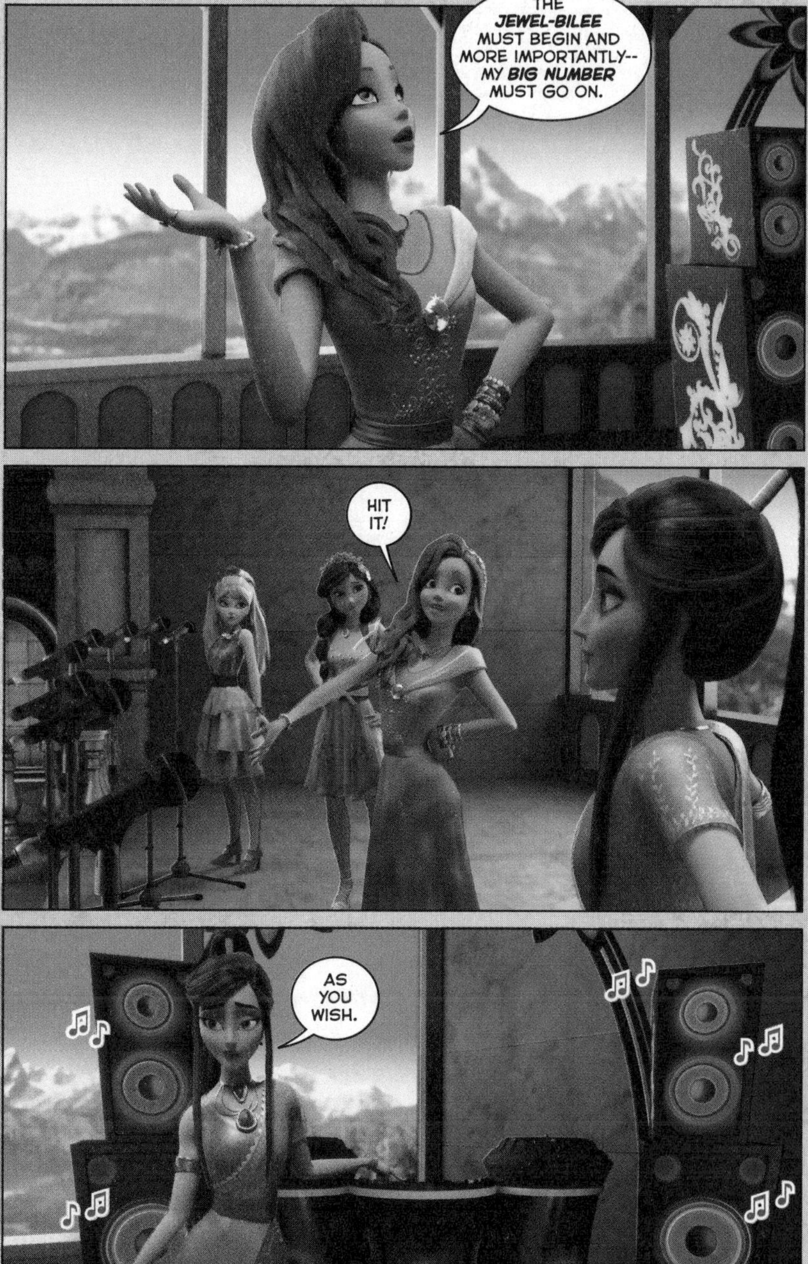
THE *JEWEL-BILEE* MUST BEGIN AND MORE IMPORTANTLY-- MY *BIG NUMBER* MUST GO ON.
HIT IT!
AS YOU WISH.

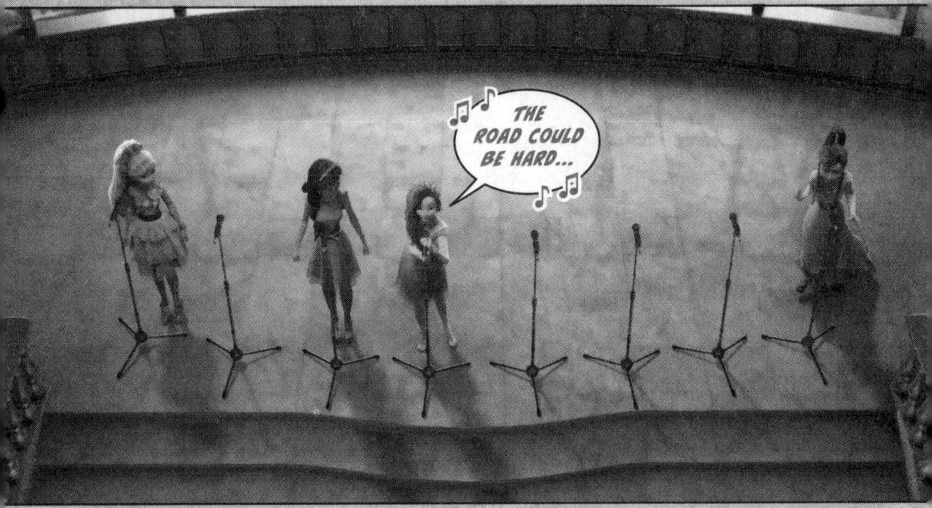
THE ROAD COULD BE HARD...

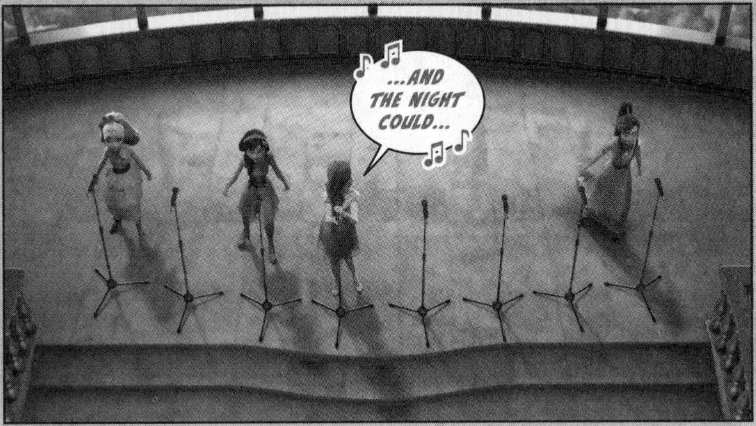
...AND THE NIGHT COULD...

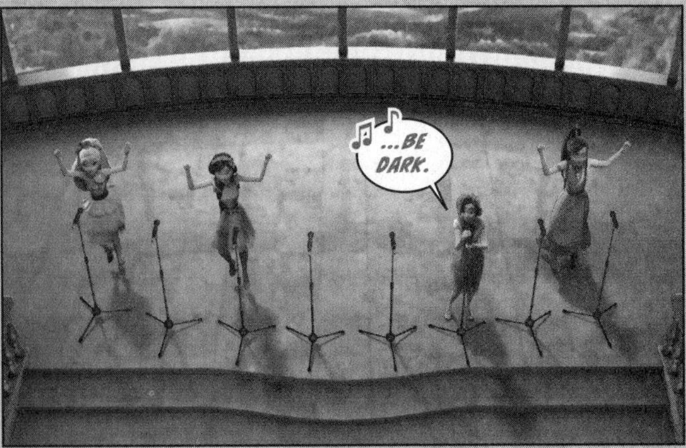
...BE DARK.

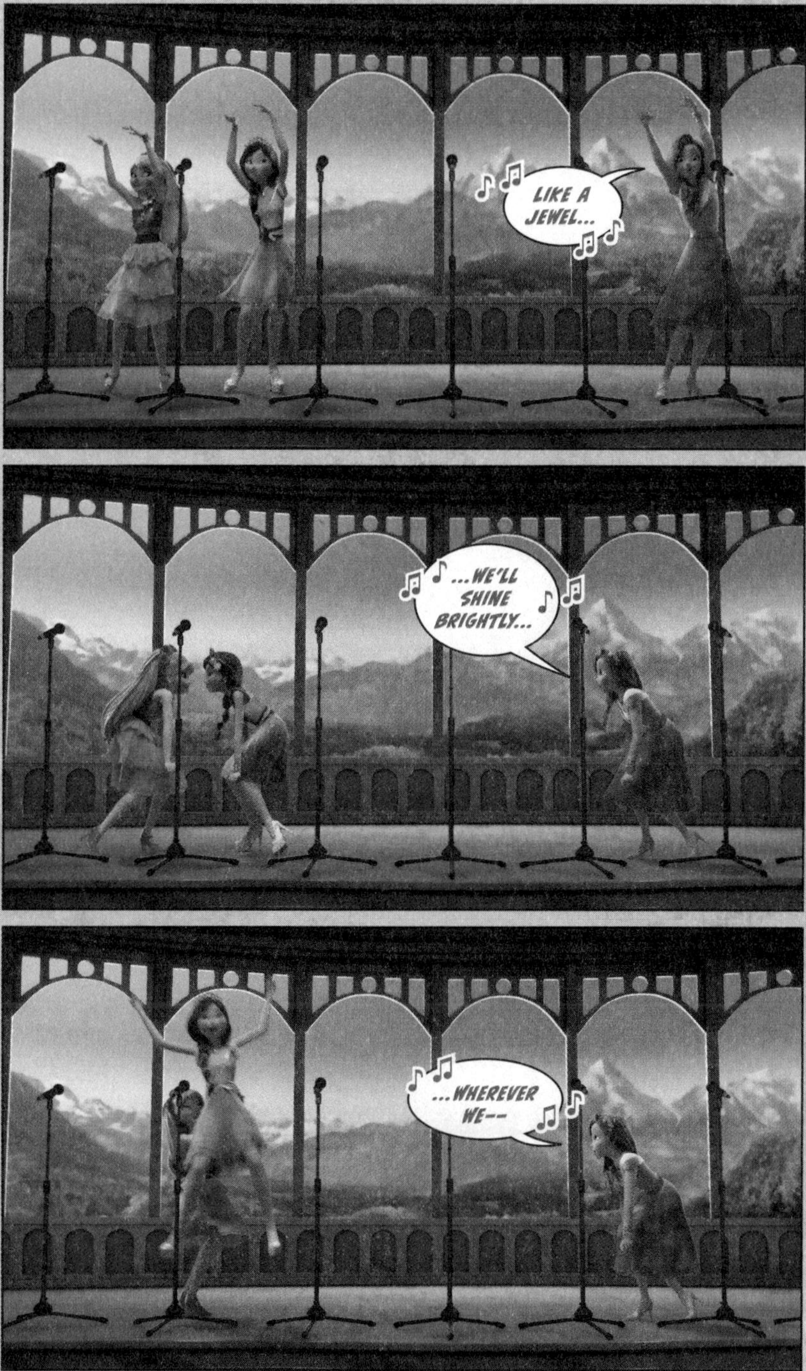
LIKE A JEWEL...
...WE'LL SHINE BRIGHTLY...
...WHEREVER WE--

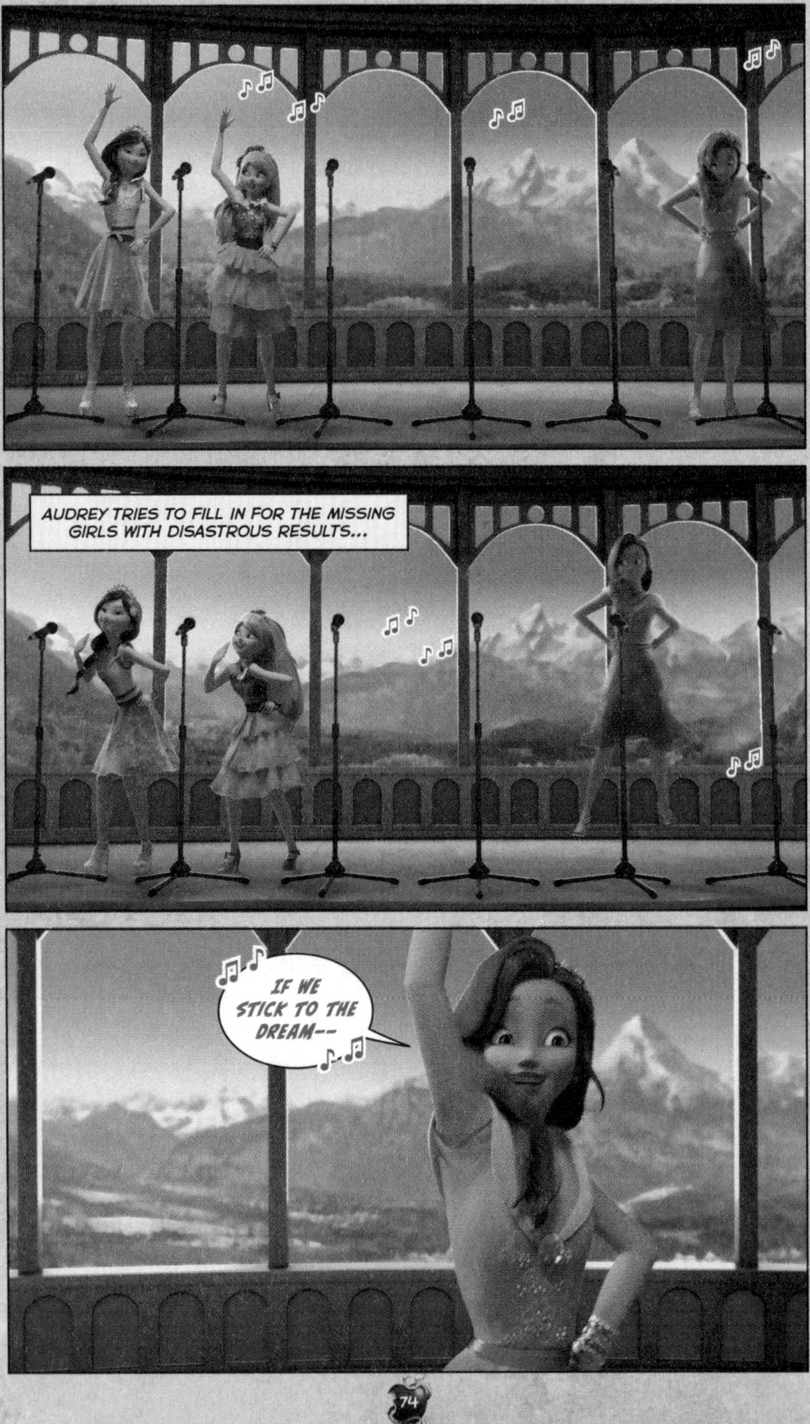
AUDREY TRIES TO FILL IN FOR THE MISSING GIRLS WITH DISASTROUS RESULTS...
IF WE STICK TO THE DREAM--

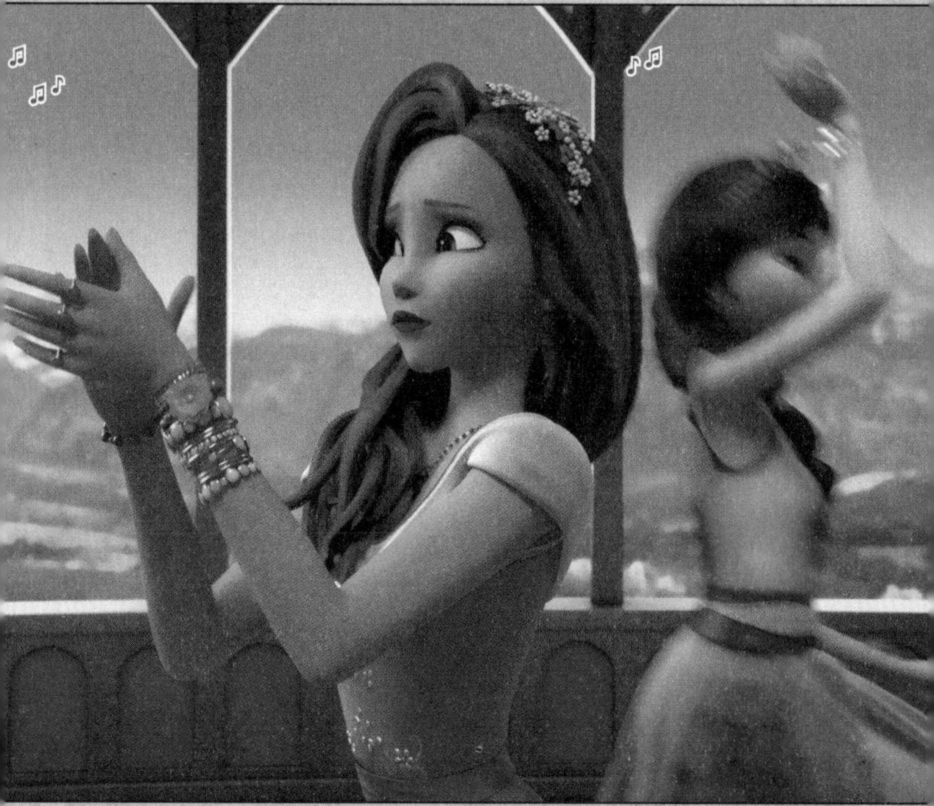

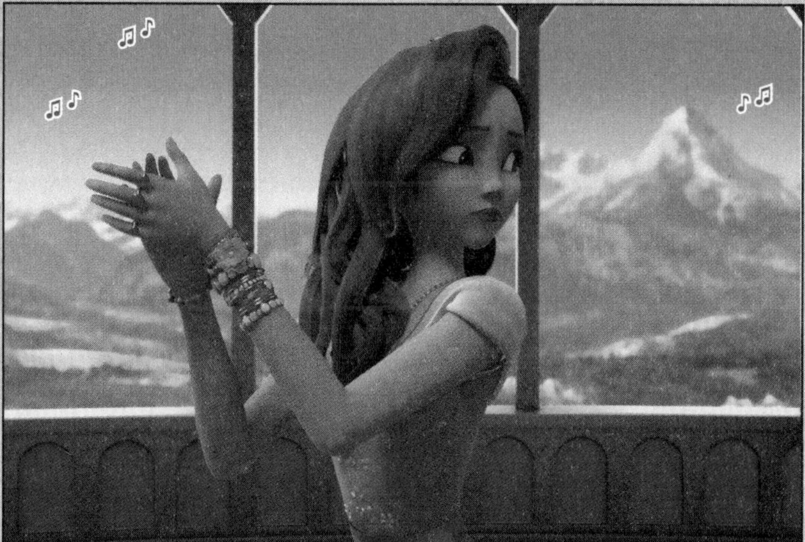

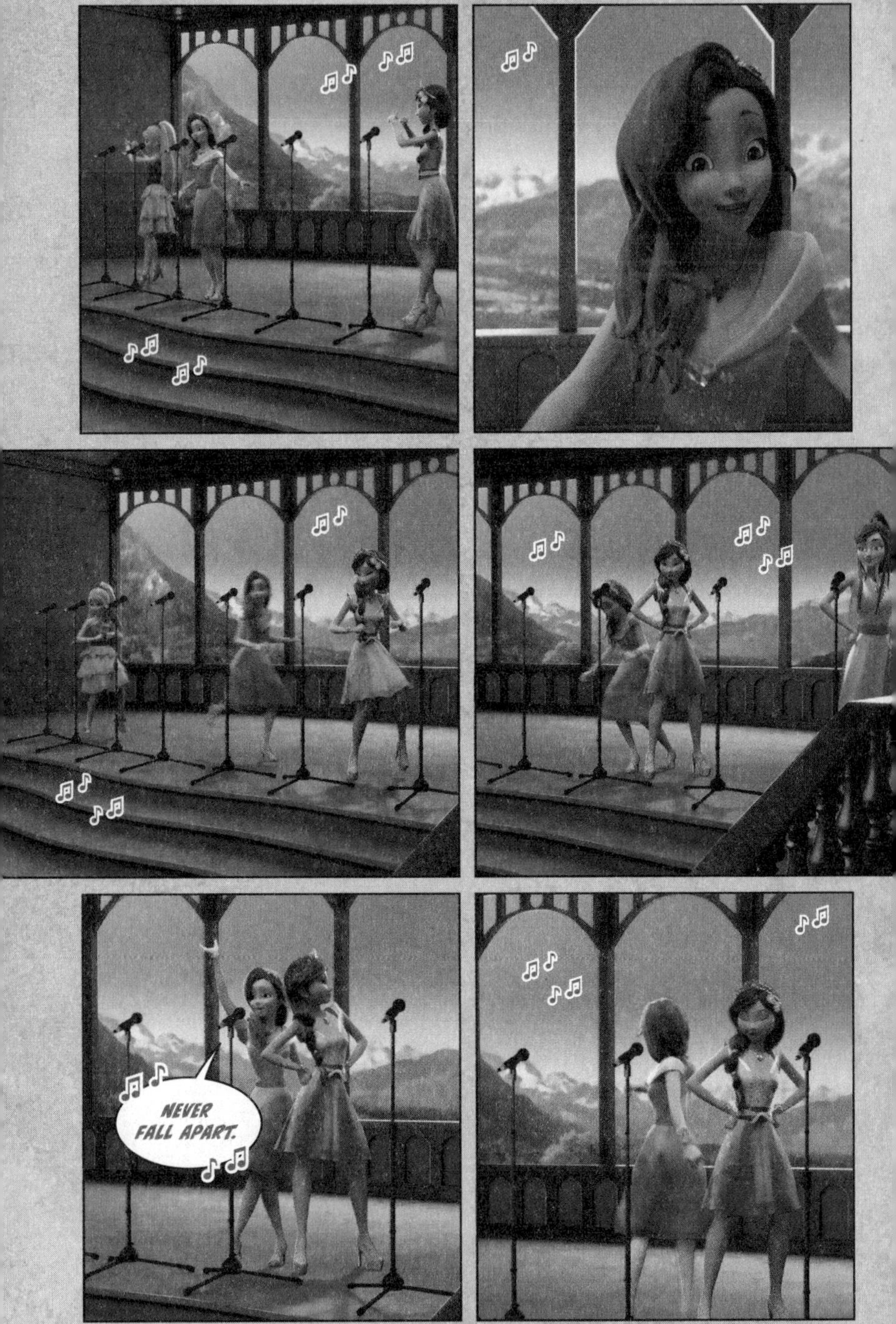
NEVER FALL APART.

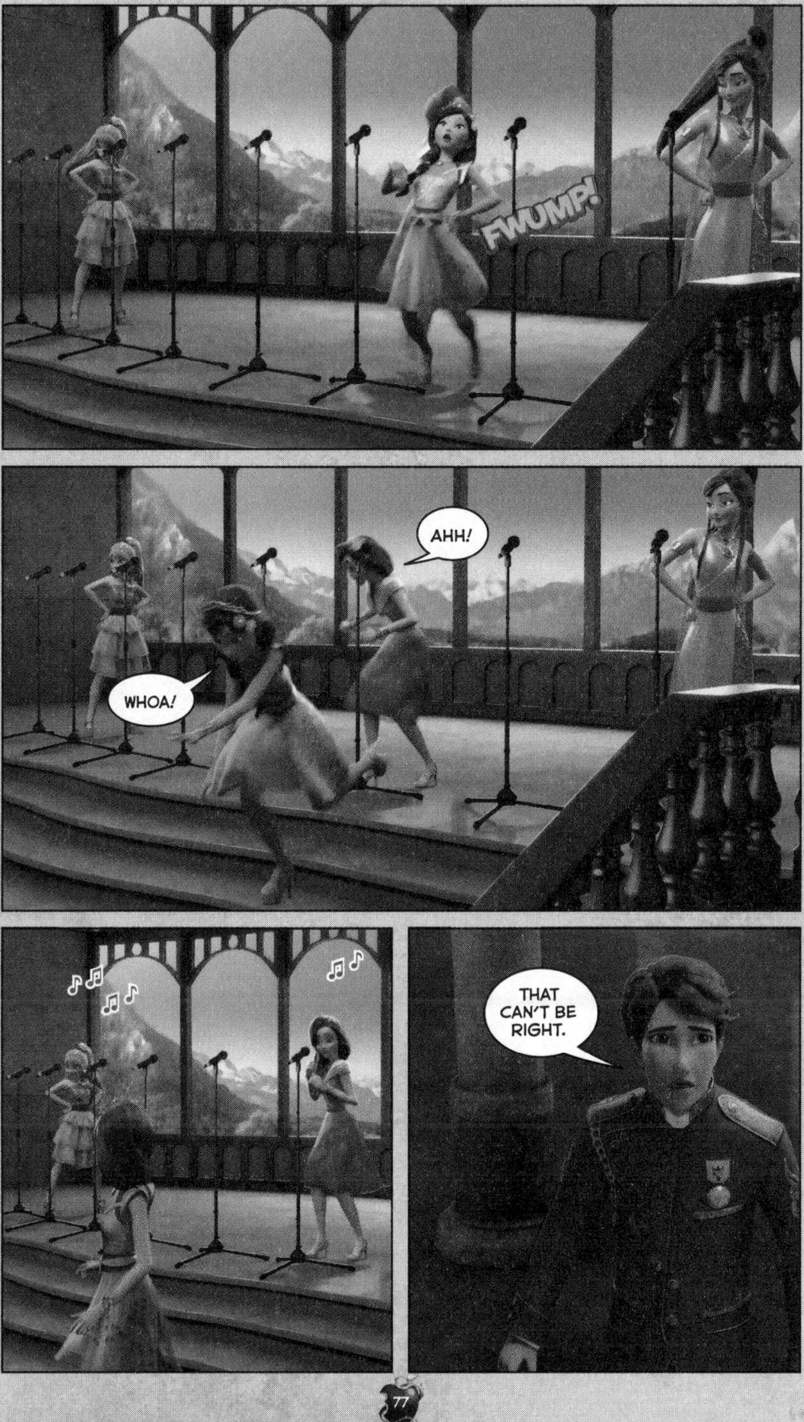
FWUMP!
AHH!
WHOA!
THAT CAN'T BE RIGHT.

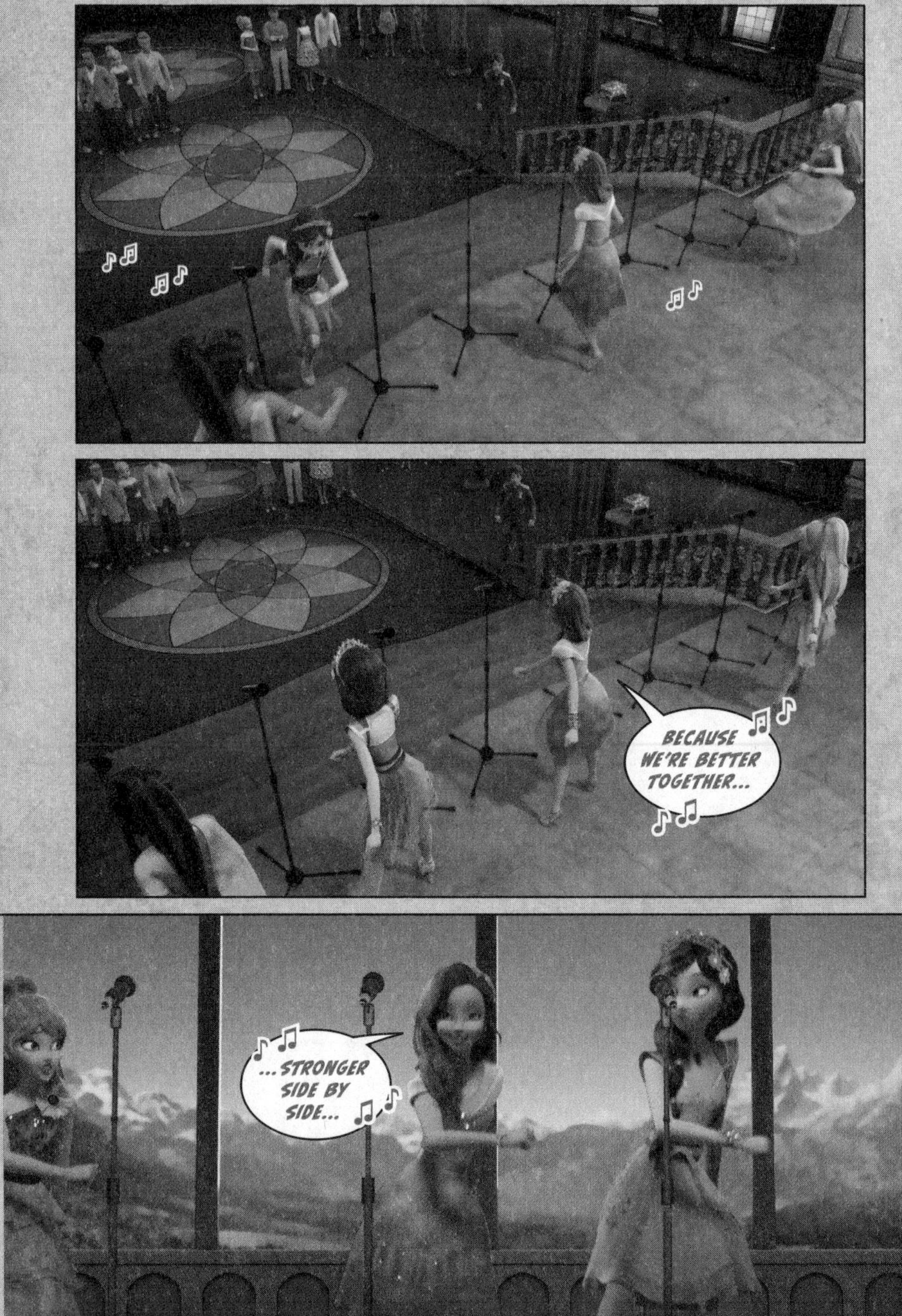
BECAUSE WE'RE BETTER TOGETHER...
...STRONGER SIDE BY SIDE...

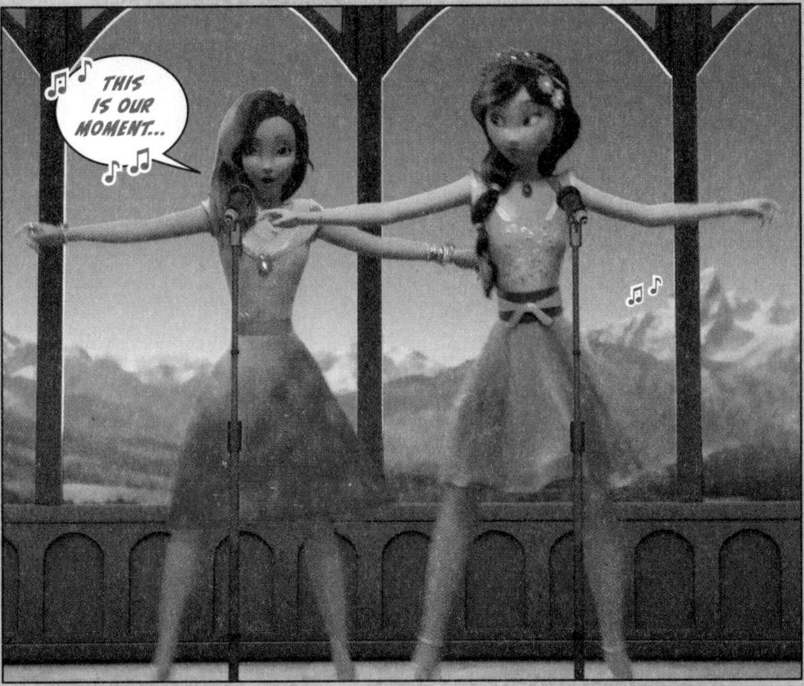
THIS IS OUR MOMENT...

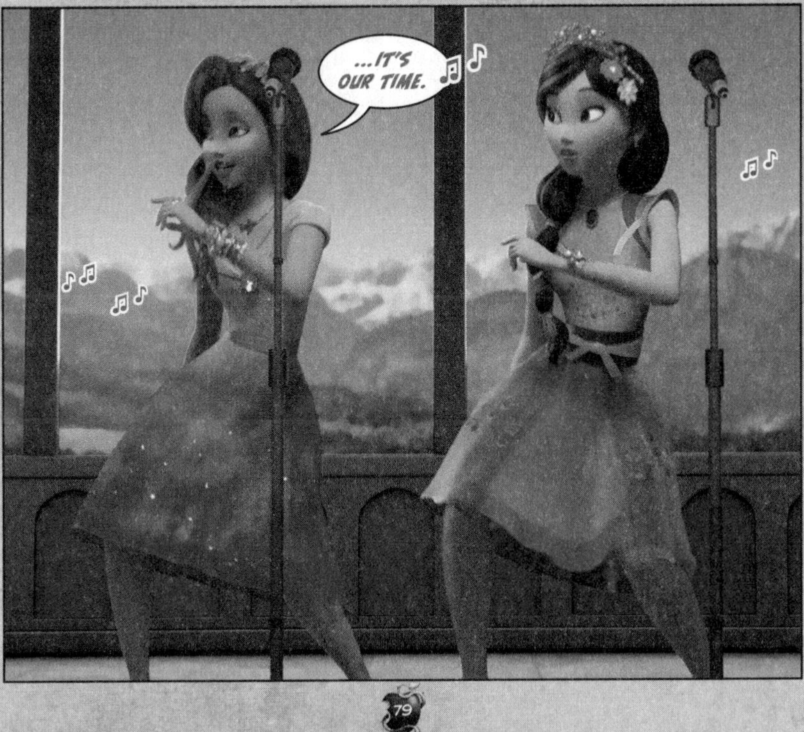
...IT'S OUR TIME.

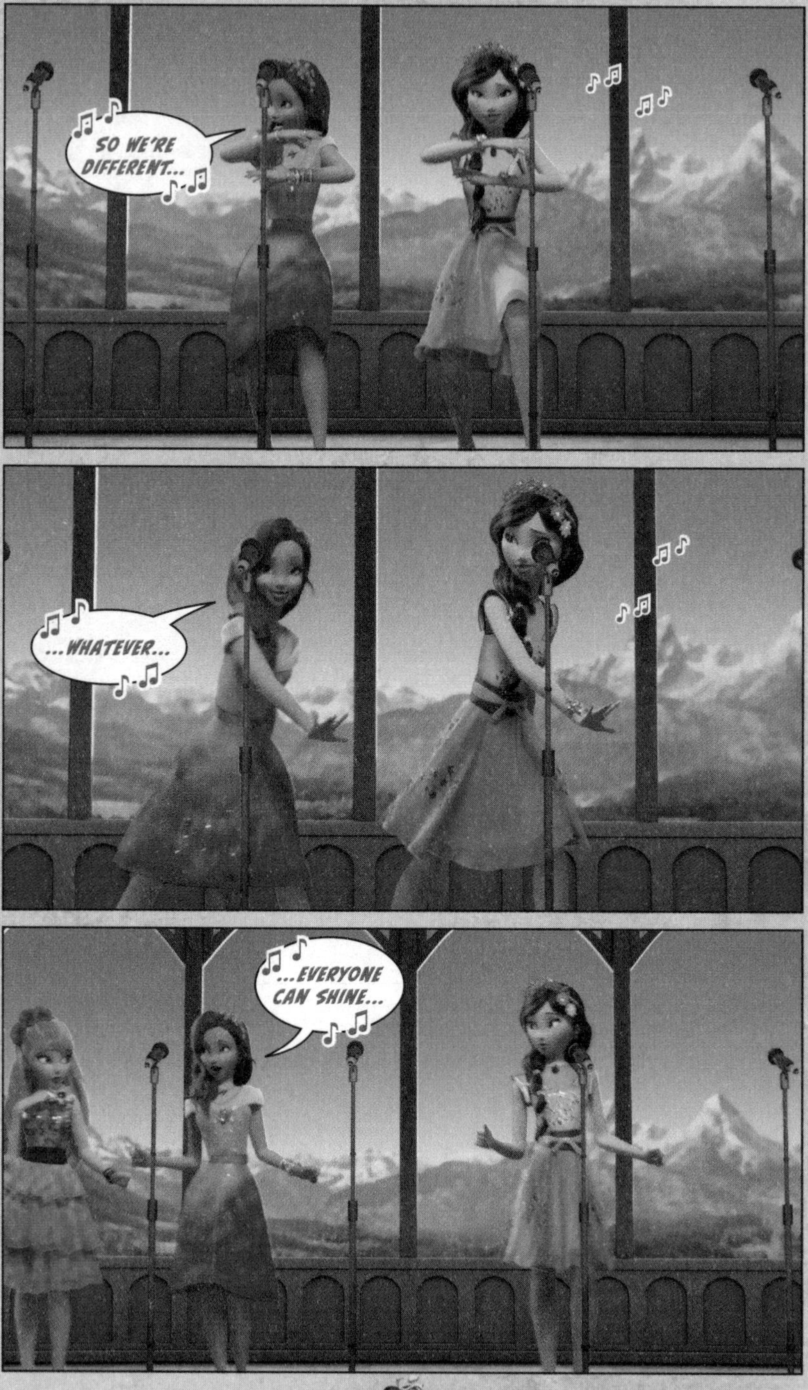
SO WE'RE DIFFERENT...
...WHATEVER...
...EVERYONE CAN SHINE...

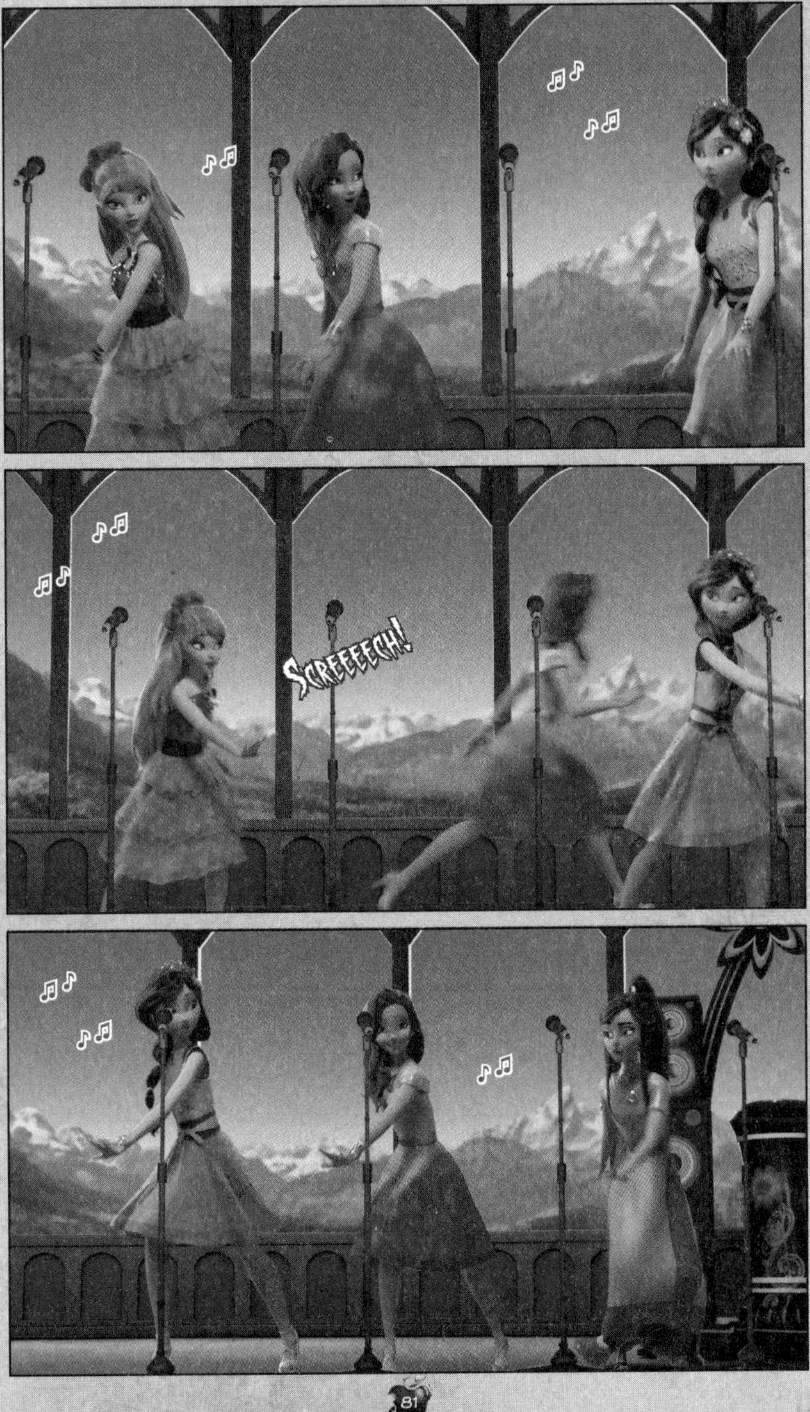
SCREEEEECH!

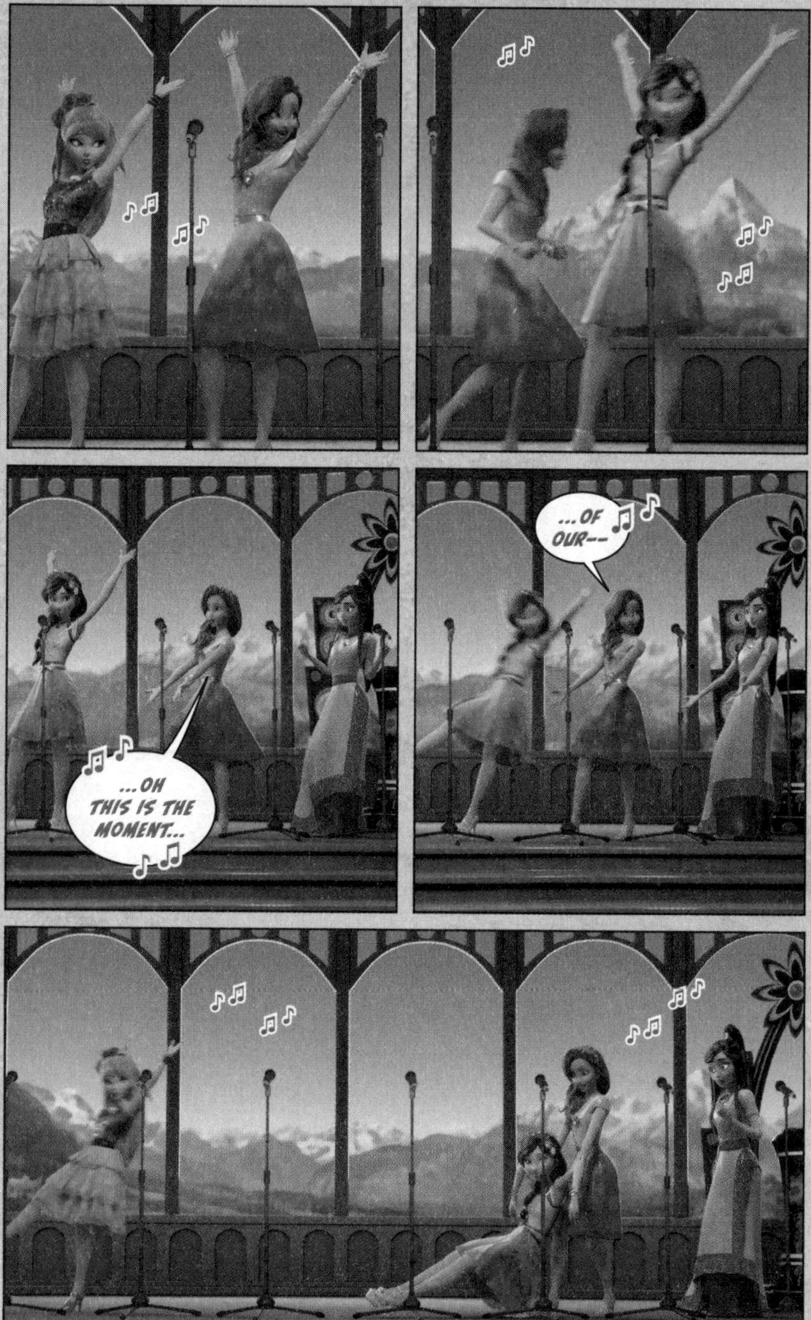
...OH THIS IS THE MOMENT...
...OF OUR--

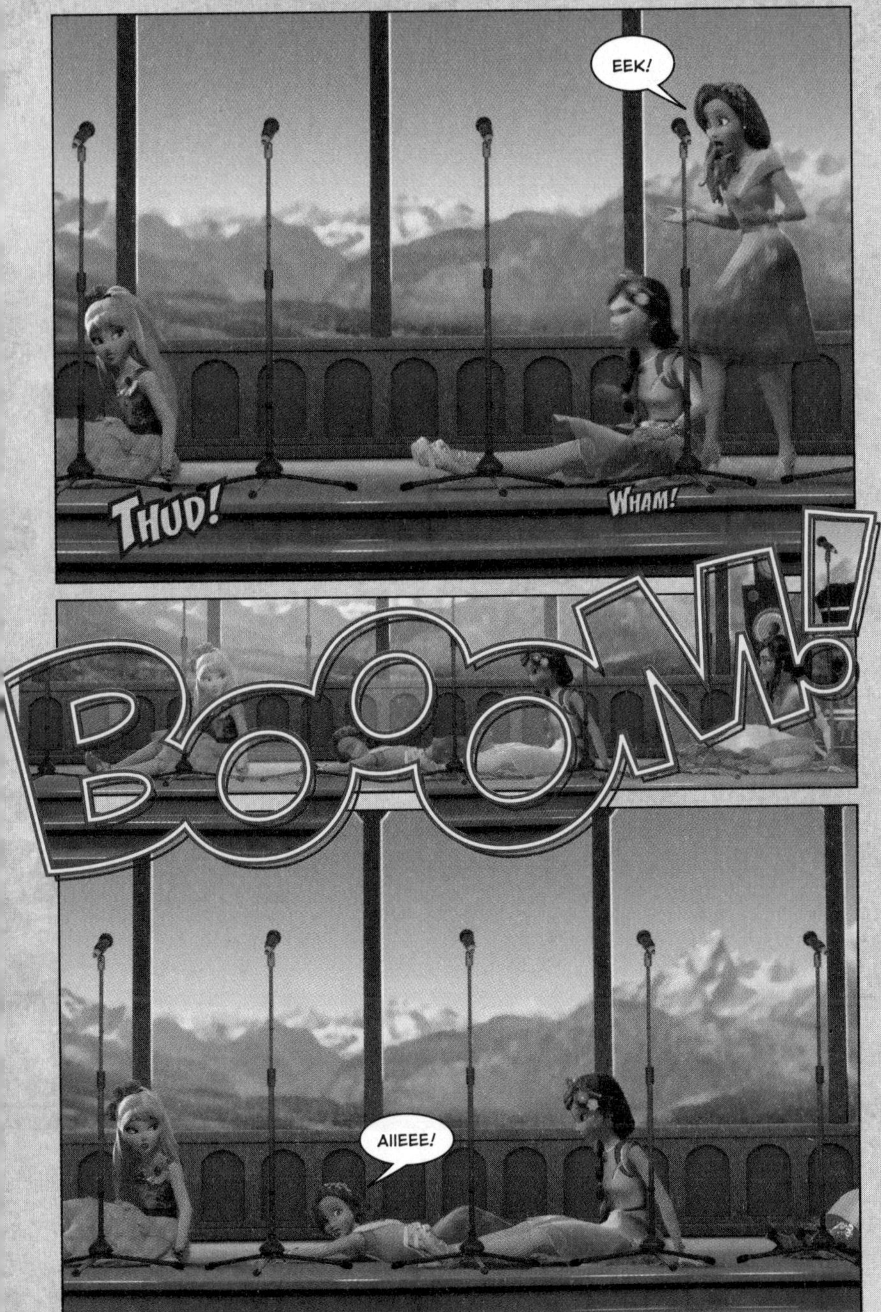
EEK!
THUD!
WHAM!
BOOOM!
AIIEEE!

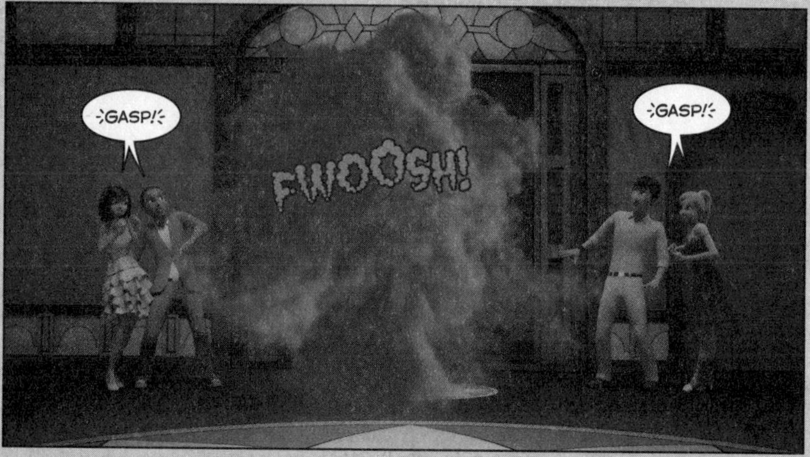
GASP!
FWOOSH!
GASP!

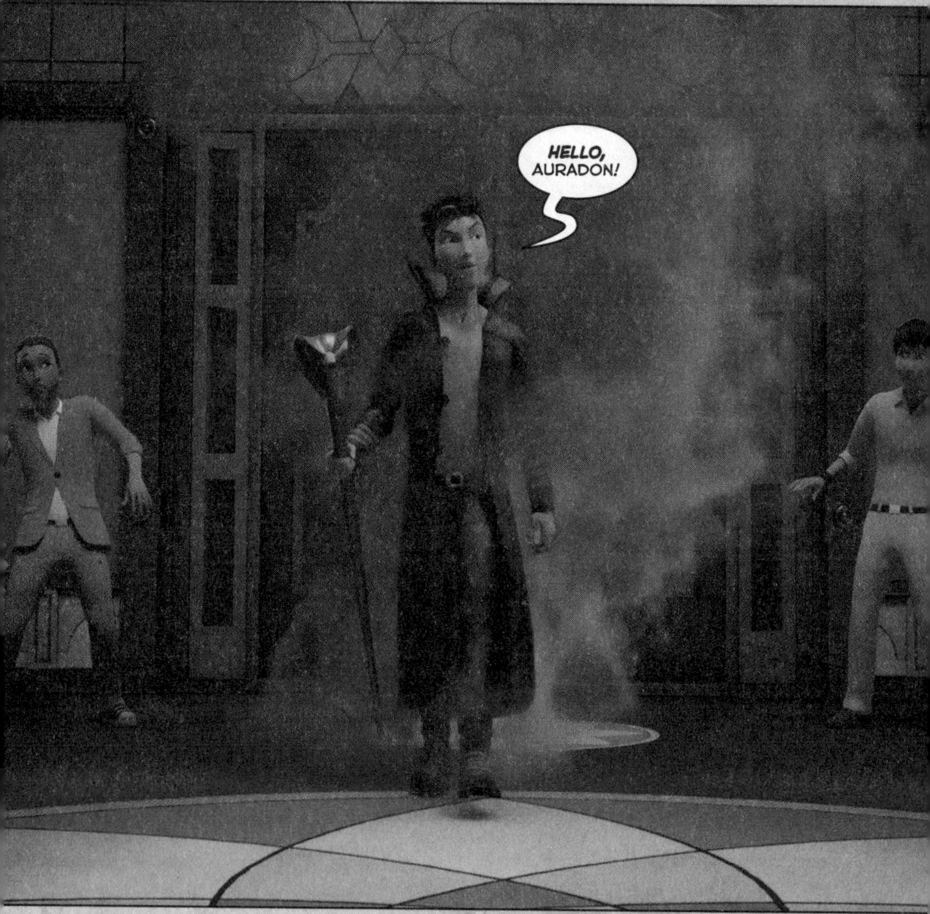
HELLO, AURADON!

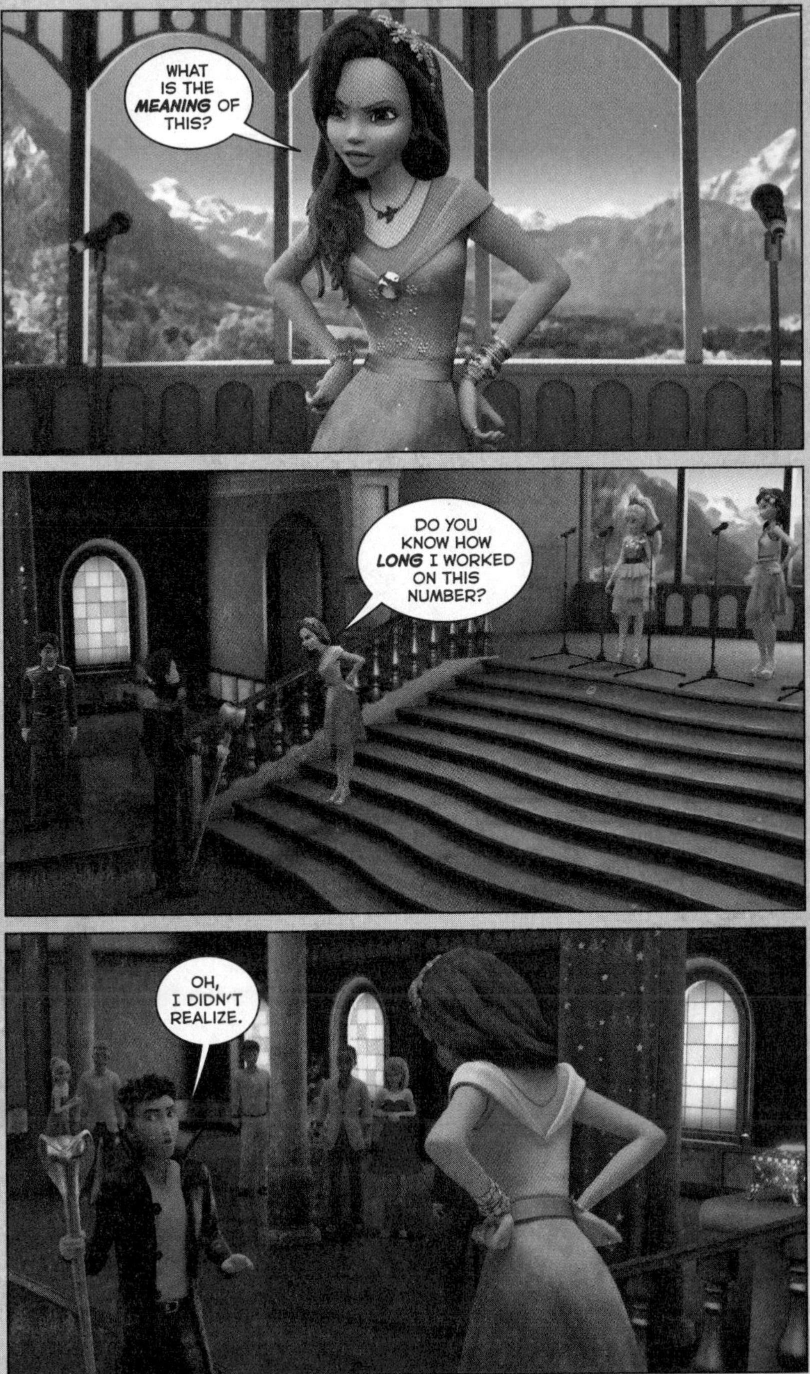
WHAT IS THE MEANING OF THIS?
DO YOU KNOW HOW LONG I WORKED ON THIS NUMBER?
OH, I DIDN'T REALIZE.

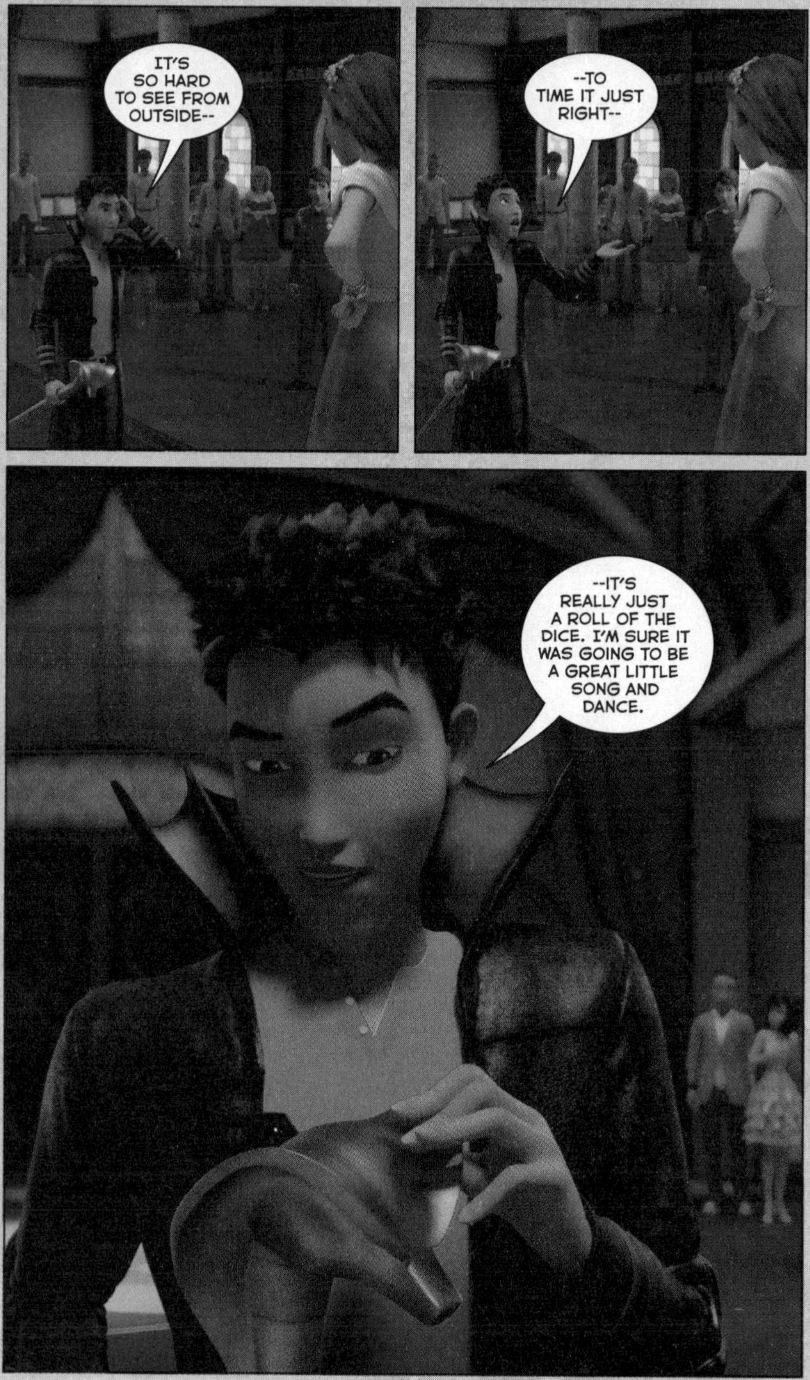
IT'S SO HARD TO SEE FROM OUTSIDE--
--TO TIME IT JUST RIGHT--
--IT'S REALLY JUST A ROLL OF THE DICE. I'M SURE IT WAS GOING TO BE A GREAT LITTLE SONG AND DANCE.

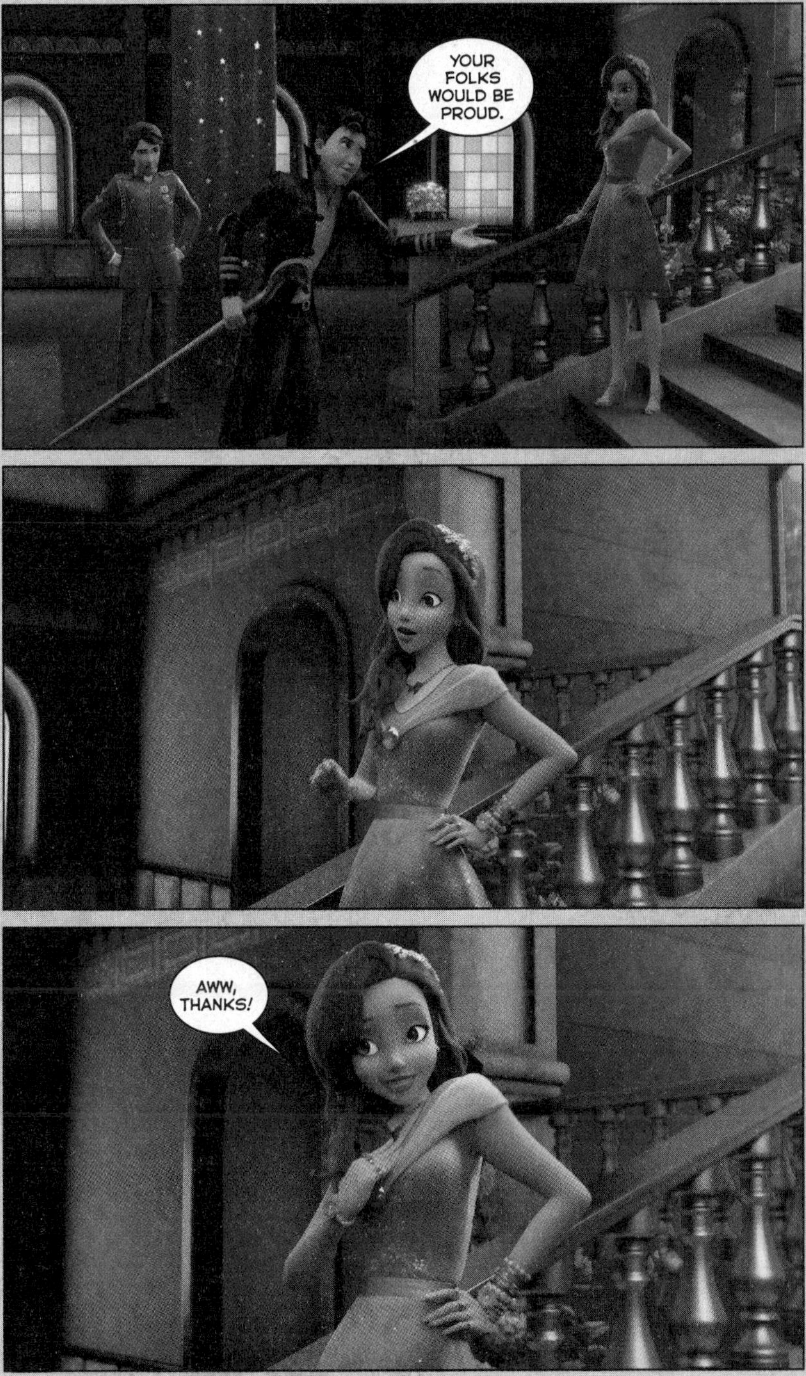
YOUR FOLKS WOULD BE PROUD.
AWW, THANKS!

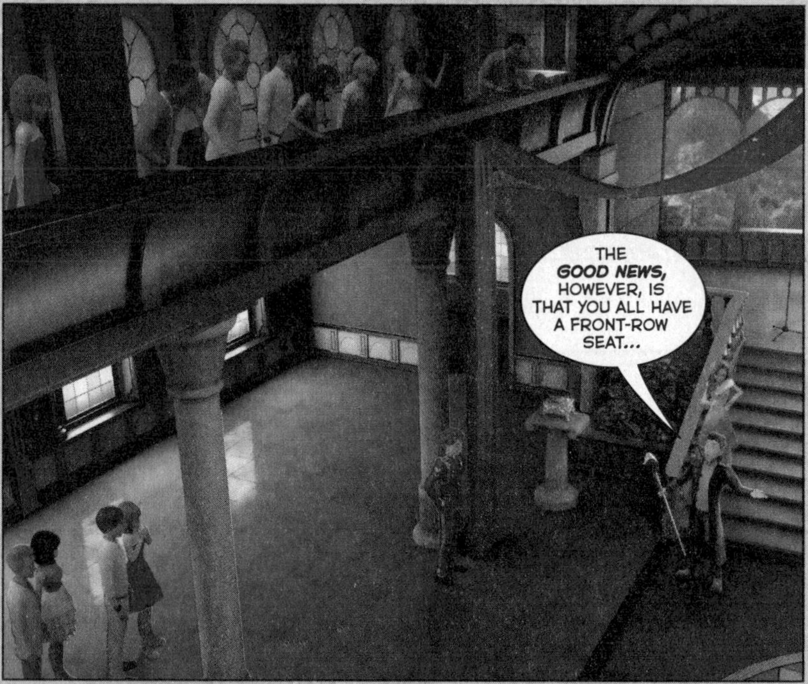
THE *GOOD NEWS,* HOWEVER, IS THAT YOU ALL HAVE A FRONT-ROW SEAT...

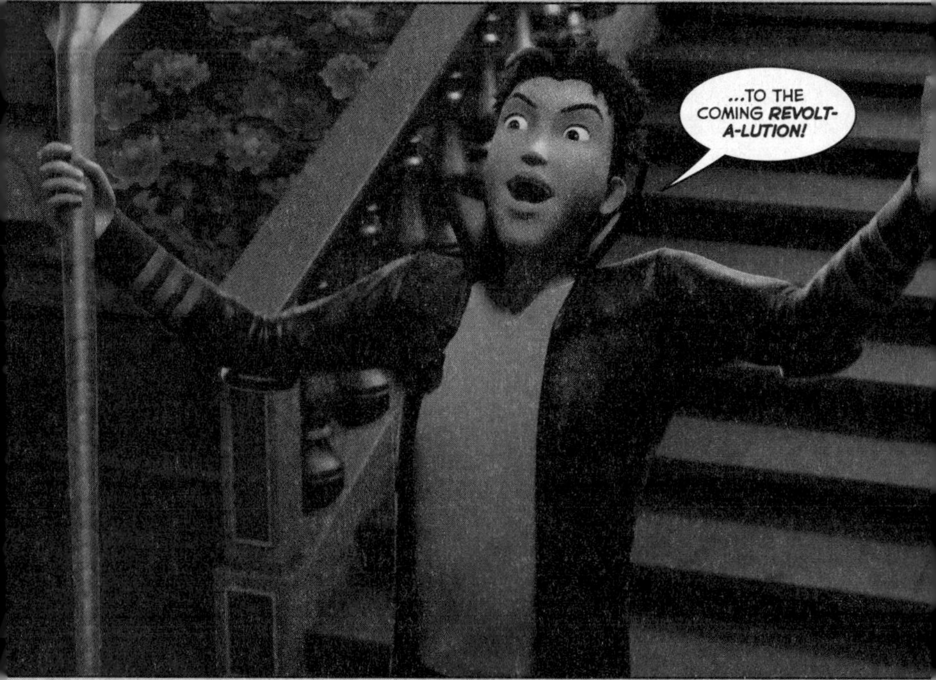
...TO THE COMING *REVOLT-A-LUTION!*

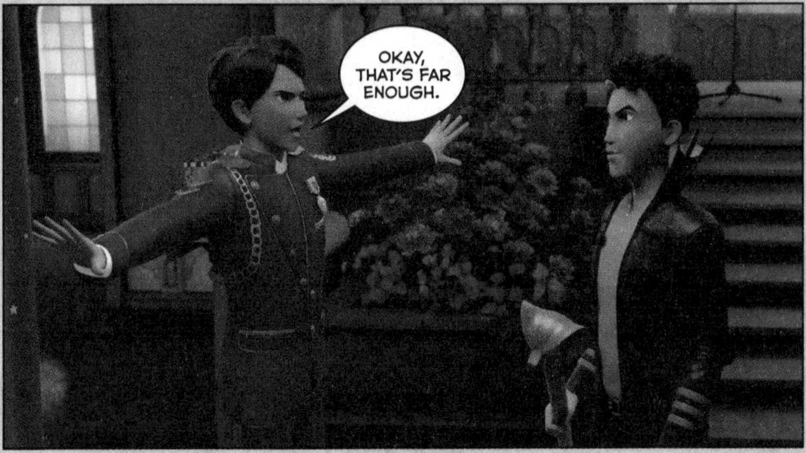
OKAY, THAT'S FAR ENOUGH.

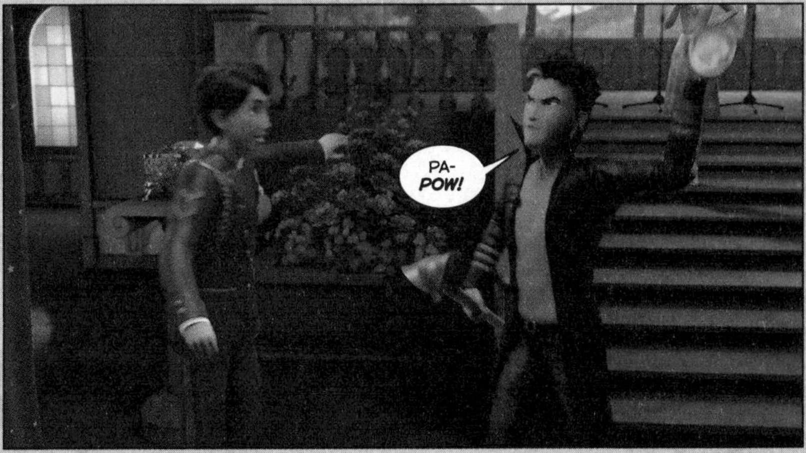
PA-POW!

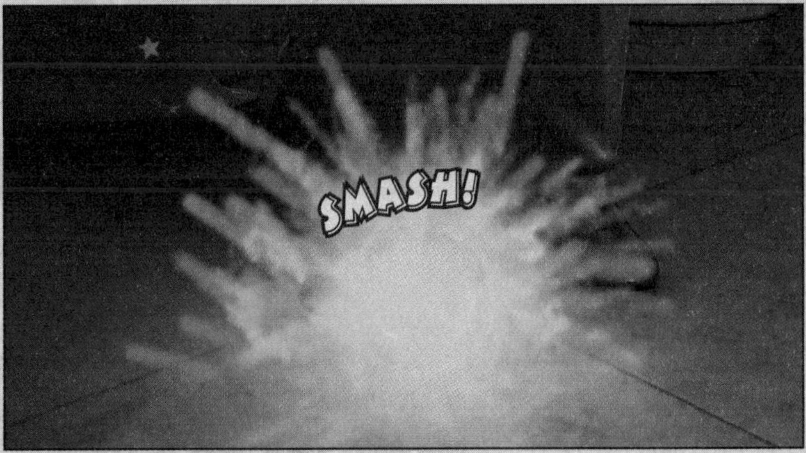
SMASH!

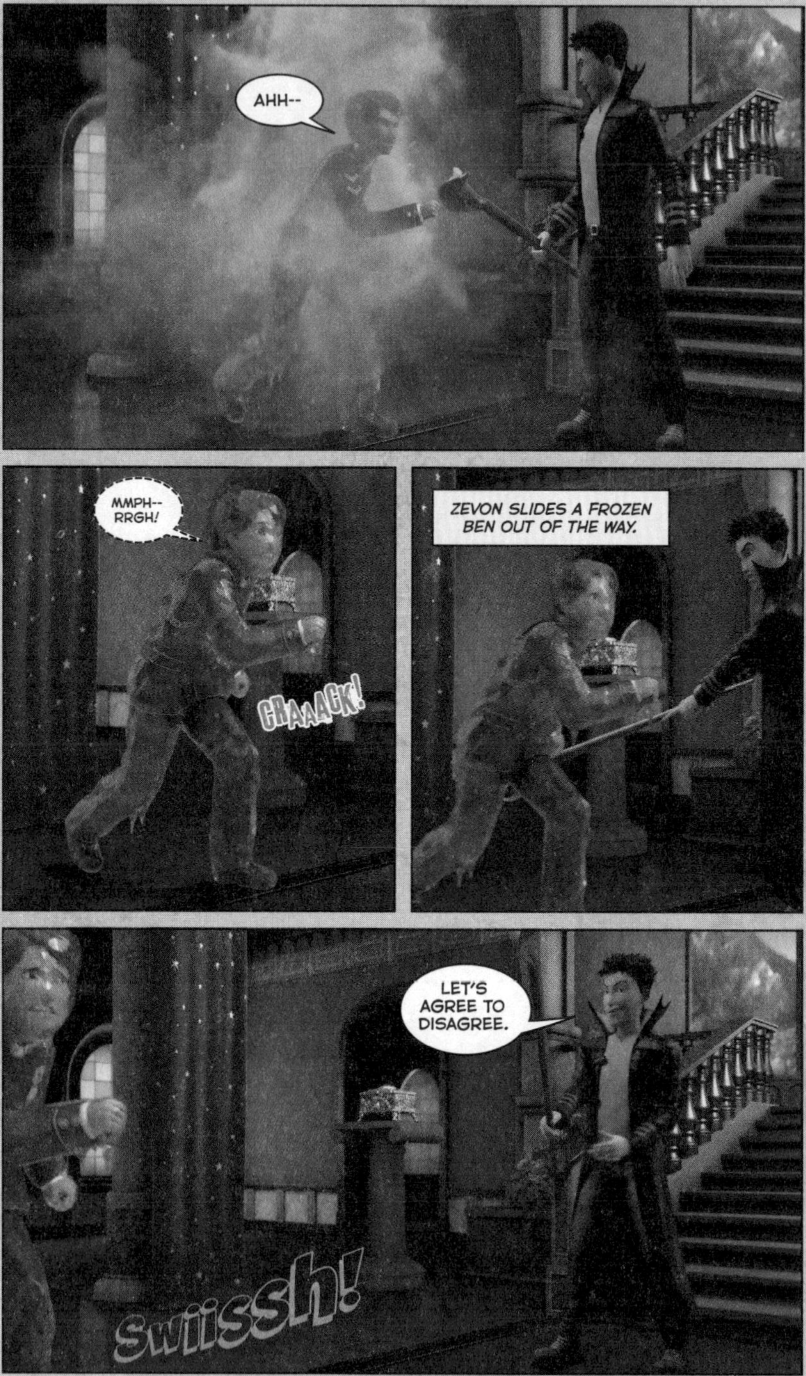
AHH--
MMPH--
RRGH!
CRAAACK!
ZEVON SLIDES A FROZEN
BEN OUT OF THE WAY.
LET'S
AGREE TO
DISAGREE.
Swiissh!

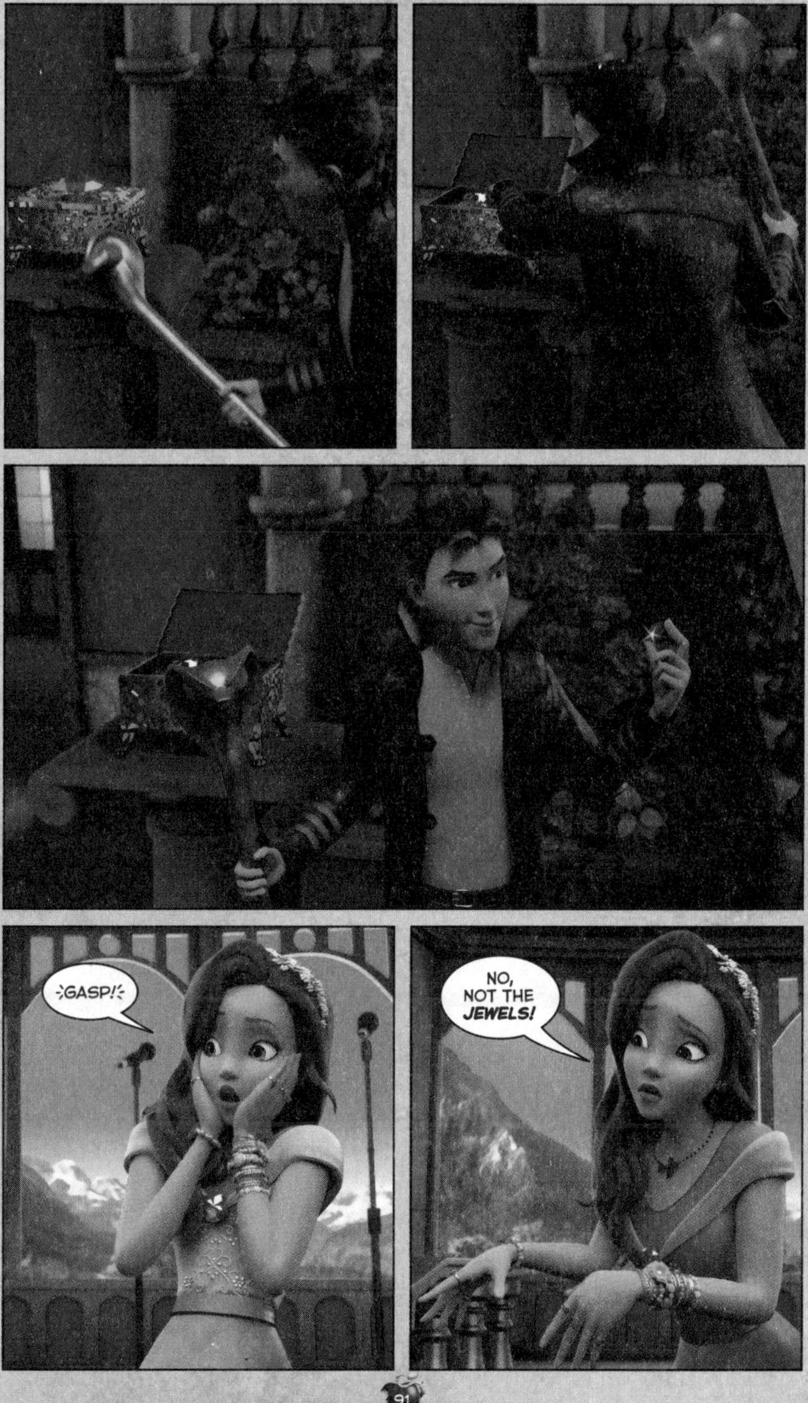

GASP!
NO, NOT THE JEWELS!

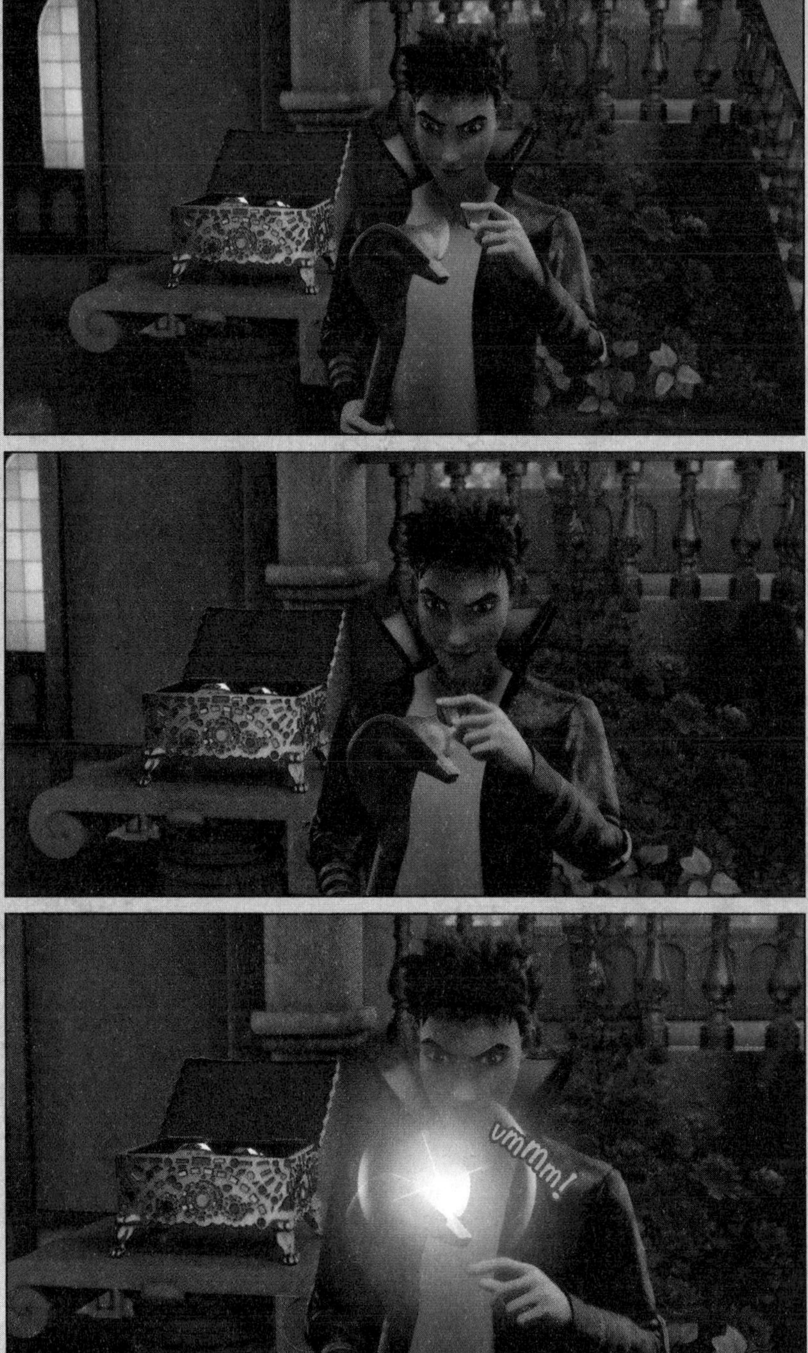
vmmm!

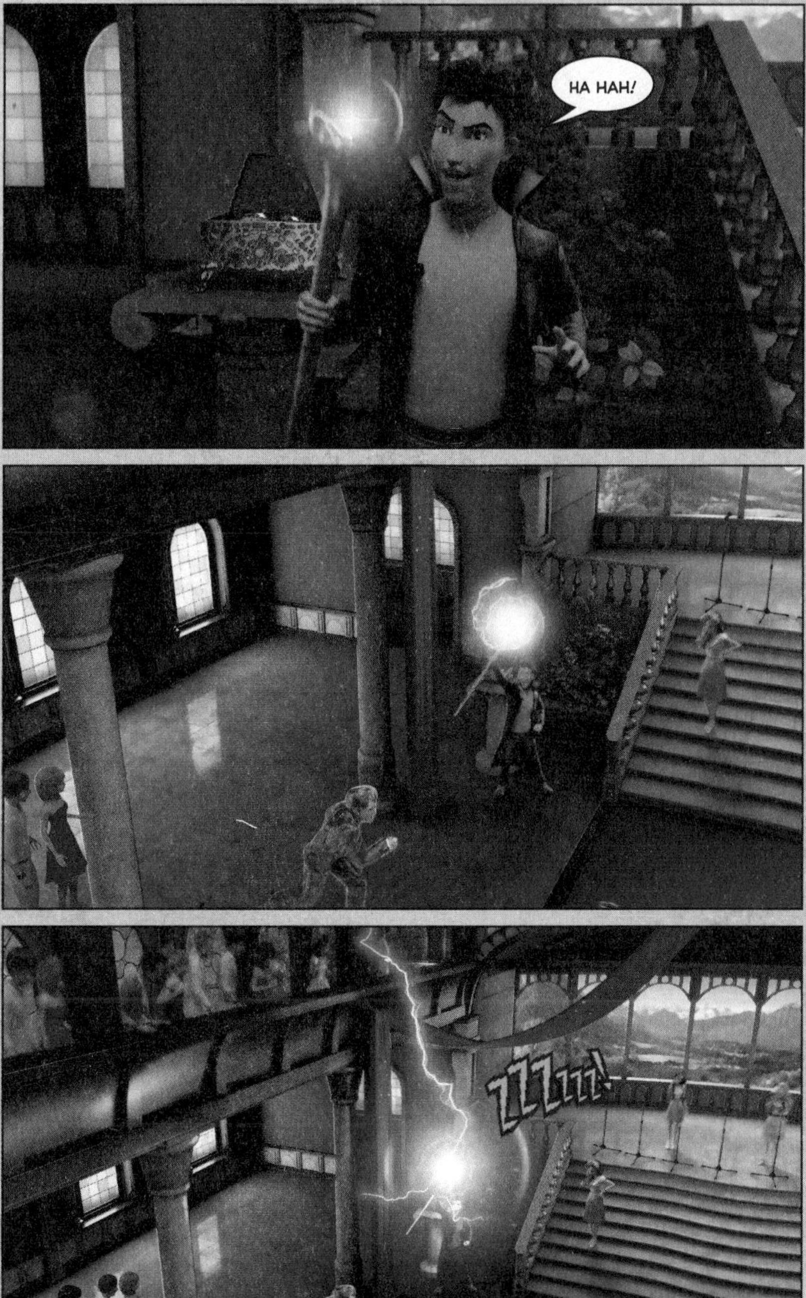
HA HAH!
ZZZzzz!

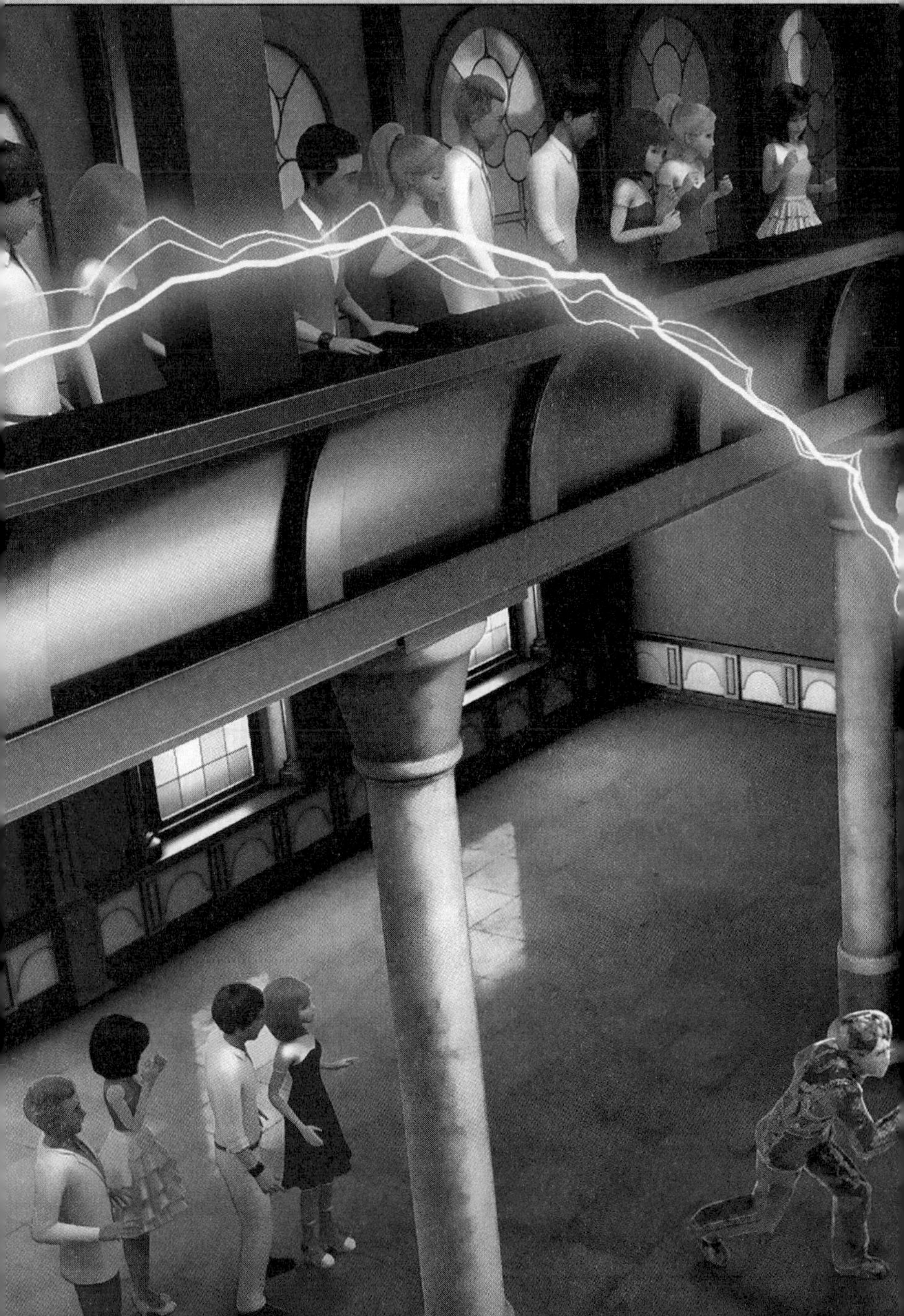

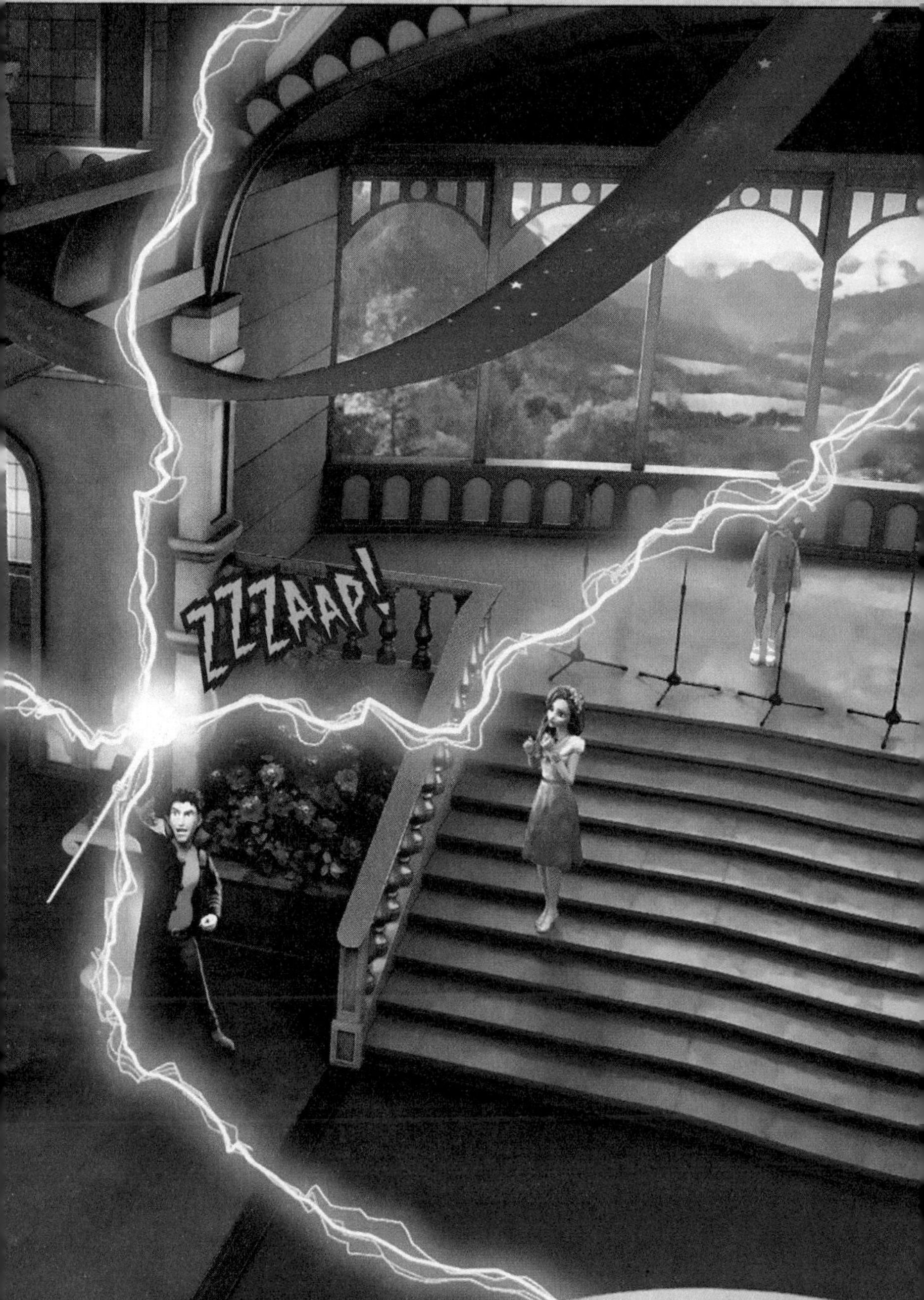
ZZZAAP!

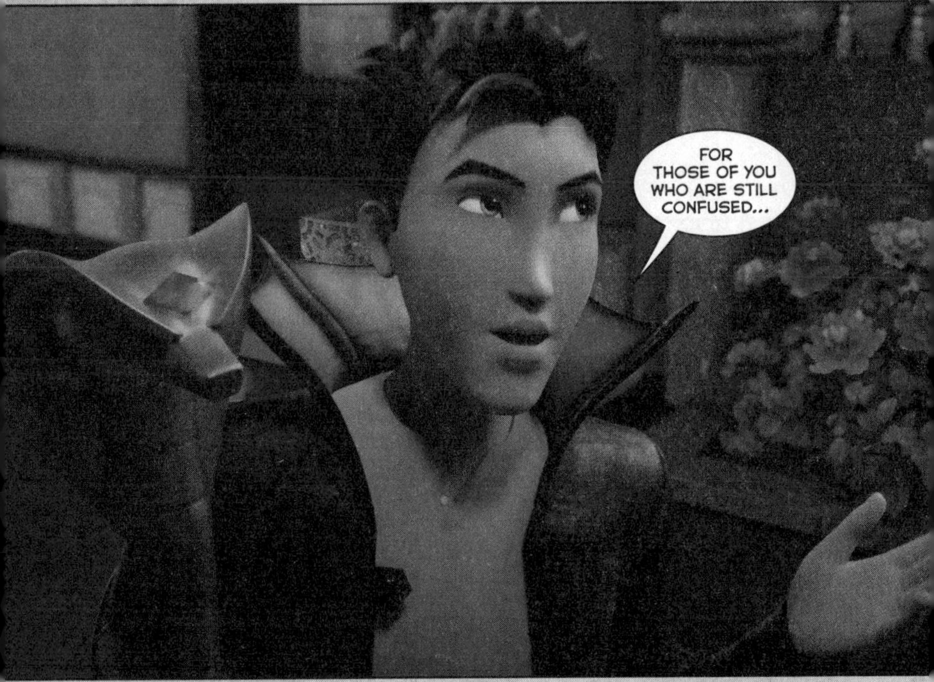
FOR THOSE OF YOU WHO ARE STILL CONFUSED...

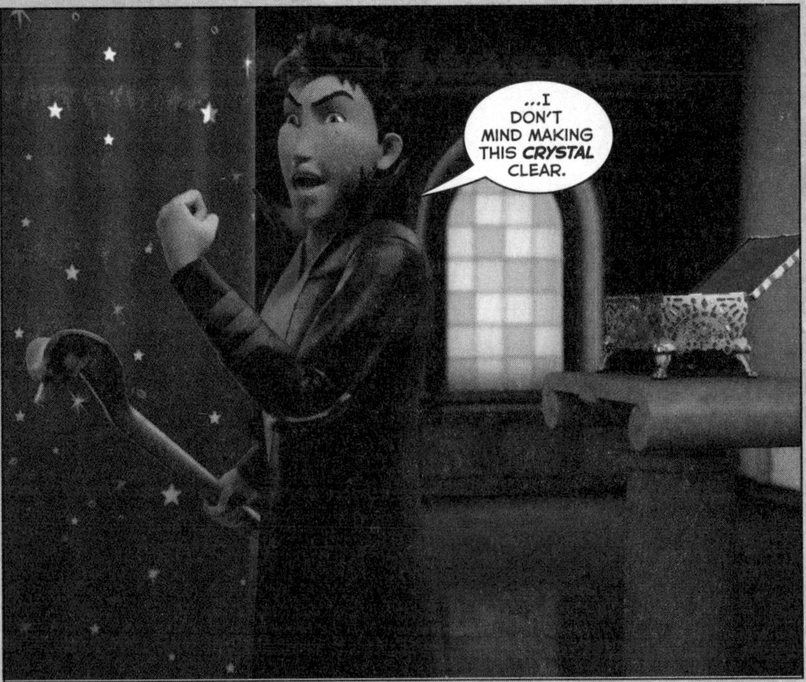
...I DON'T MIND MAKING THIS **CRYSTAL** CLEAR.

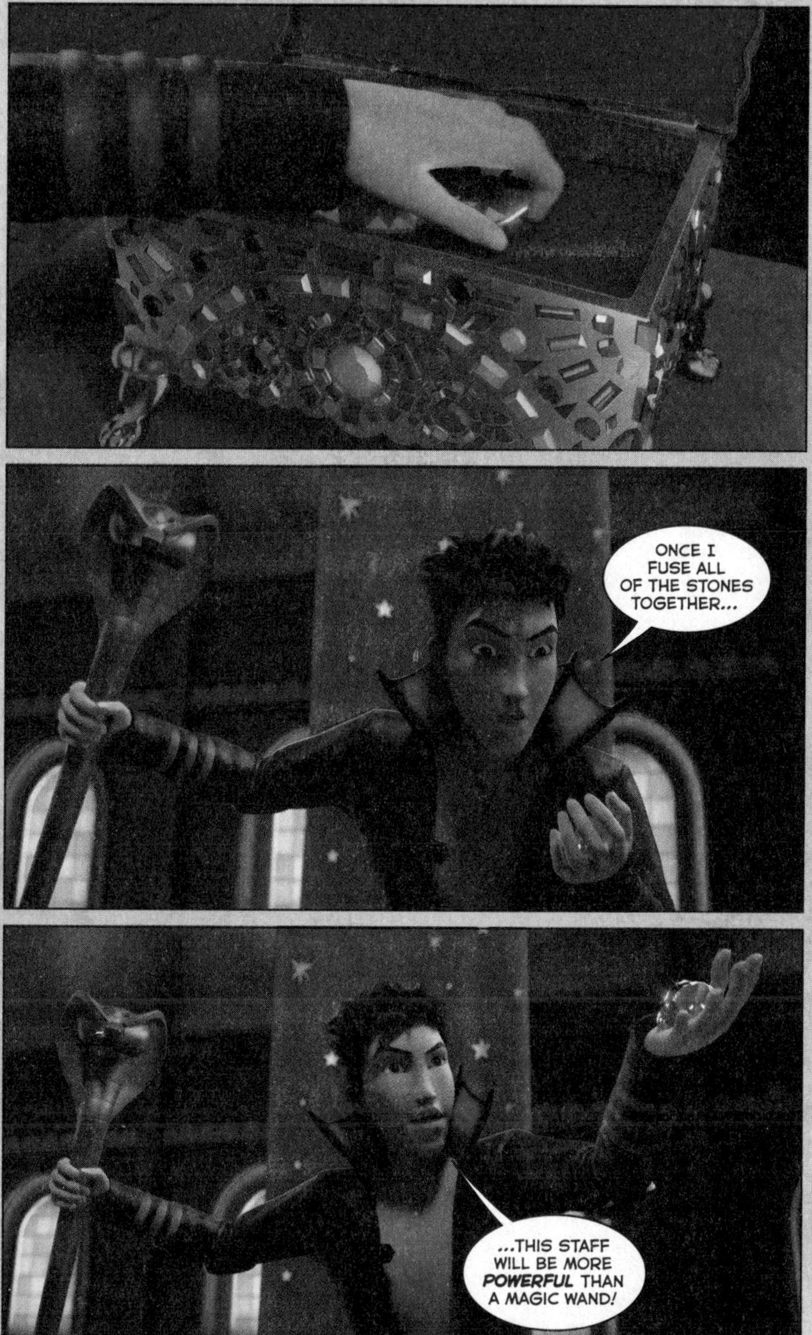
ONCE I FUSE ALL OF THE STONES TOGETHER...
...THIS STAFF WILL BE MORE *POWERFUL* THAN A MAGIC WAND!

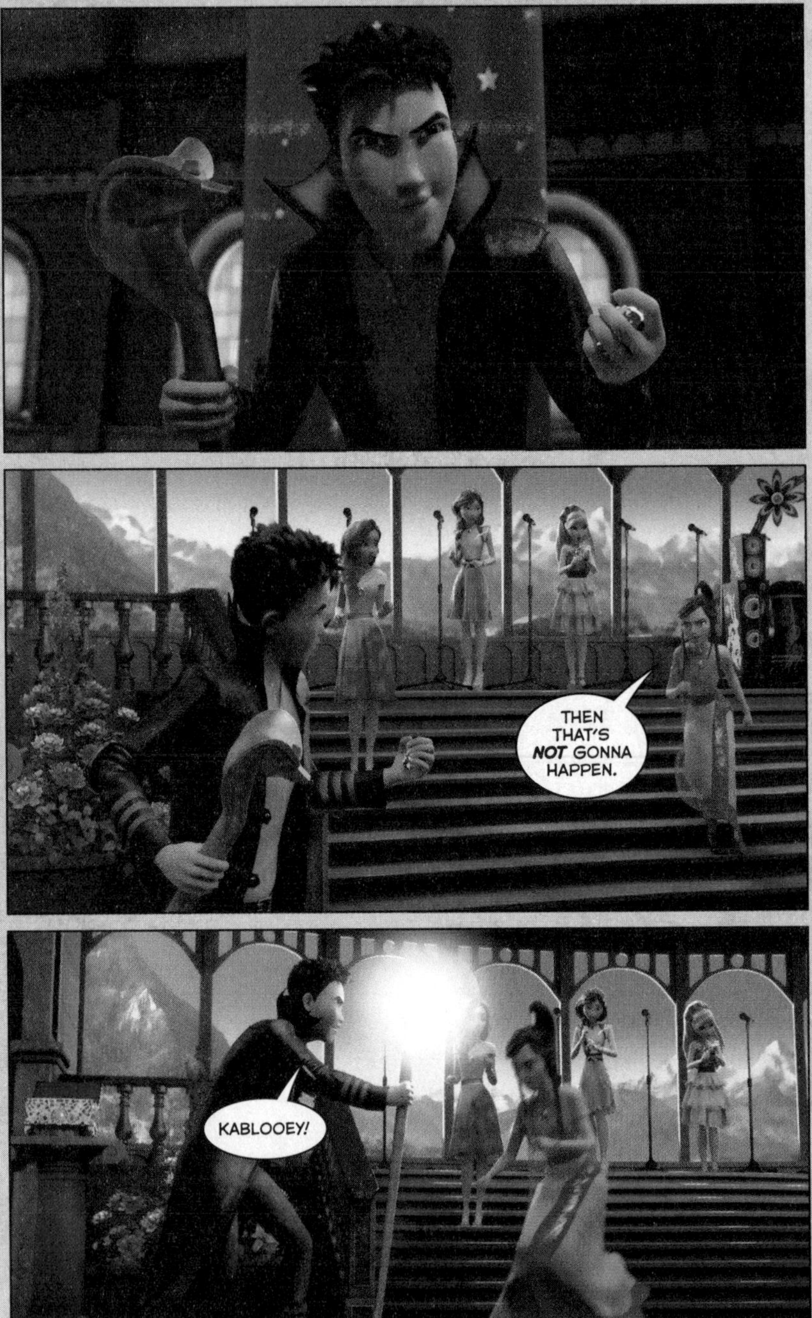
THEN THAT'S ***NOT*** GONNA HAPPEN.
KABLOOEY!

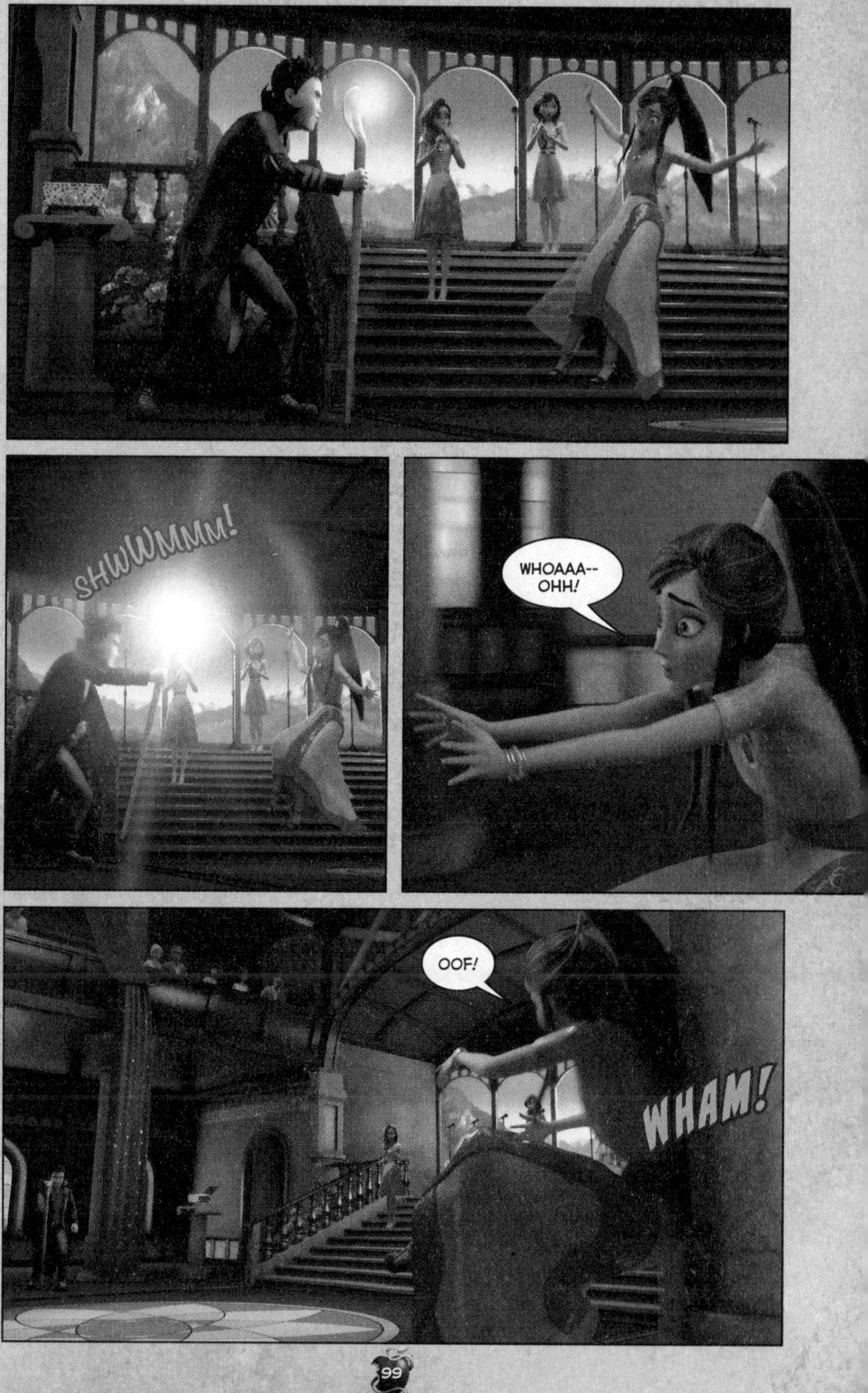
SHWWMMM!
WHOAAA--
OHH!
OOF!
WHAM!

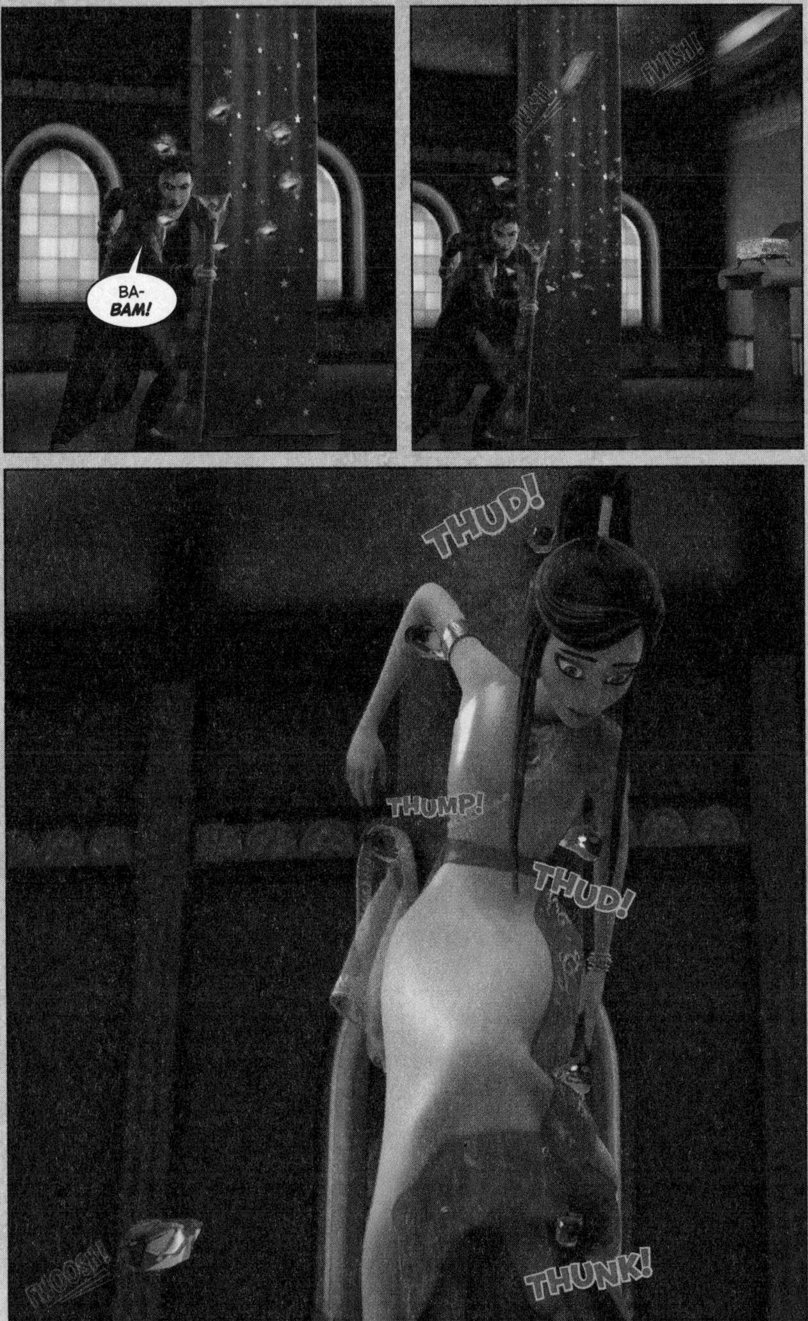
BA-
BAM!
FWISH!
THUD!
THUMP!
THUD!
FWOOSH!
THUNK!

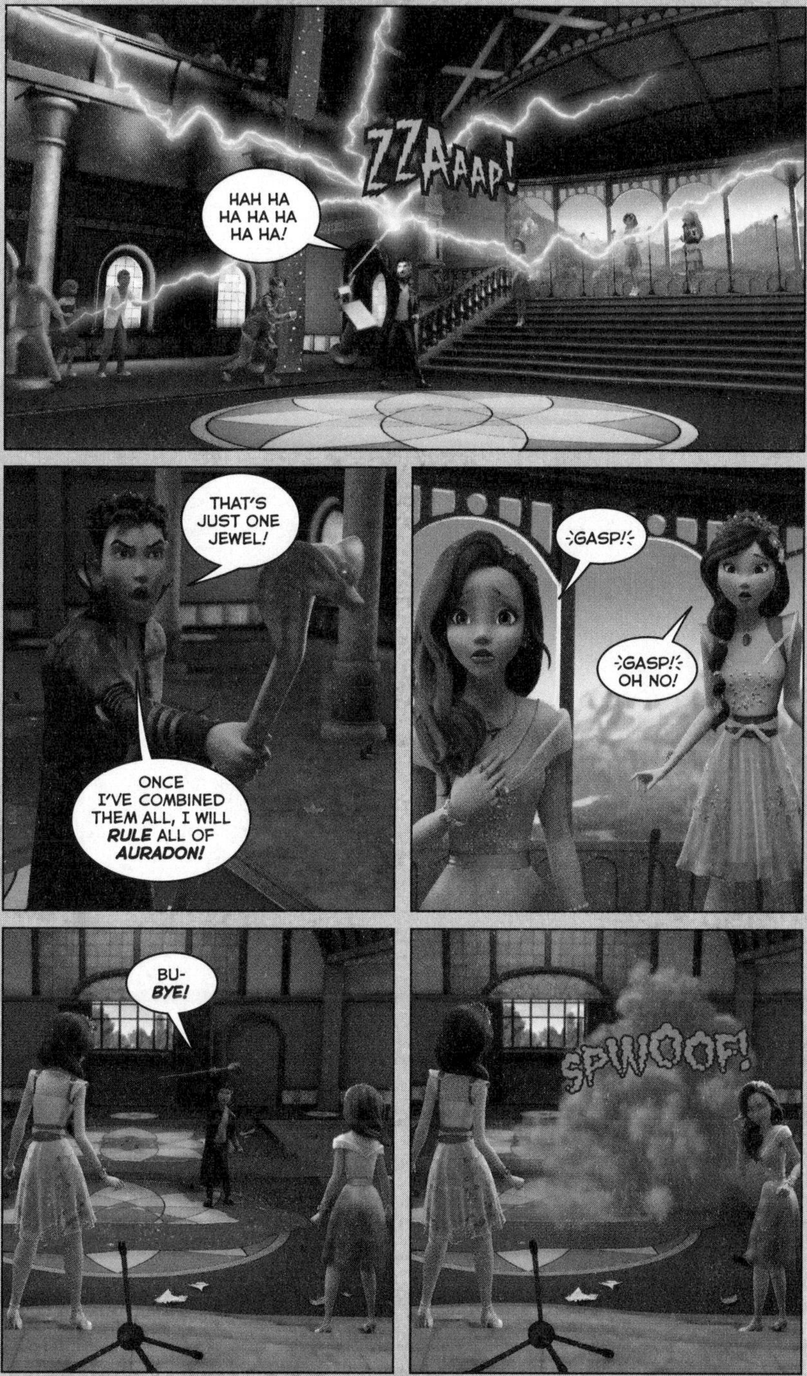
ZZAAAP!
HAH HA HA HA HA HA HA!
THAT'S JUST ONE JEWEL!
ONCE I'VE COMBINED THEM ALL, I WILL RULE ALL OF AURADON!
GASP!
GASP! OH NO!
BU-BYE!
SPWOOF!

CHAPTER 29: MAL-LONE

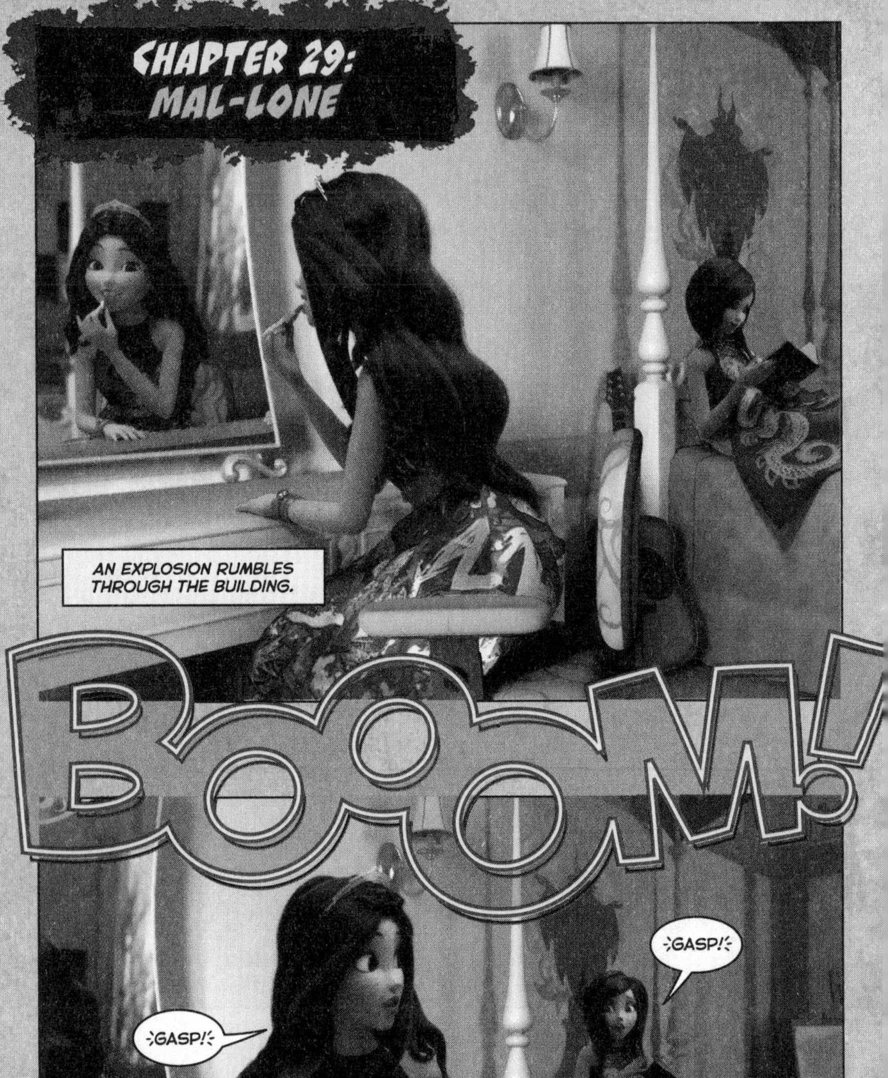

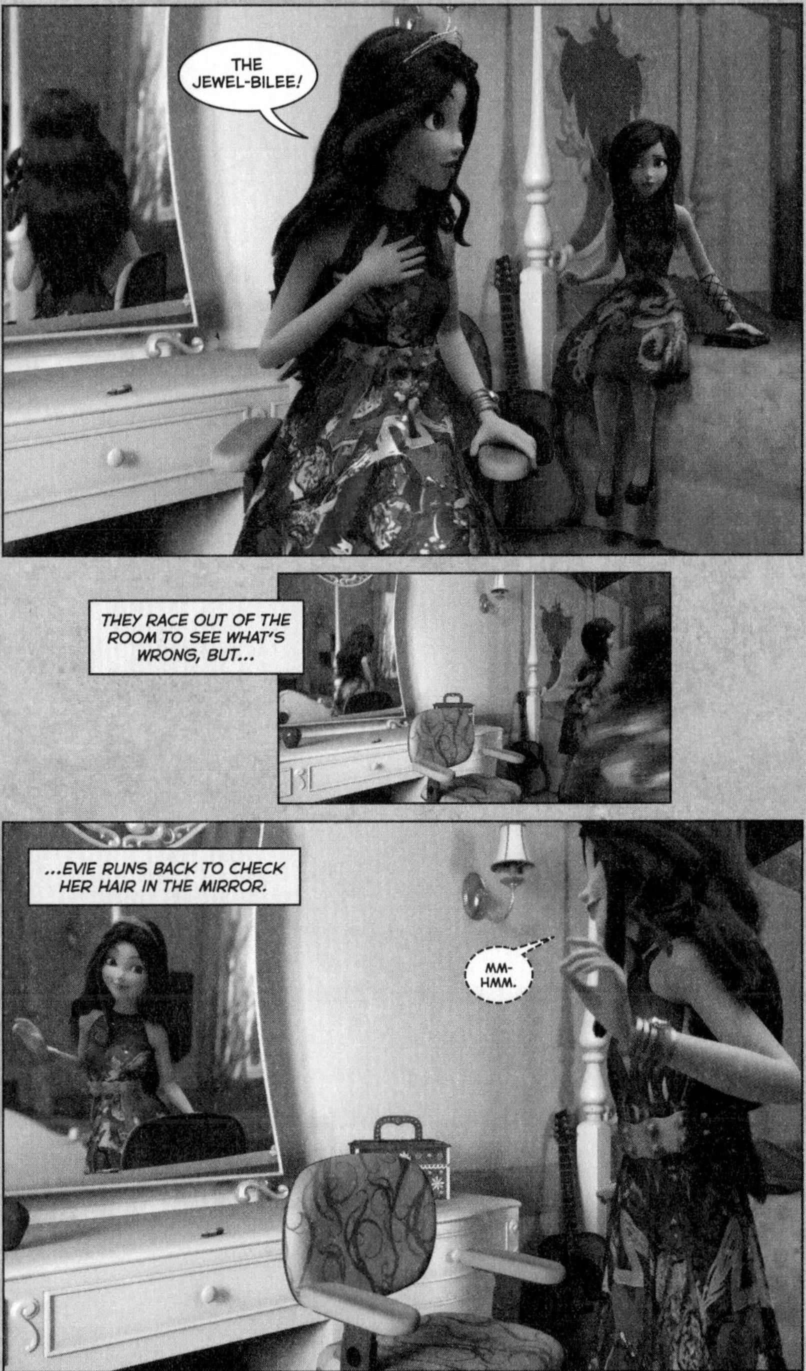
THE JEWEL-BILEE!
THEY RACE OUT OF THE ROOM TO SEE WHAT'S WRONG, BUT...
...EVIE RUNS BACK TO CHECK HER HAIR IN THE MIRROR.
MM-HMM.

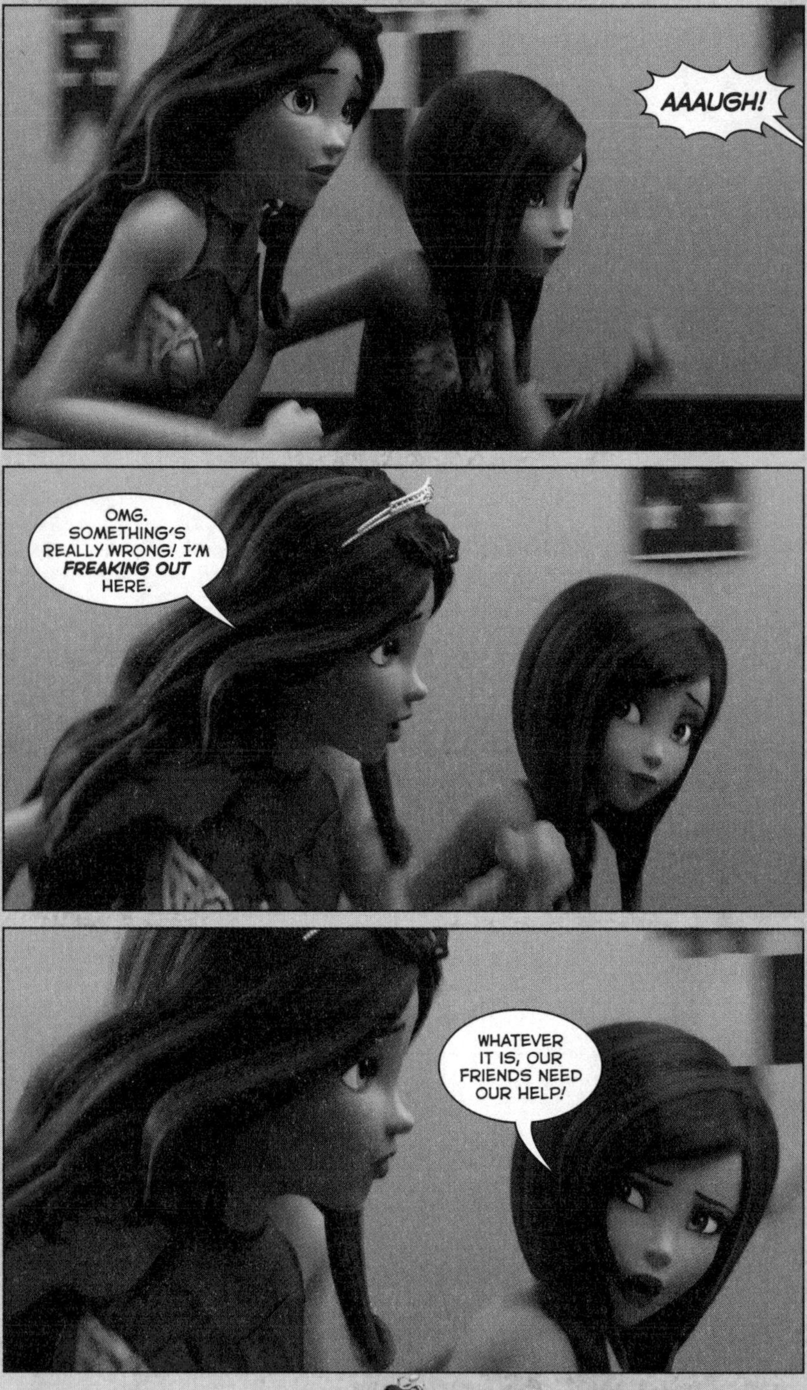

AAAUGH!
OMG. SOMETHING'S REALLY WRONG! I'M FREAKING OUT HERE.
WHATEVER IT IS, OUR FRIENDS NEED OUR HELP!

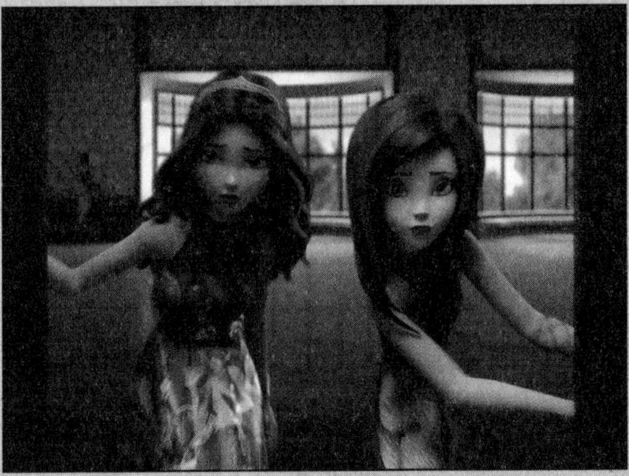

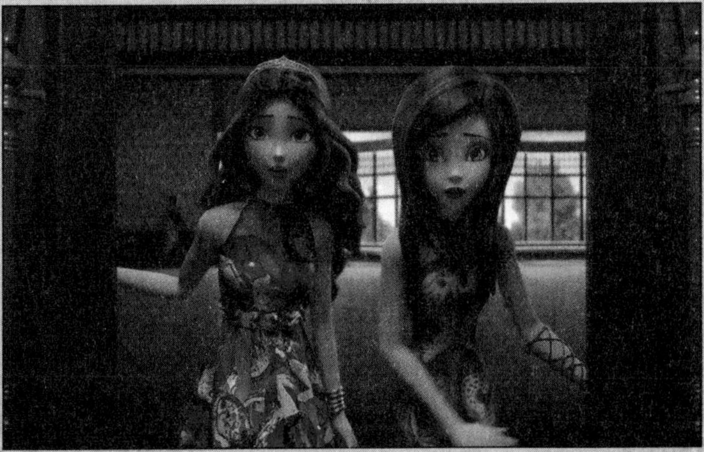

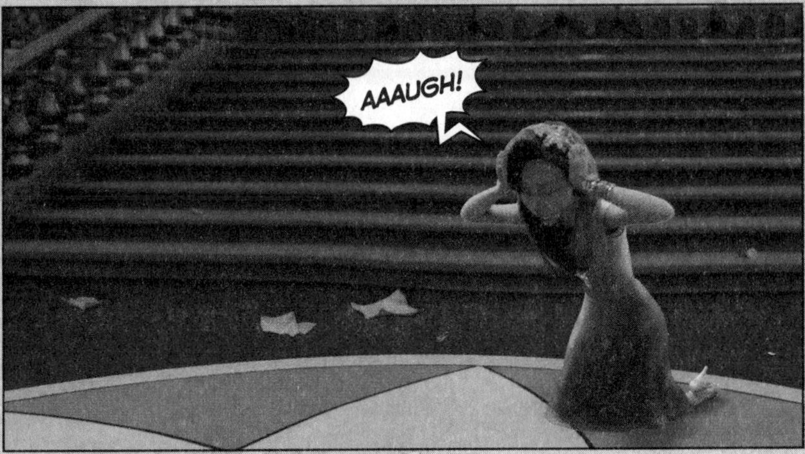
AAAUGH!

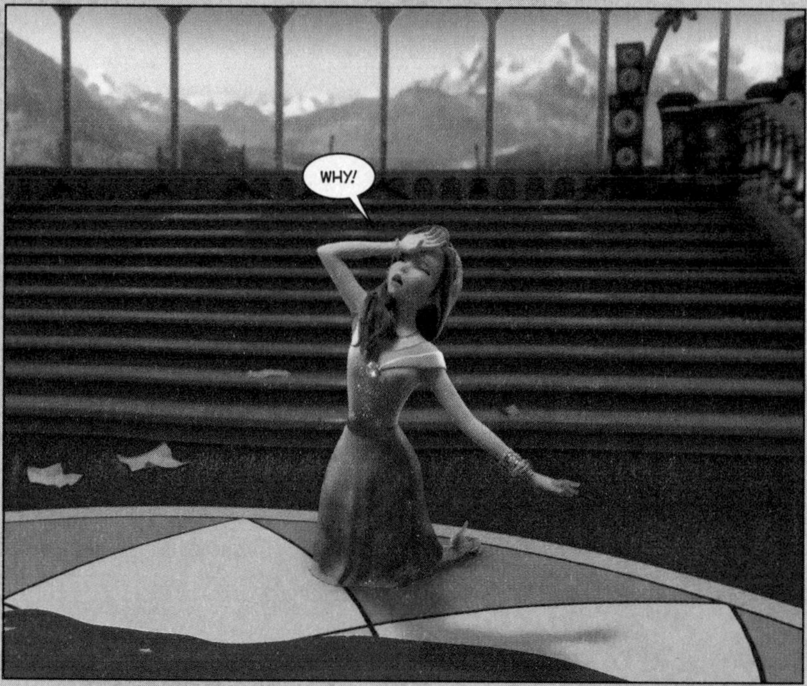
WHY!

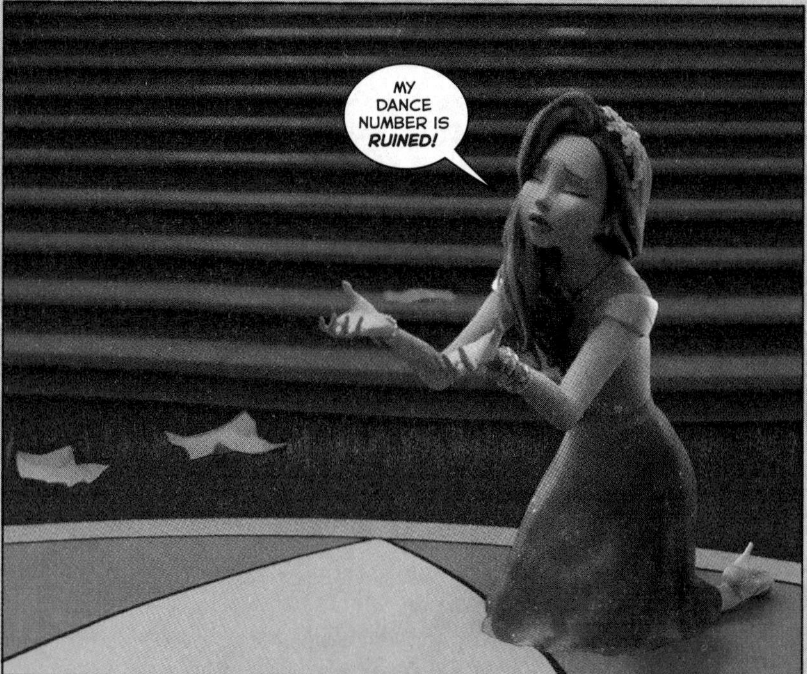
MY DANCE NUMBER IS ***RUINED!***

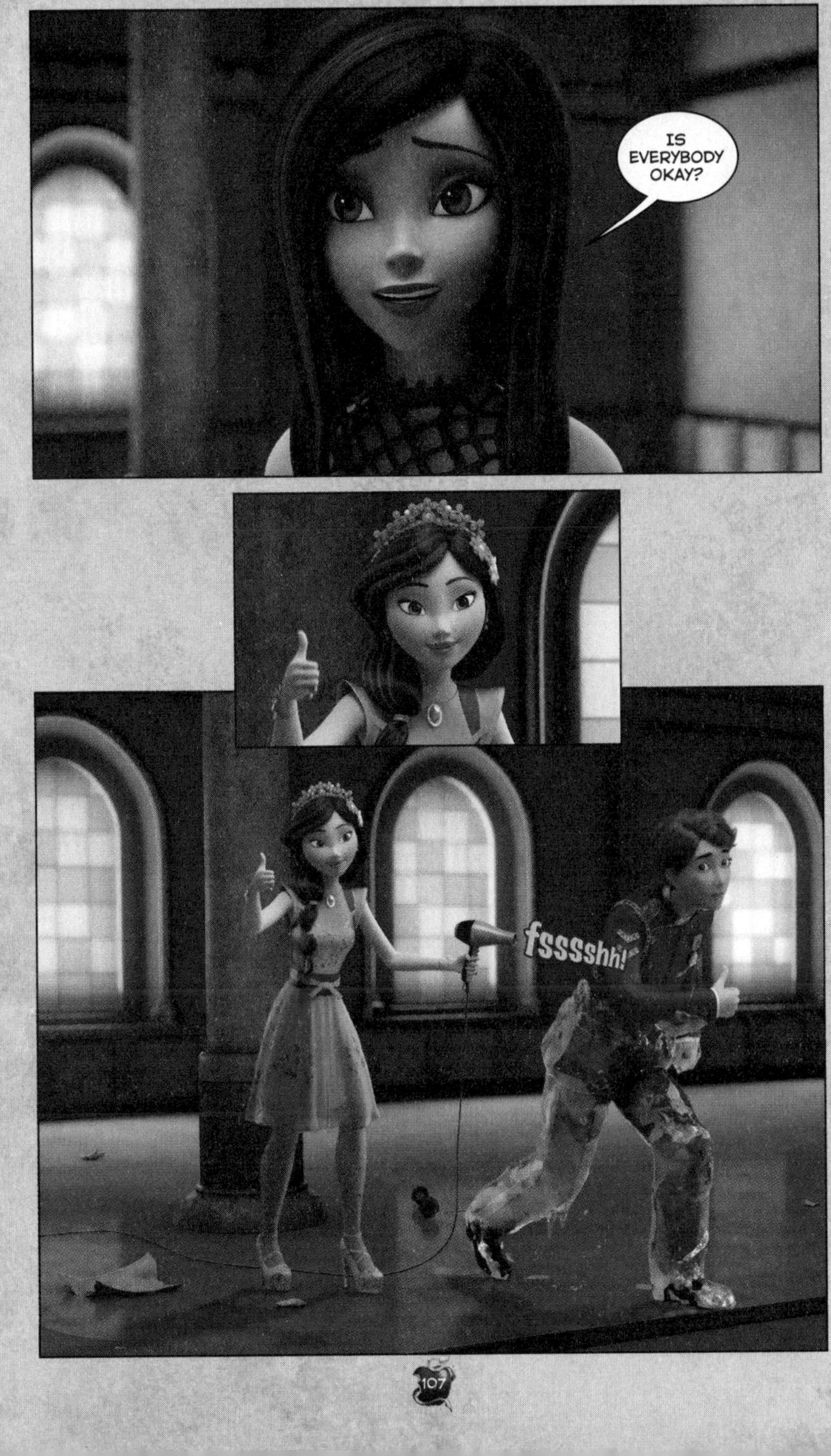
IS EVERYBODY OKAY?
fssssh!

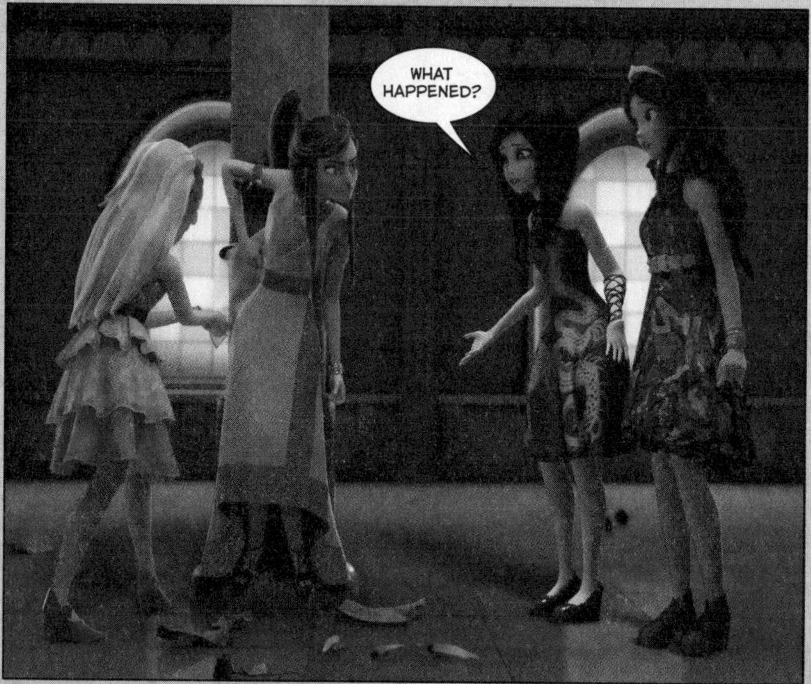
WHAT HAPPENED?

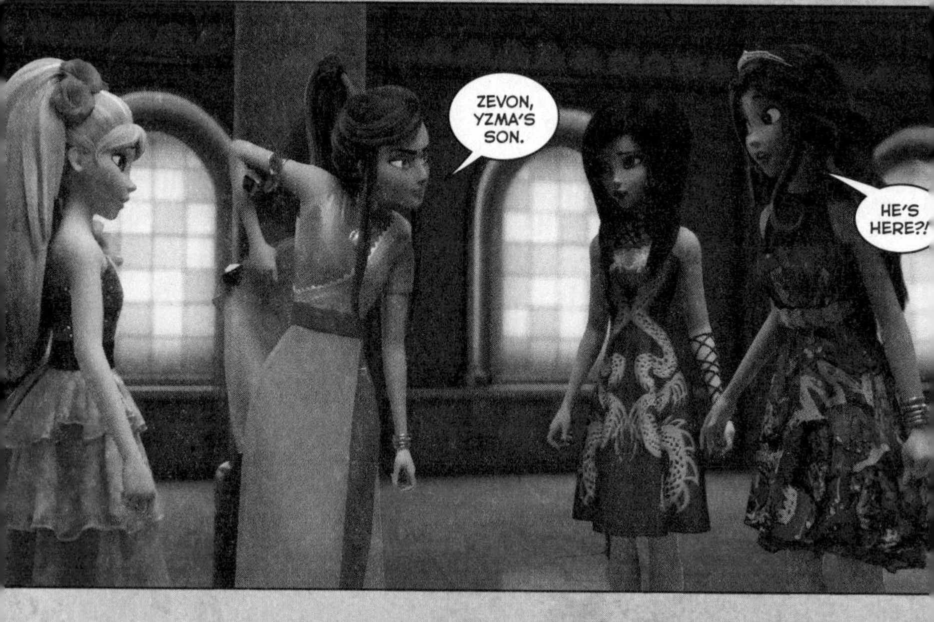
ZEVON, YZMA'S SON.
HE'S HERE?!

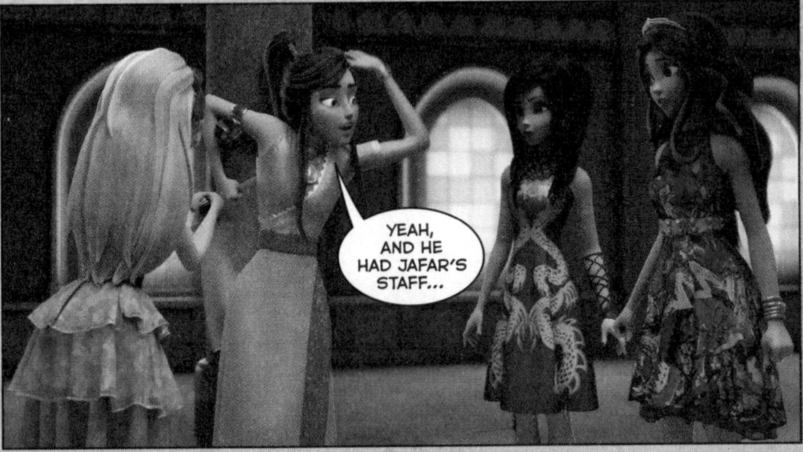
YEAH, AND HE HAD JAFAR'S STAFF...

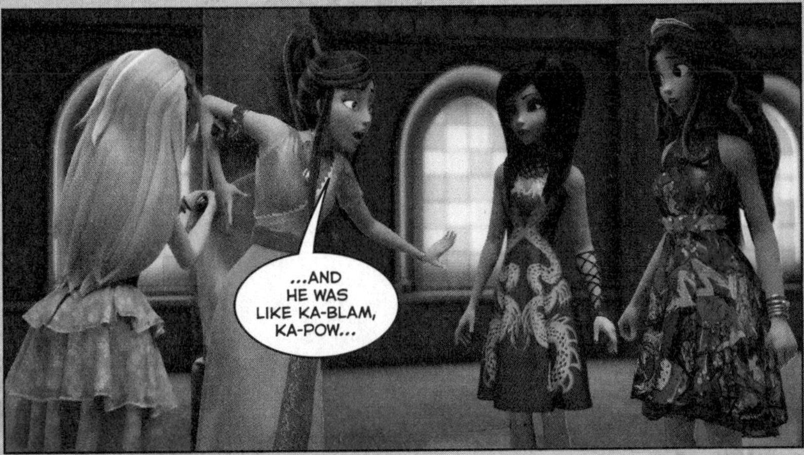
...AND HE WAS LIKE KA-BLAM, KA-POW...

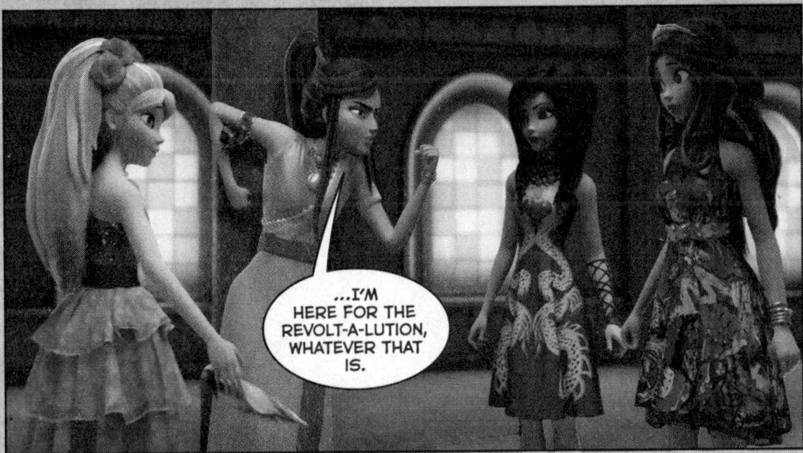
...I'M HERE FOR THE REVOLT-A-LUTION, WHATEVER THAT IS.

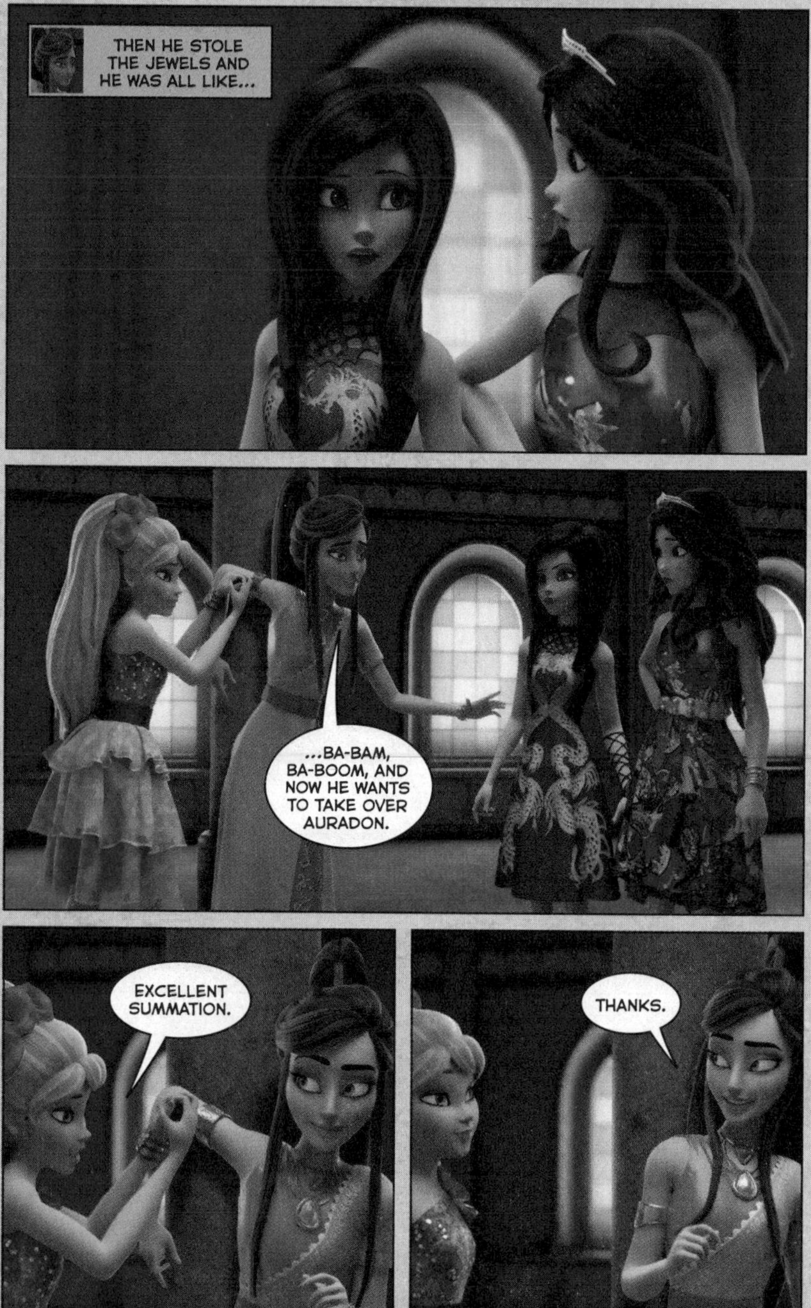
THEN HE STOLE THE JEWELS AND HE WAS ALL LIKE...
...BA-BAM, BA-BOOM, AND NOW HE WANTS TO TAKE OVER AURADON.
EXCELLENT SUMMATION.
THANKS.

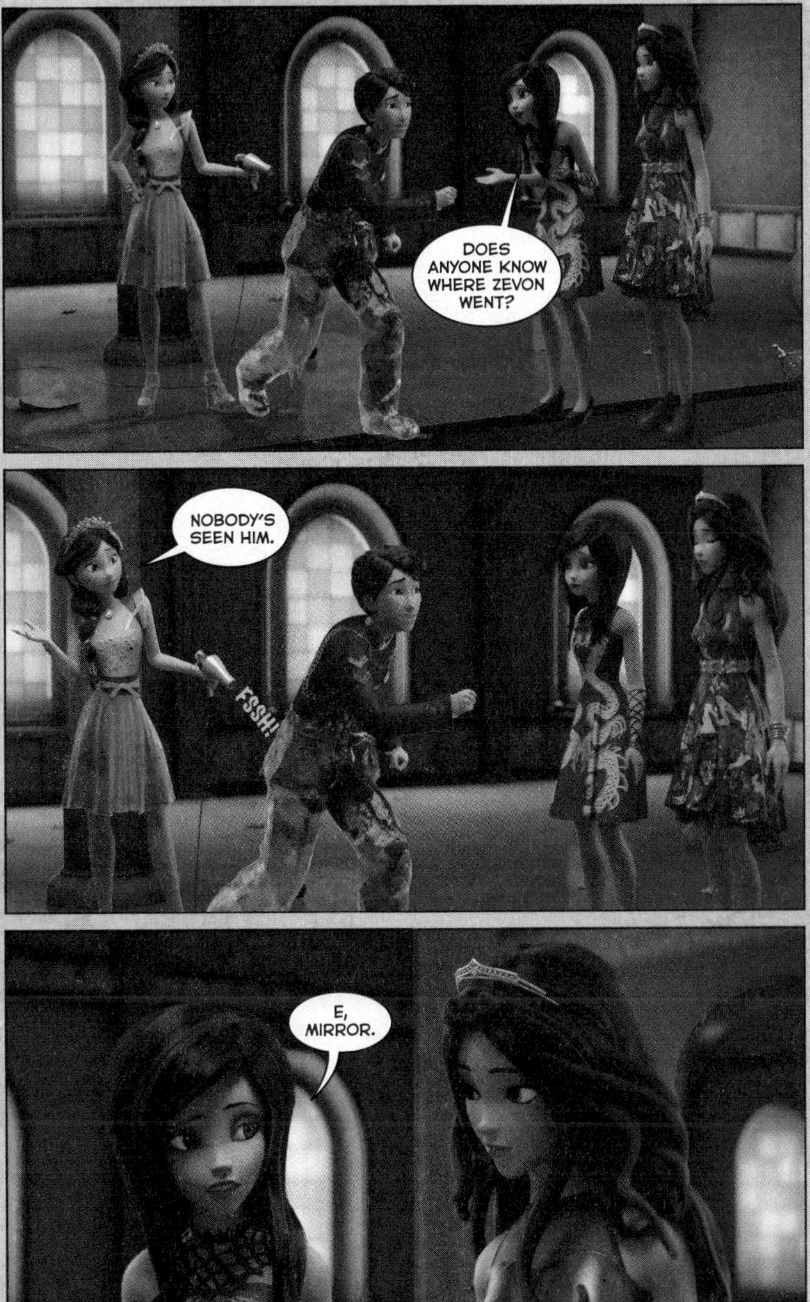
DOES ANYONE KNOW WHERE ZEVON WENT?
NOBODY'S SEEN HIM.
FSSH!
E, MIRROR.

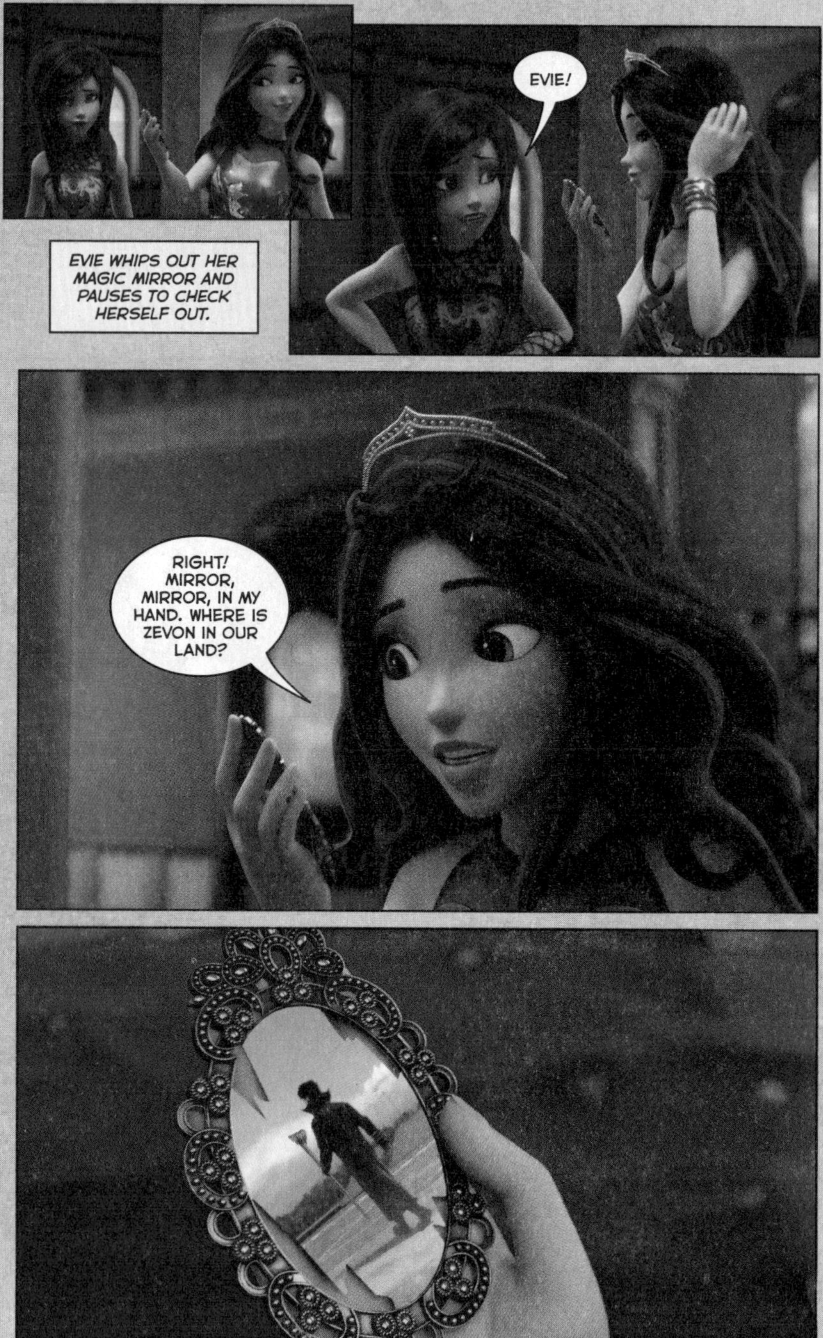
EVIE!
EVIE WHIPS OUT HER MAGIC MIRROR AND PAUSES TO CHECK HERSELF OUT.
RIGHT! MIRROR, MIRROR, IN MY HAND. WHERE IS ZEVON IN OUR LAND?

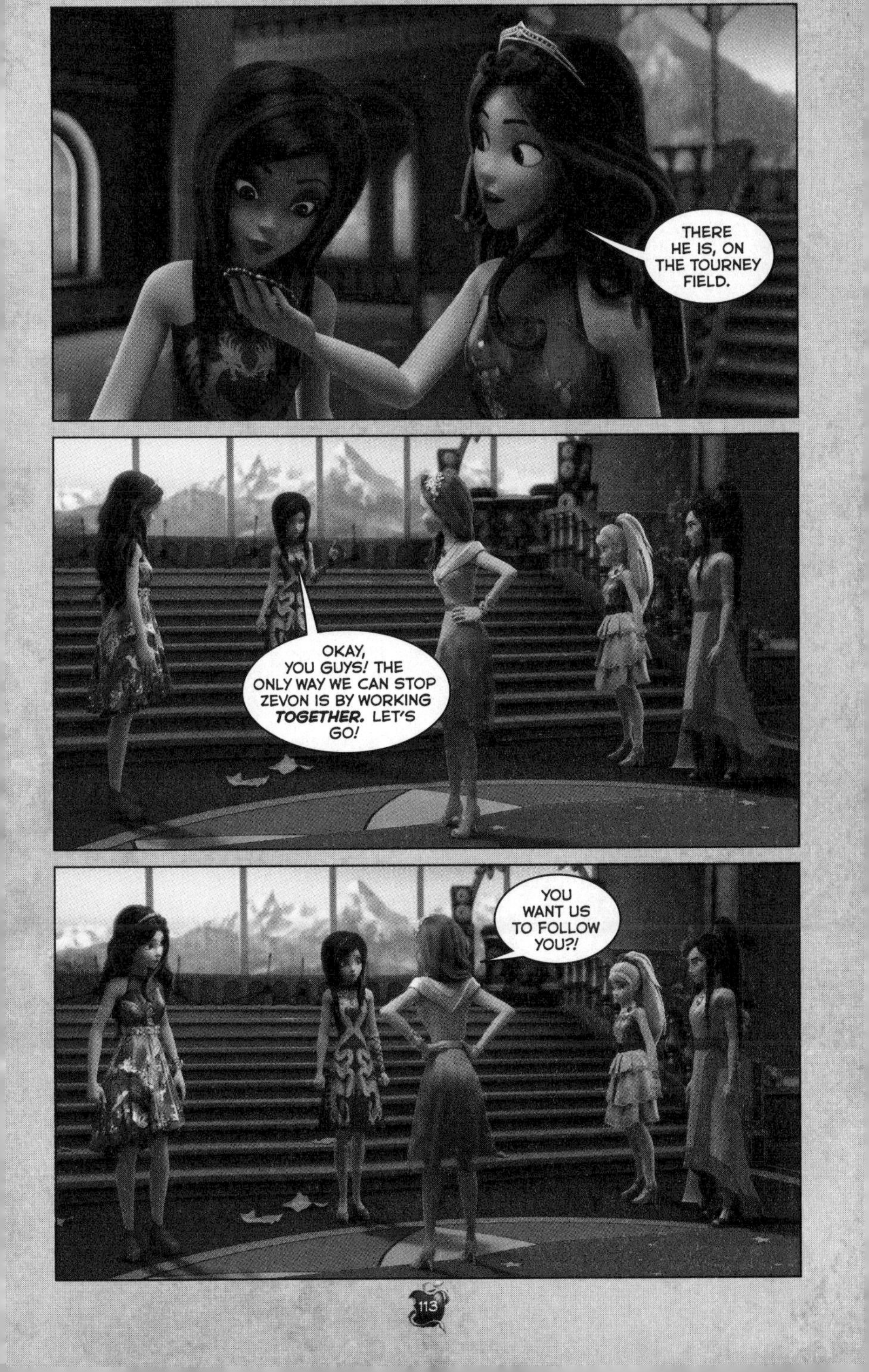
THERE HE IS, ON THE TOURNEY FIELD.
OKAY, YOU GUYS! THE ONLY WAY WE CAN STOP ZEVON IS BY WORKING **TOGETHER.** LET'S GO!
YOU WANT US TO FOLLOW YOU?!

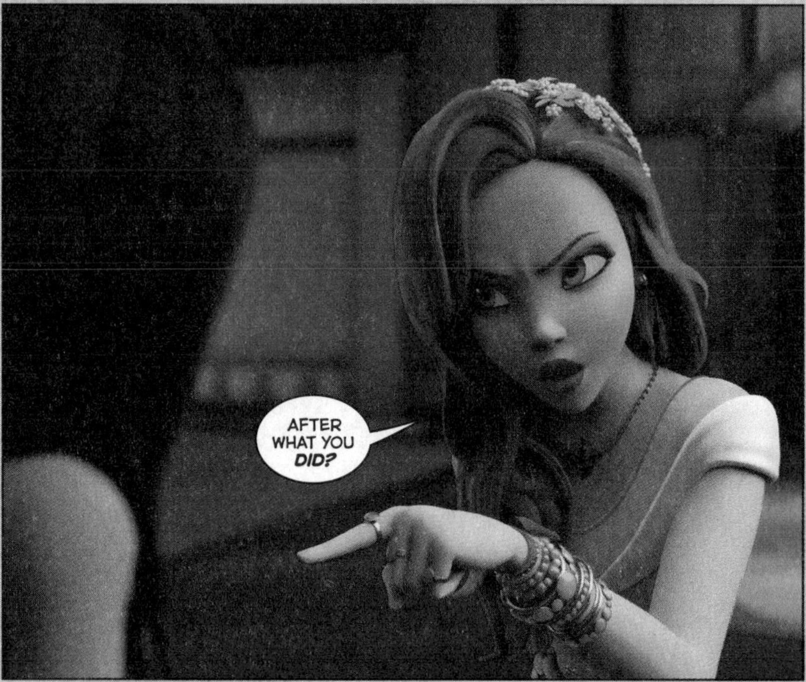
AFTER WHAT YOU *DID?*

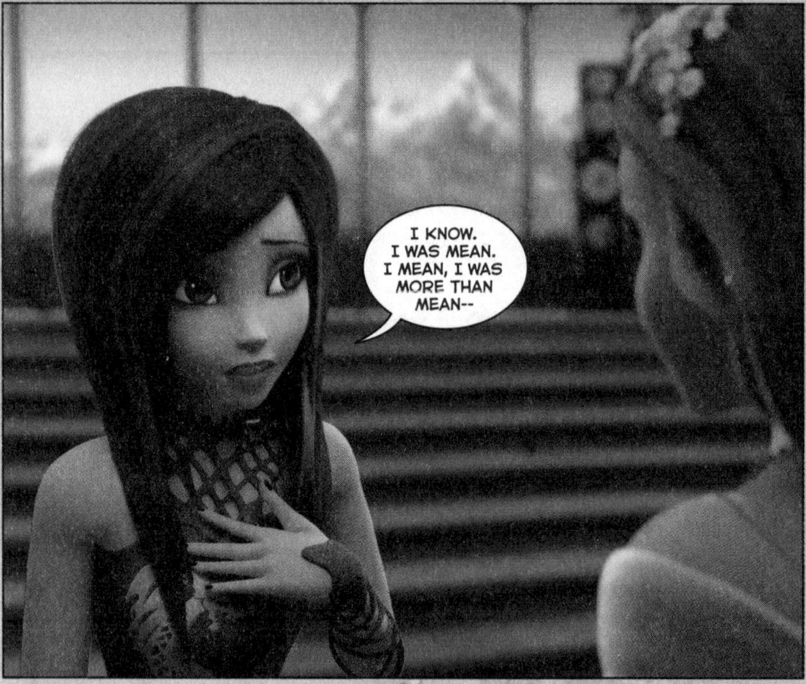
I KNOW. I WAS MEAN. I MEAN, I WAS MORE THAN MEAN--

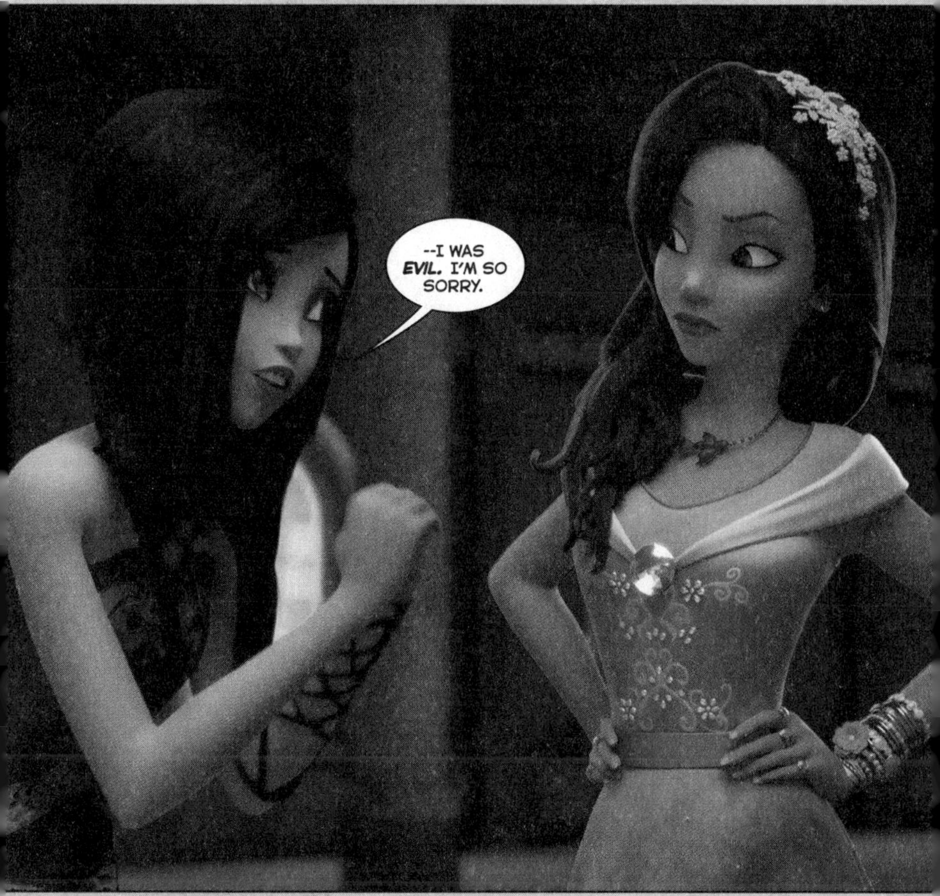
--I WAS *EVIL.* I'M SO SORRY.

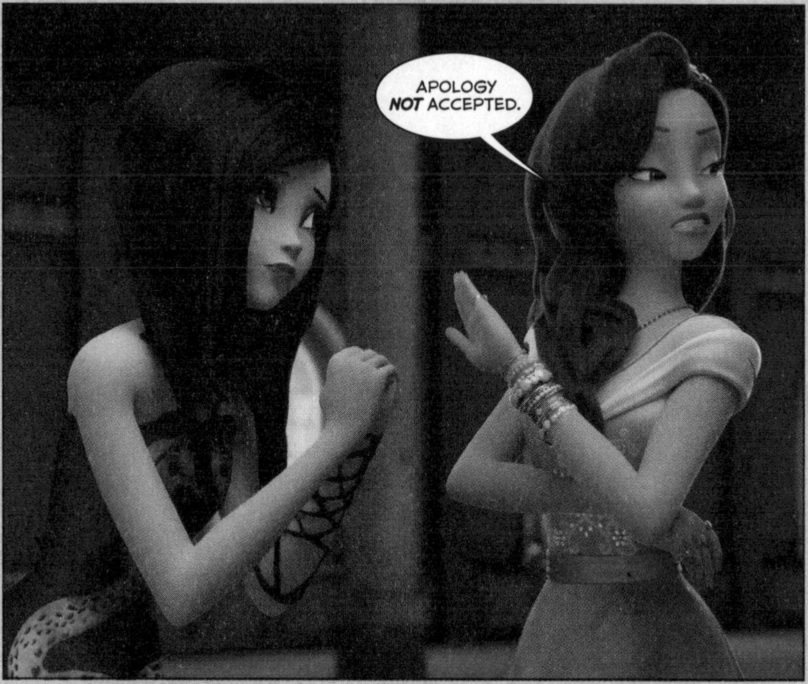
APOLOGY **NOT** ACCEPTED.

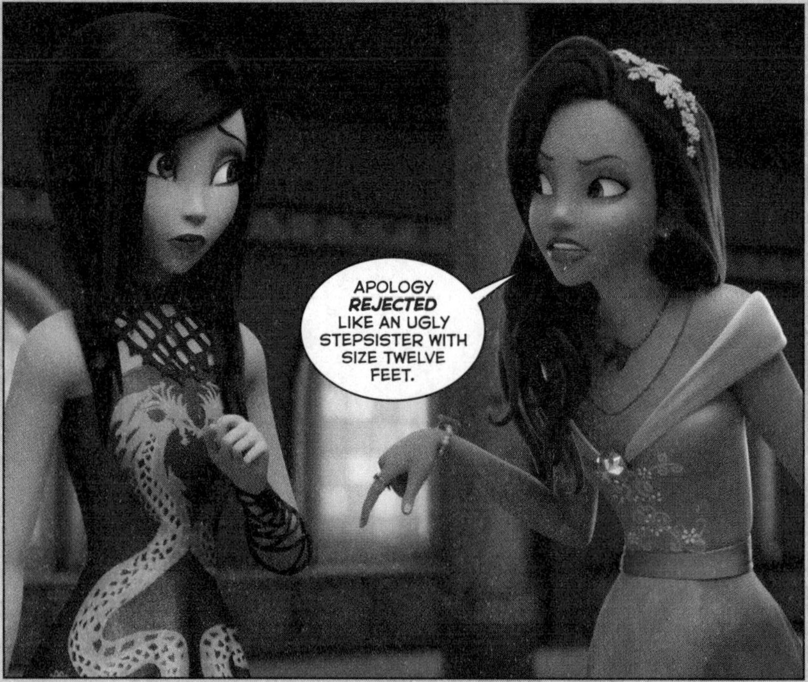
APOLOGY **REJECTED** LIKE AN UGLY STEPSISTER WITH SIZE TWELVE FEET.

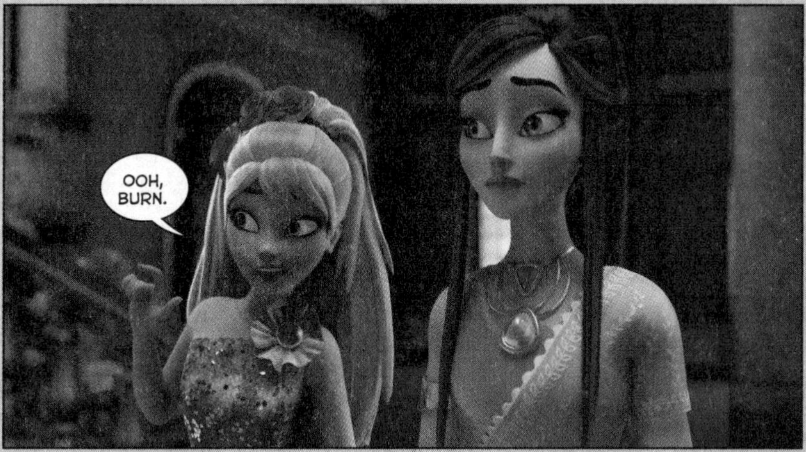
OOH, BURN.

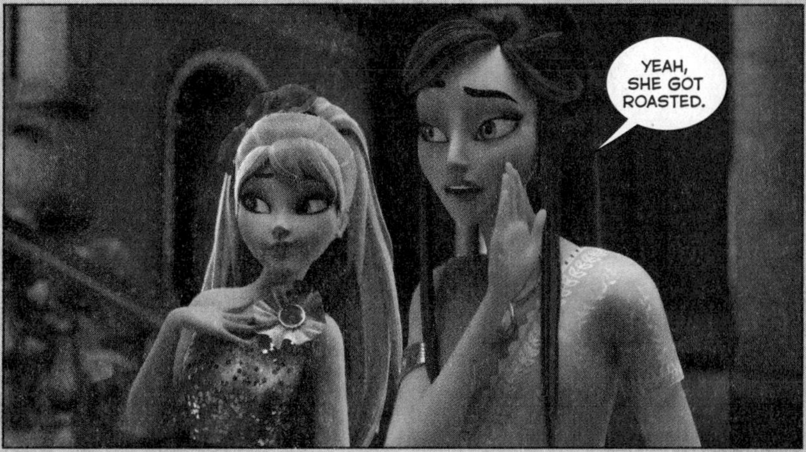
YEAH, SHE GOT ROASTED.

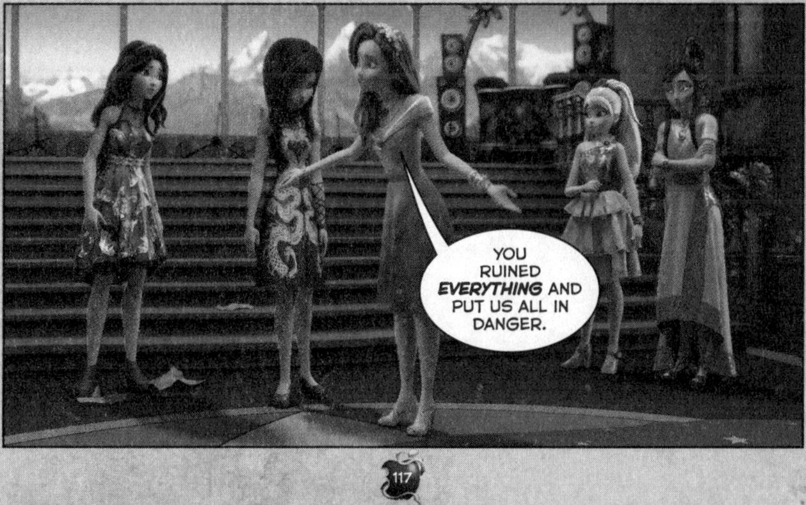
YOU RUINED *EVERYTHING* AND PUT US ALL IN DANGER.

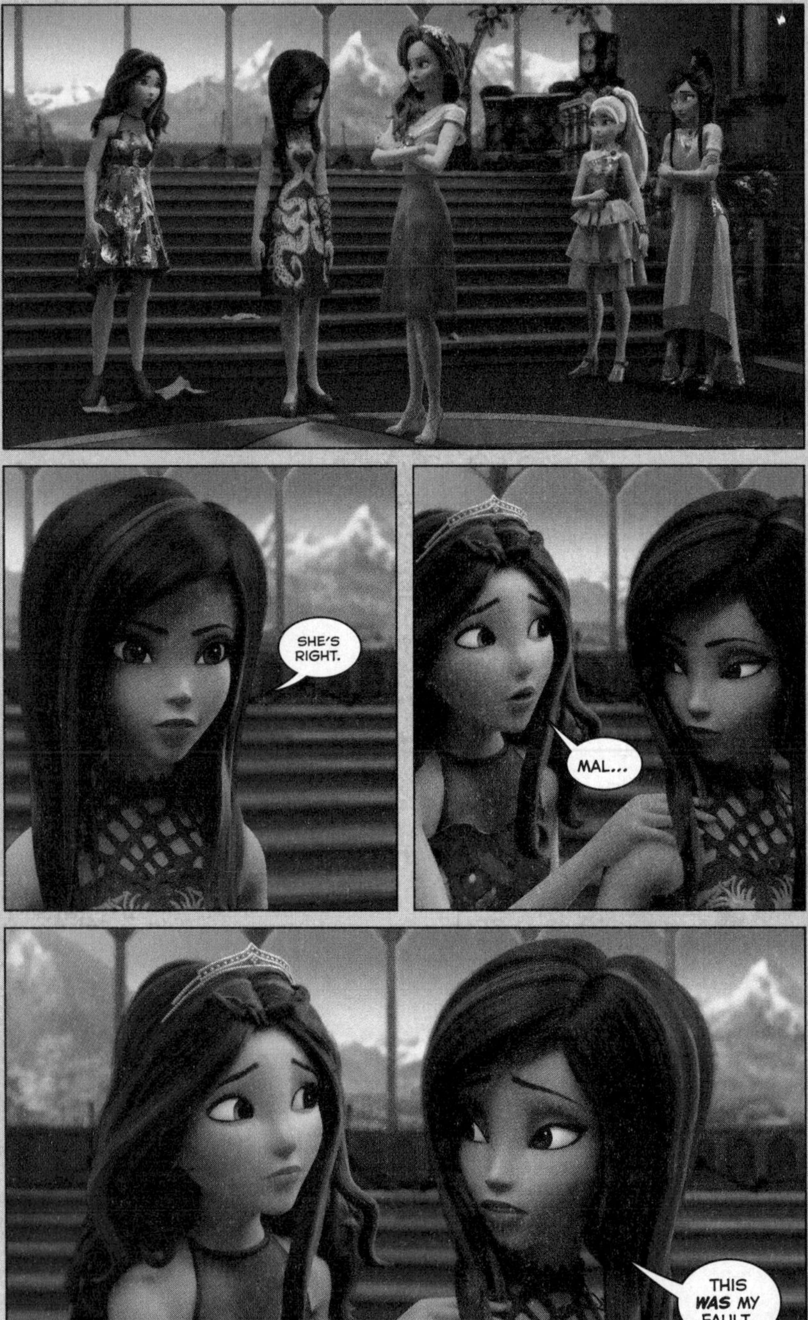
SHE'S RIGHT.
MAL...
THIS WAS MY FAULT.

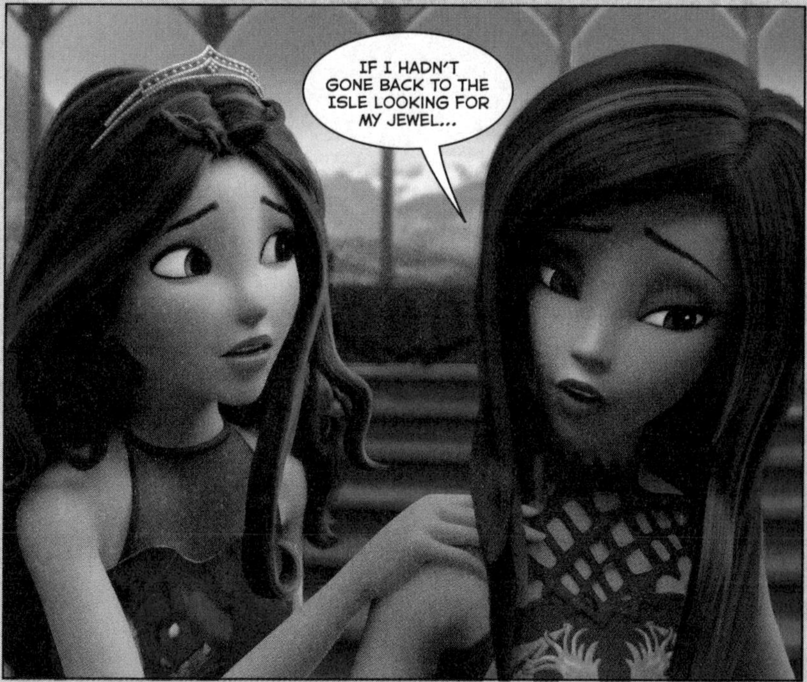
IF I HADN'T GONE BACK TO THE ISLE LOOKING FOR MY JEWEL...

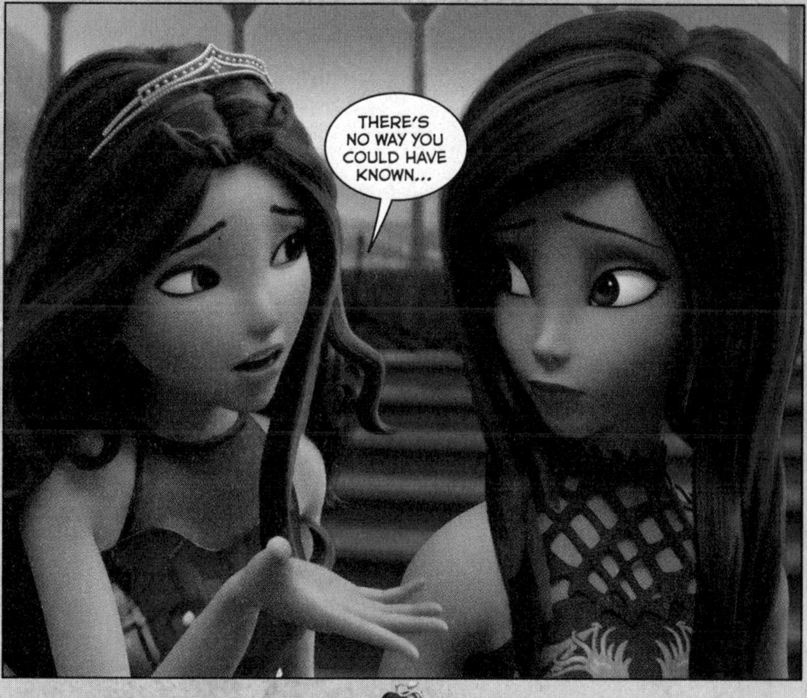
THERE'S NO WAY YOU COULD HAVE KNOWN...

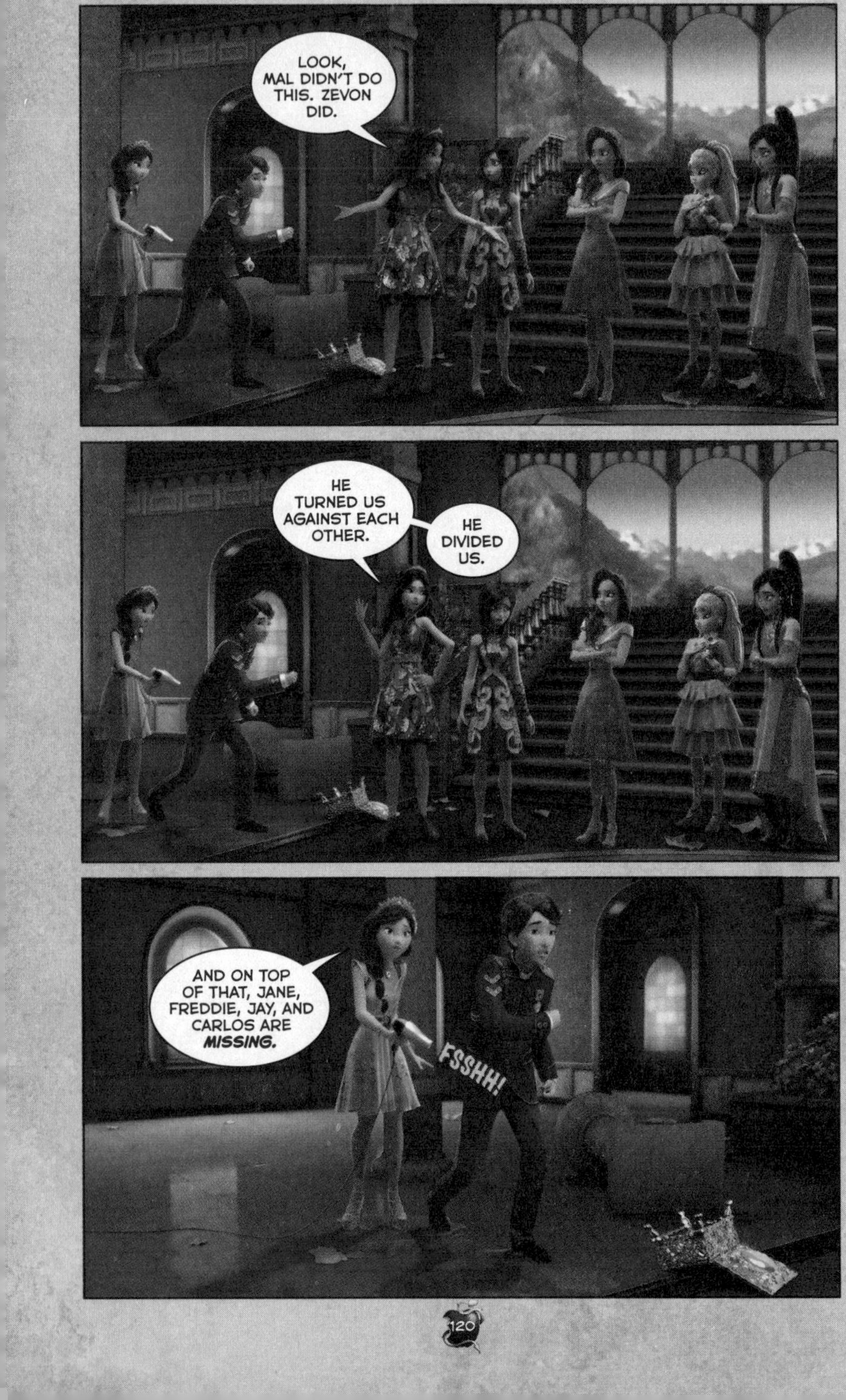
LOOK, MAL DIDN'T DO THIS. ZEVON DID.
HE TURNED US AGAINST EACH OTHER.
HE DIVIDED US.
AND ON TOP OF THAT, JANE, FREDDIE, JAY, AND CARLOS ARE *MISSING.*
FSSHH!

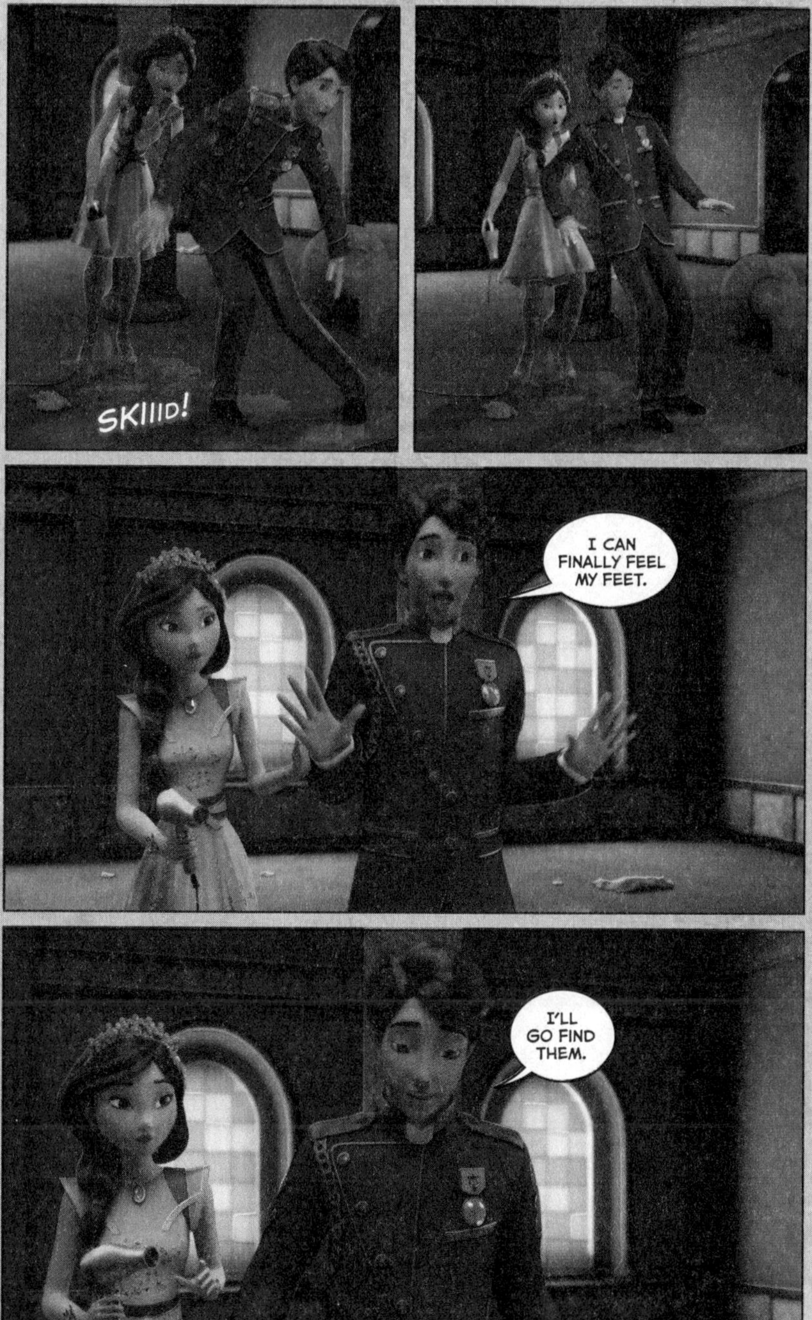

SKIIID!
I CAN FINALLY FEEL MY FEET.
I'LL GO FIND THEM.

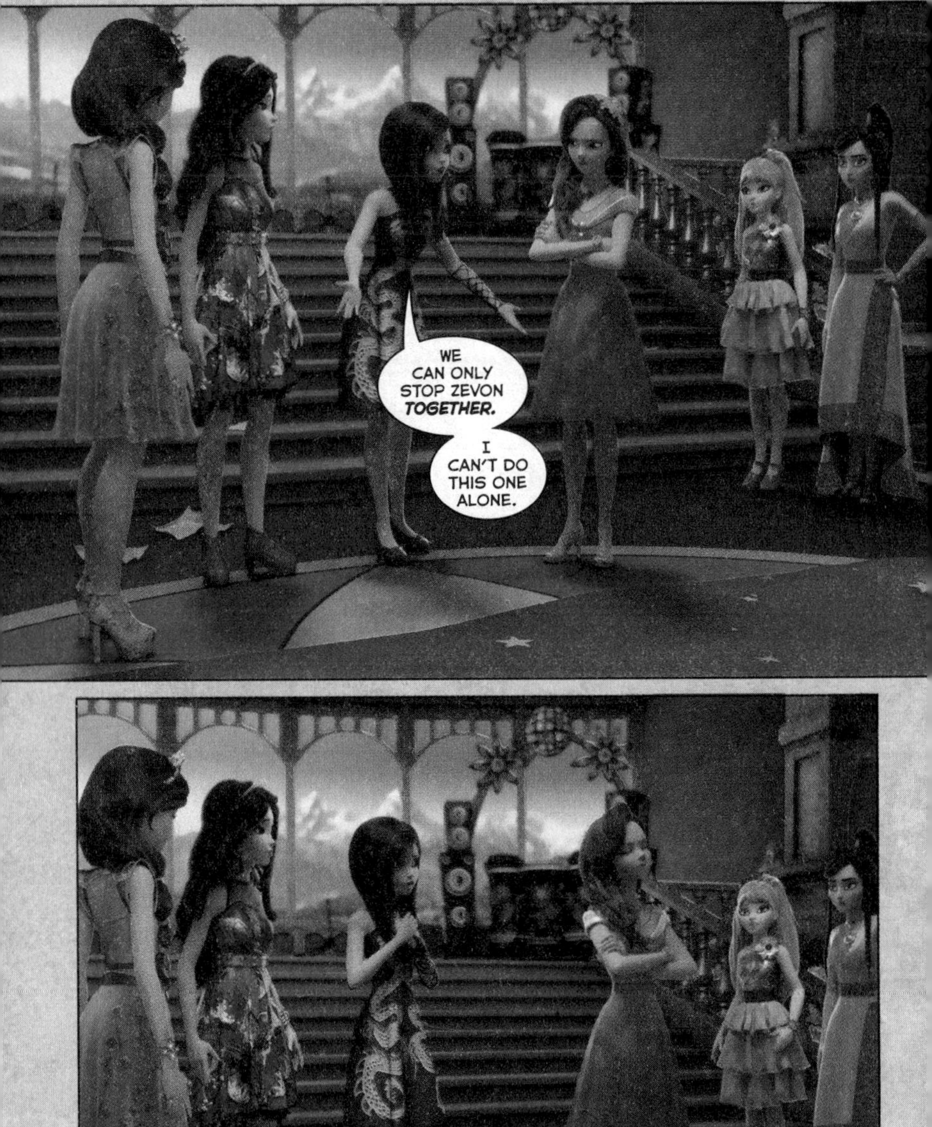
WE CAN ONLY STOP ZEVON *TOGETHER.*
I CAN'T DO THIS ONE ALONE.

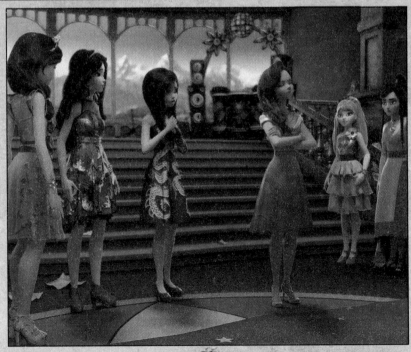

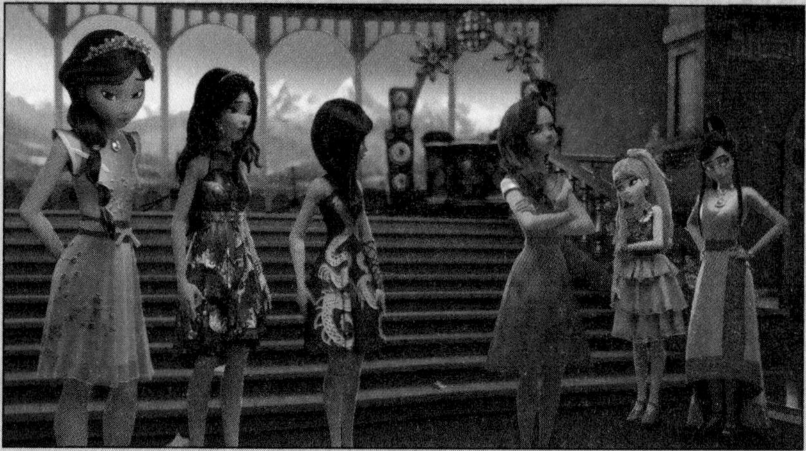

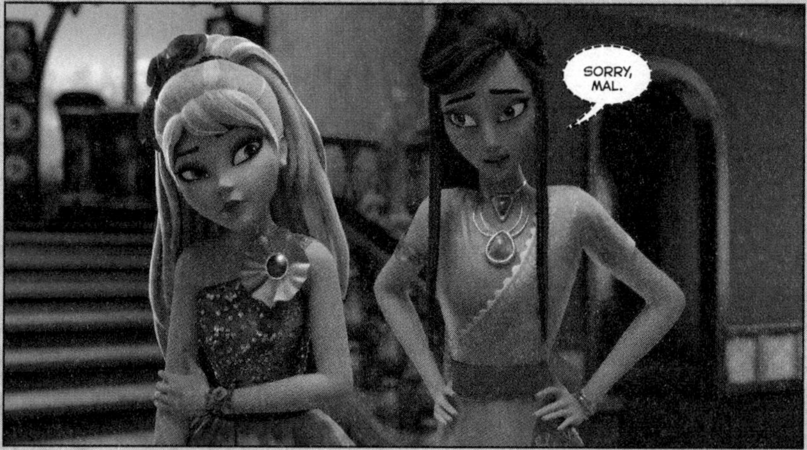
SORRY, MAL.

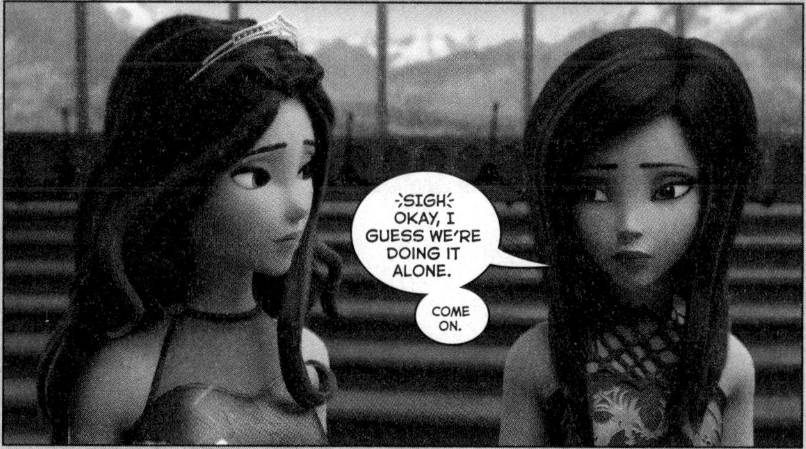
-SIGH-
OKAY, I GUESS WE'RE DOING IT ALONE.
COME ON.

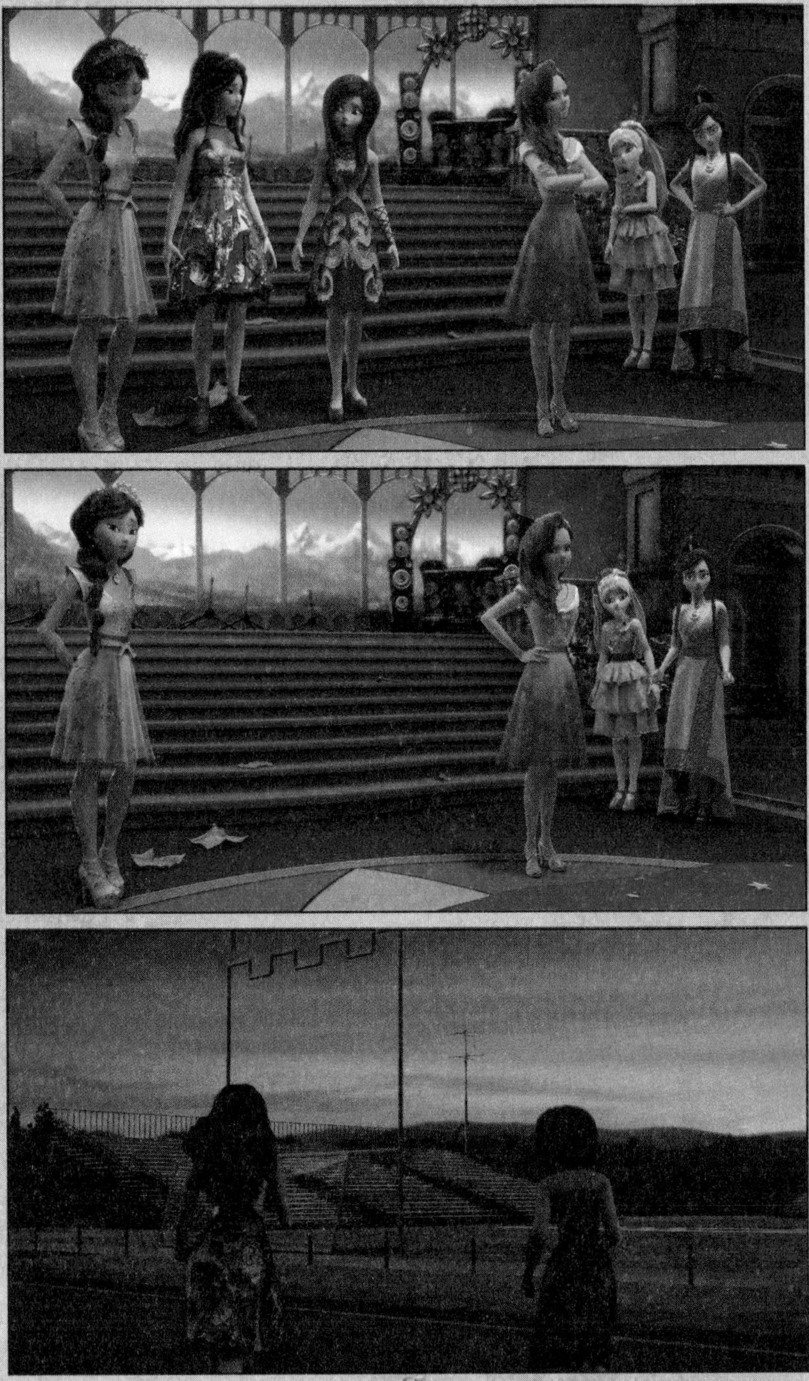

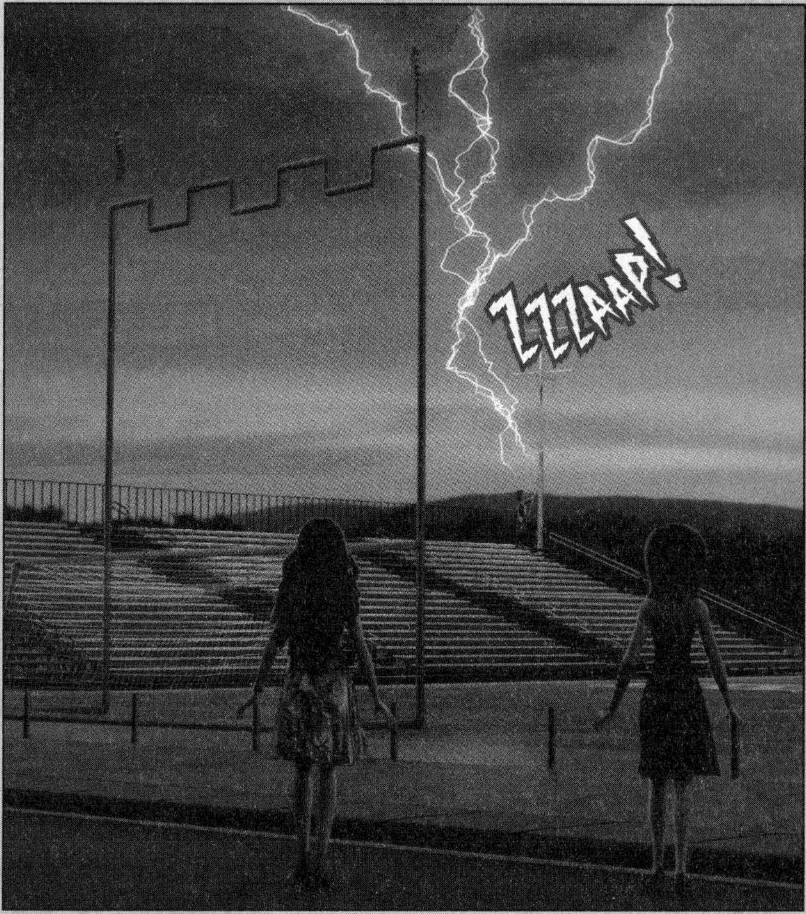
ZZZAAP!

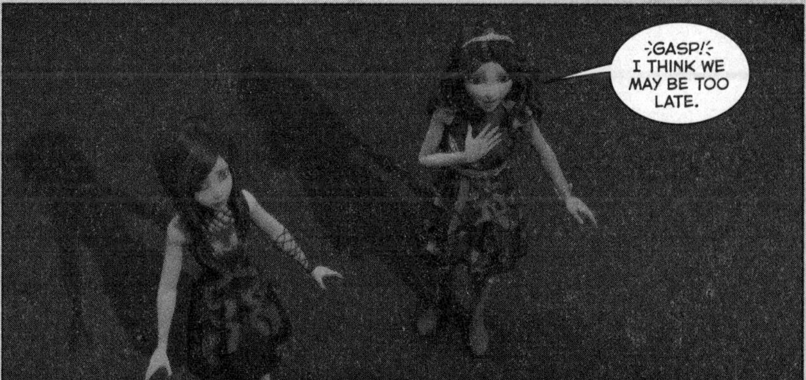
GASP! I THINK WE MAY BE TOO LATE.

CHAPTER 30: TRAPPED

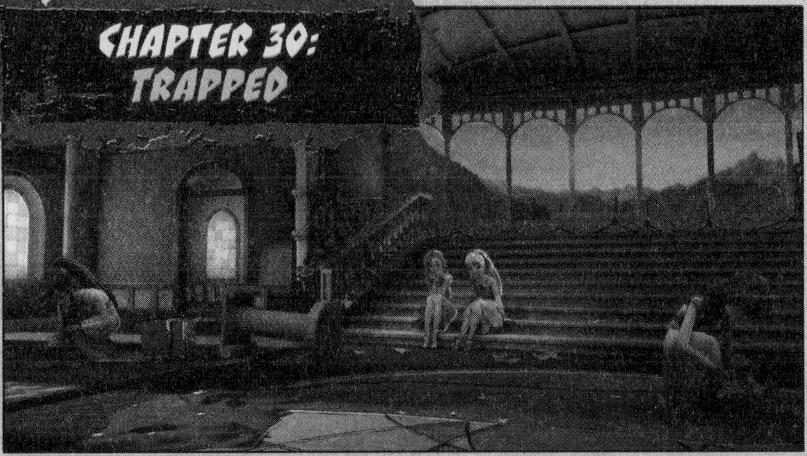

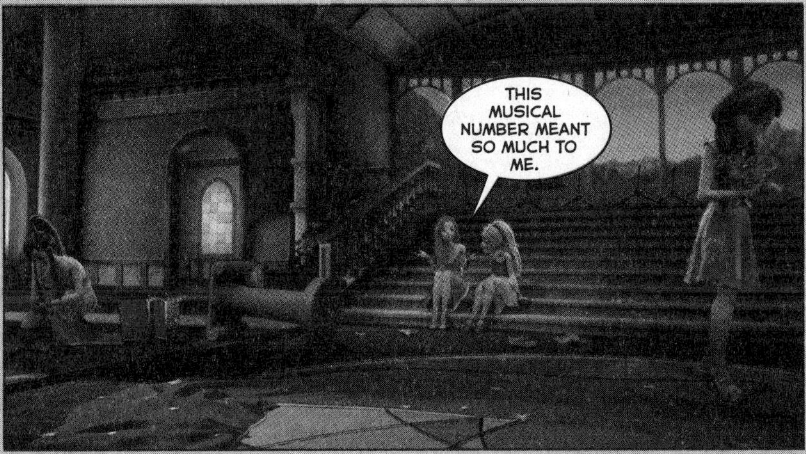
THIS MUSICAL NUMBER MEANT SO MUCH TO ME.

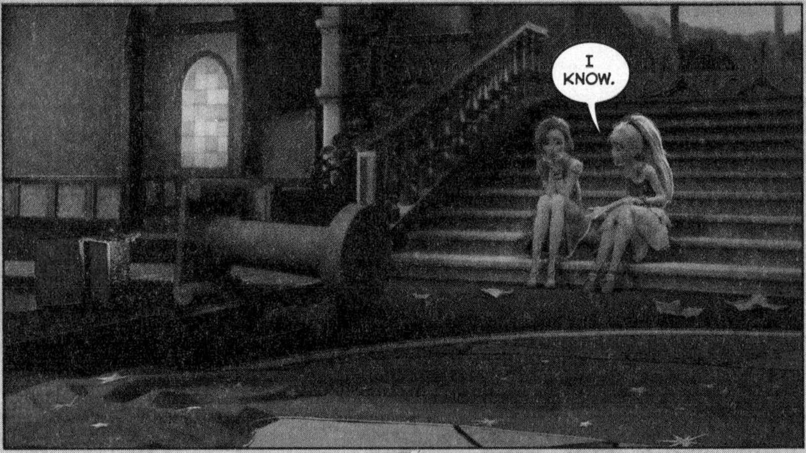
I KNOW.

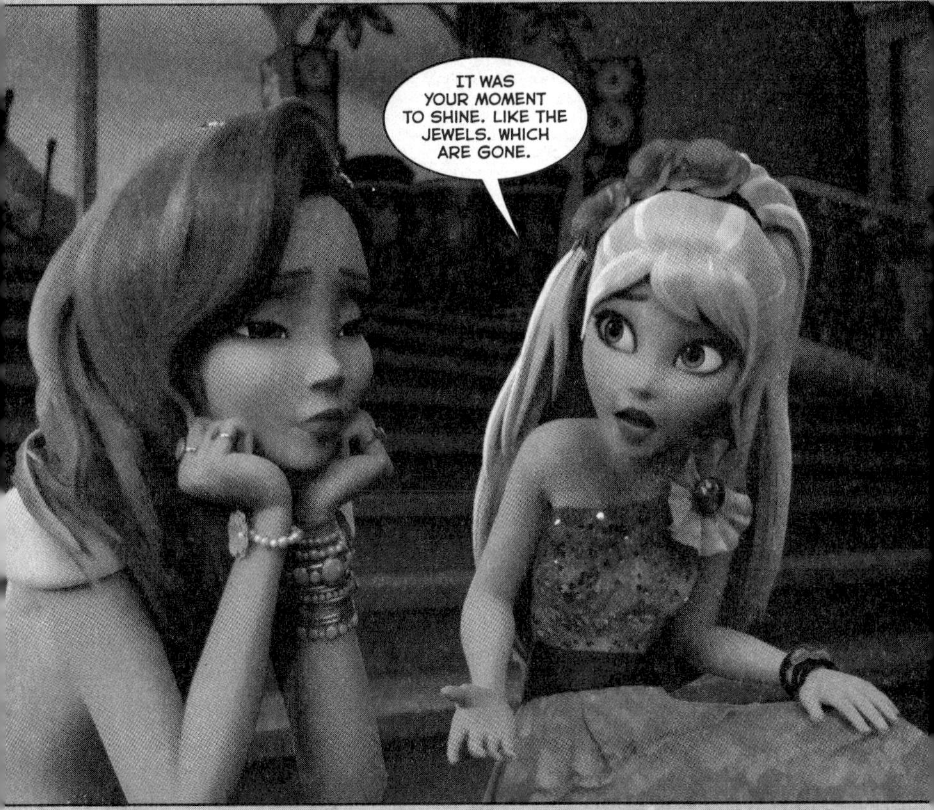
IT WAS YOUR MOMENT TO SHINE. LIKE THE JEWELS. WHICH ARE GONE.

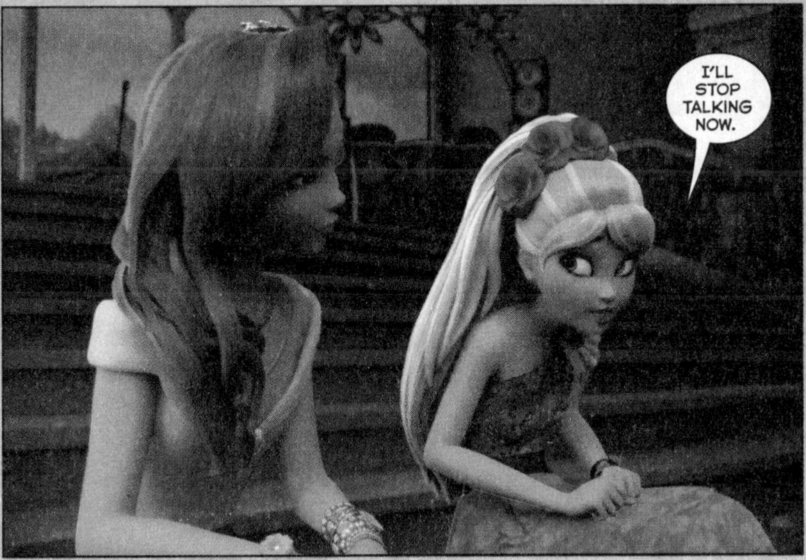
I'LL STOP TALKING NOW.

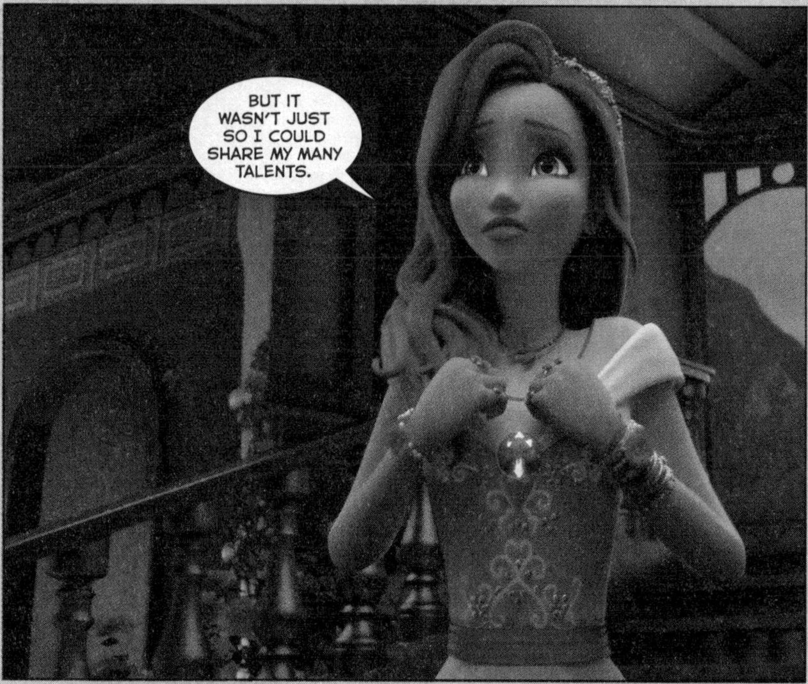
BUT IT WASN'T JUST SO I COULD SHARE MY MANY TALENTS.

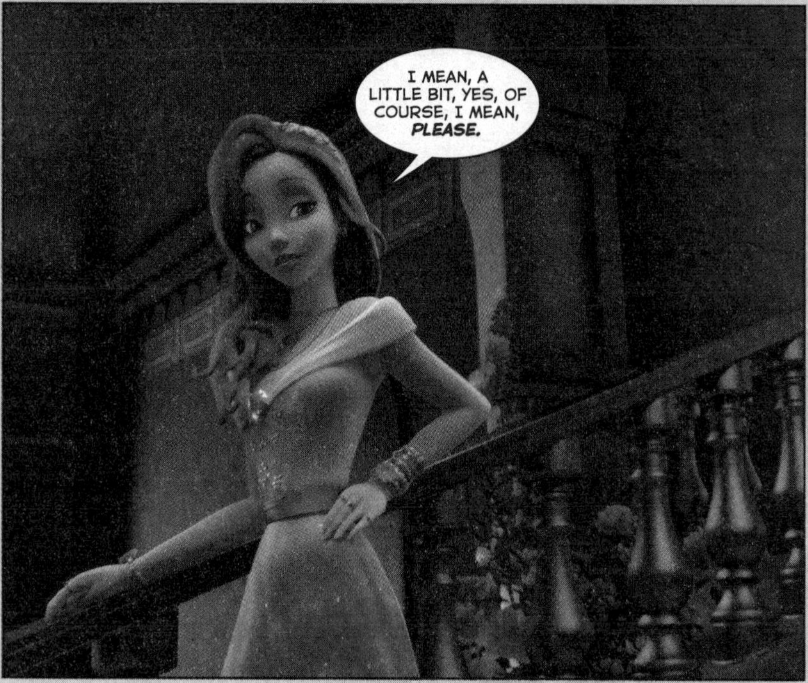
I MEAN, A LITTLE BIT, YES, OF COURSE, I MEAN, *PLEASE.*

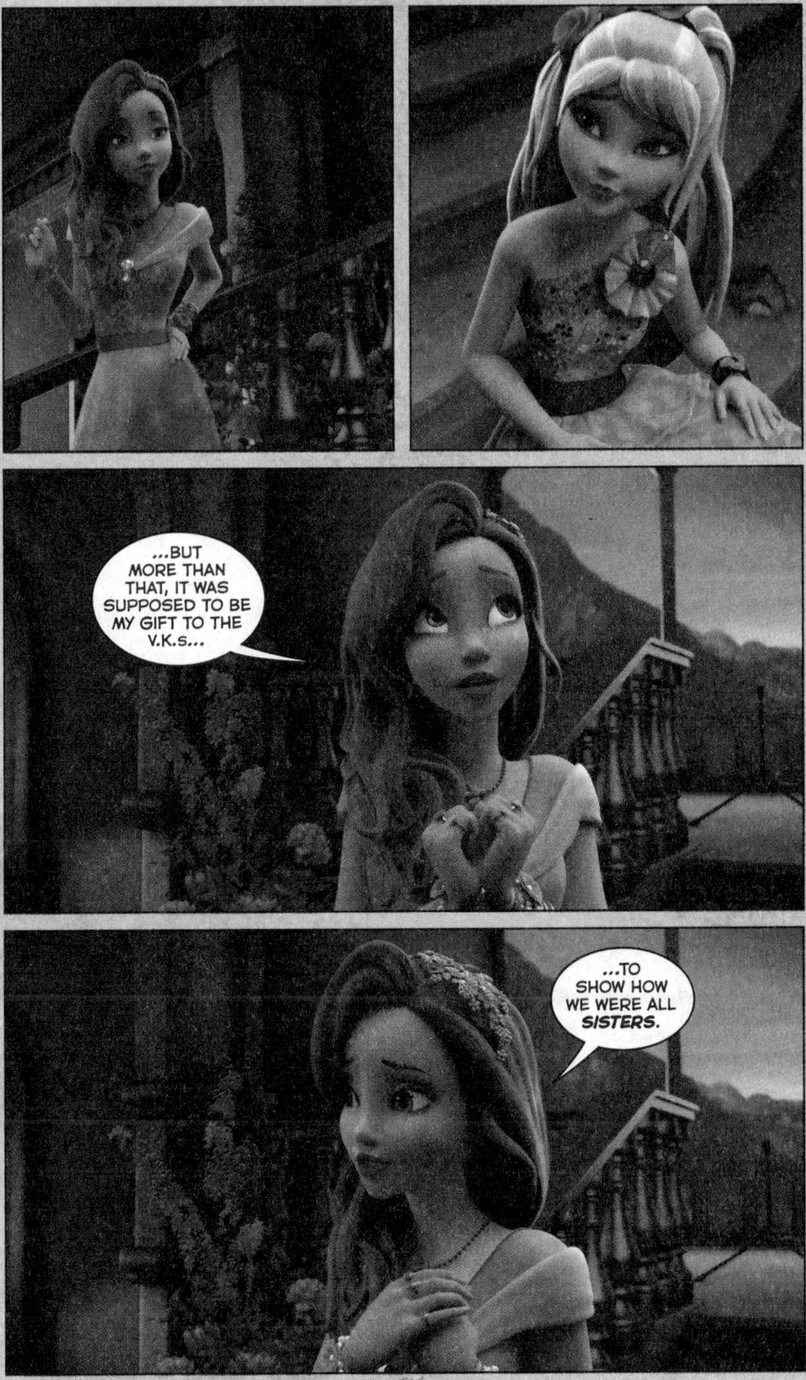
...BUT MORE THAN THAT, IT WAS SUPPOSED TO BE MY GIFT TO THE V.K.s...
...TO SHOW HOW WE WERE ALL **SISTERS.**

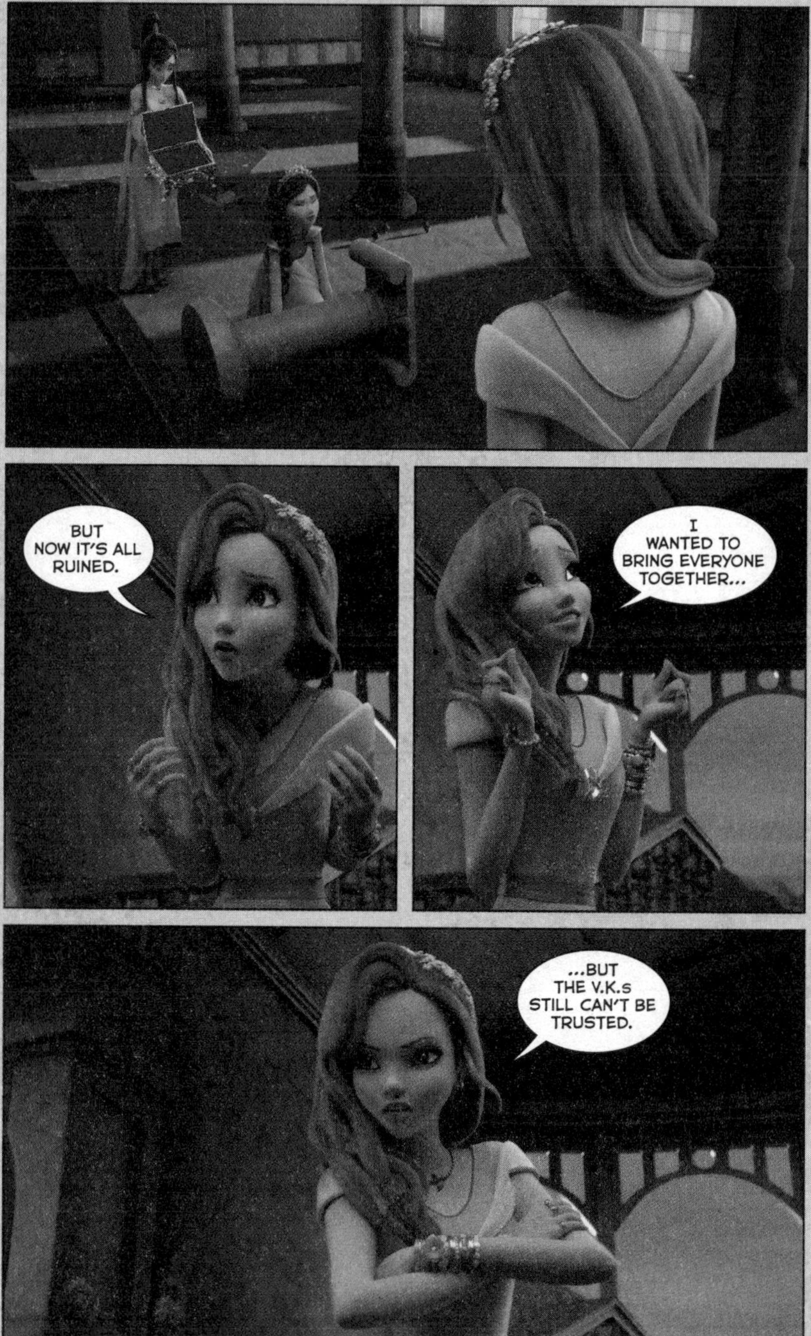

BUT NOW IT'S ALL RUINED.
I WANTED TO BRING EVERYONE TOGETHER...
...BUT THE V.K.s STILL CAN'T BE TRUSTED.

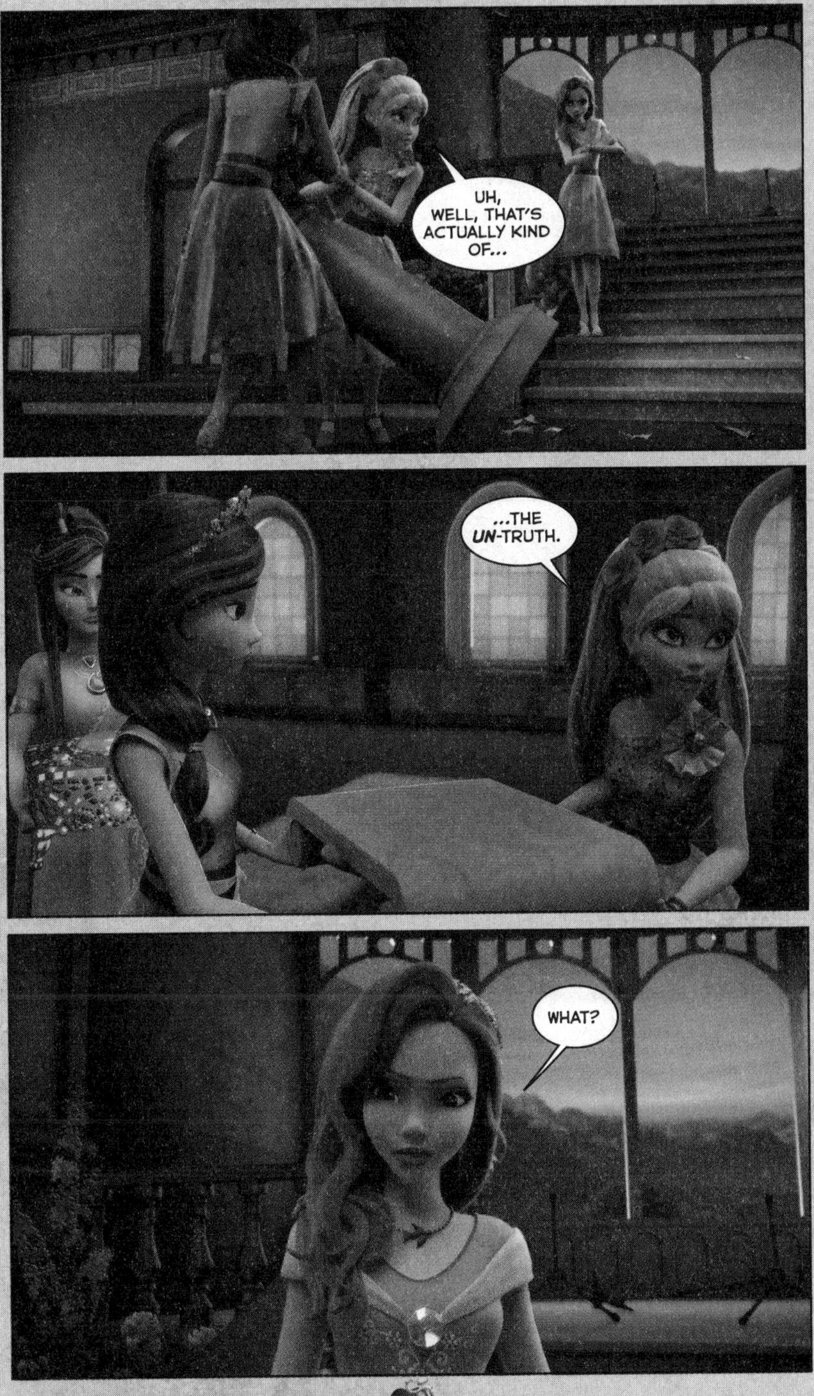
UH, WELL, THAT'S ACTUALLY KIND OF...
...THE *UN*-TRUTH.
WHAT?

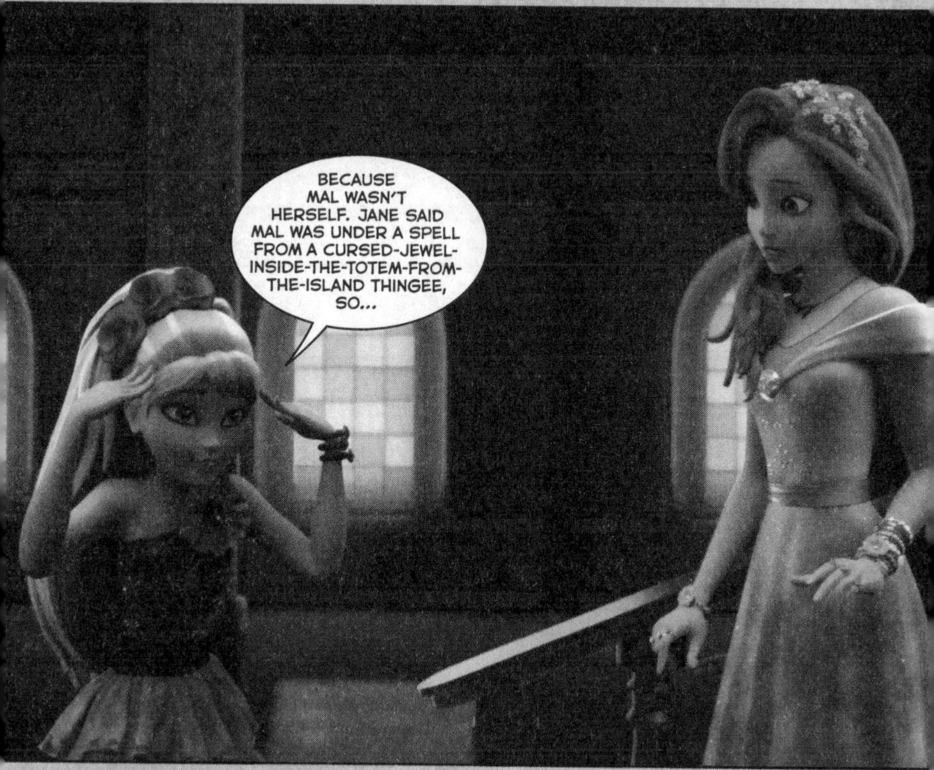
BECAUSE MAL WASN'T HERSELF. JANE SAID MAL WAS UNDER A SPELL FROM A CURSED-JEWEL-INSIDE-THE-TOTEM-FROM-THE-ISLAND THINGEE, SO...

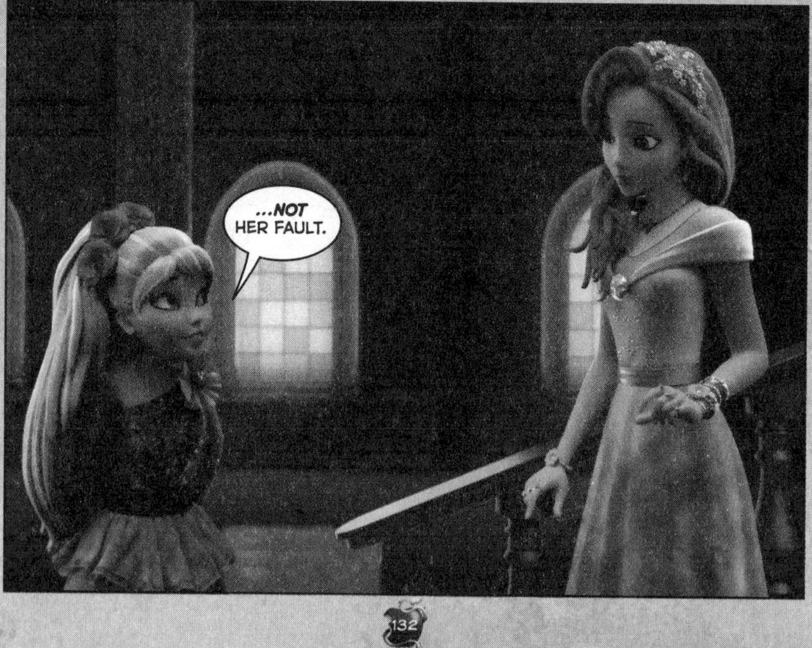
...***NOT*** HER FAULT.

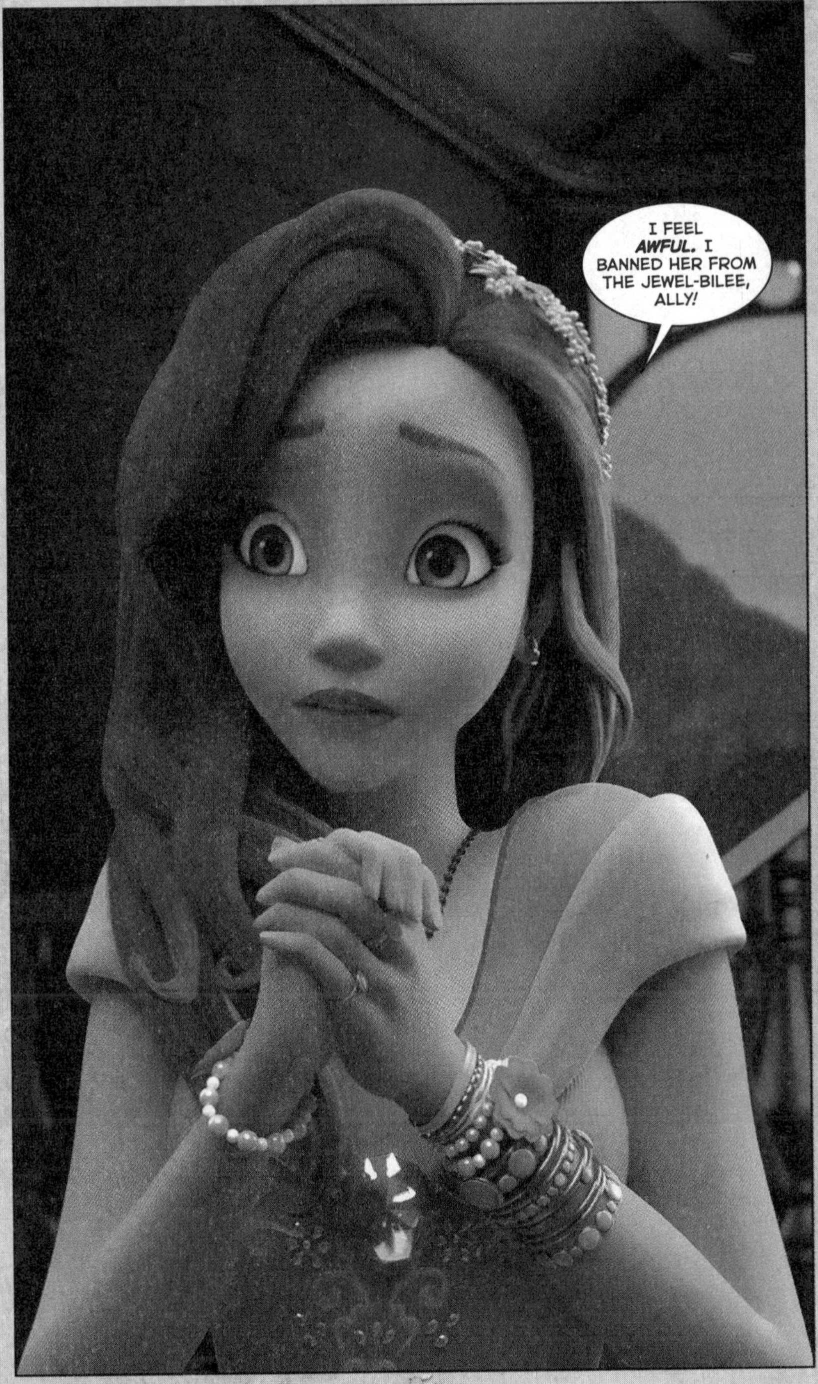
I FEEL **AWFUL.** I BANNED HER FROM THE JEWEL-BILEE, ALLY!

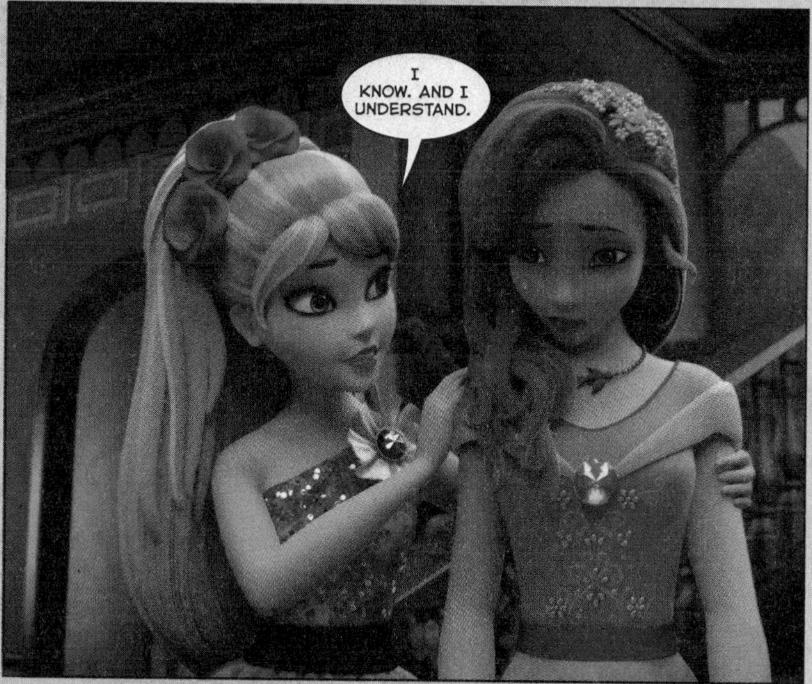
I KNOW. AND I UNDERSTAND.

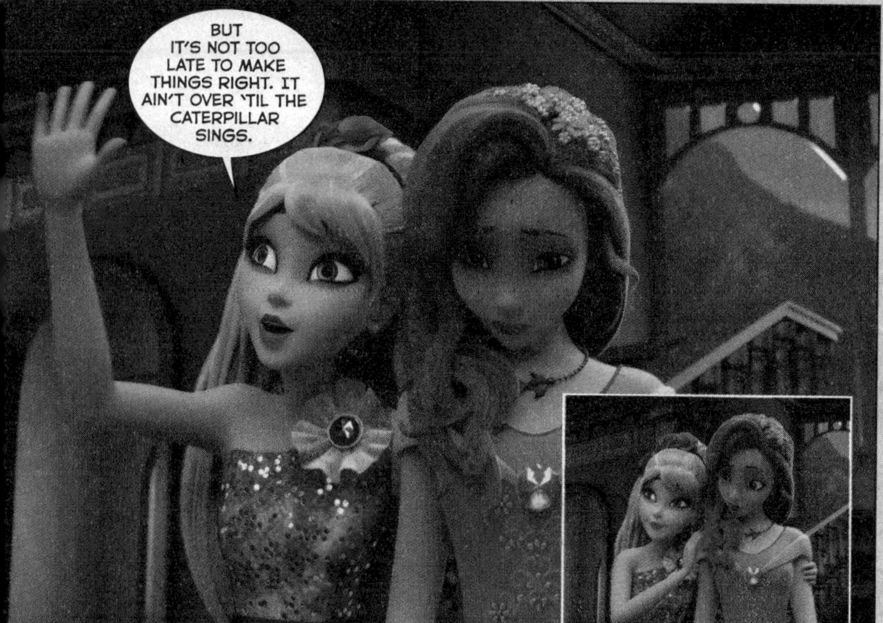
BUT IT'S NOT TOO LATE TO MAKE THINGS RIGHT. IT AIN'T OVER 'TIL THE CATERPILLAR SINGS.

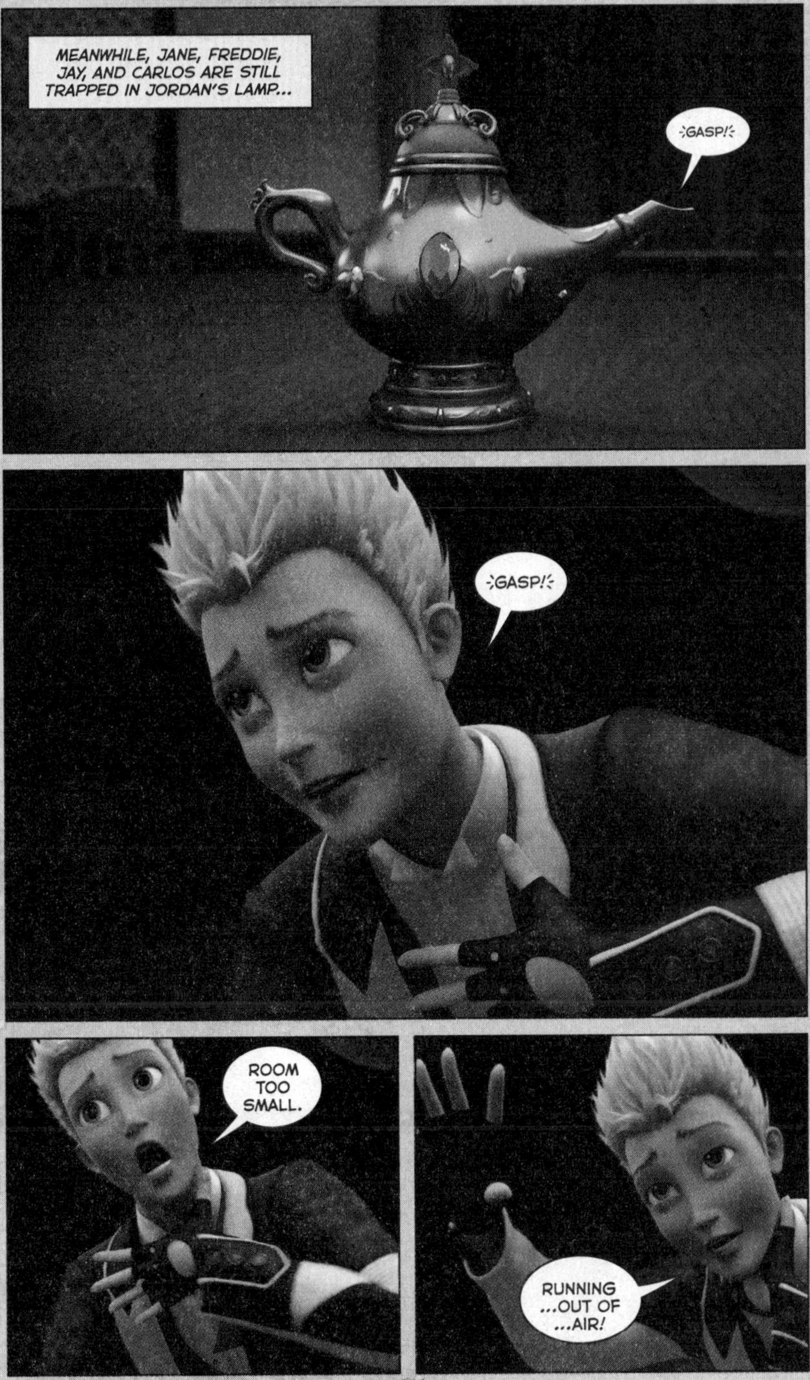
MEANWHILE, JANE, FREDDIE, JAY, AND CARLOS ARE STILL TRAPPED IN JORDAN'S LAMP...
GASP!
GASP!
ROOM TOO SMALL.
RUNNING ...OUT OF ...AIR!

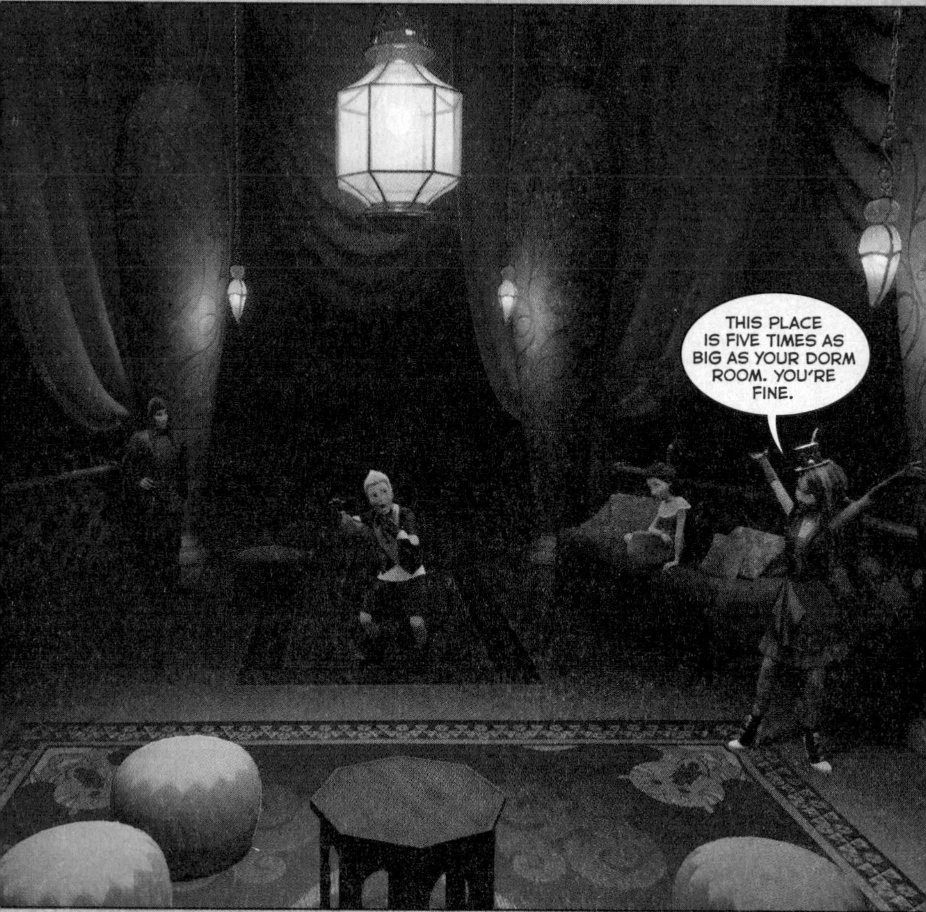
THIS PLACE IS FIVE TIMES AS BIG AS YOUR DORM ROOM. YOU'RE FINE.

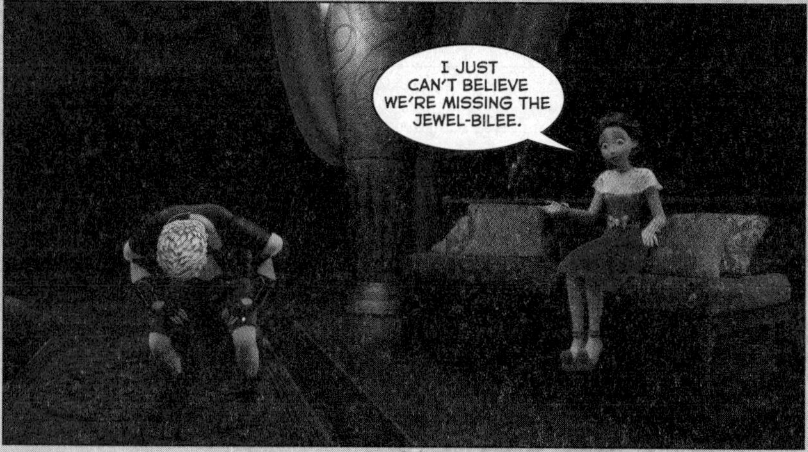
I JUST CAN'T BELIEVE WE'RE MISSING THE JEWEL-BILEE.

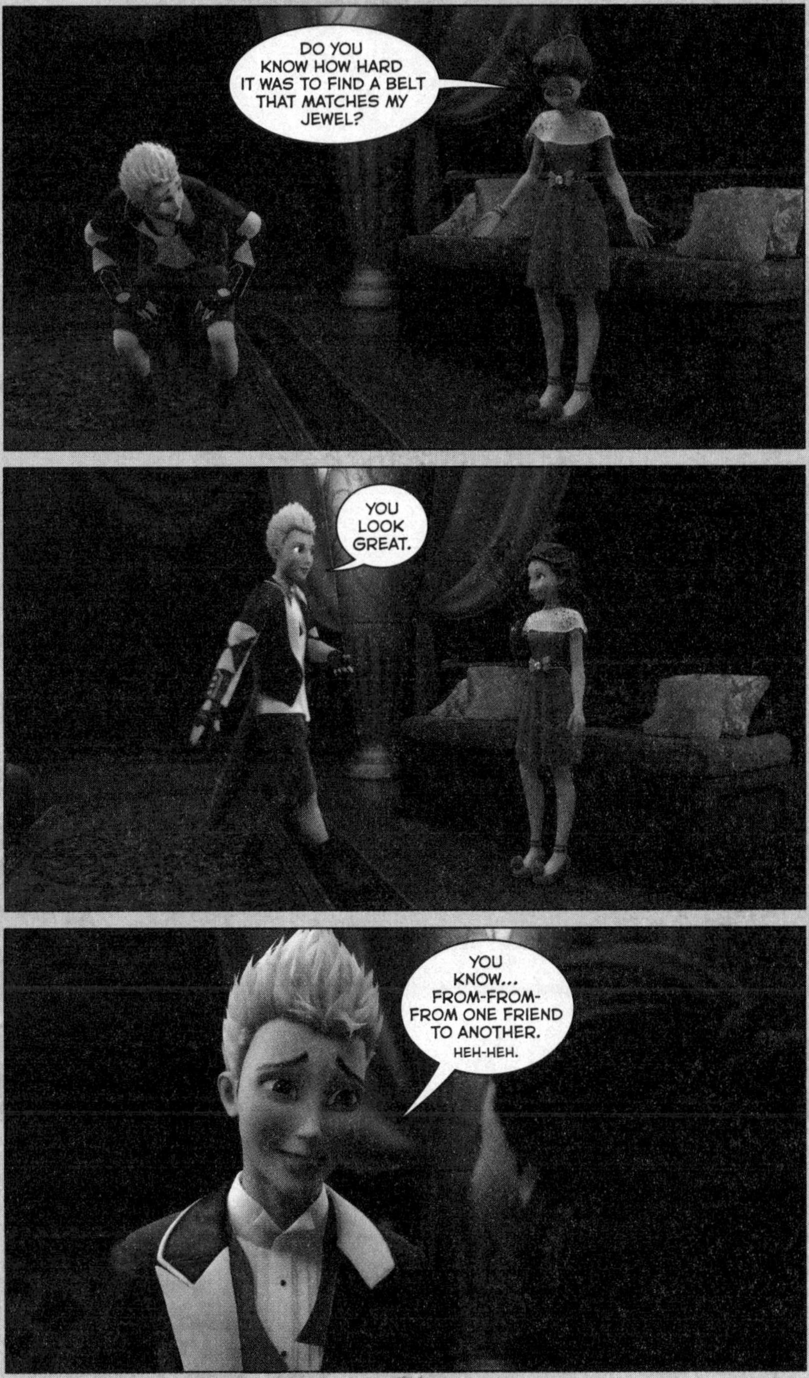
DO YOU KNOW HOW HARD IT WAS TO FIND A BELT THAT MATCHES MY JEWEL?
YOU LOOK GREAT.
YOU KNOW... FROM-FROM-FROM ONE FRIEND TO ANOTHER. HEH-HEH.

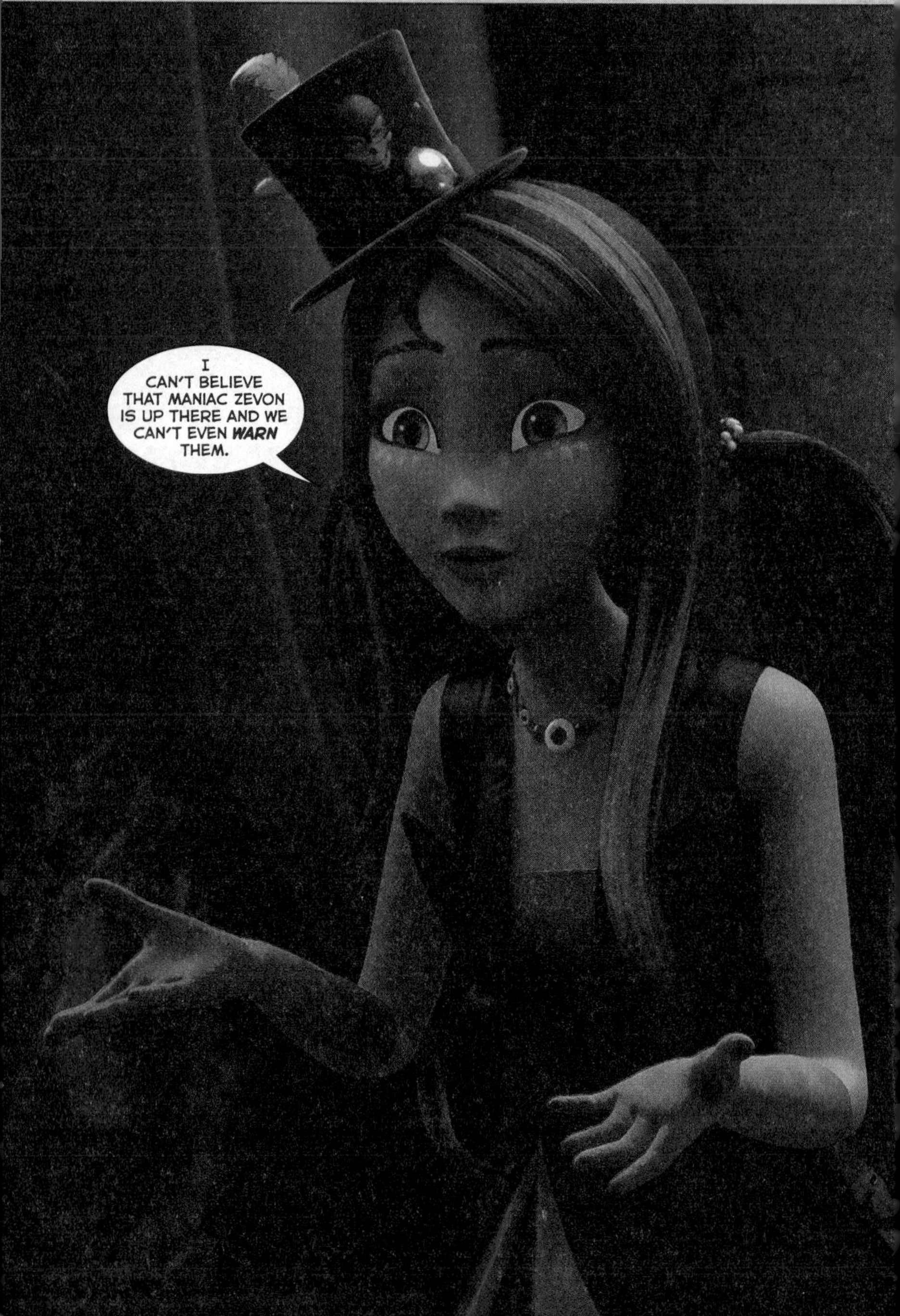
I CAN'T BELIEVE THAT MANIAC ZEVON IS UP THERE AND WE CAN'T EVEN *WARN* THEM.

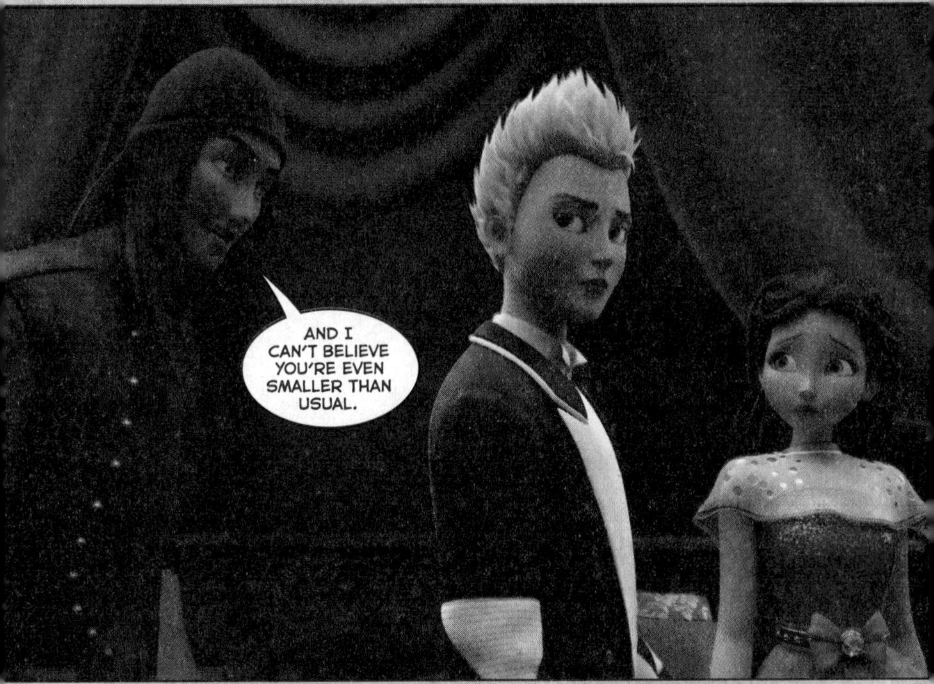
AND I CAN'T BELIEVE YOU'RE EVEN SMALLER THAN USUAL.

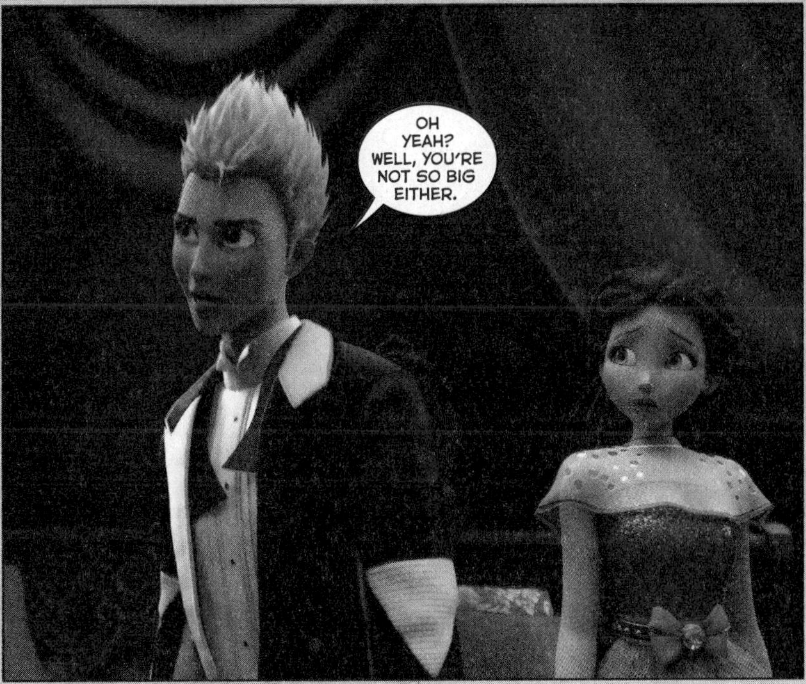
OH YEAH? WELL, YOU'RE NOT SO BIG EITHER.

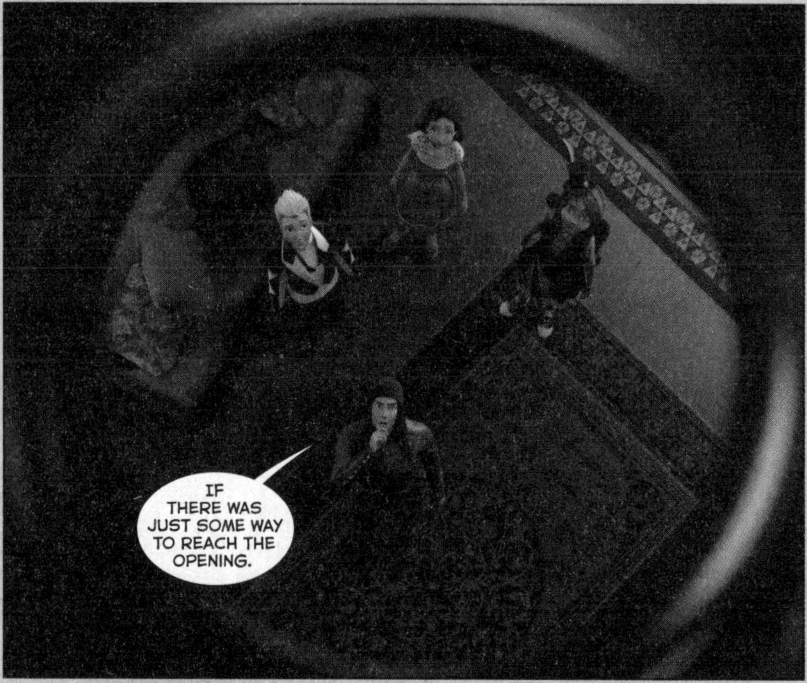
IF THERE WAS JUST SOME WAY TO REACH THE OPENING.

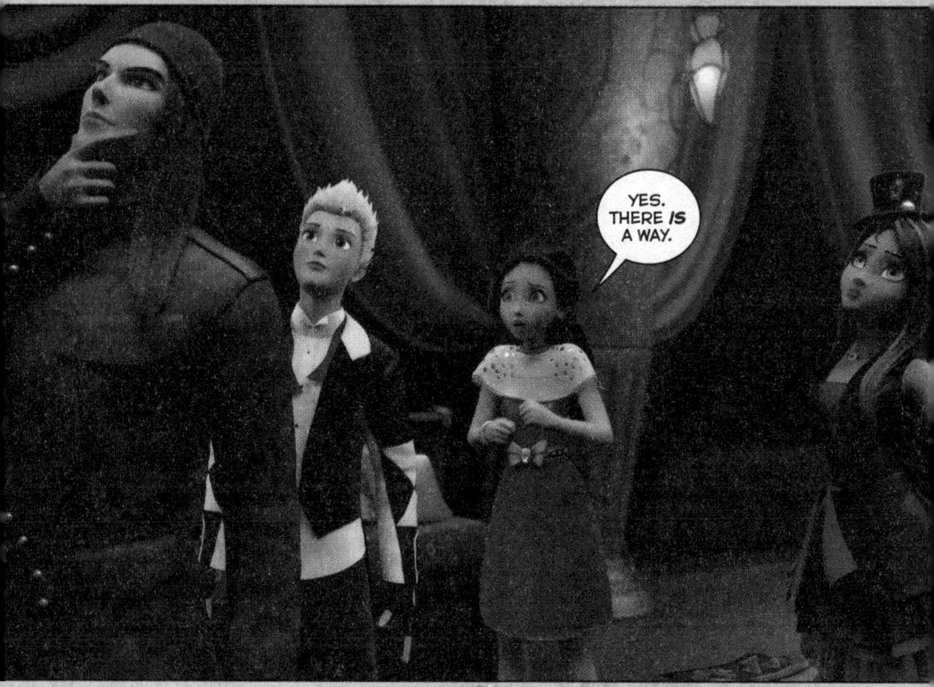
YES. THERE IS A WAY.

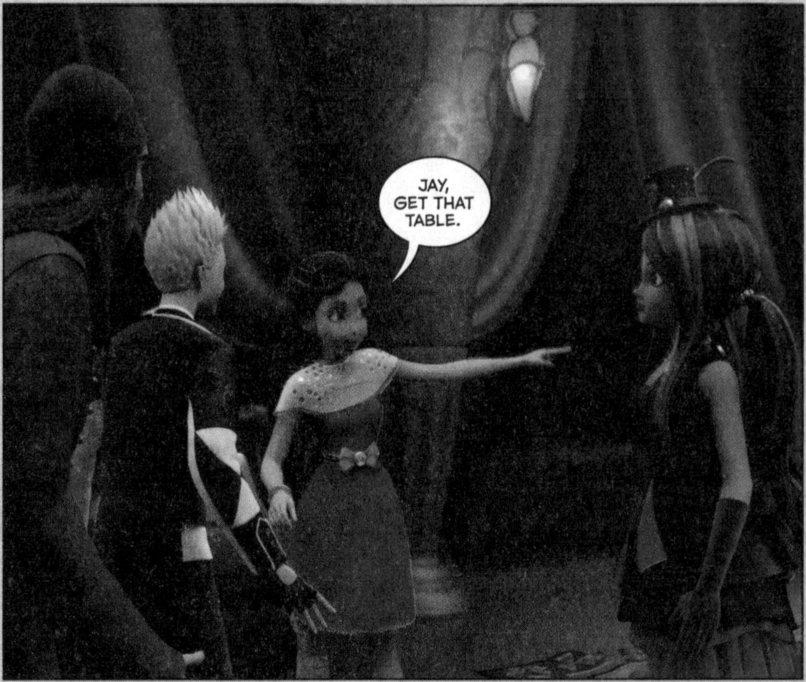
JAY, GET THAT TABLE.

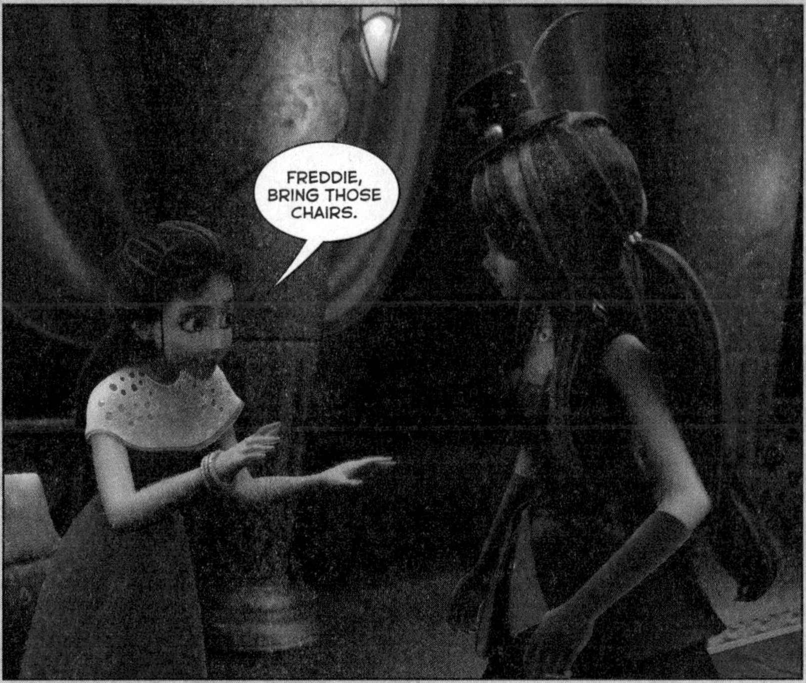
FREDDIE, BRING THOSE CHAIRS.

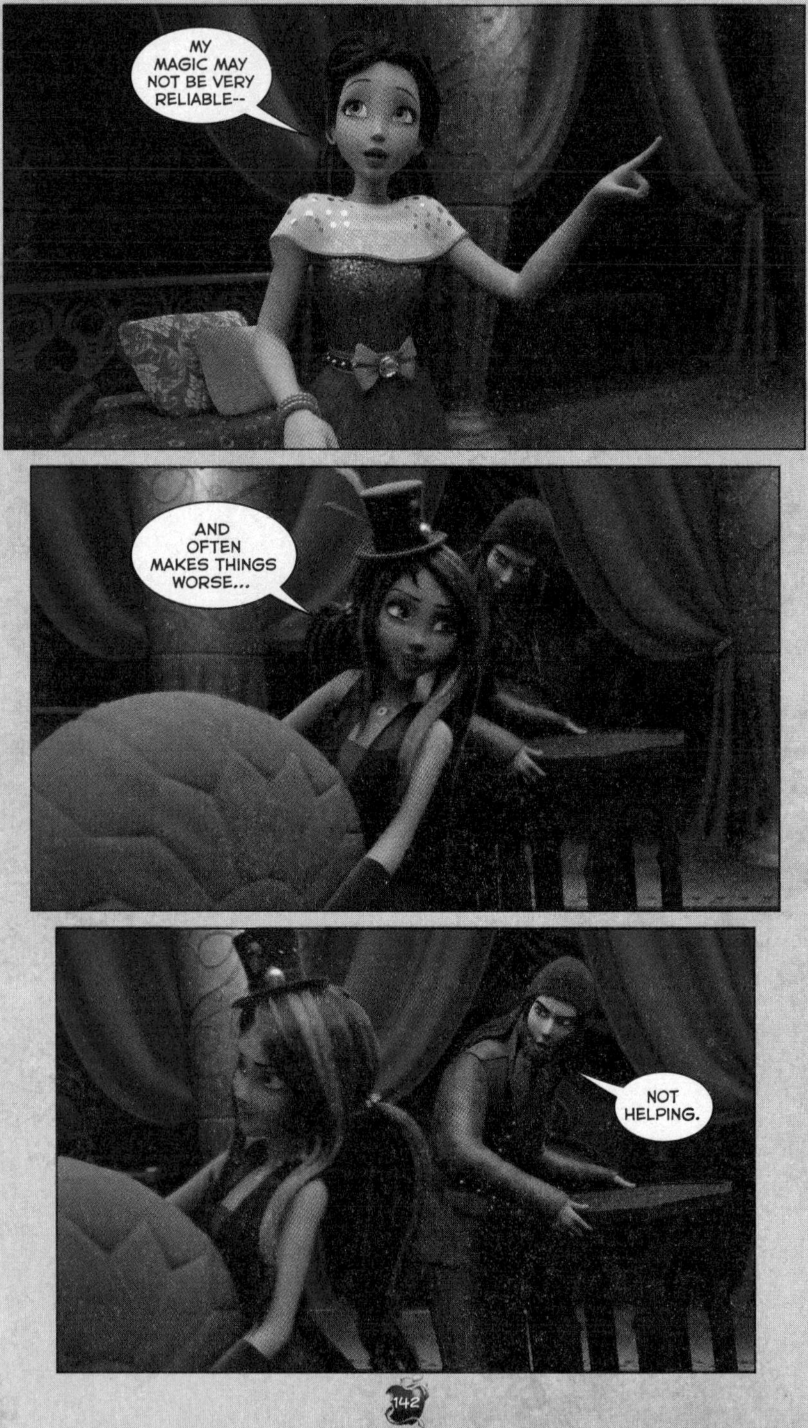
MY MAGIC MAY NOT BE VERY RELIABLE--
AND OFTEN MAKES THINGS WORSE...
NOT HELPING.

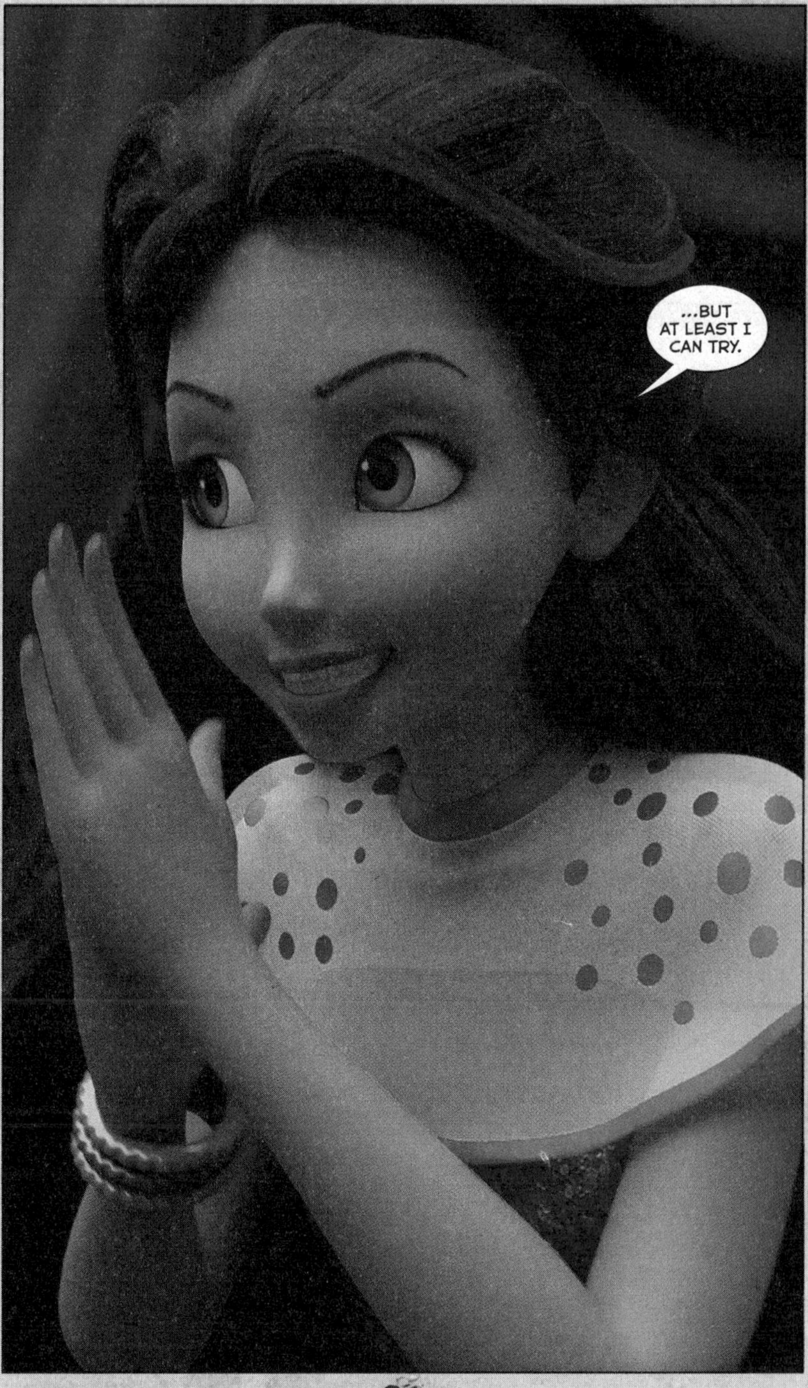
...BUT AT LEAST I CAN TRY.

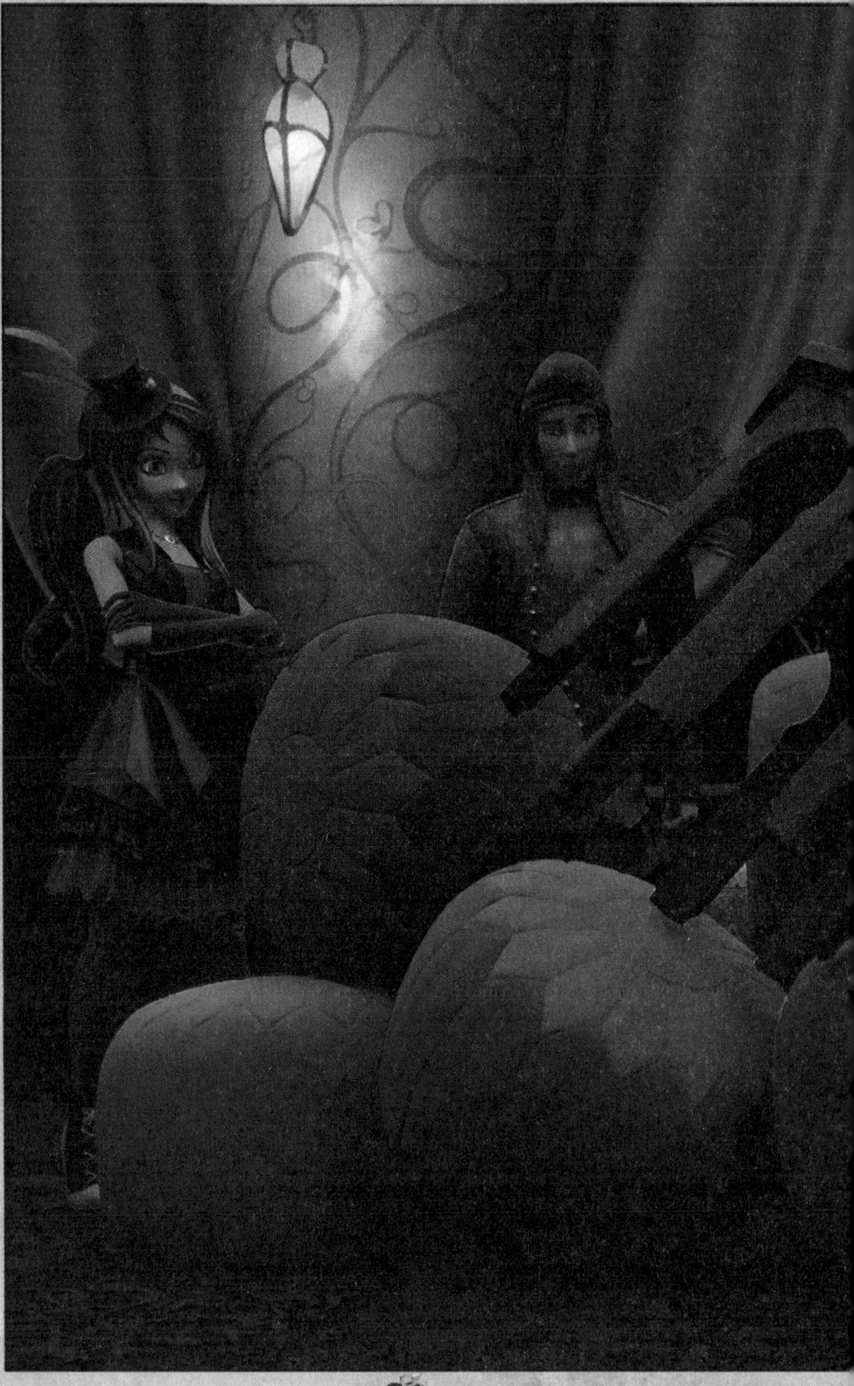

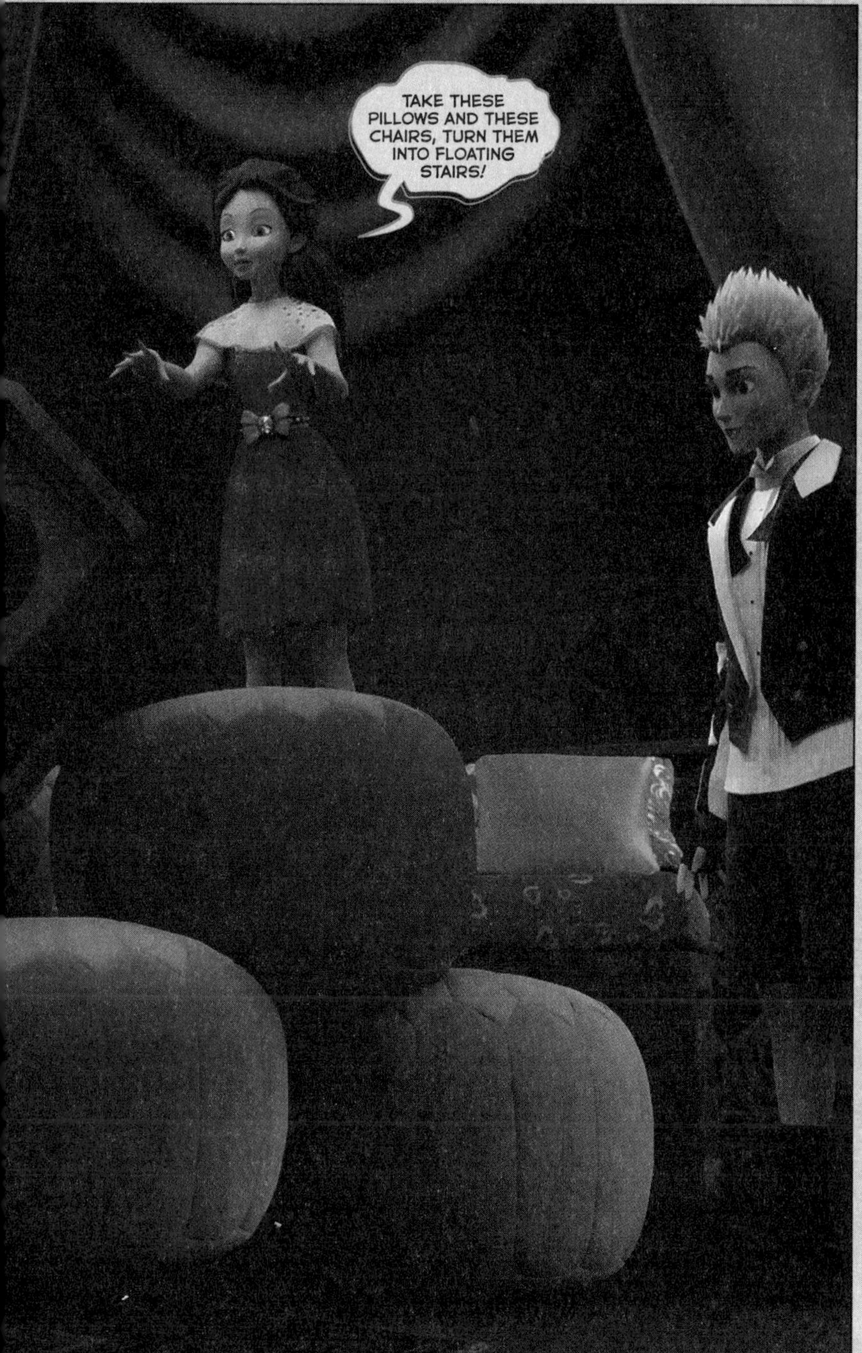
TAKE THESE PILLOWS AND THESE CHAIRS, TURN THEM INTO FLOATING STAIRS!

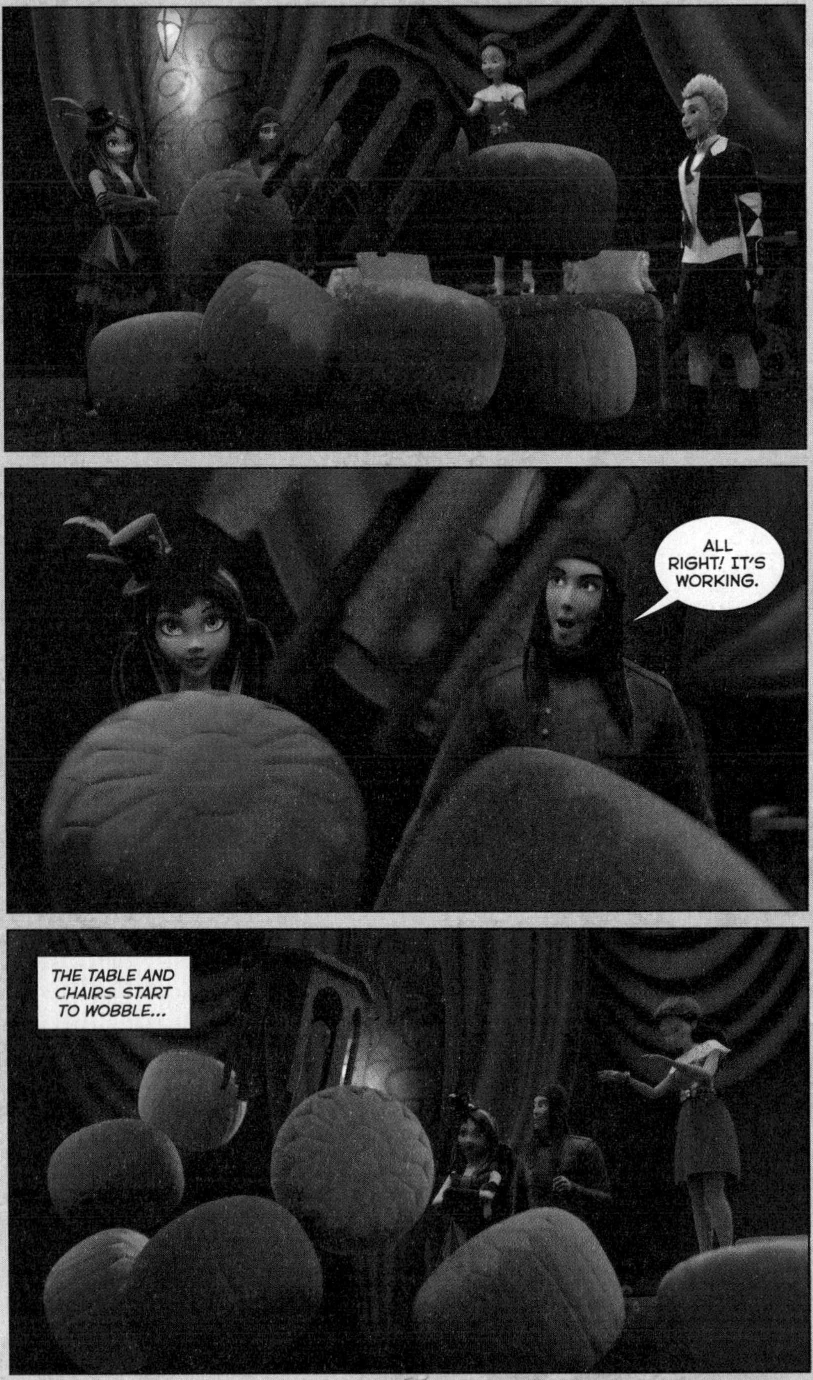
ALL RIGHT! IT'S WORKING.
THE TABLE AND CHAIRS START TO WOBBLE...

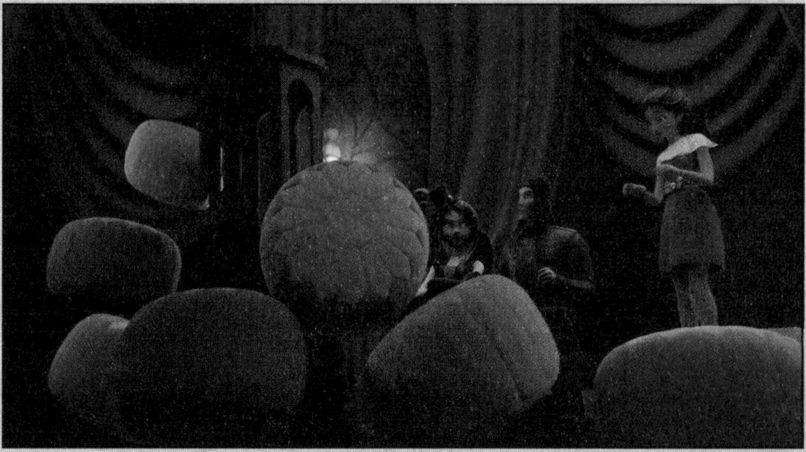

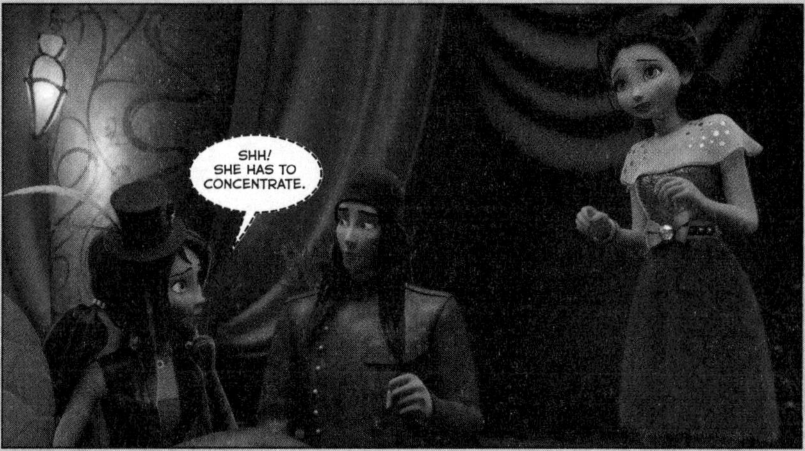
SHH! SHE HAS TO CONCENTRATE.

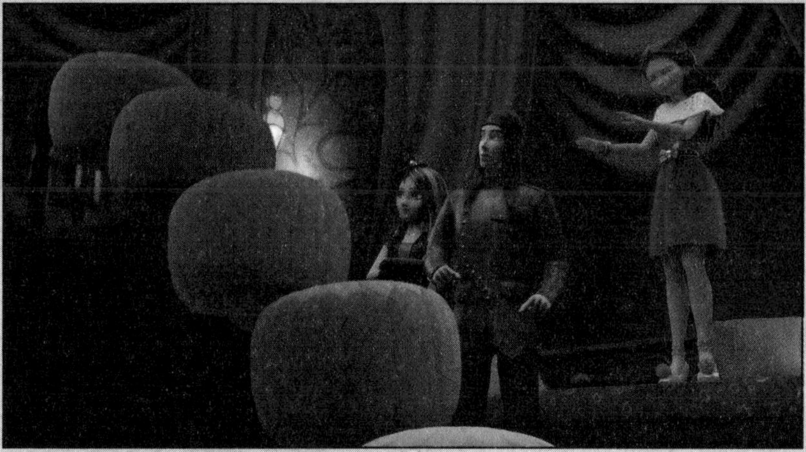

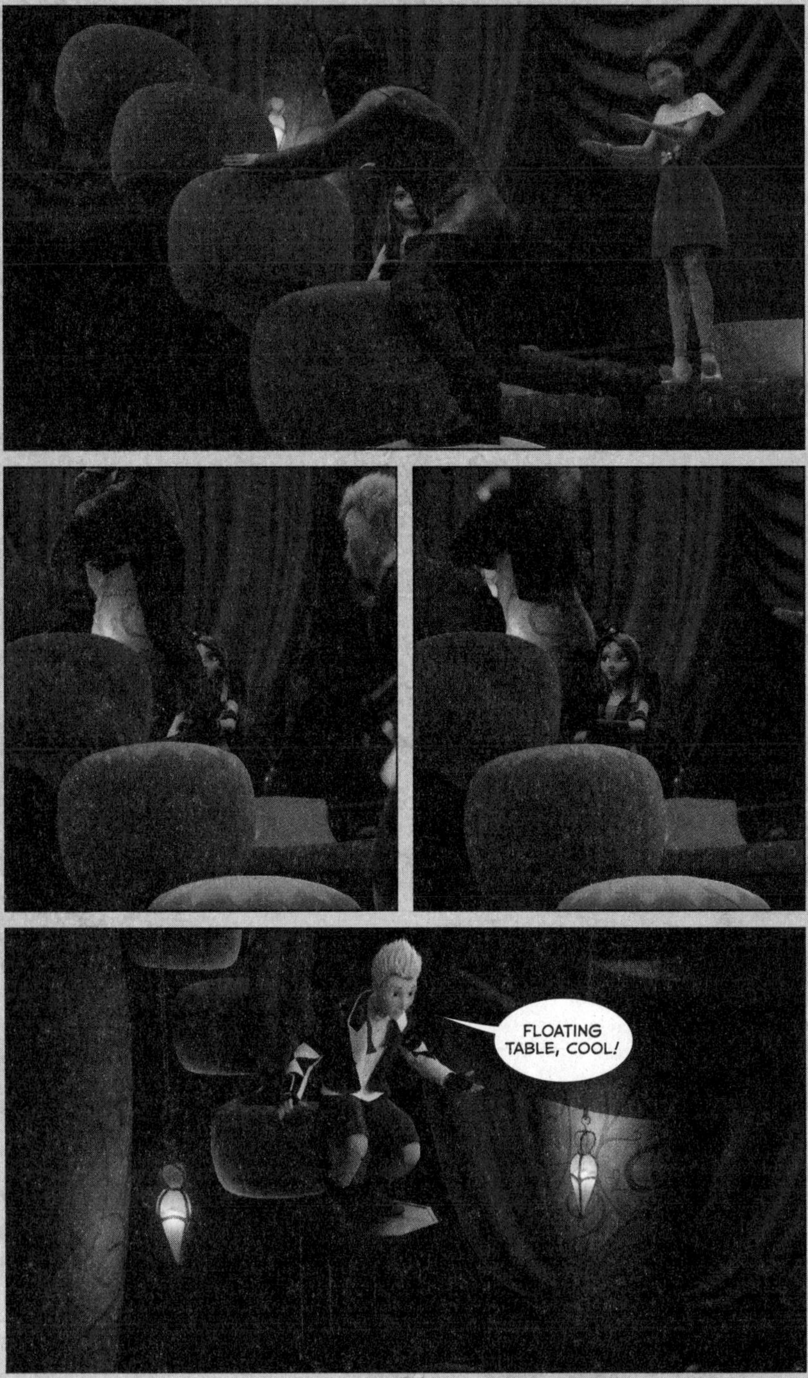
FLOATING
TABLE, COOL!

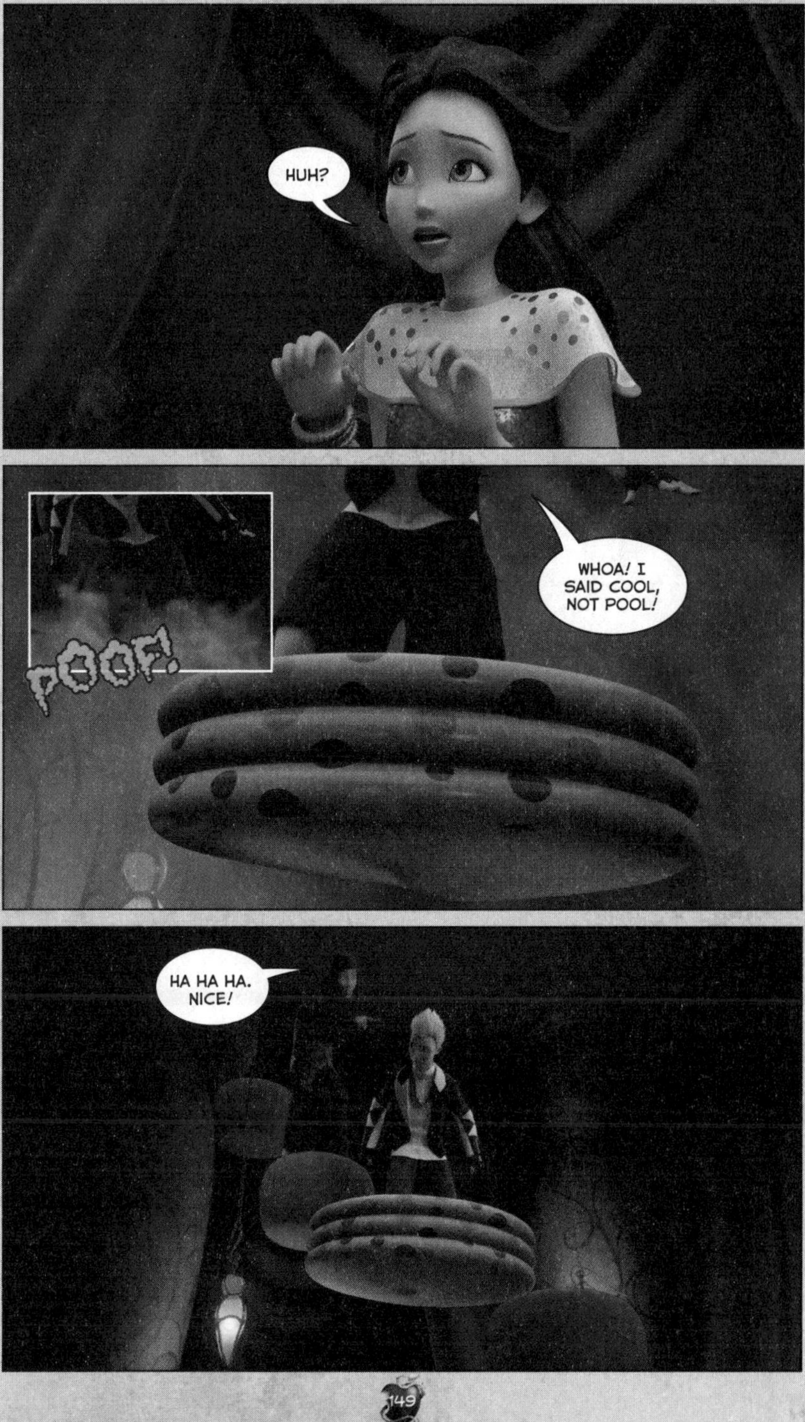
HUH?
WHOA! I SAID COOL, NOT POOL!
POOF!
HA HA HA. NICE!

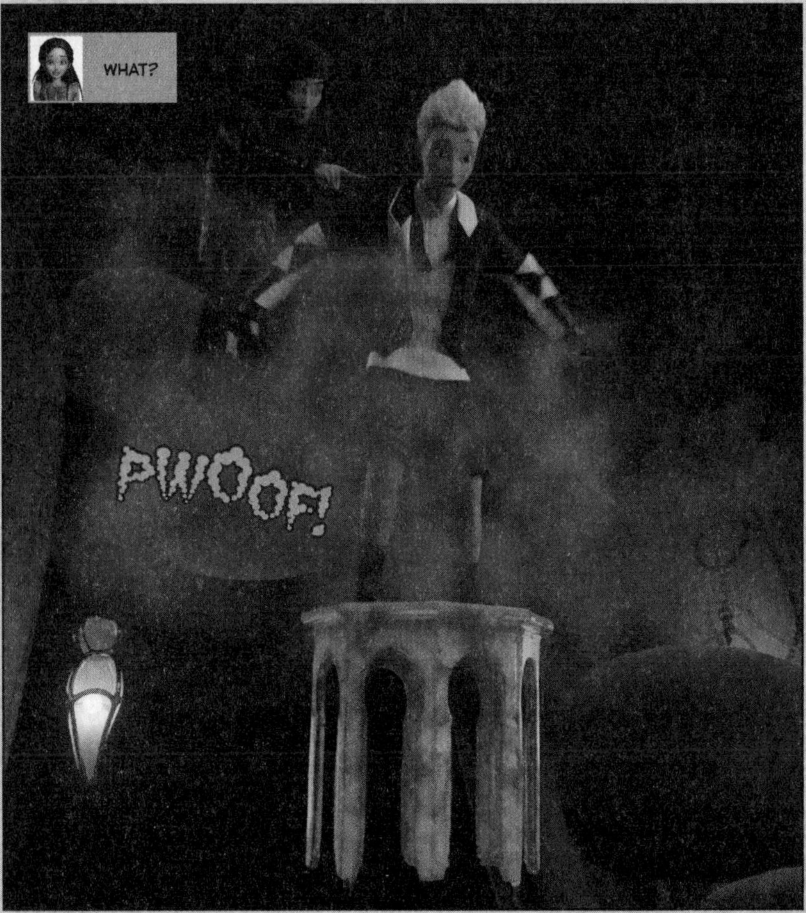
WHAT?
PWOOF!

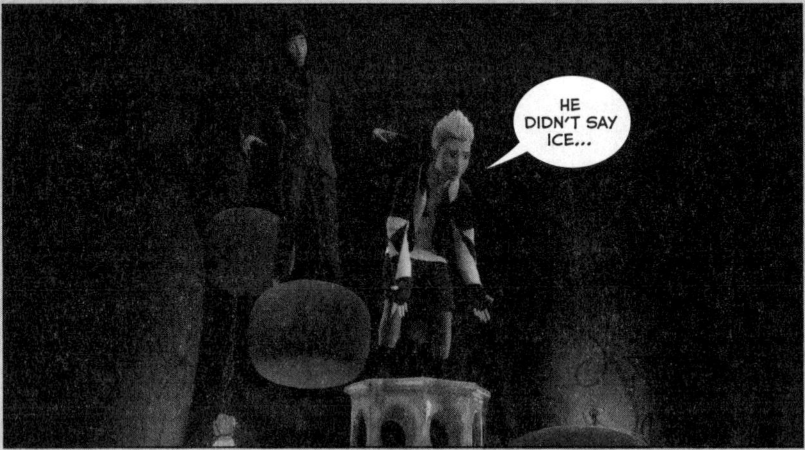
HE DIDN'T SAY ICE...

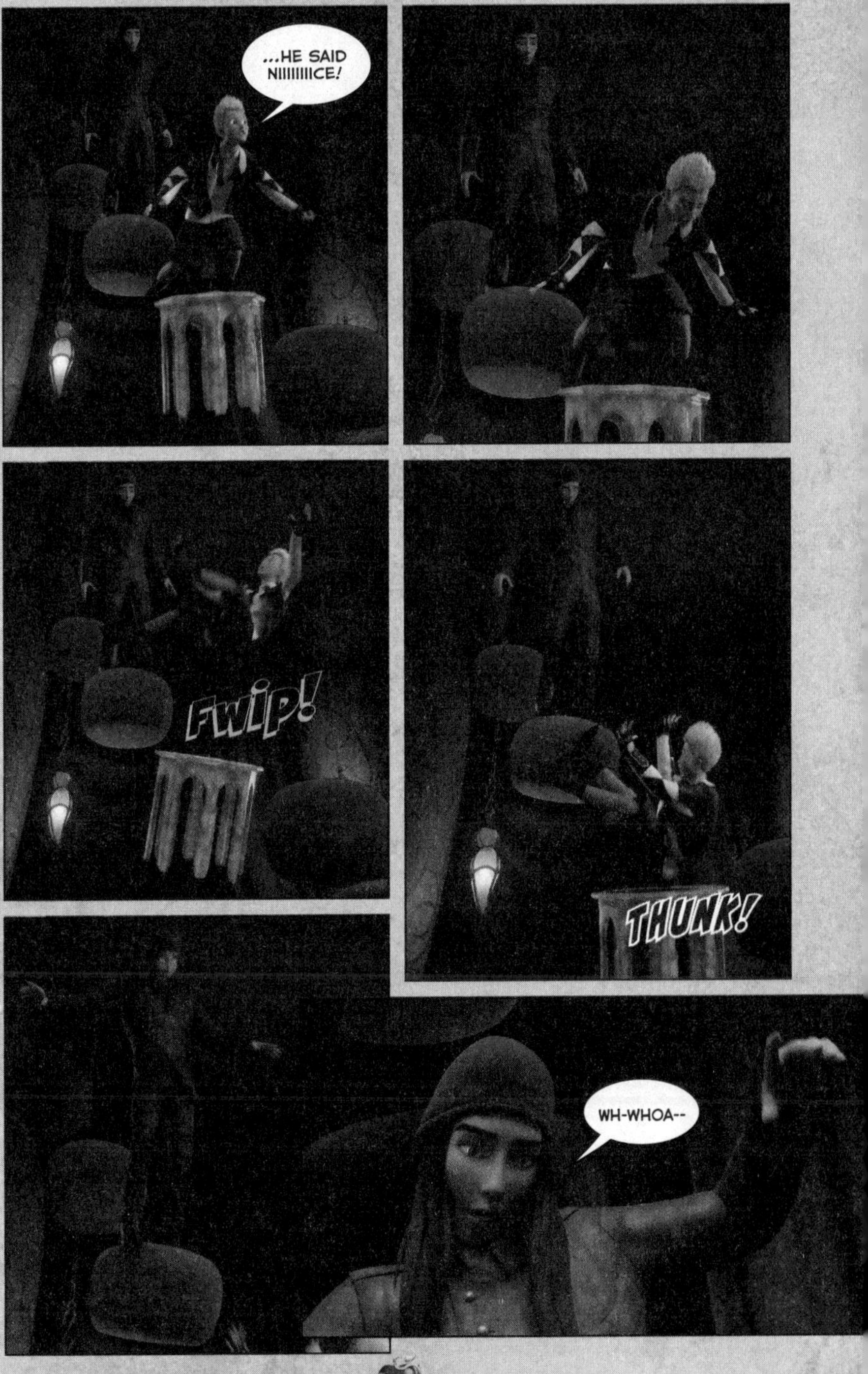
...HE SAID NIIIIIIICE!
FWIP!
THUNK!
WH-WHOA--

WHOA--
OHH--AHHHH!

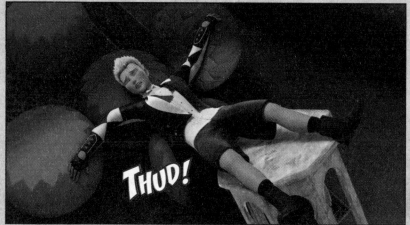

THUD!

WHAM!

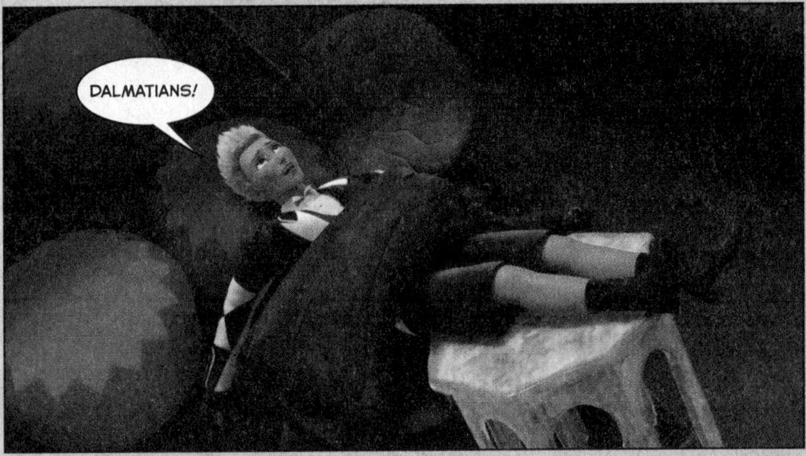
DALMATIANS!

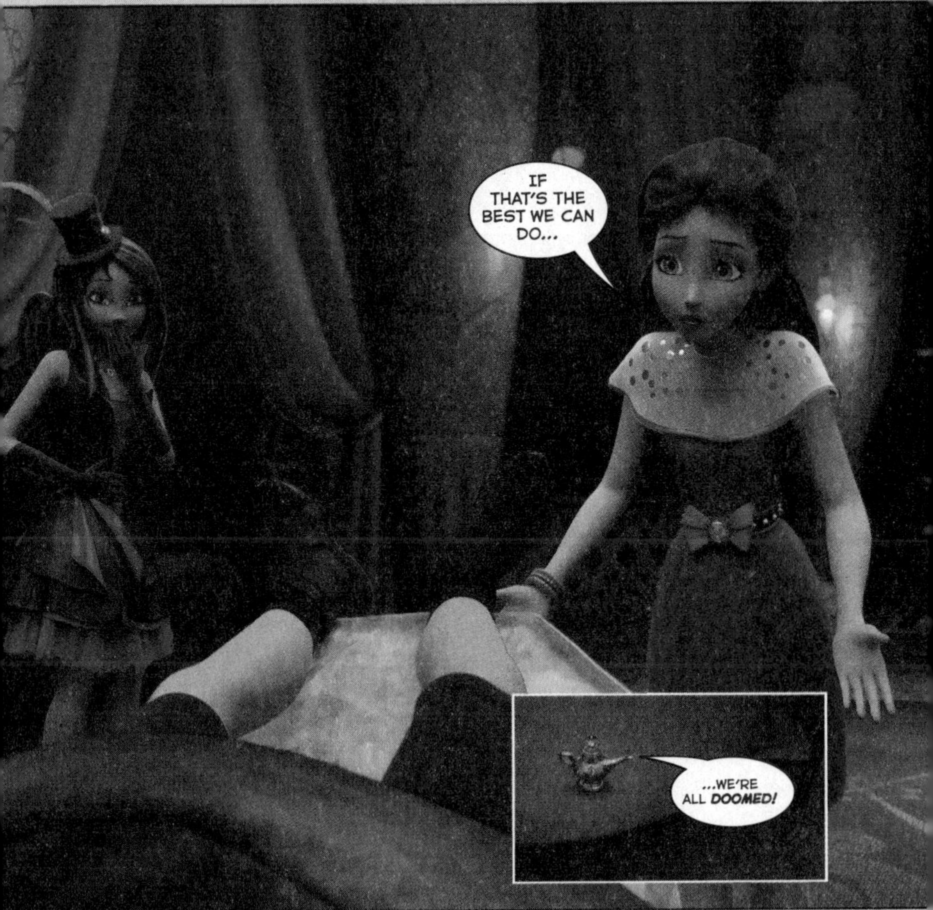
IF THAT'S THE BEST WE CAN DO...
...WE'RE ALL **DOOMED!**

CHAPTER 31: FACE TO FACE

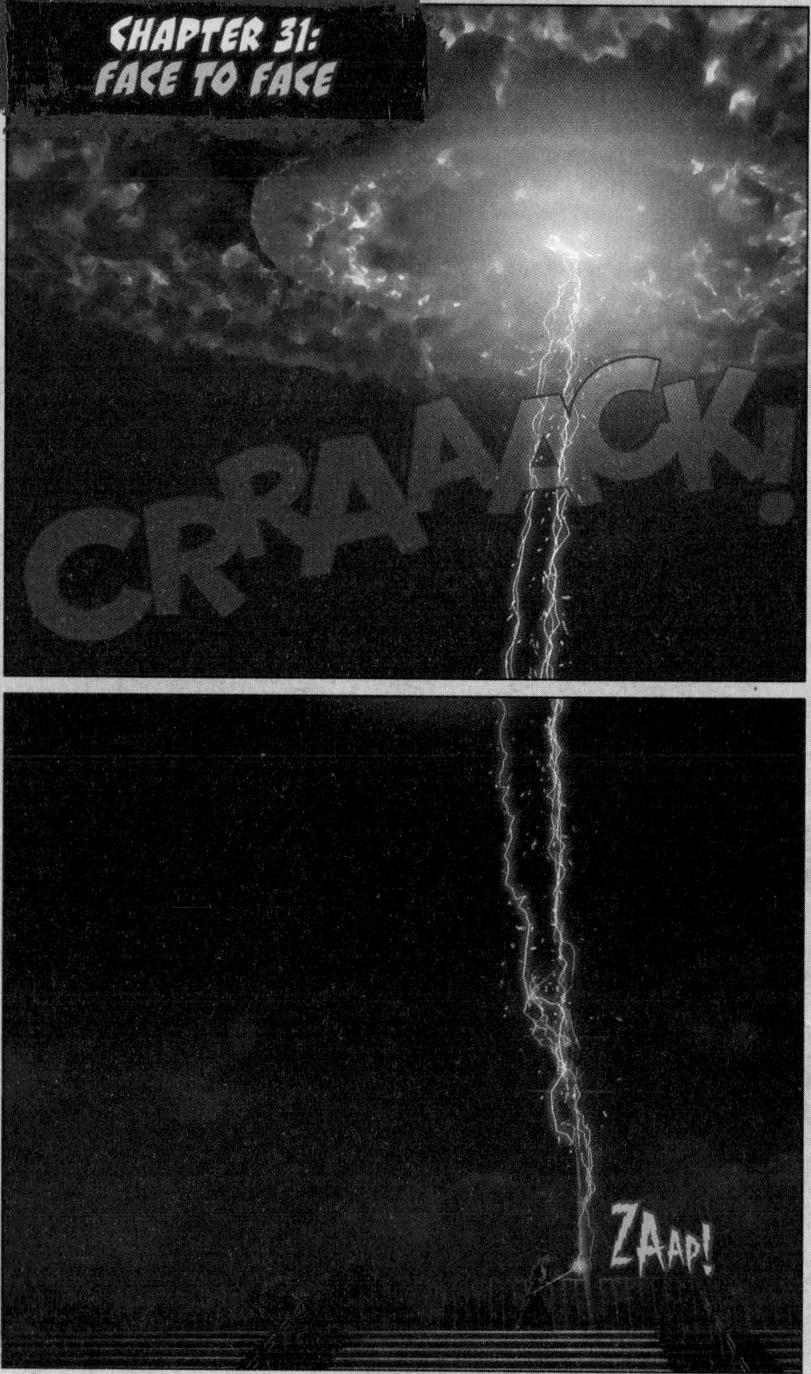
CRAAACK!
ZAAP!

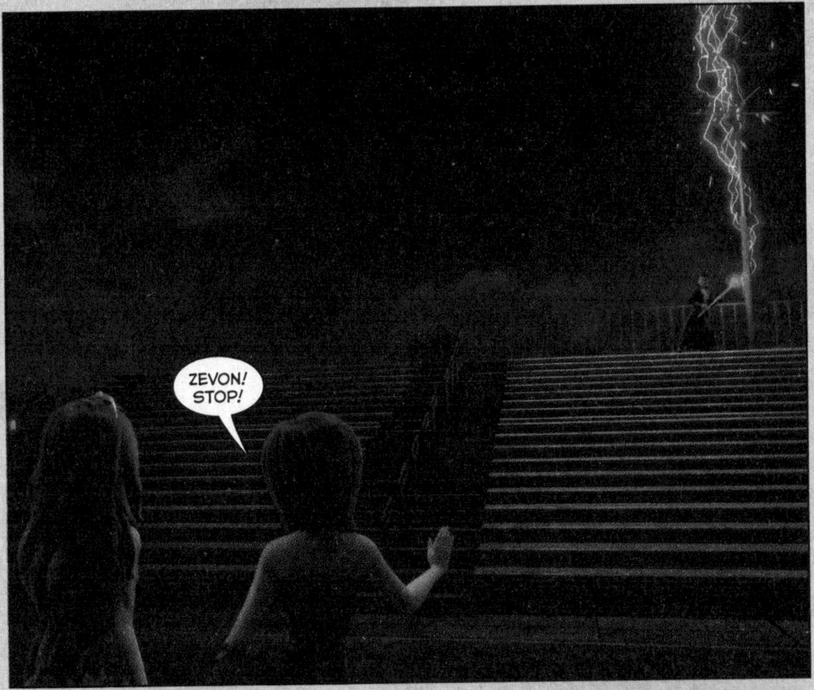
ZEVON! STOP!

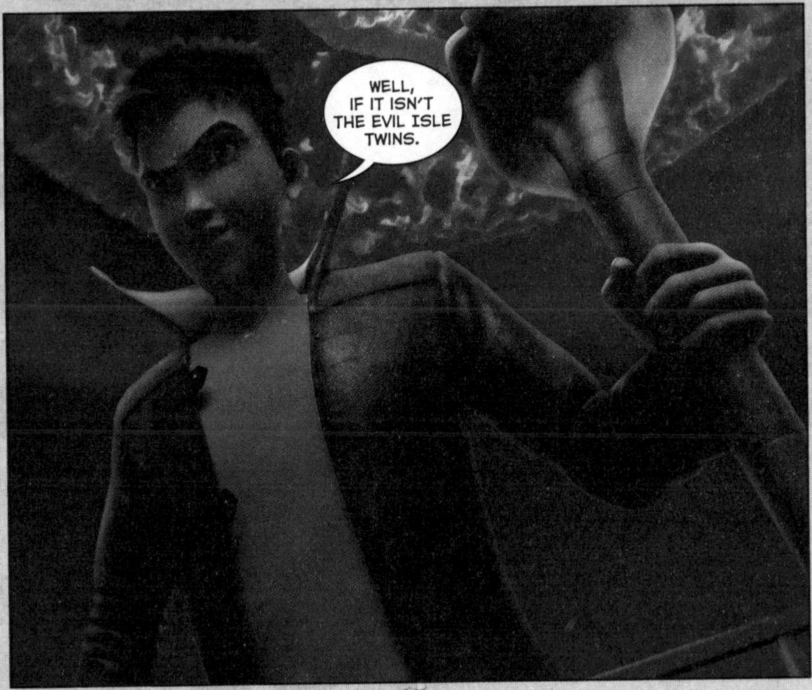
WELL, IF IT ISN'T THE EVIL ISLE TWINS.

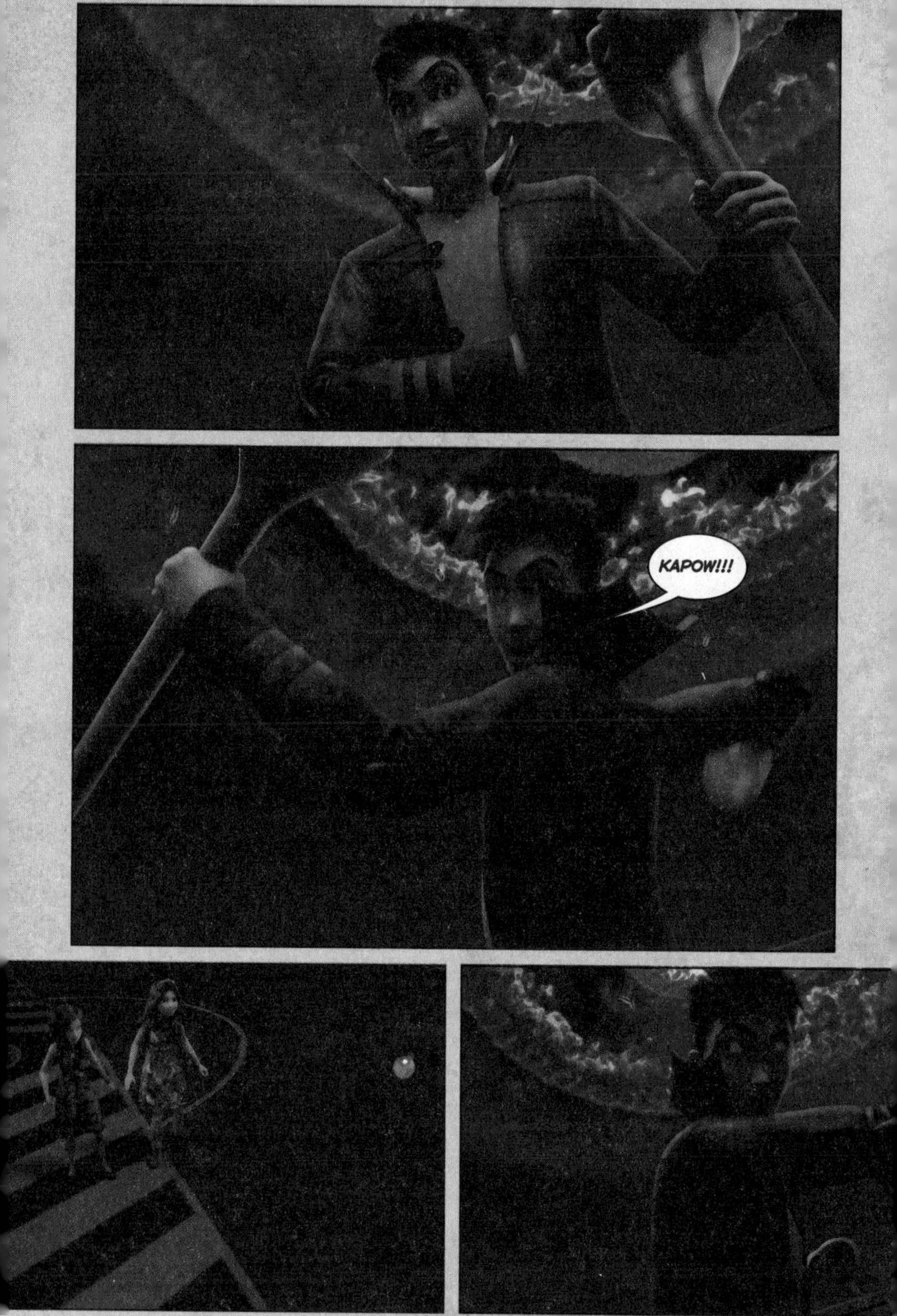
KAPOW!!!

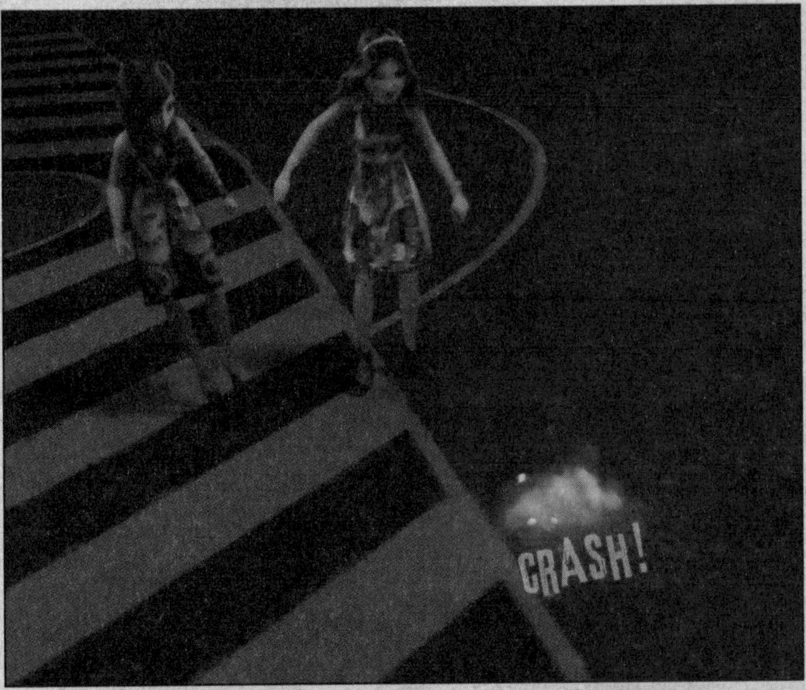
CRASH!

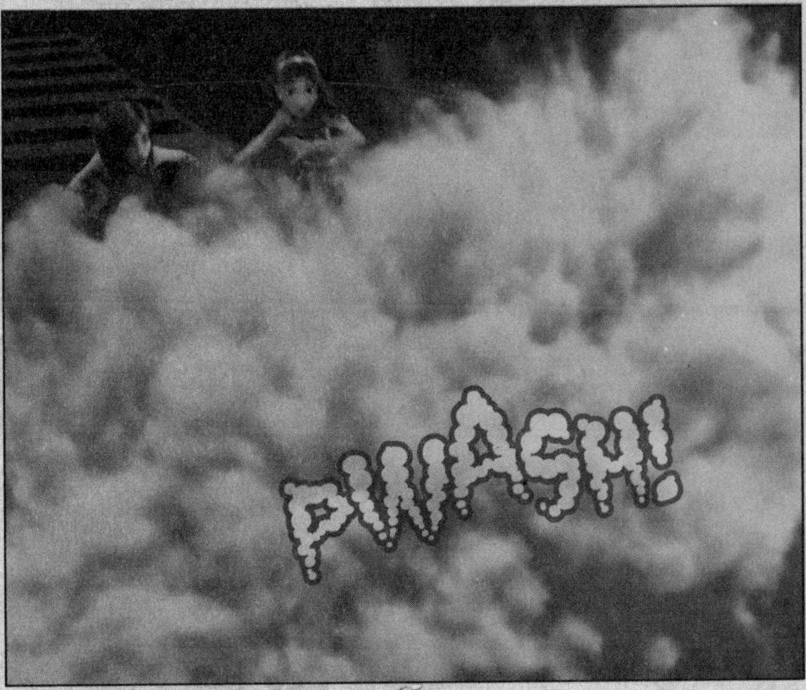
PWASH!

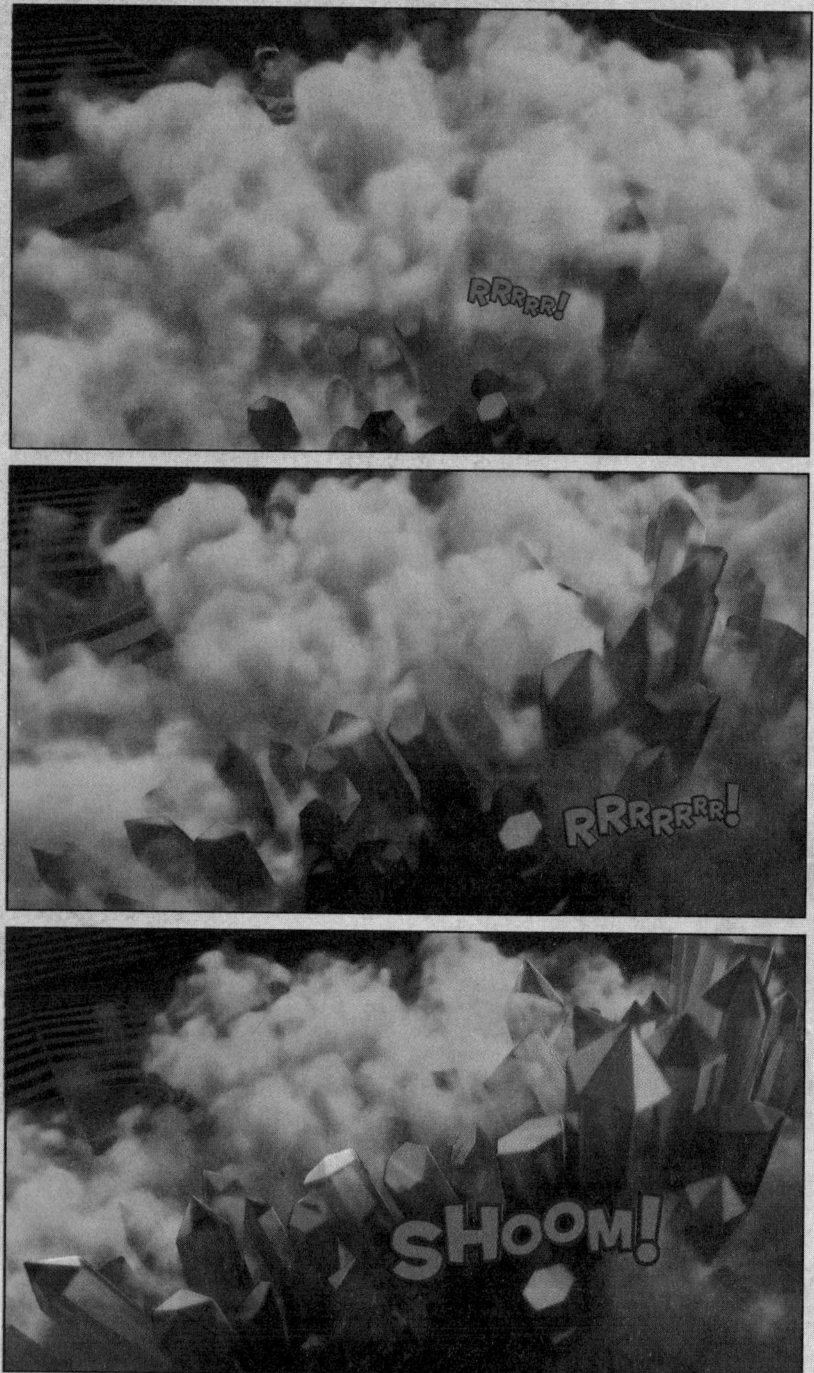
RRRRR!
RRRRRRR!
SHOOM!

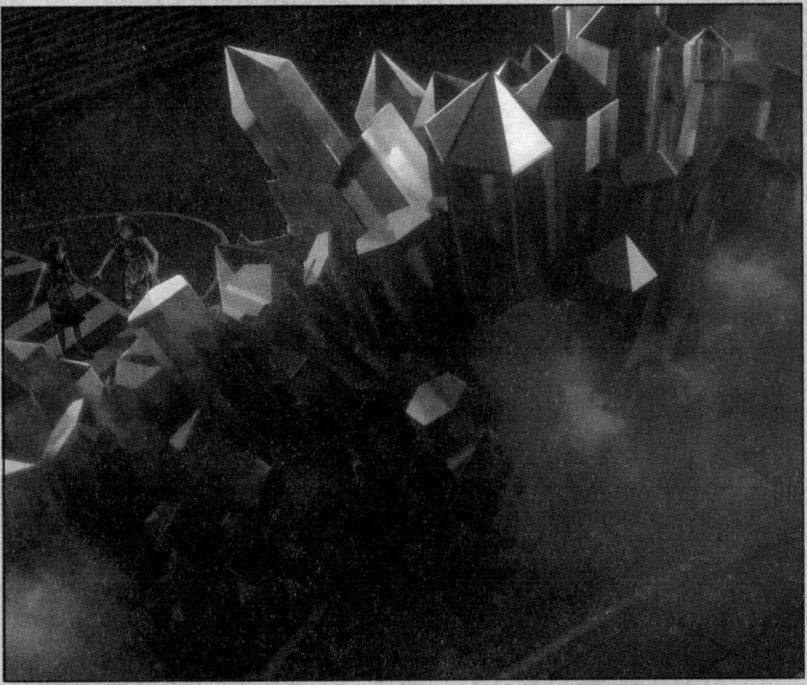

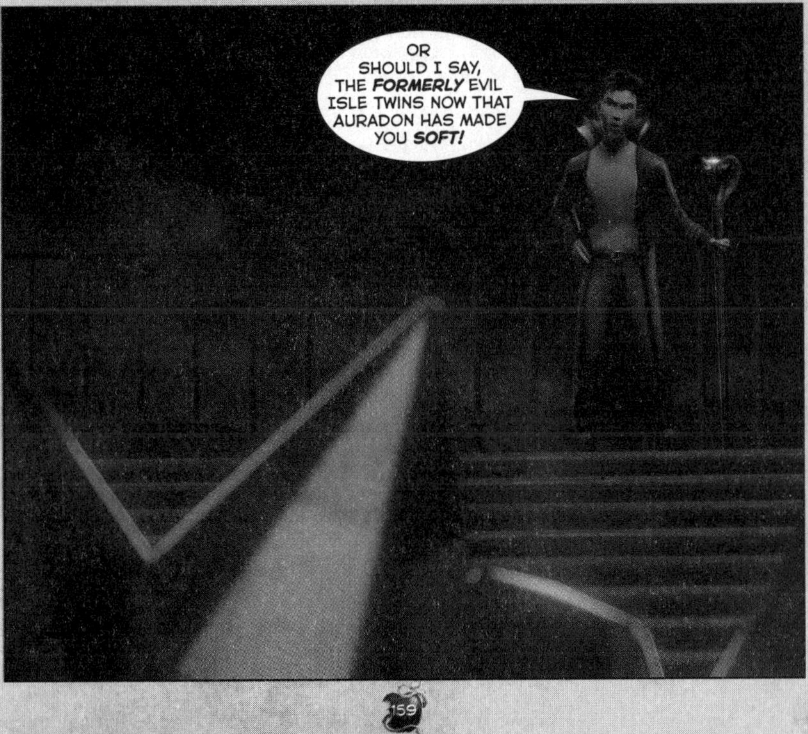
OR SHOULD I SAY, THE **FORMERLY** EVIL ISLE TWINS NOW THAT AURADON HAS MADE YOU **SOFT!**

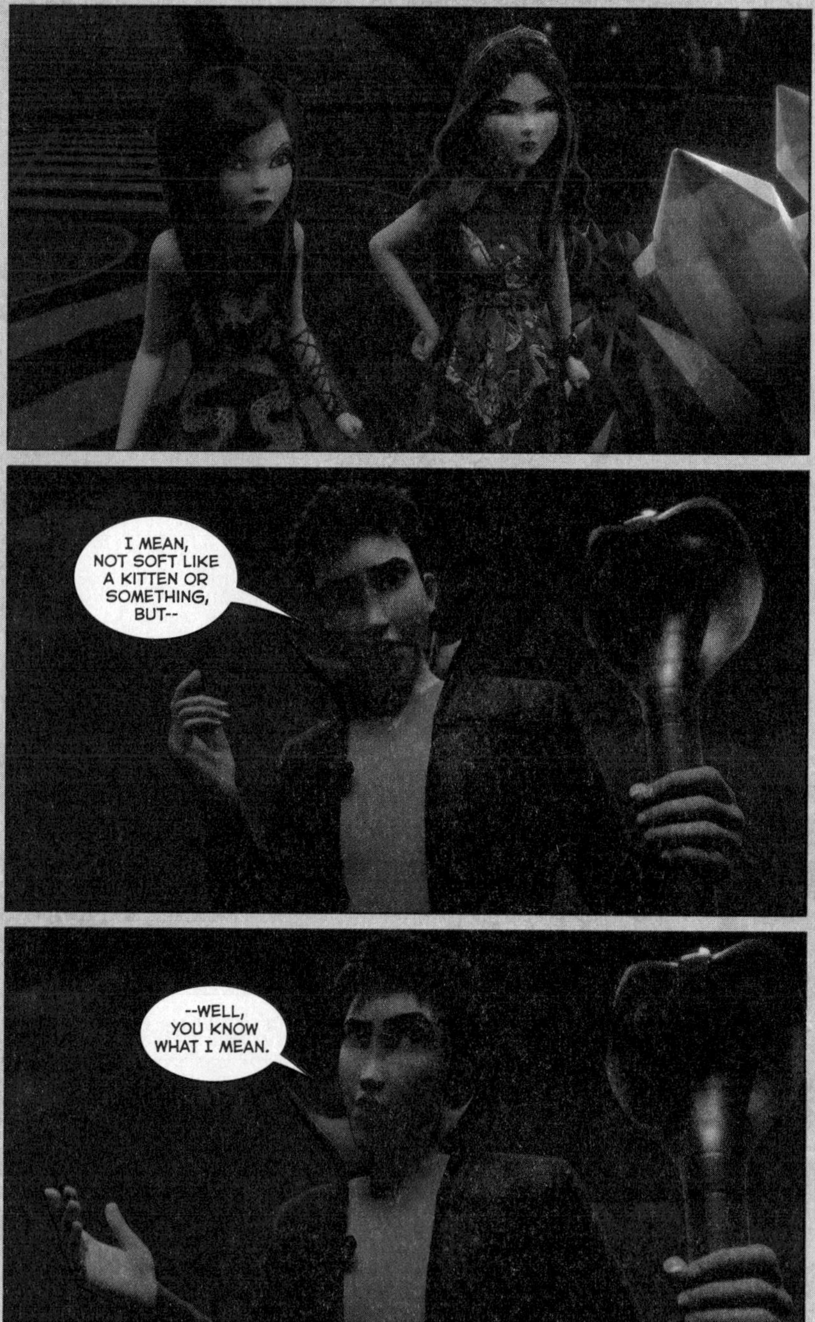
I MEAN, NOT SOFT LIKE A KITTEN OR SOMETHING, BUT--
--WELL, YOU KNOW WHAT I MEAN.

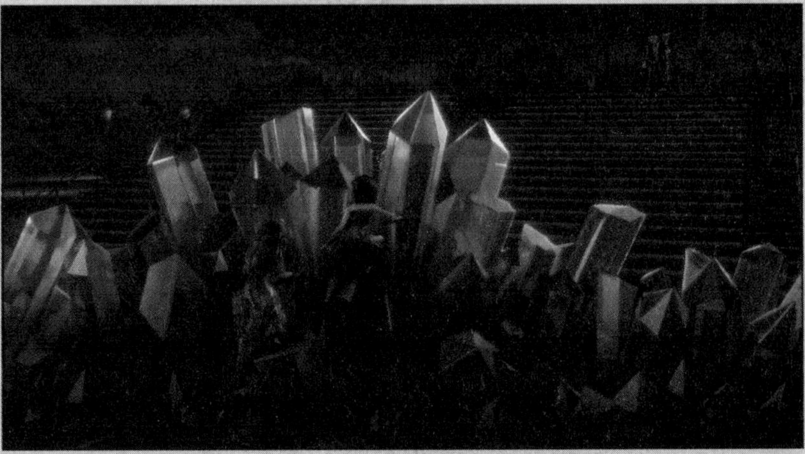

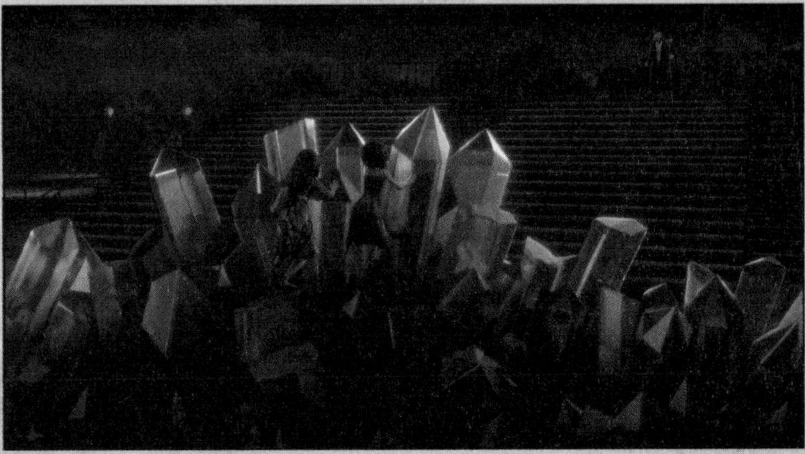

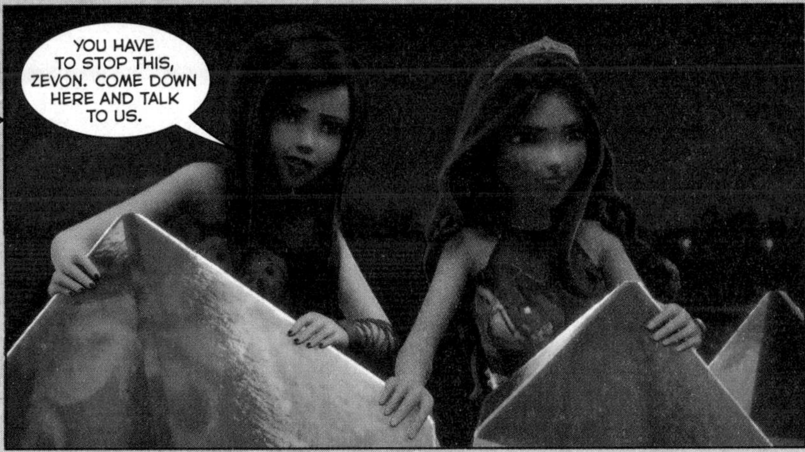
YOU HAVE TO STOP THIS, ZEVON. COME DOWN HERE AND TALK TO US.

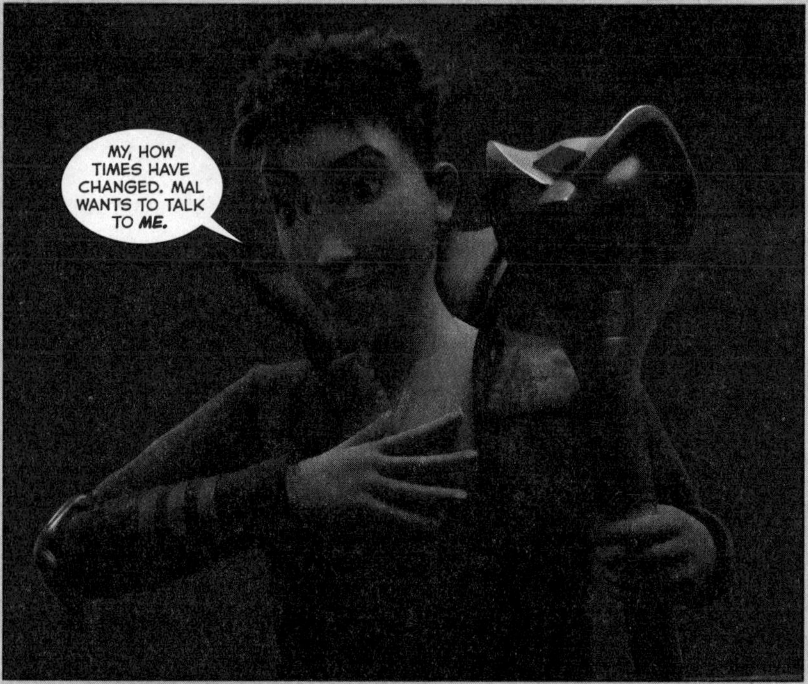
MY, HOW TIMES HAVE CHANGED. MAL WANTS TO TALK TO *ME.*

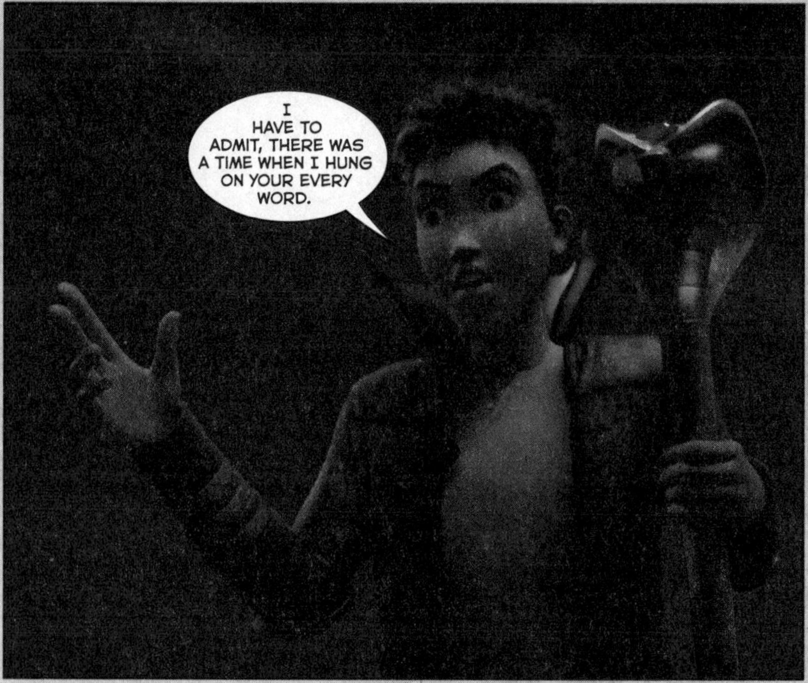
I HAVE TO ADMIT, THERE WAS A TIME WHEN I HUNG ON YOUR EVERY WORD.

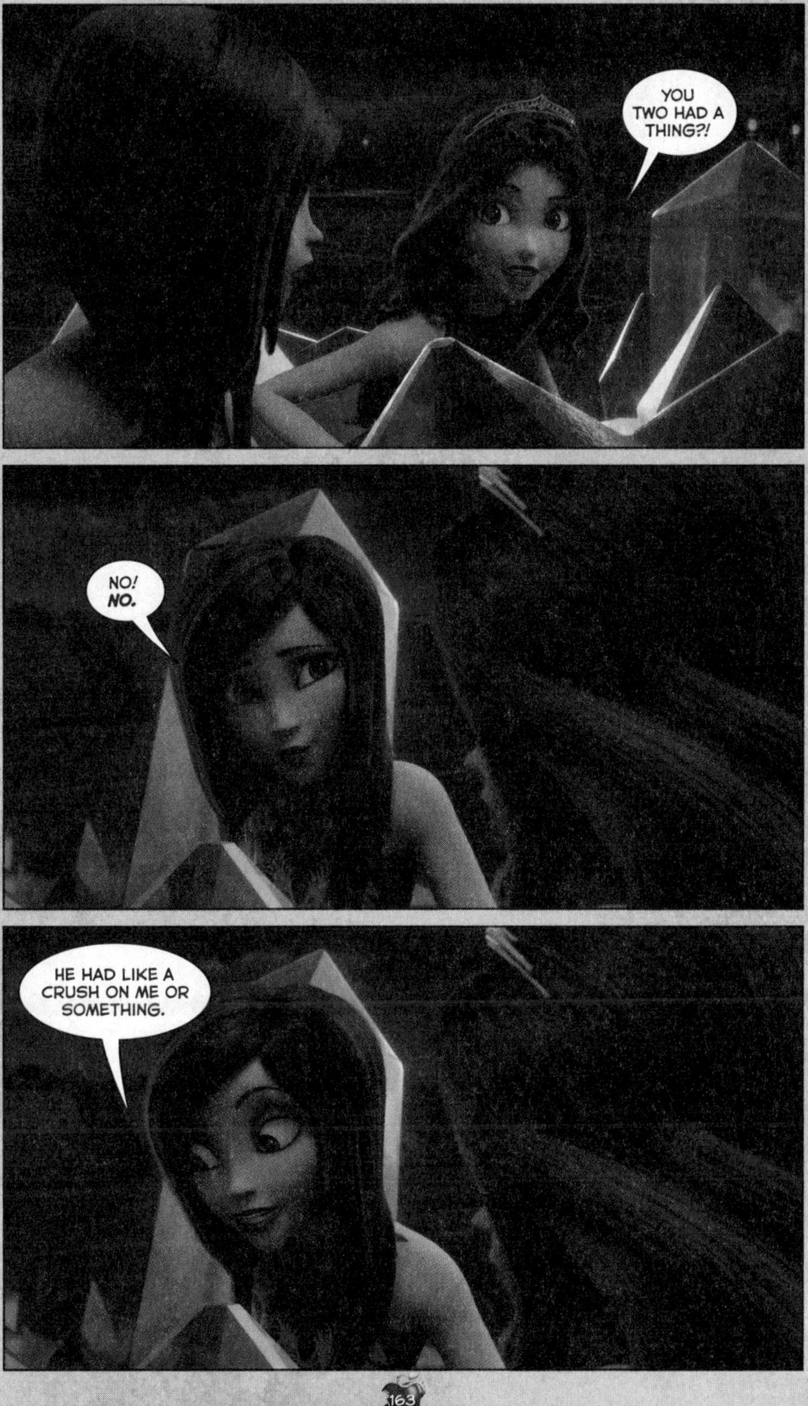
YOU TWO HAD A THING?!
NO! NO.
HE HAD LIKE A CRUSH ON ME OR SOMETHING.

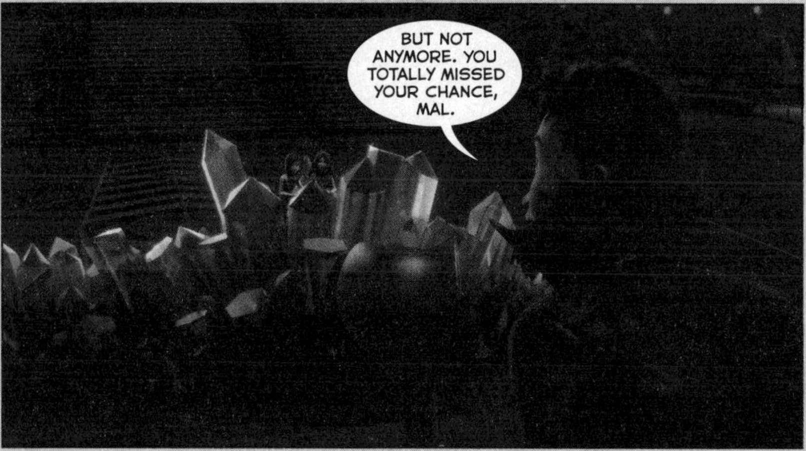
BUT NOT ANYMORE. YOU TOTALLY MISSED YOUR CHANCE, MAL.

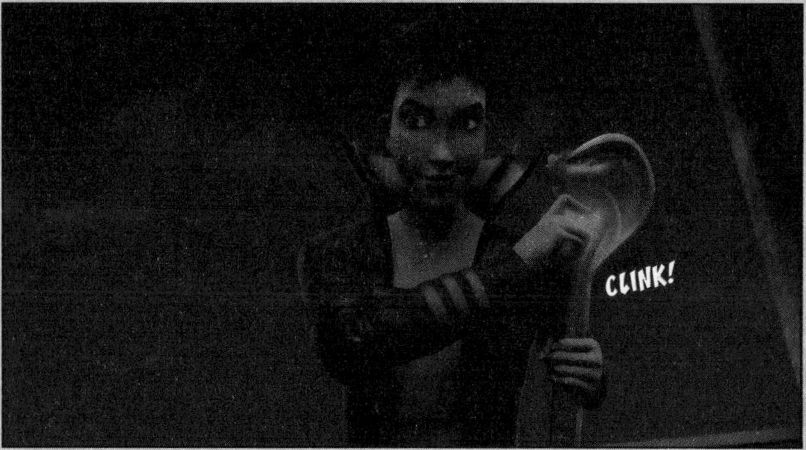
CLINK!

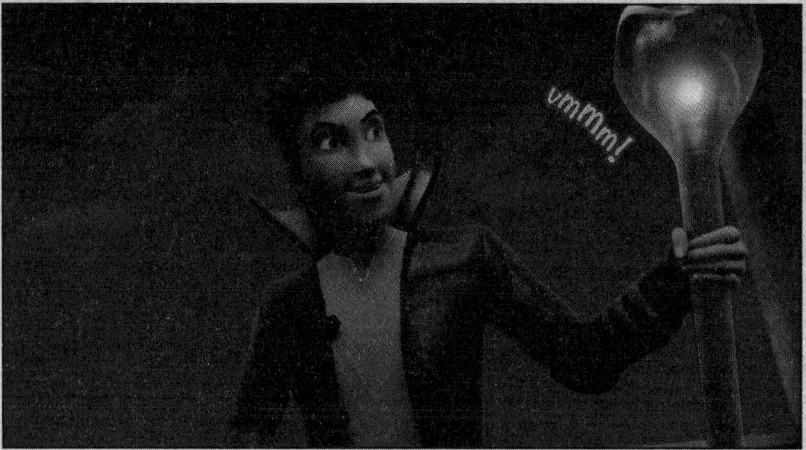
VMMM!

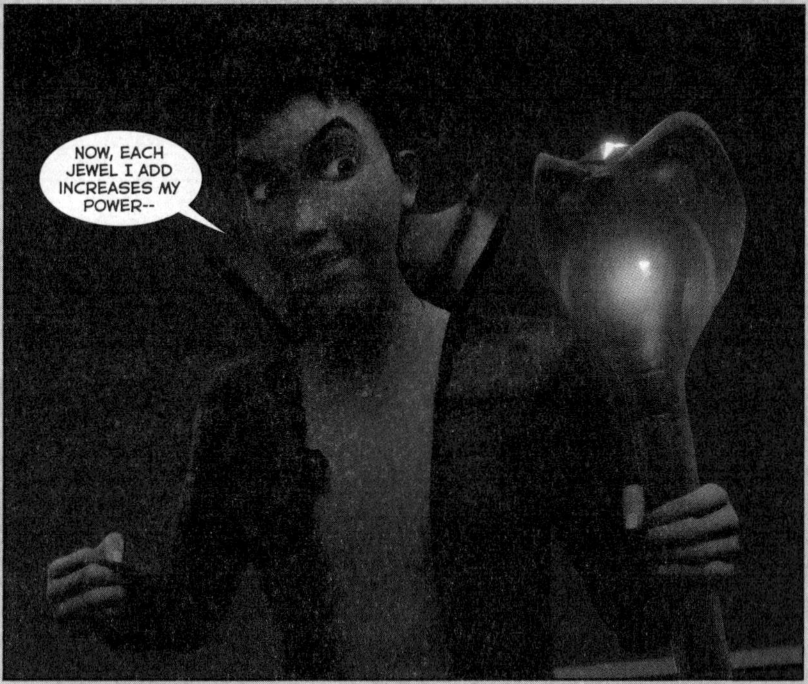
NOW, EACH JEWEL I ADD INCREASES MY POWER--

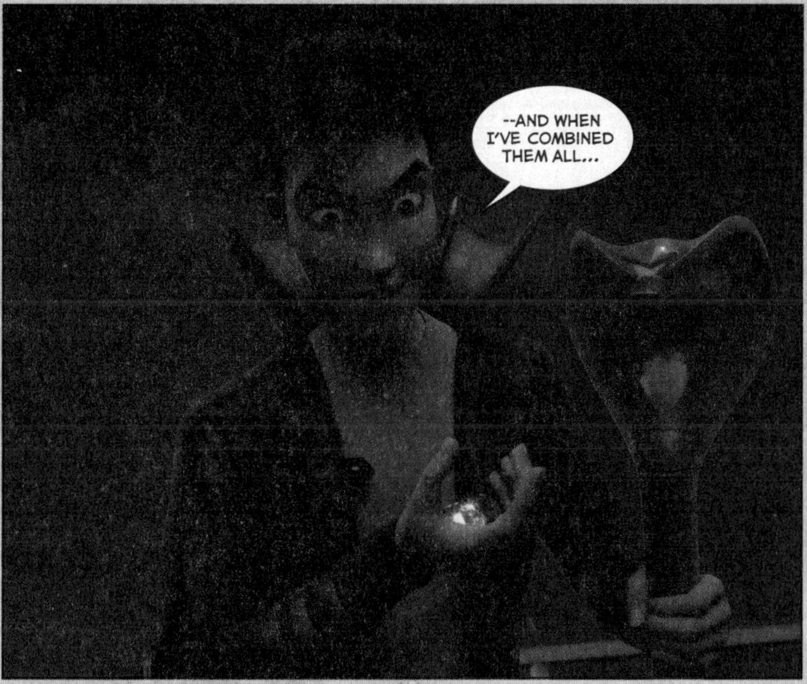
--AND WHEN I'VE COMBINED THEM ALL...

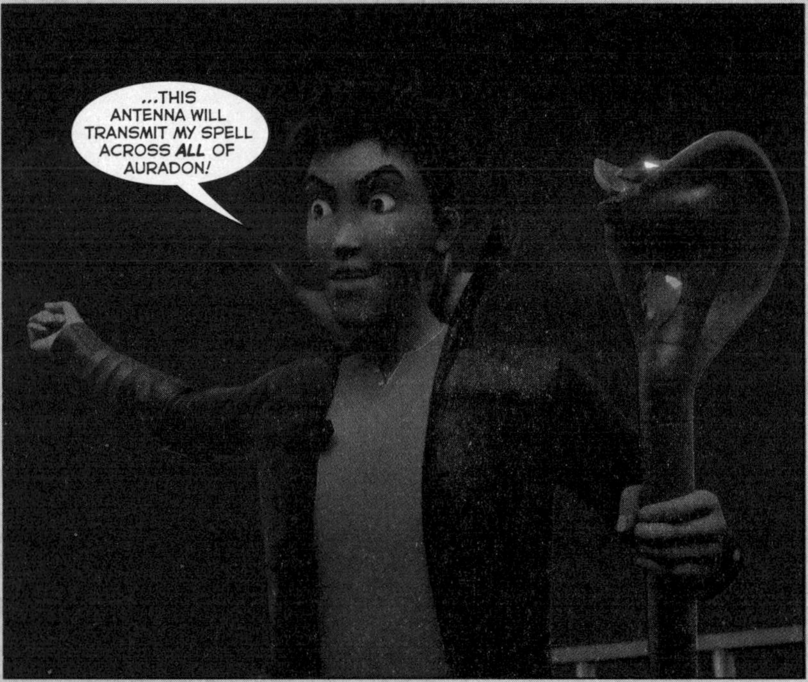
...THIS ANTENNA WILL TRANSMIT MY SPELL ACROSS ALL OF AURADON!

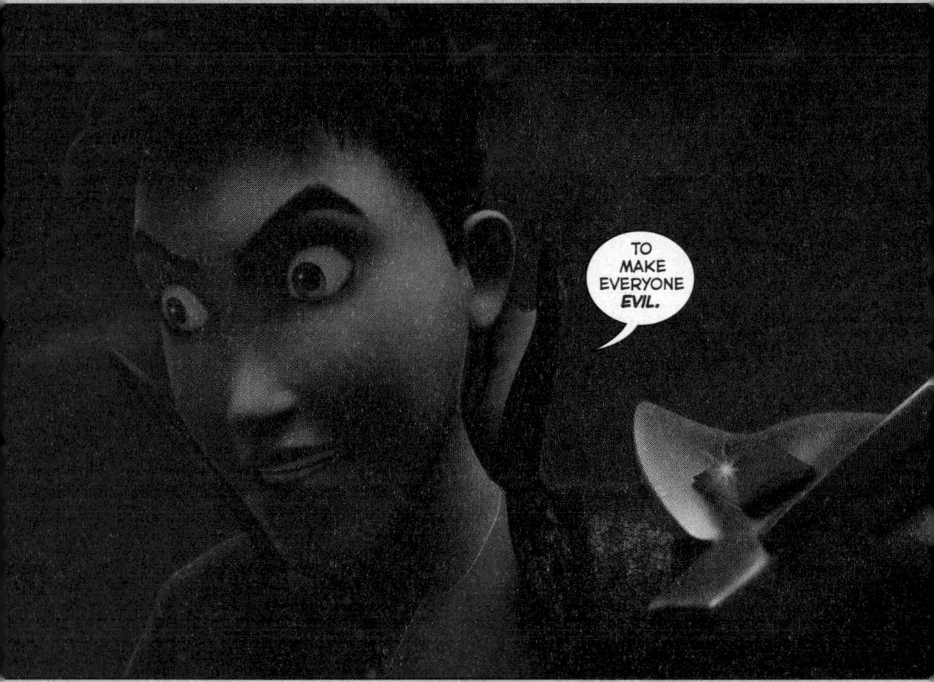
TO MAKE EVERYONE EVIL.

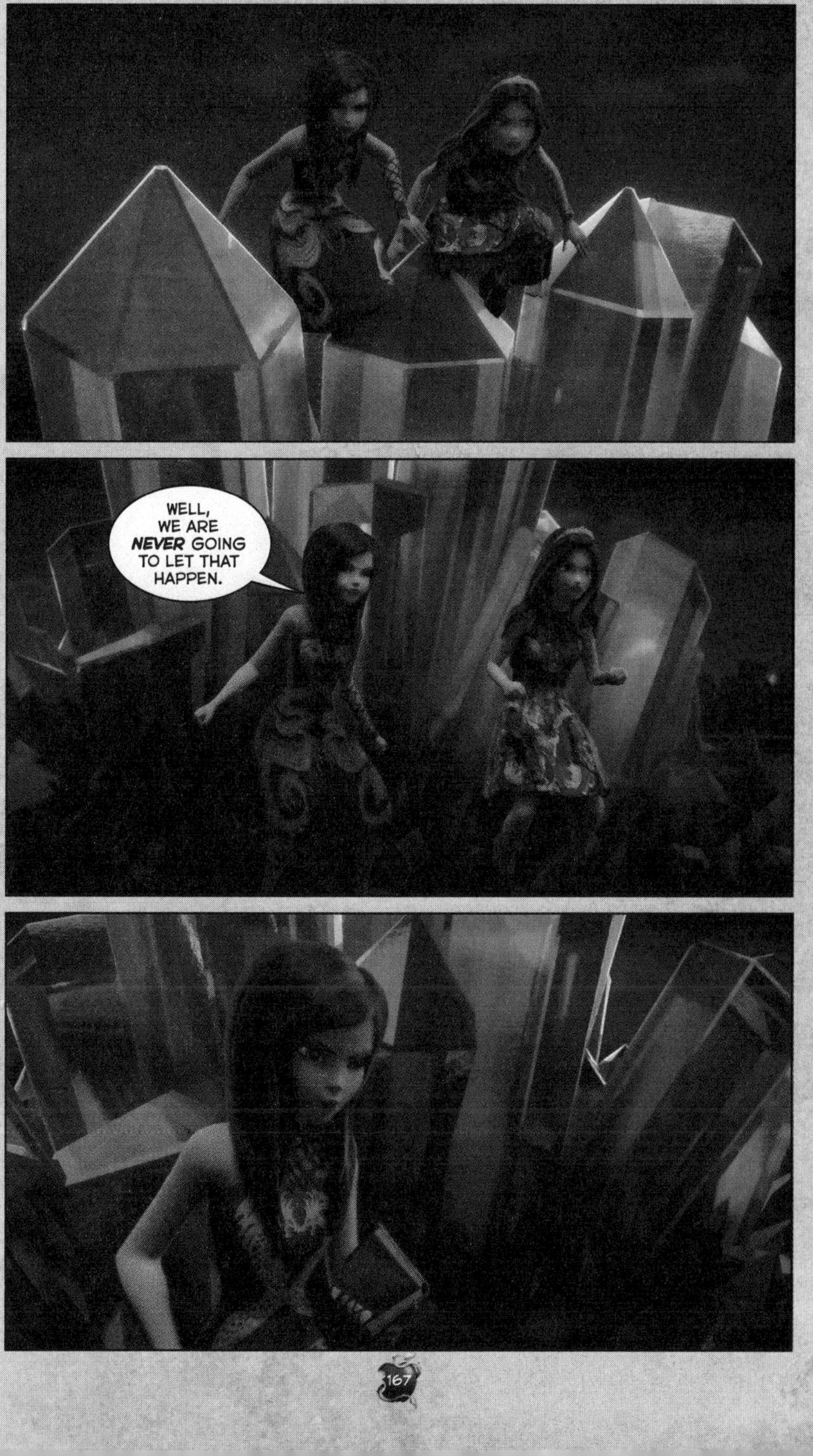
WELL, WE ARE **NEVER** GOING TO LET THAT HAPPEN.

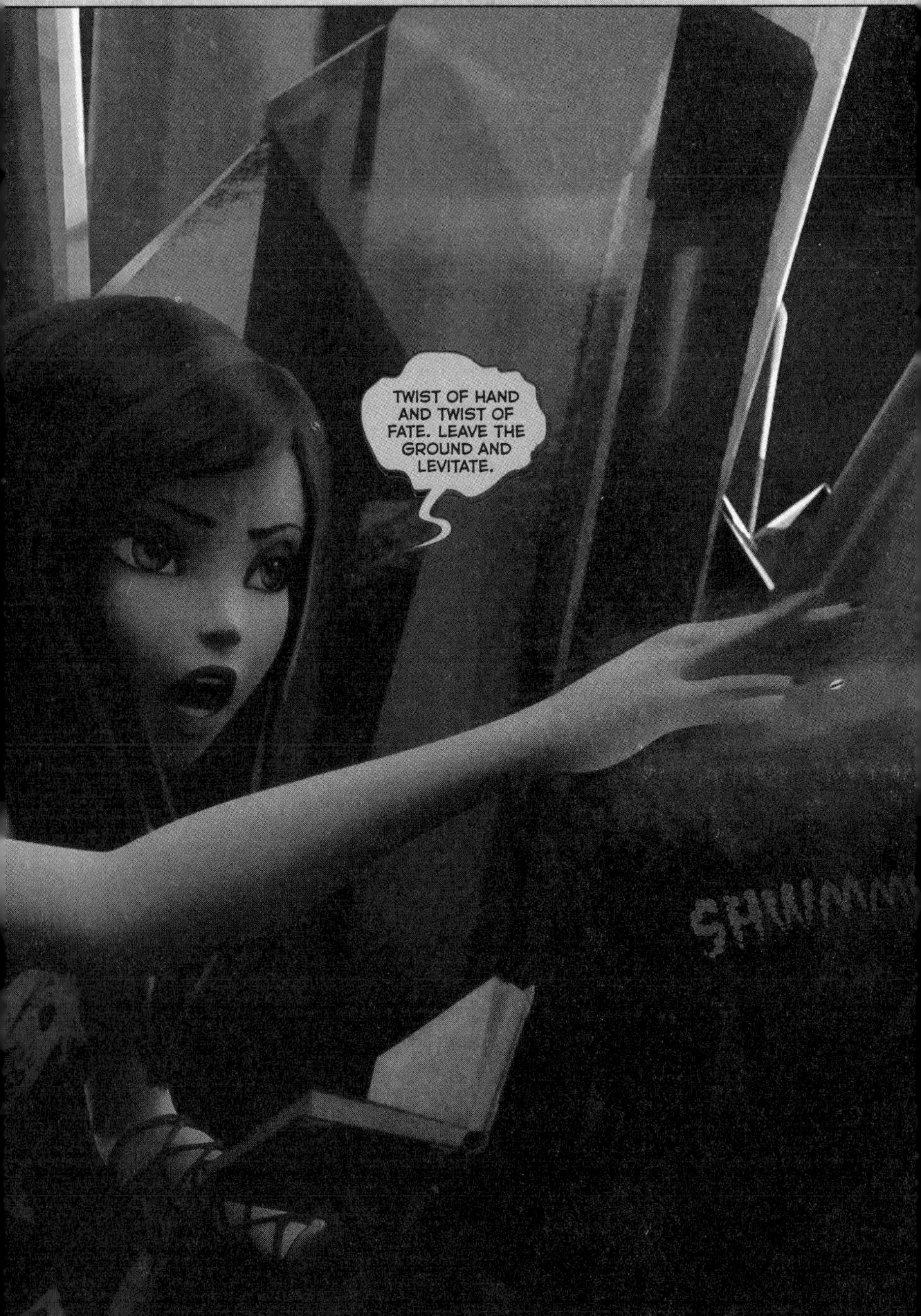
TWIST OF HAND AND TWIST OF FATE. LEAVE THE GROUND AND LEVITATE.

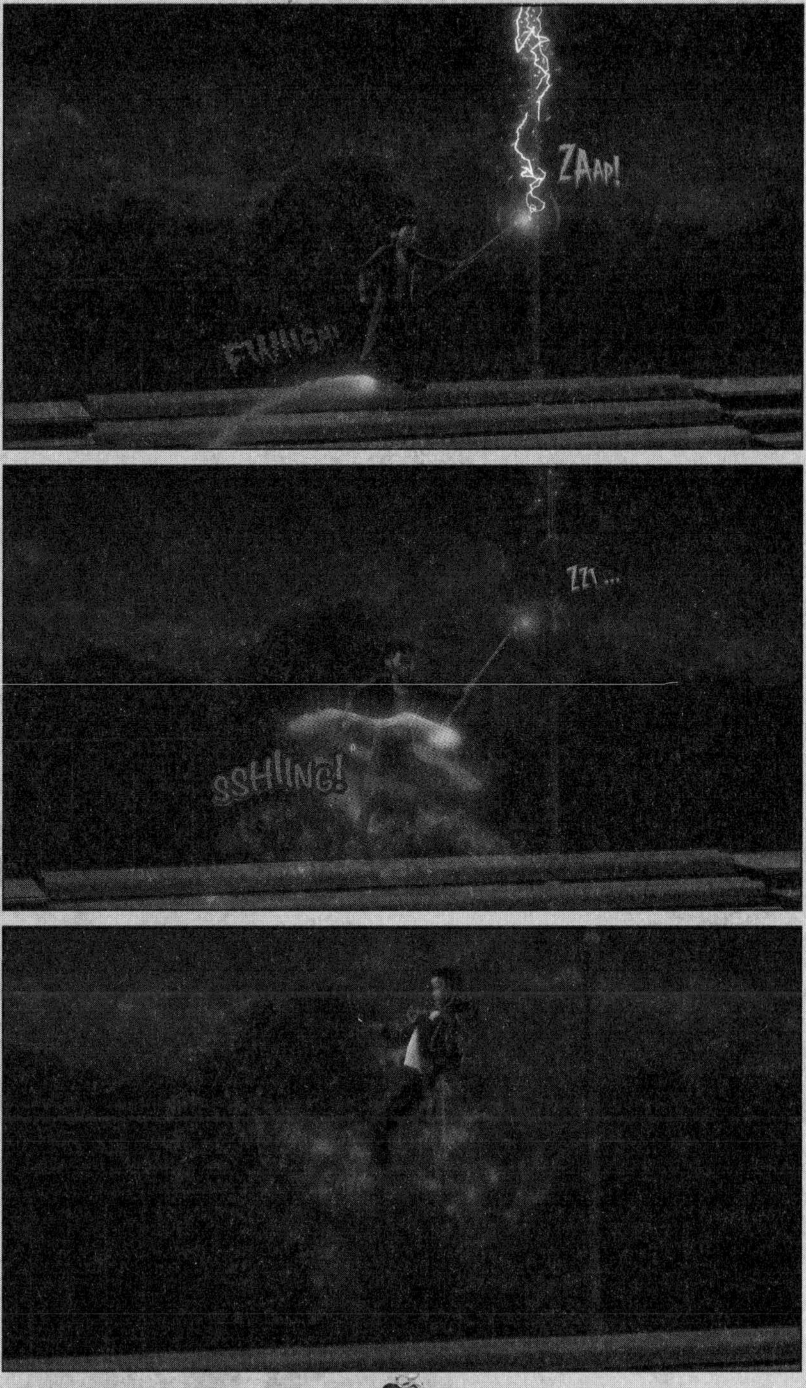
ZAAP!
ZZT...
SSHIING!

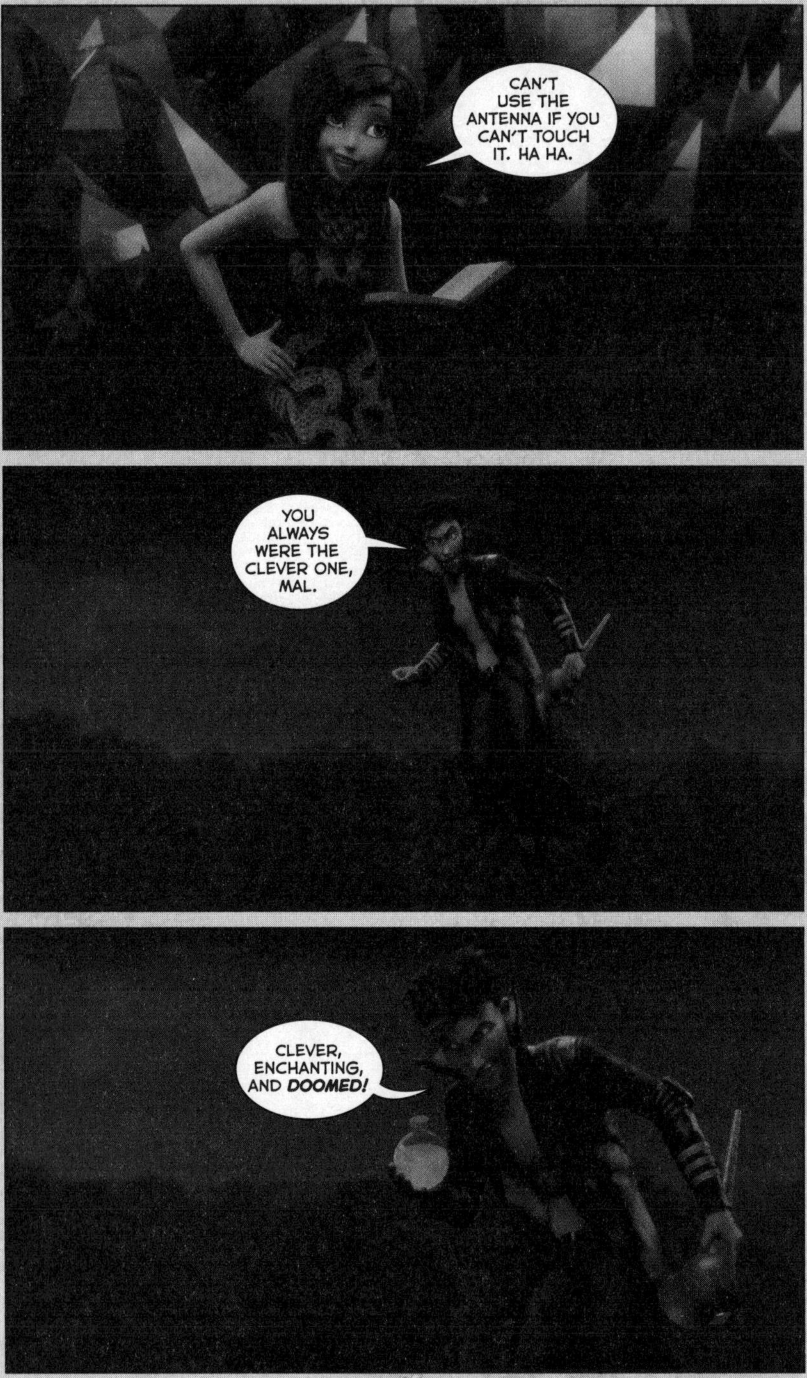
CAN'T USE THE ANTENNA IF YOU CAN'T TOUCH IT. HA HA.
YOU ALWAYS WERE THE CLEVER ONE, MAL.
CLEVER, ENCHANTING, AND ***DOOMED!***

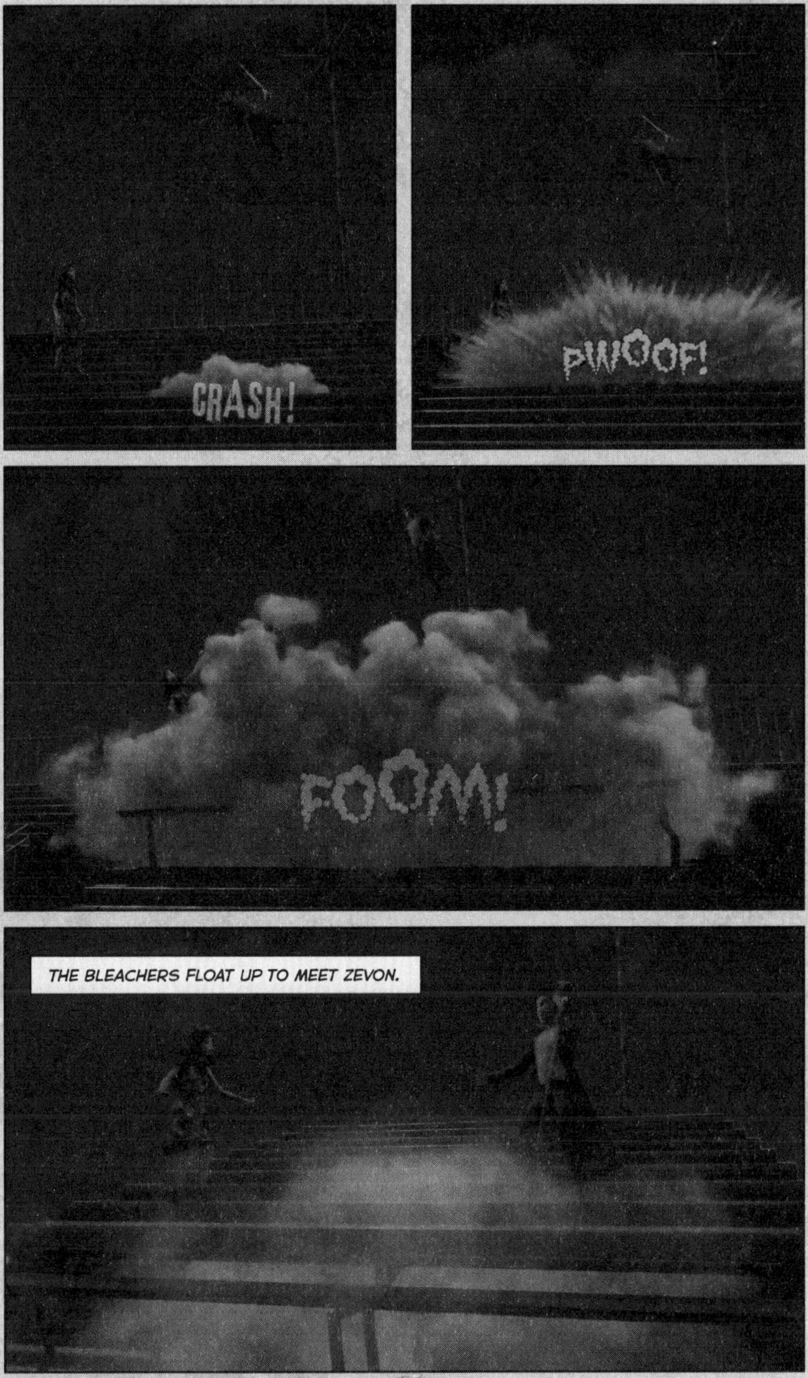
CRASH!
PWOOF!
FOOM!
THE BLEACHERS FLOAT UP TO MEET ZEVON.

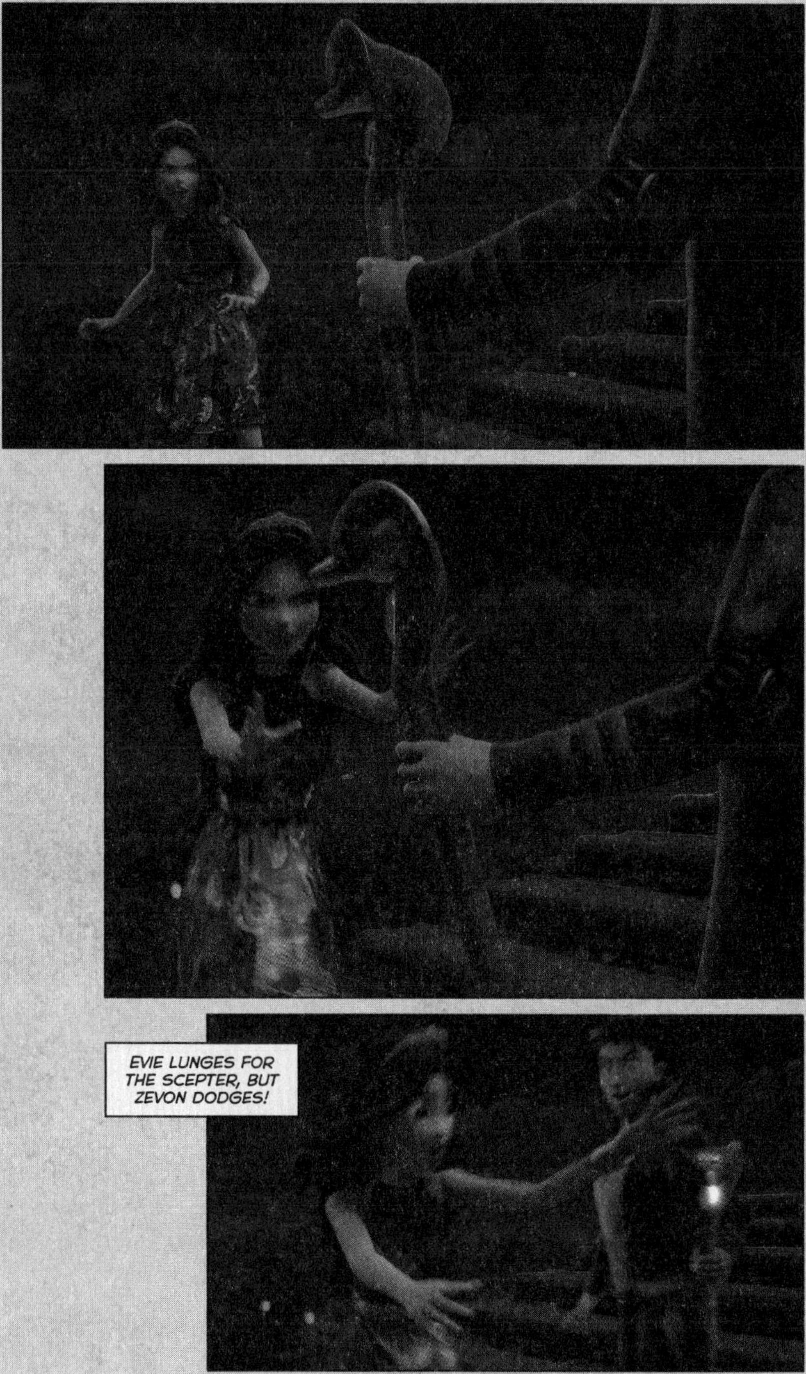
EVIE LUNGES FOR THE SCEPTER, BUT ZEVON DODGES!

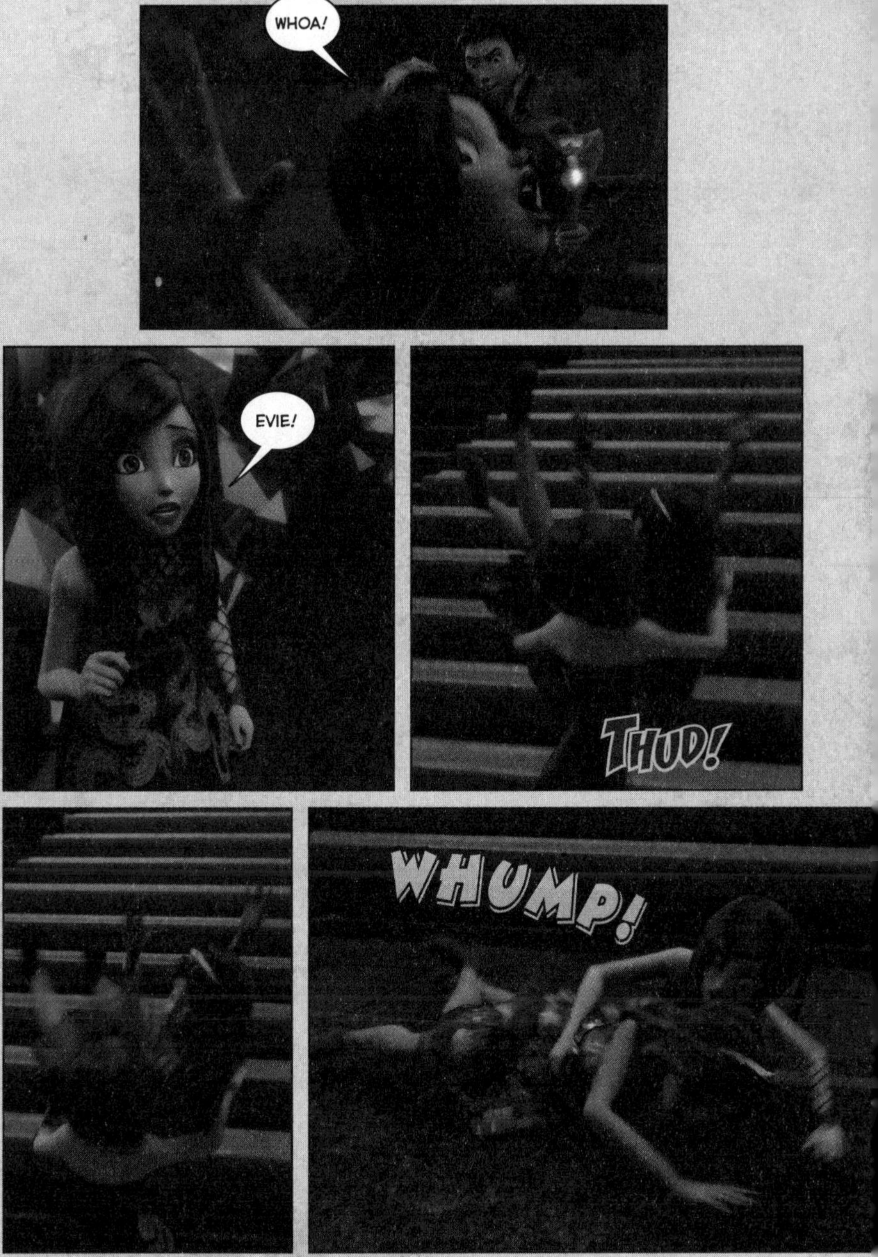
WHOA!
EVIE!
THUD!
WHUMP!

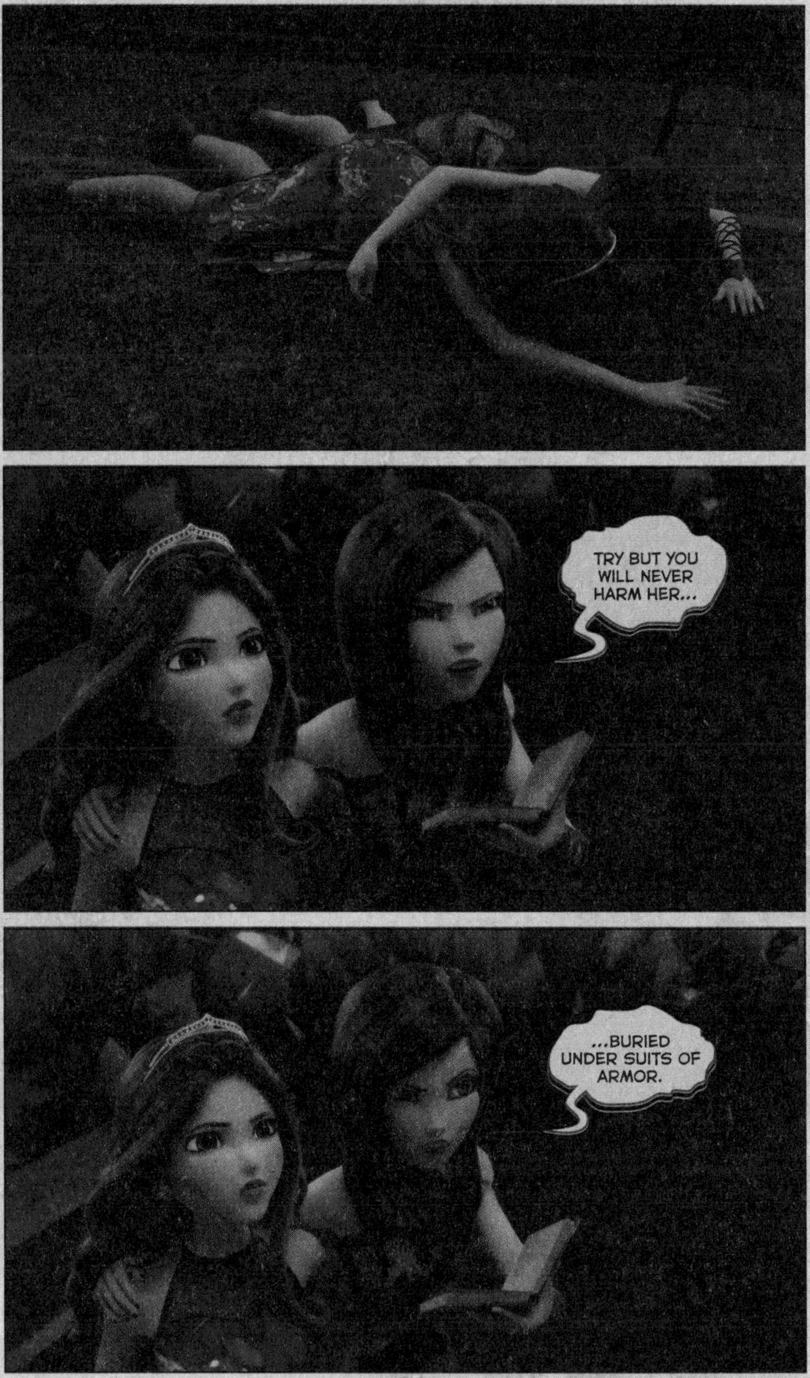
TRY BUT YOU WILL NEVER HARM HER...
...BURIED UNDER SUITS OF ARMOR.

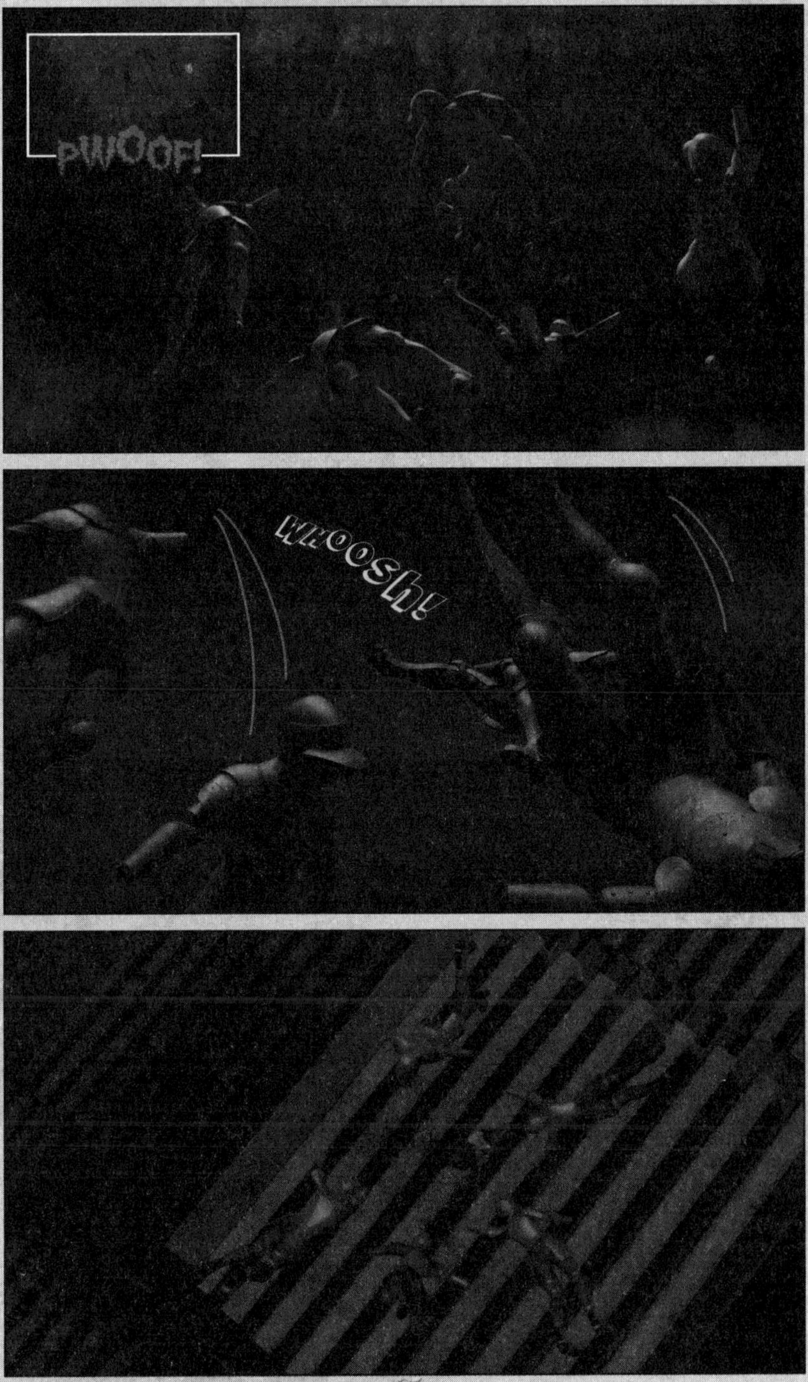
PWOOF!
WHOOSH!

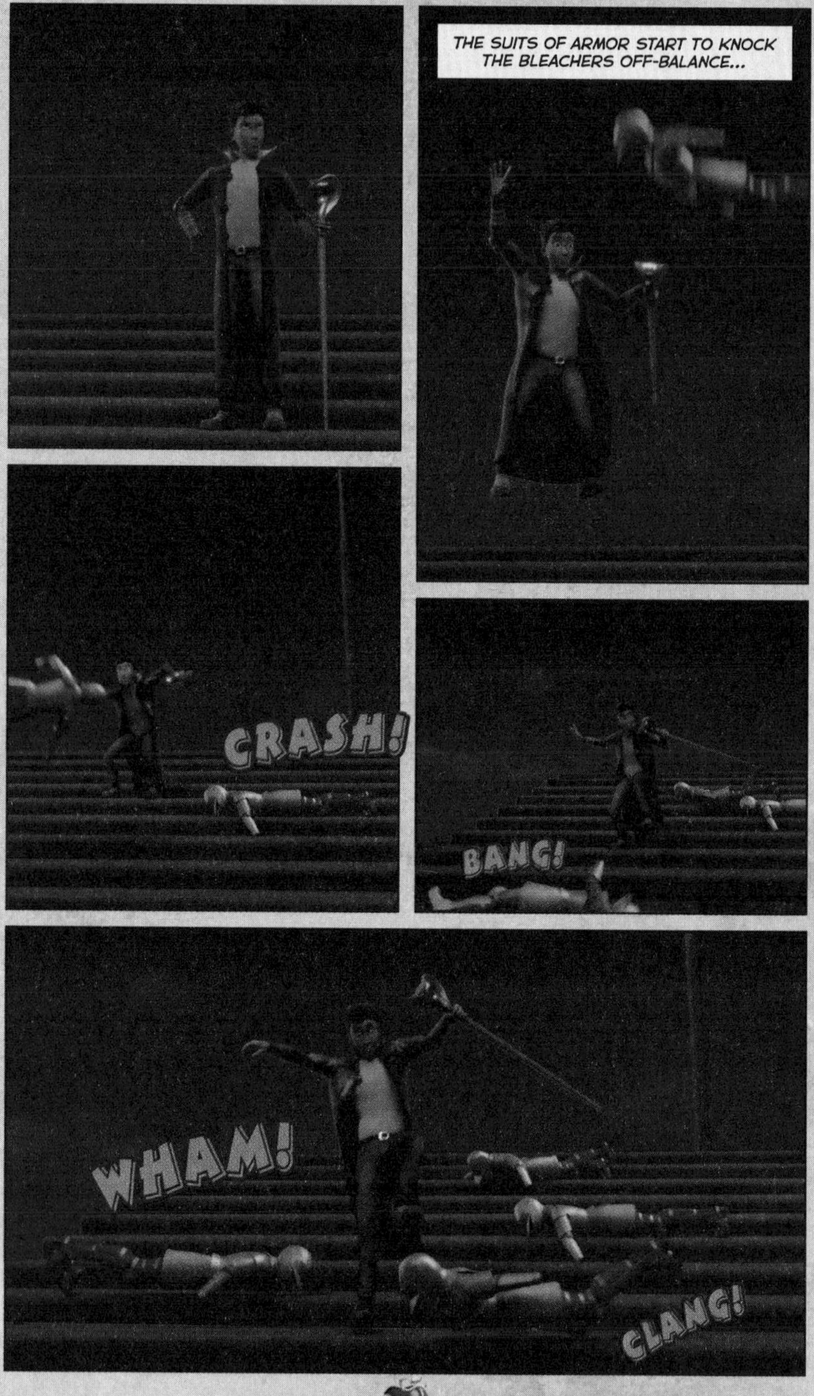
THE SUITS OF ARMOR START TO KNOCK THE BLEACHERS OFF-BALANCE...
CRASH!
BANG!
WHAM!
CLANG!

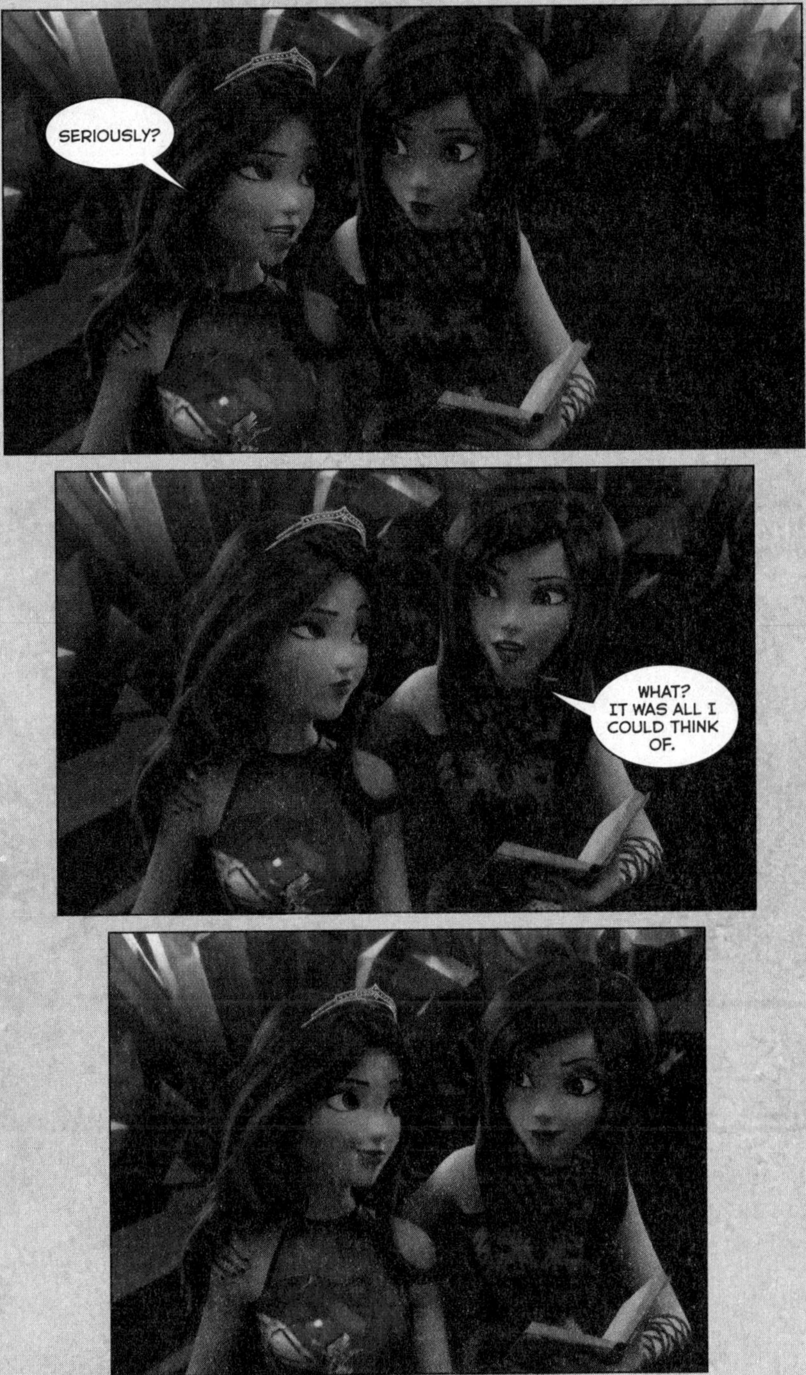
SERIOUSLY?
WHAT? IT WAS ALL I COULD THINK OF.

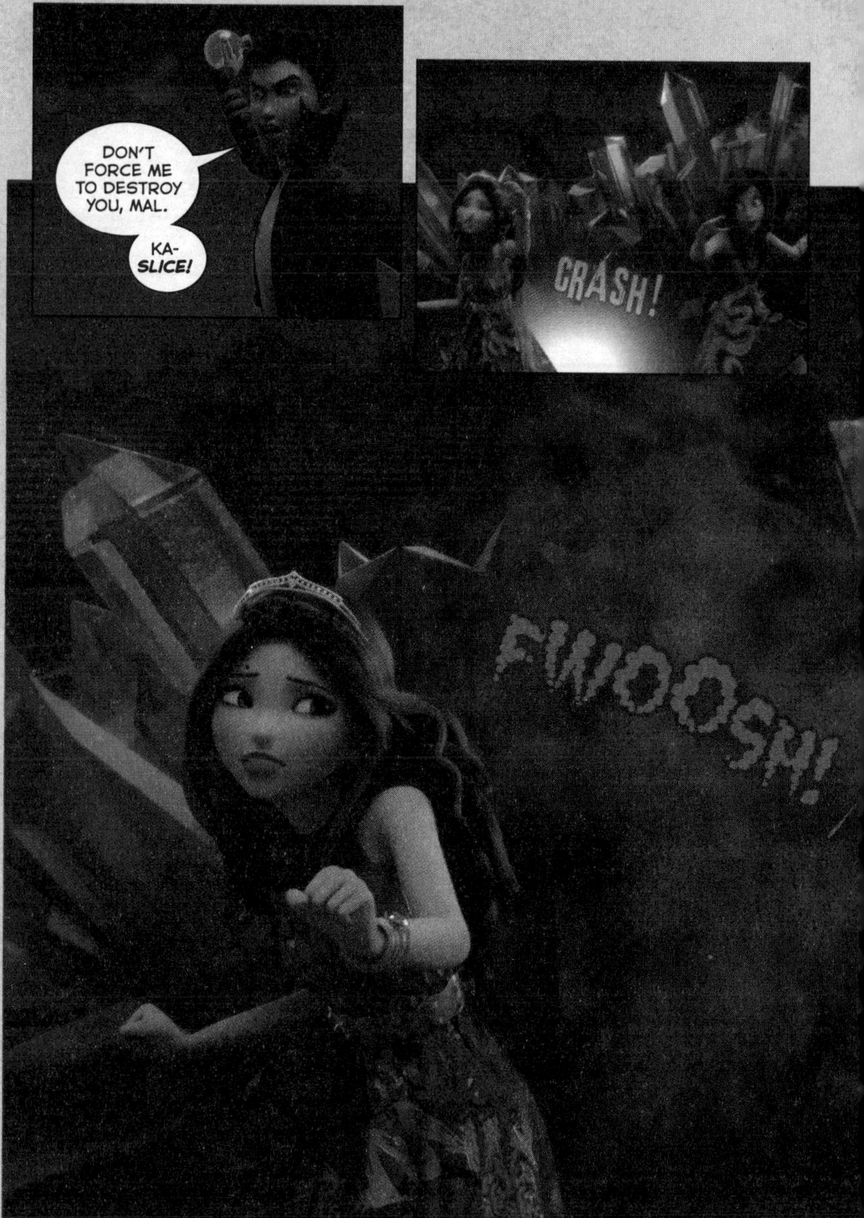
DON'T FORCE ME TO DESTROY YOU, MAL.
KA-SLICE!
CRASH!
FWOOSH!

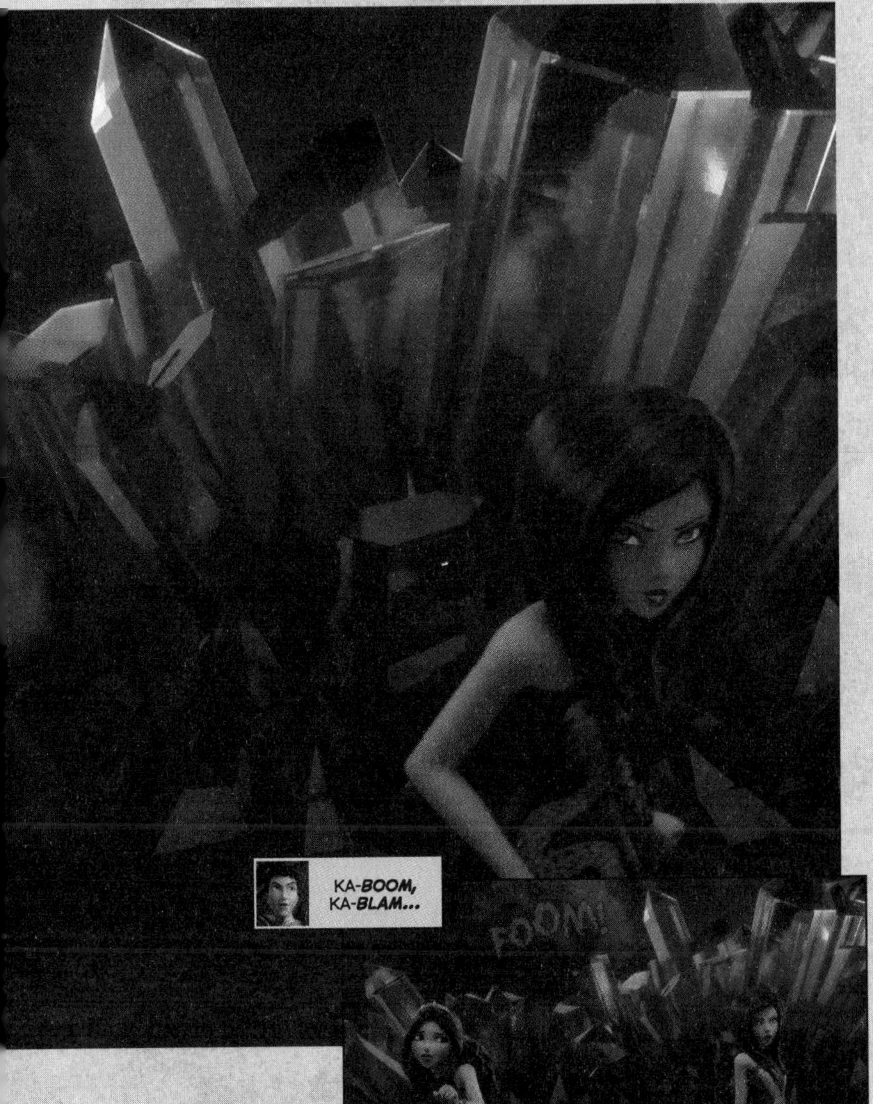
KA-BOOM,
KA-BLAM...
FOOM!

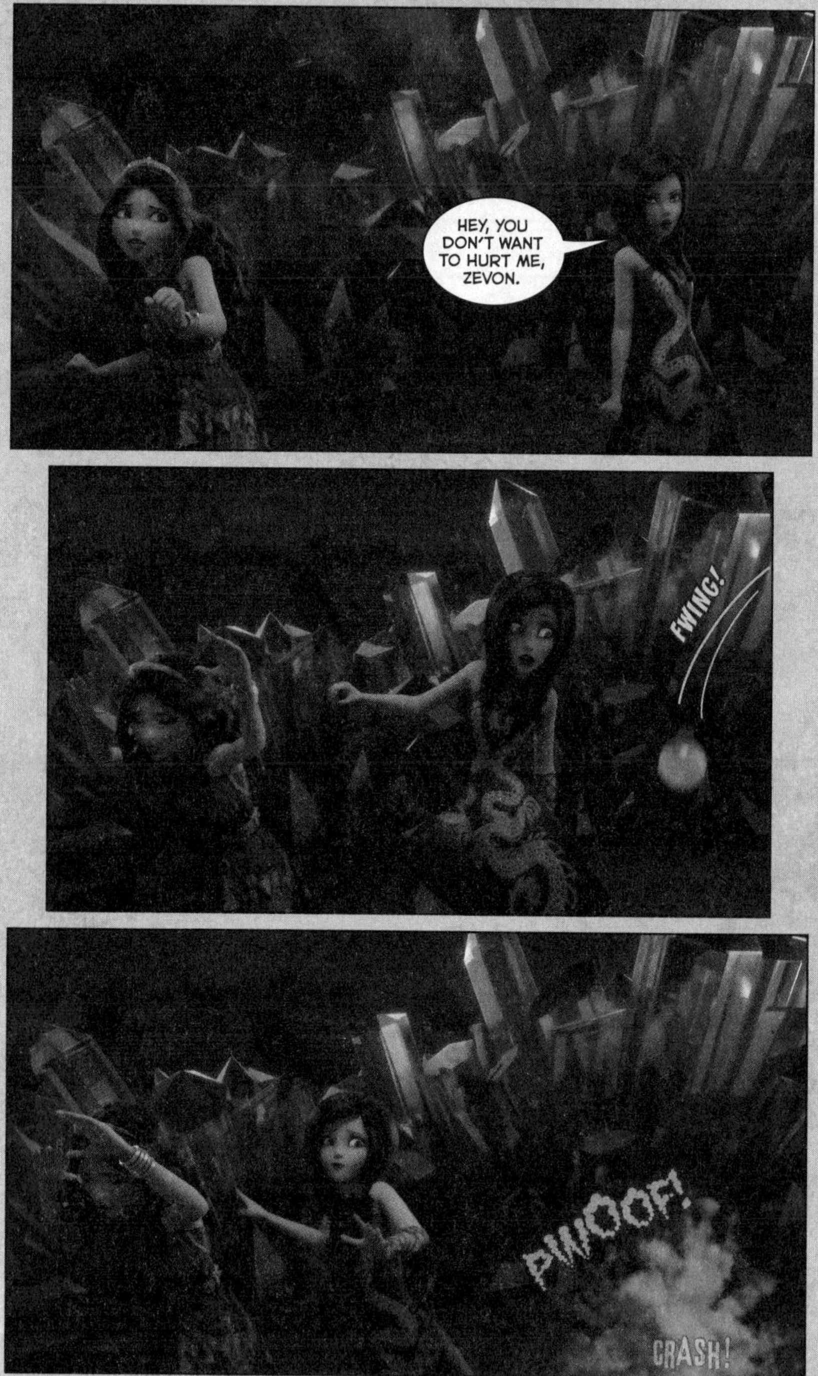
HEY, YOU DON'T WANT TO HURT ME, ZEVON.
FWING!
PWOOF!
CRASH!

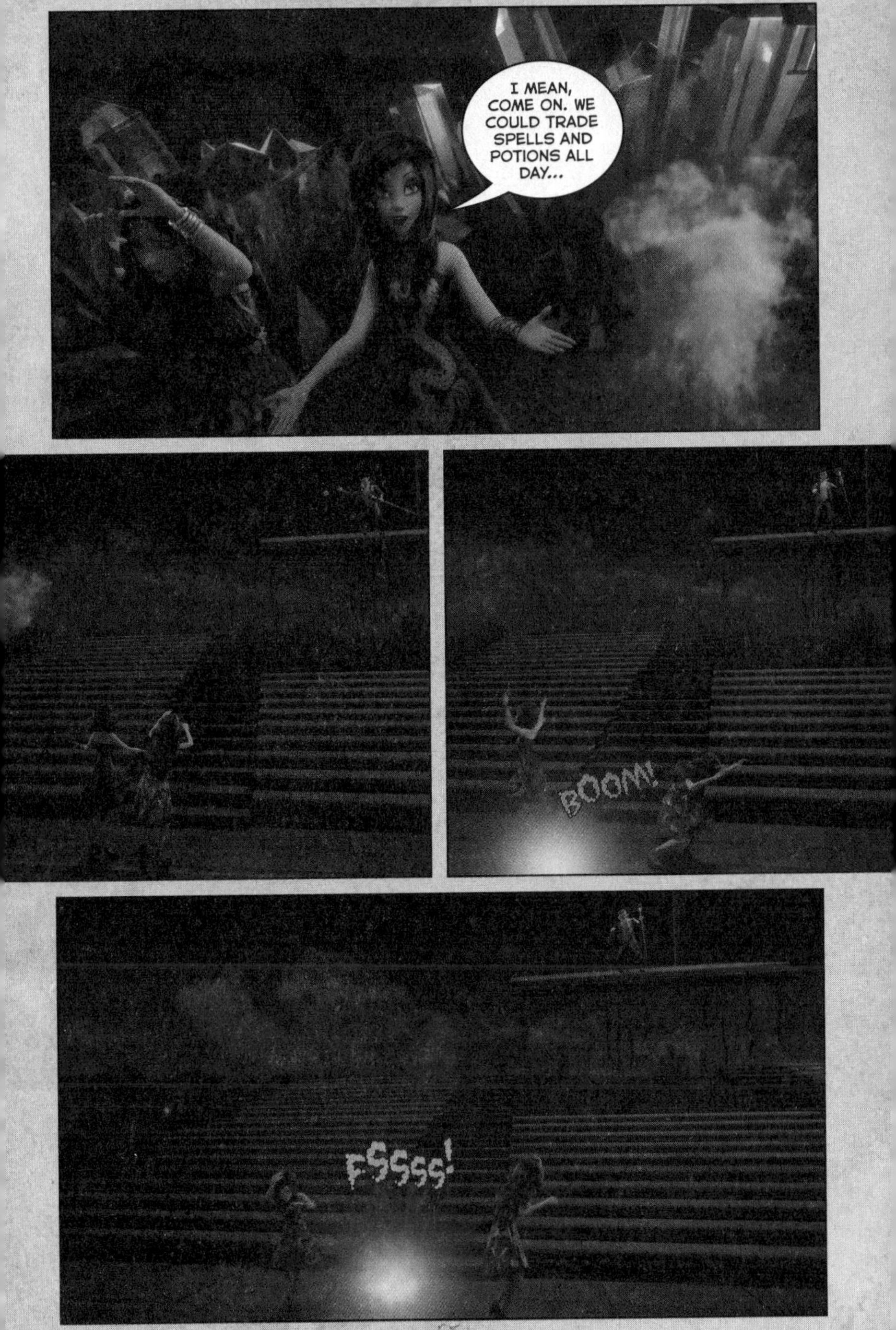
I MEAN, COME ON. WE COULD TRADE SPELLS AND POTIONS ALL DAY...
BOOM!
FSSSS!

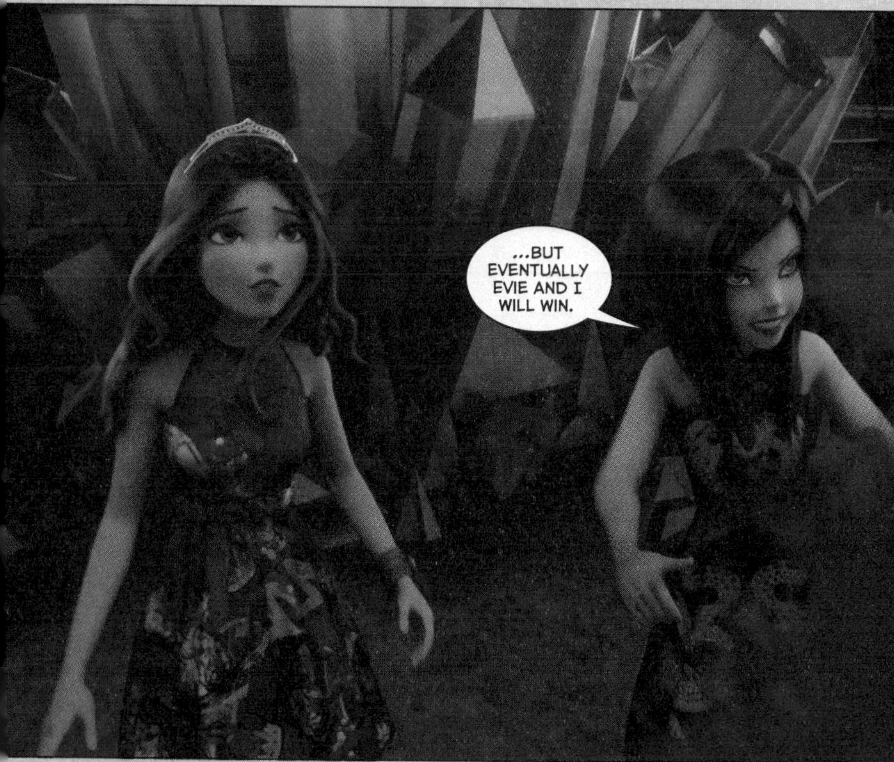
...BUT EVENTUALLY EVIE AND I WILL WIN.

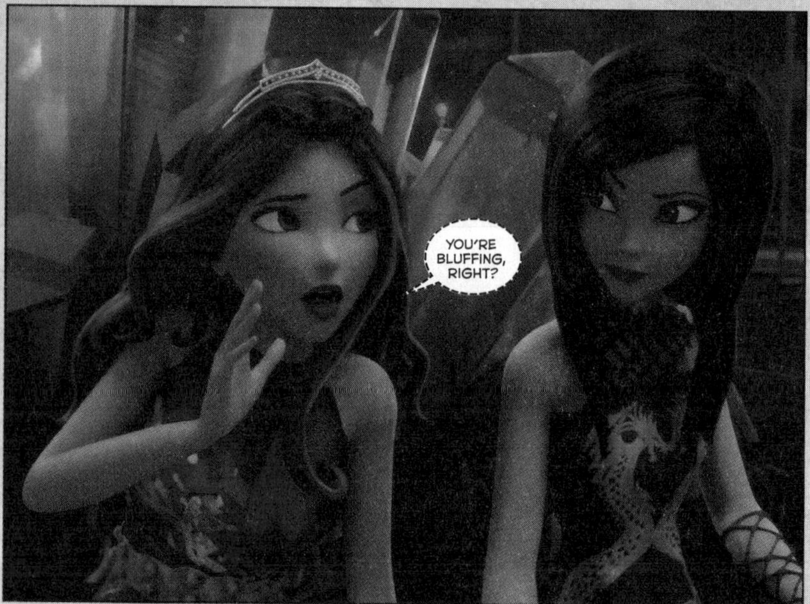
YOU'RE BLUFFING, RIGHT?

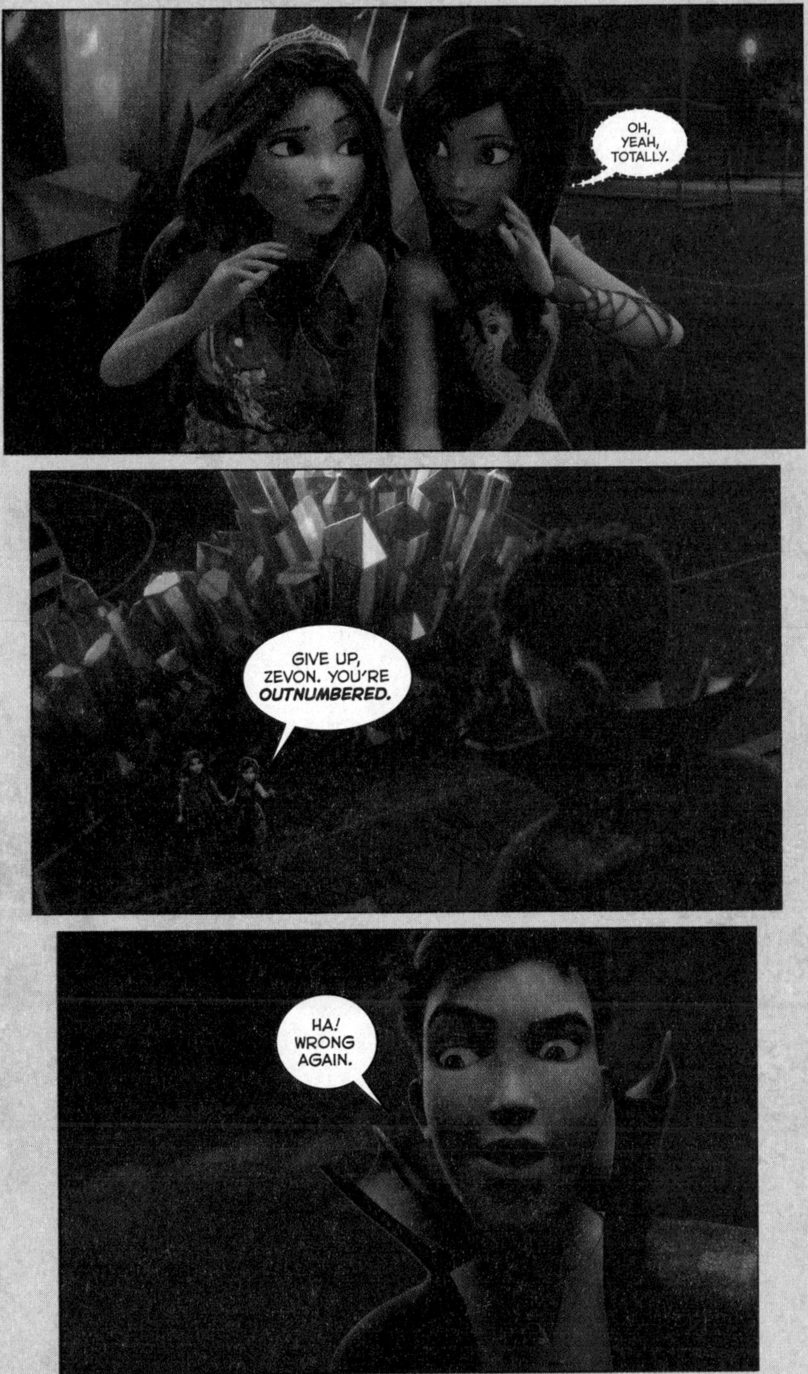
OH, YEAH, TOTALLY.
GIVE UP, ZEVON. YOU'RE ***OUTNUMBERED.***
HA! WRONG AGAIN.

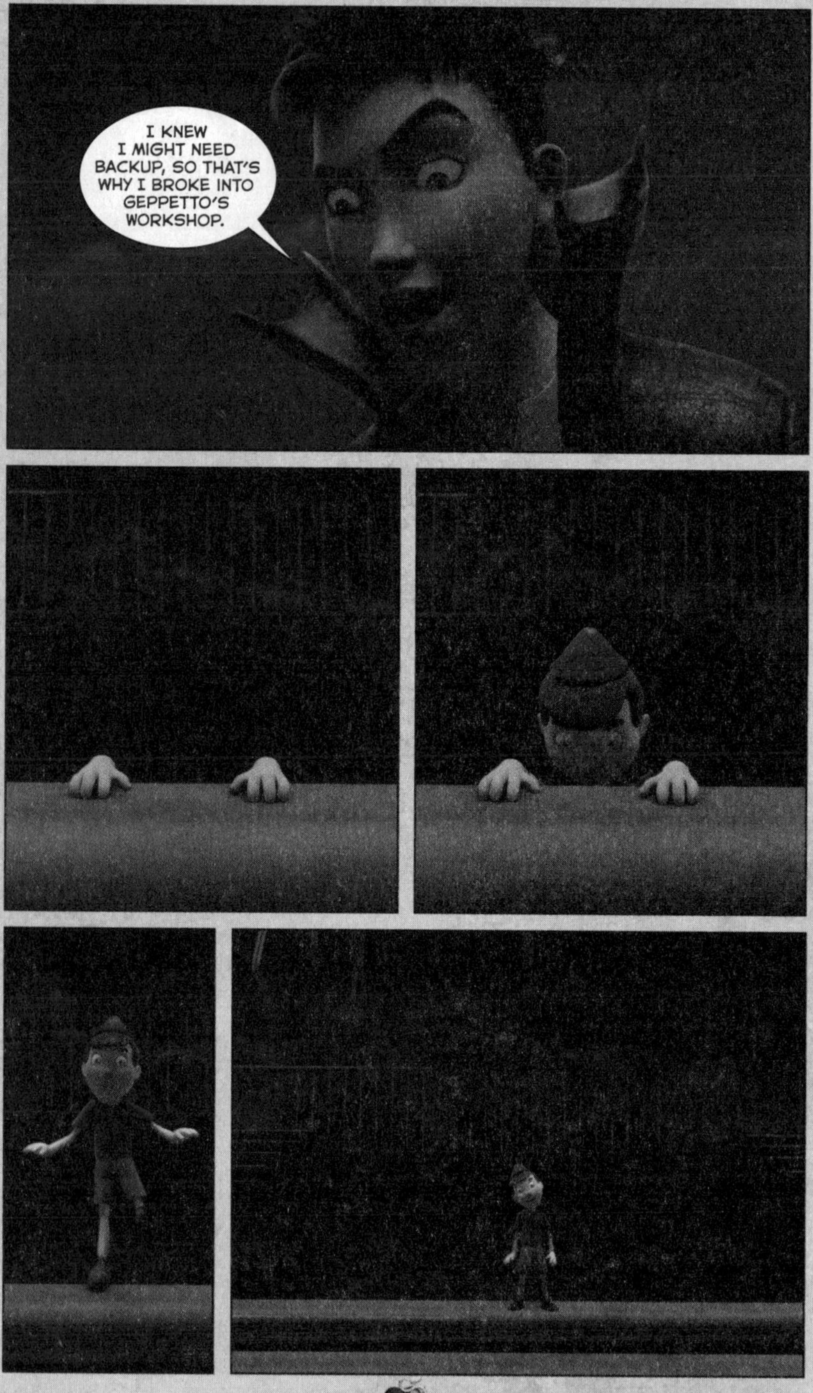
I KNEW I MIGHT NEED BACKUP, SO THAT'S WHY I BROKE INTO GEPPETTO'S WORKSHOP.

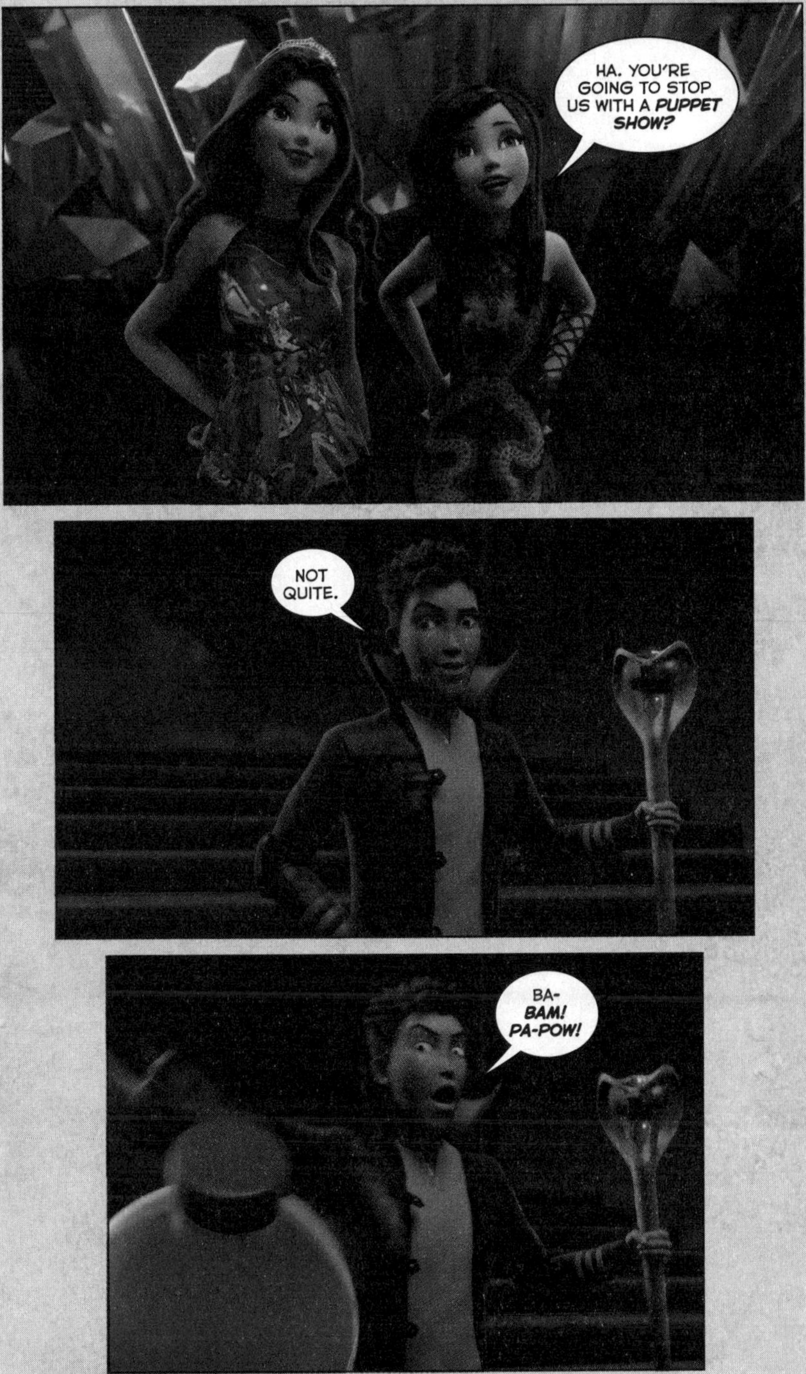
HA. YOU'RE GOING TO STOP US WITH A *PUPPET SHOW?*
NOT QUITE.
BA-*BAM! PA-POW!*

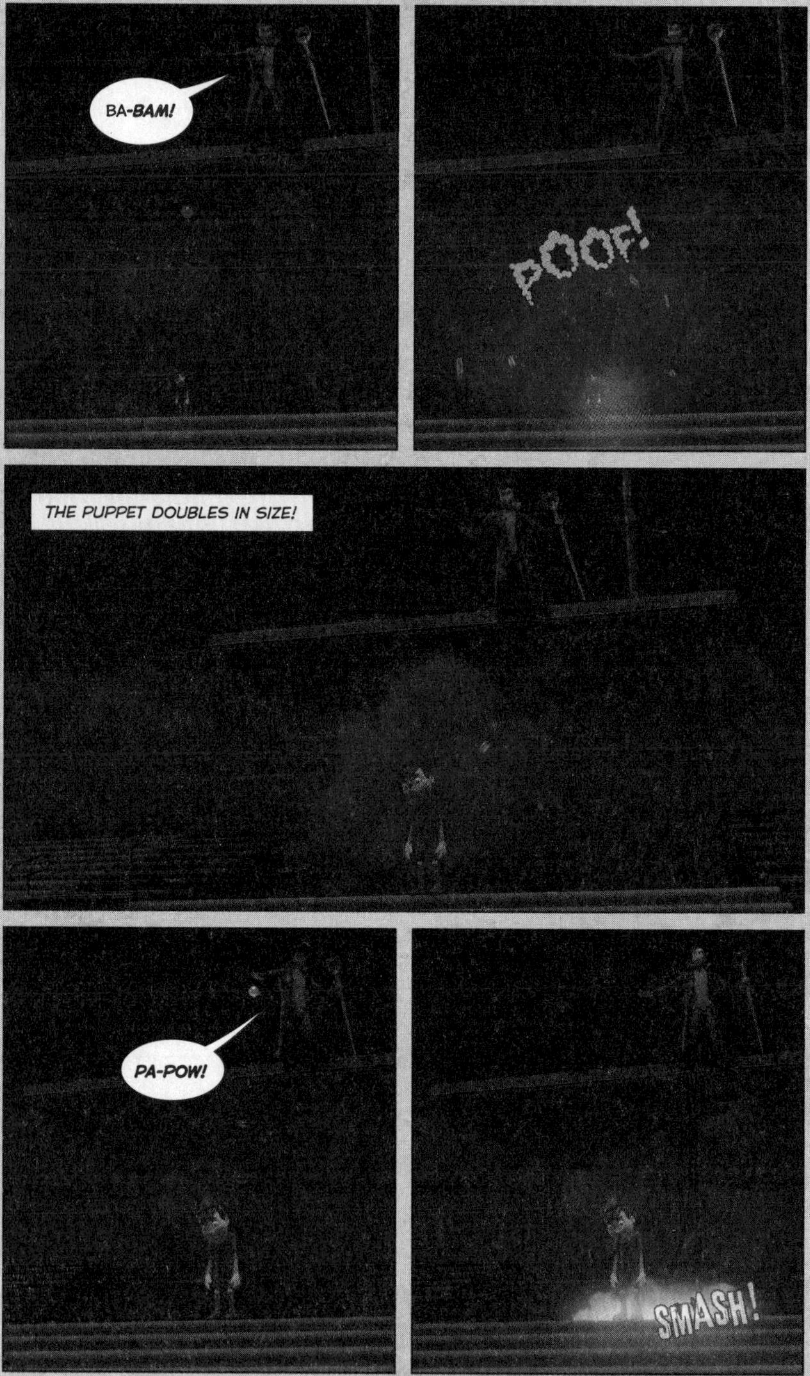
BA-BAM!
POOF!
THE PUPPET DOUBLES IN SIZE!
PA-POW!
SMASH!

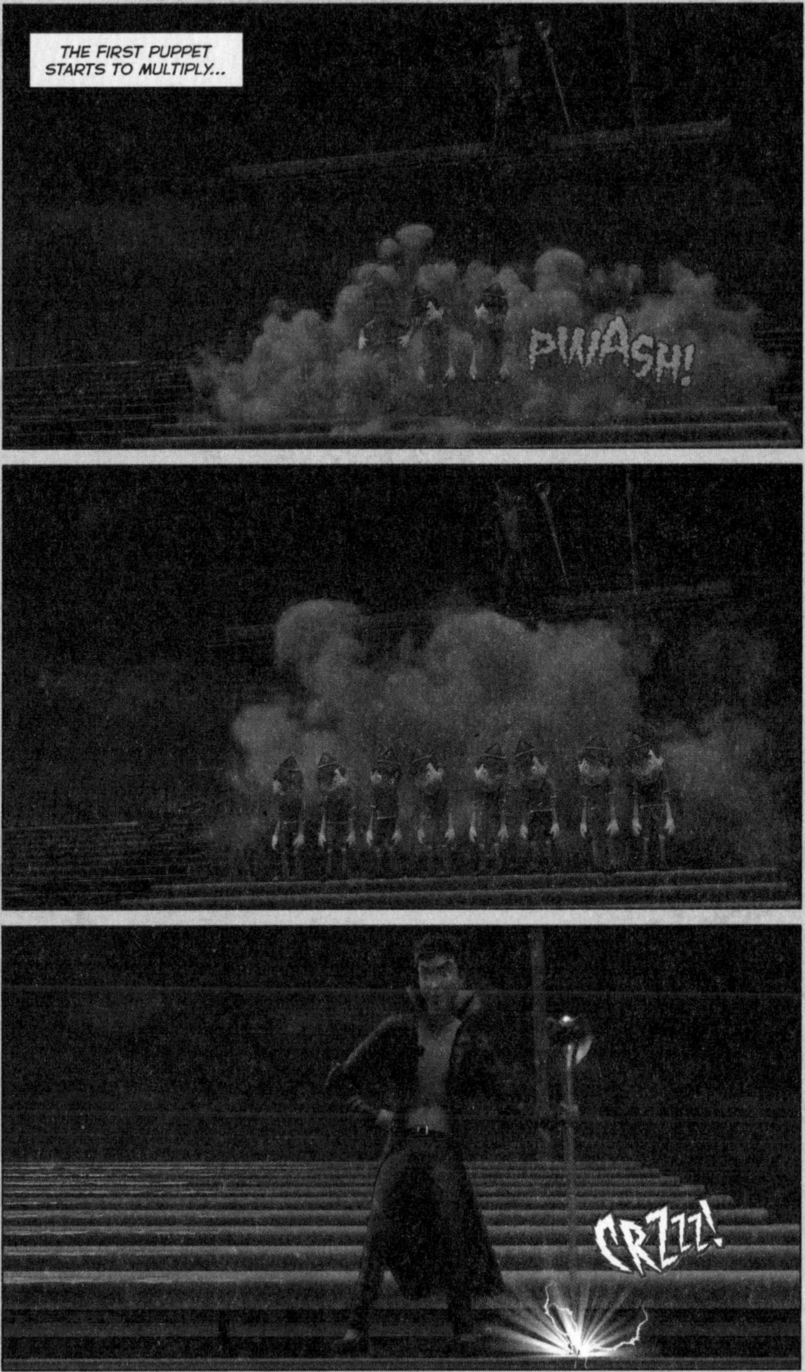
THE FIRST PUPPET STARTS TO MULTIPLY...
PWASH!
CRZZZ!

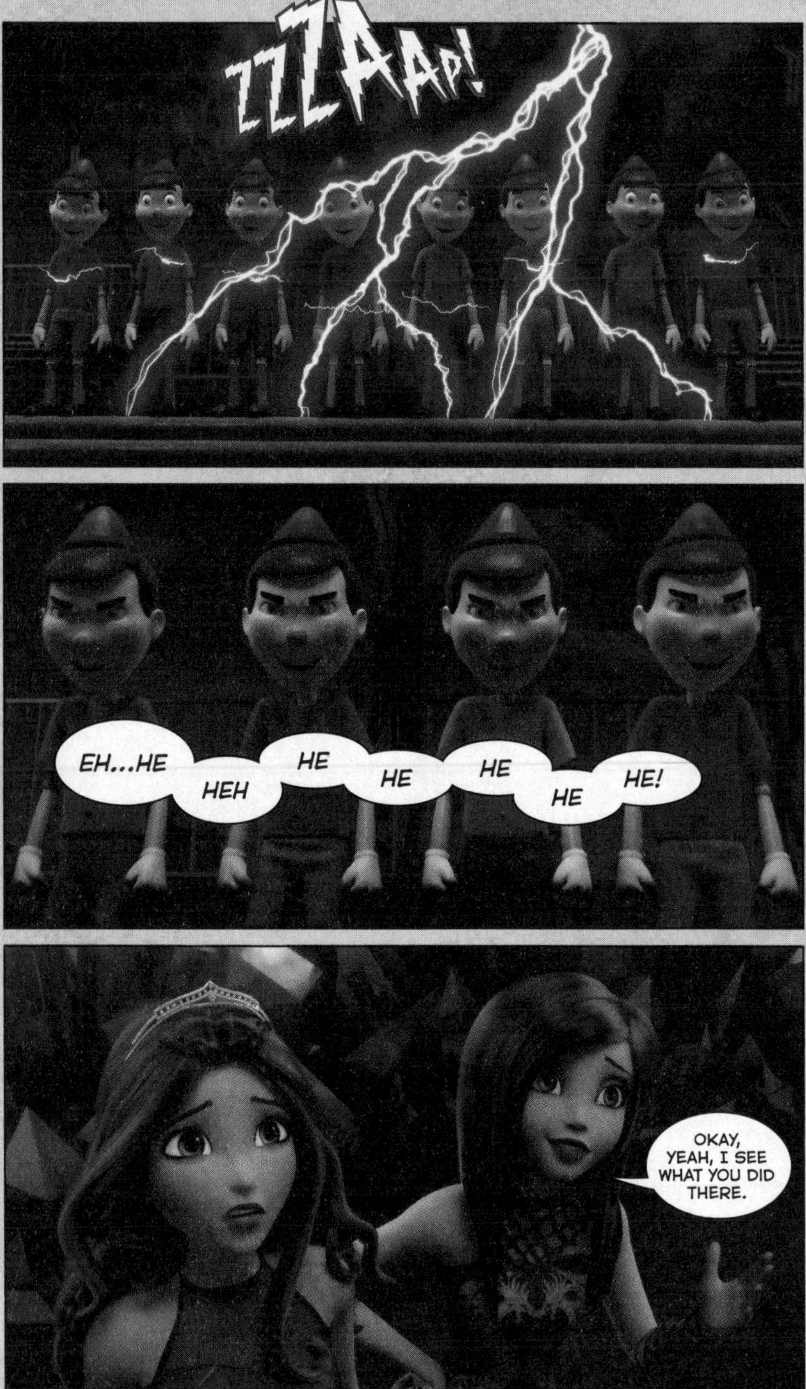
ZZZAAP!
EH...HE
HEH
HE
HE
HE
HE
HE!
OKAY, YEAH, I SEE WHAT YOU DID THERE.

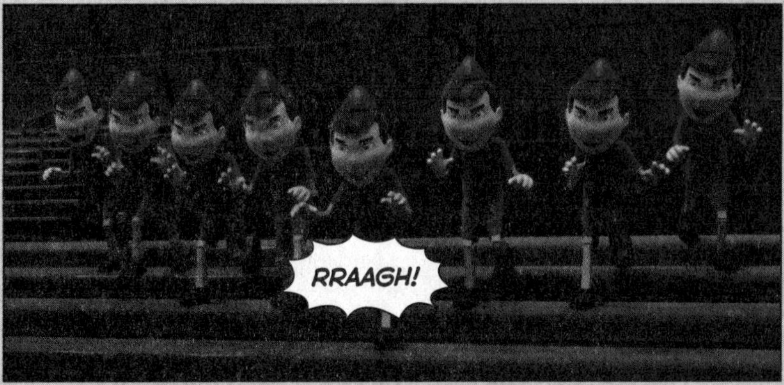
RRAAGH!

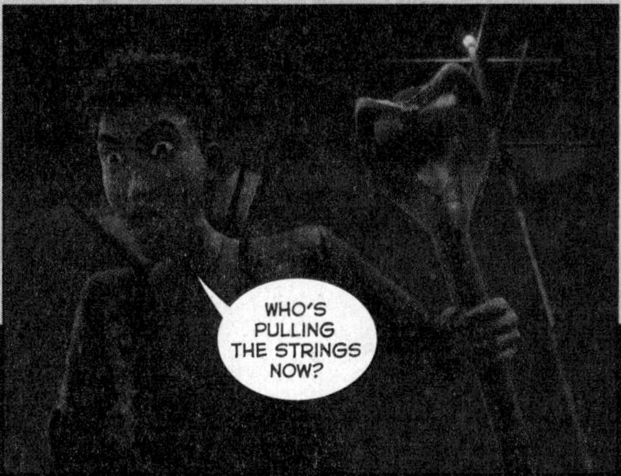
WHO'S PULLING THE STRINGS NOW?

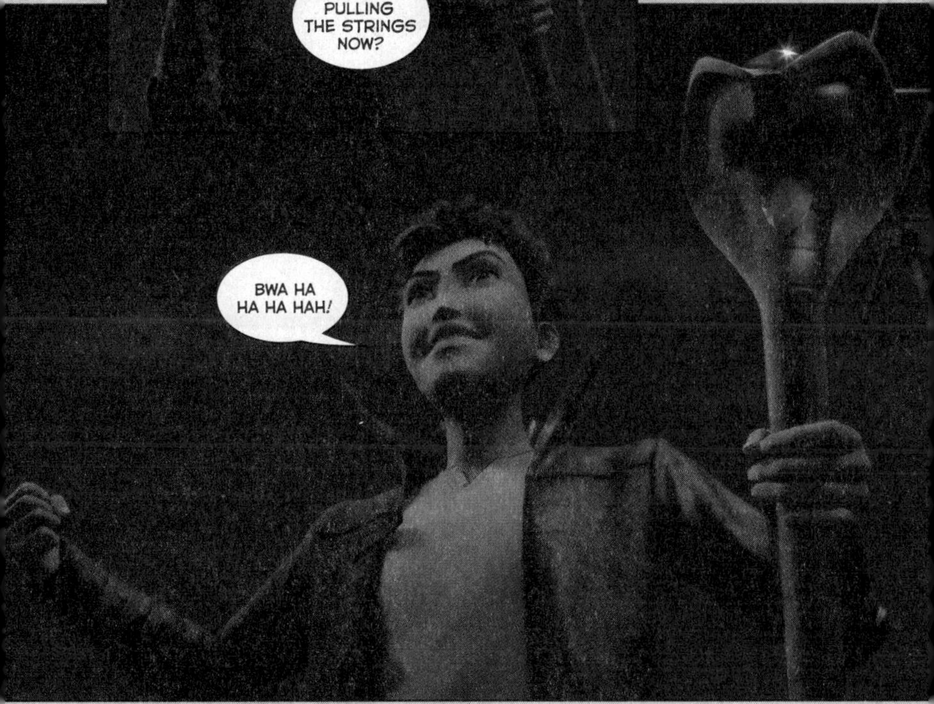
BWA HA HA HA HAH!

CHAPTER 32: UNITED WE STAND

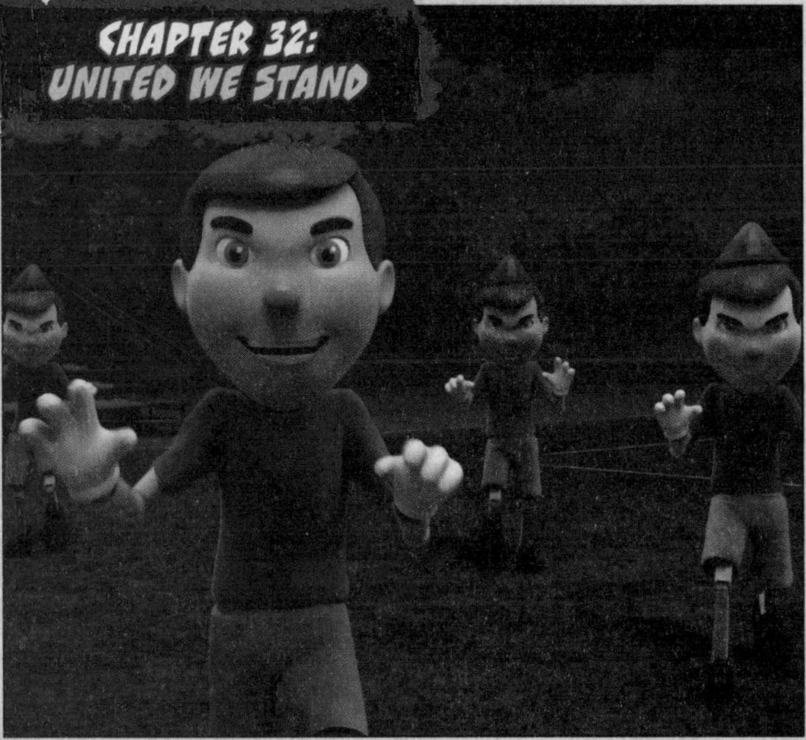

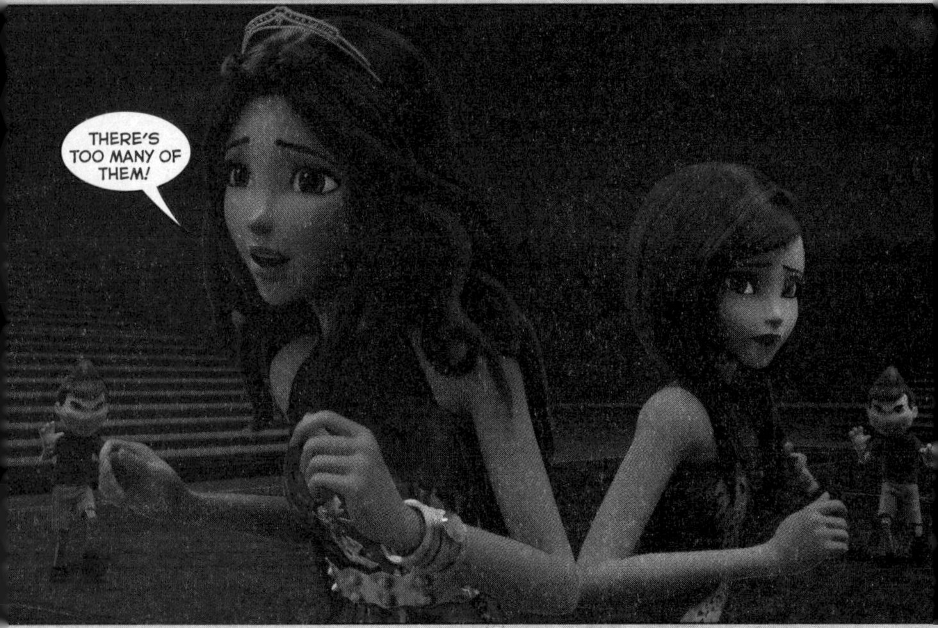
THERE'S TOO MANY OF THEM!

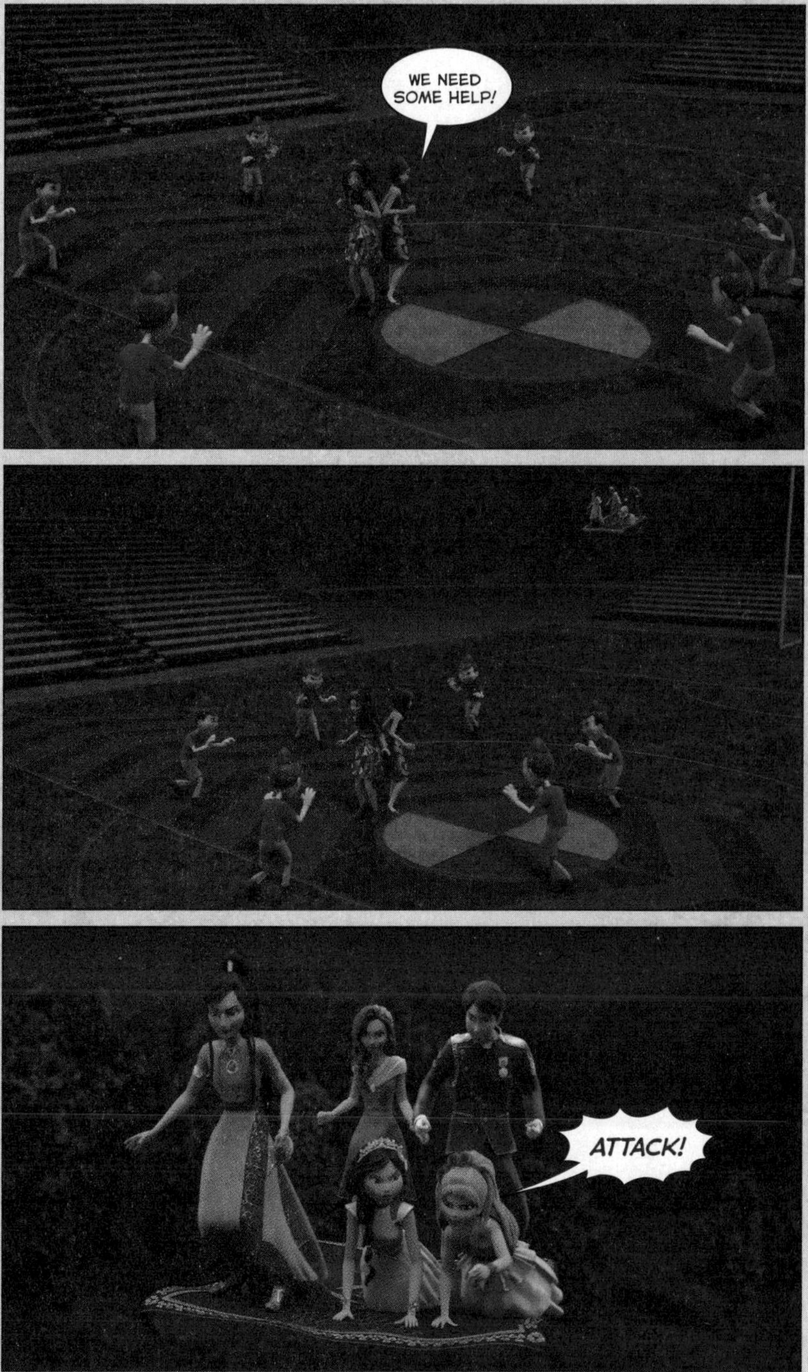
WE NEED SOME HELP!
ATTACK!

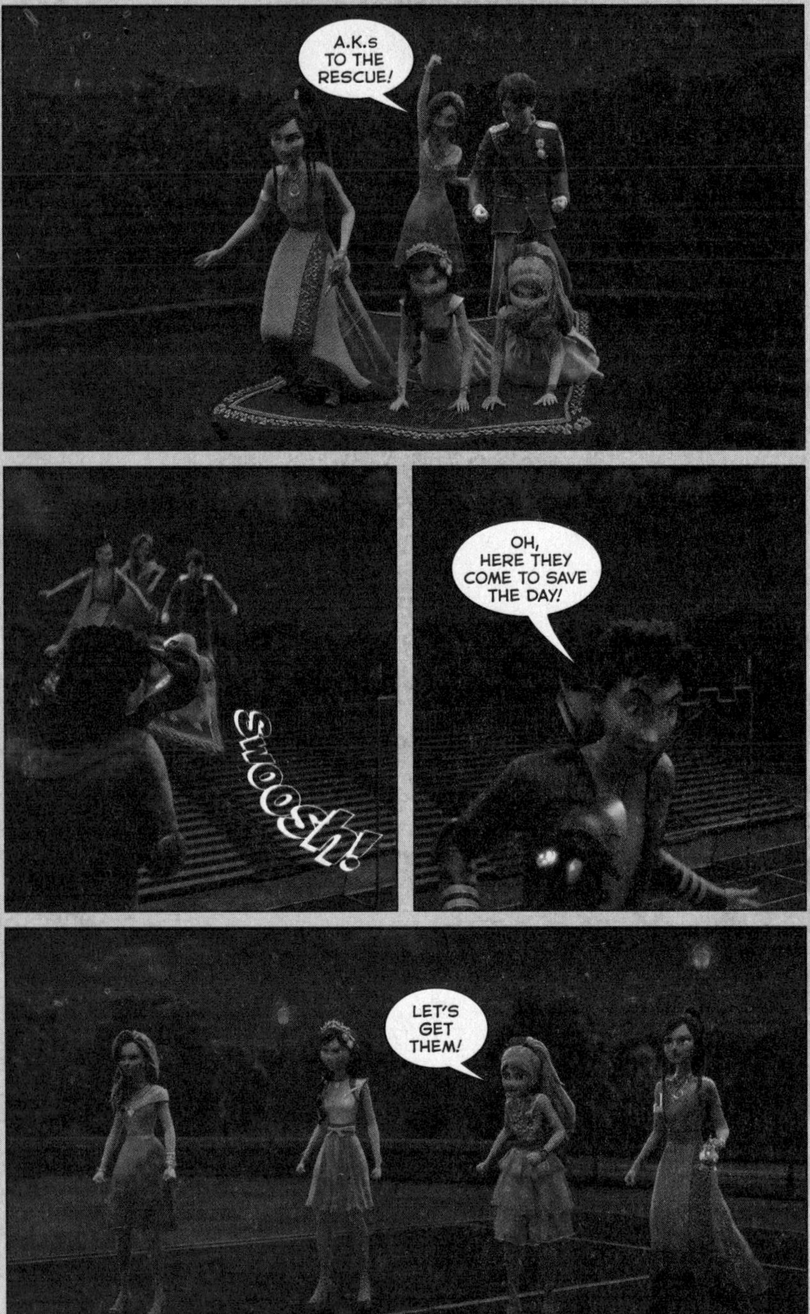
A.K.s TO THE RESCUE!
SWOOSH!
OH, HERE THEY COME TO SAVE THE DAY!
LET'S GET THEM!

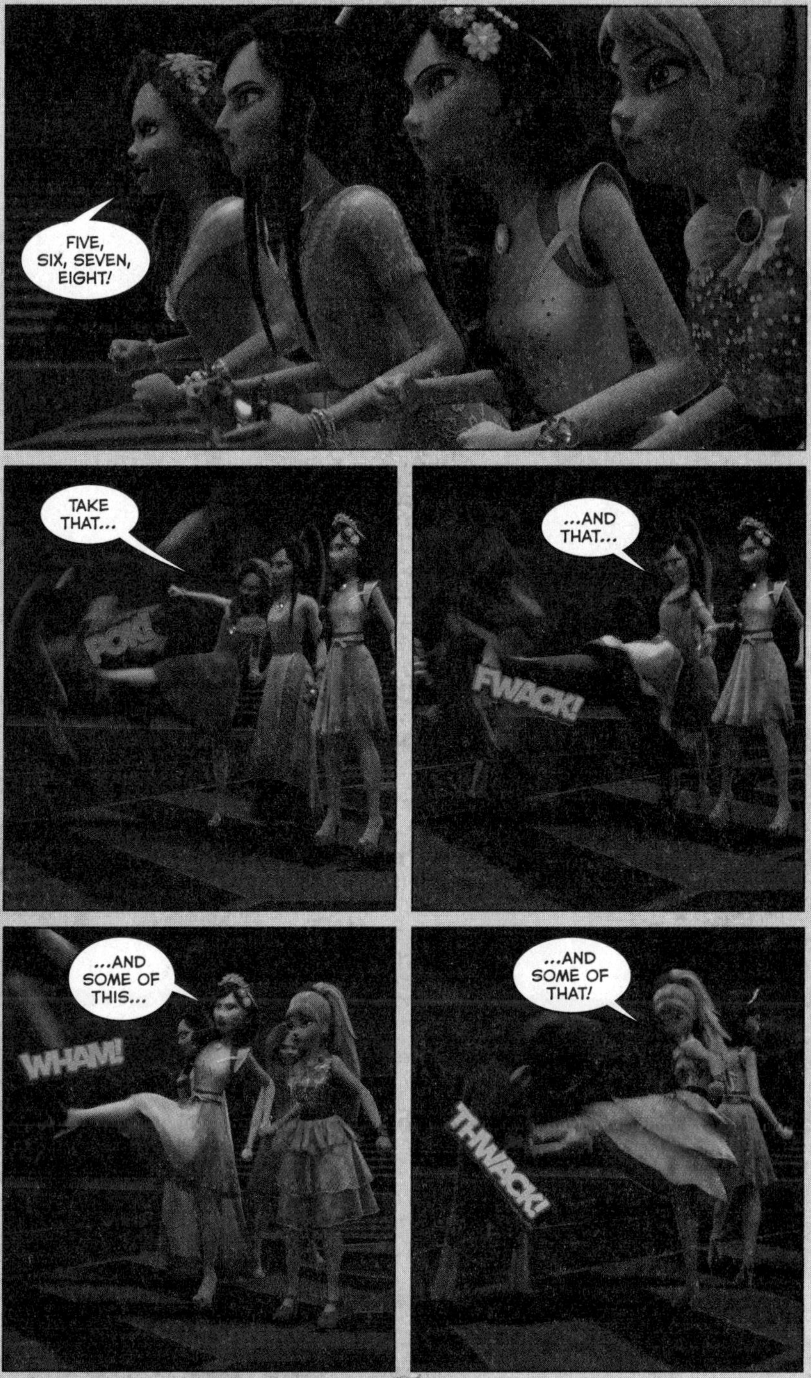
FIVE, SIX, SEVEN, EIGHT!
TAKE THAT...
POW!
...AND THAT...
FWACK!
...AND SOME OF THIS...
WHAM!
...AND SOME OF THAT!
THWACK!

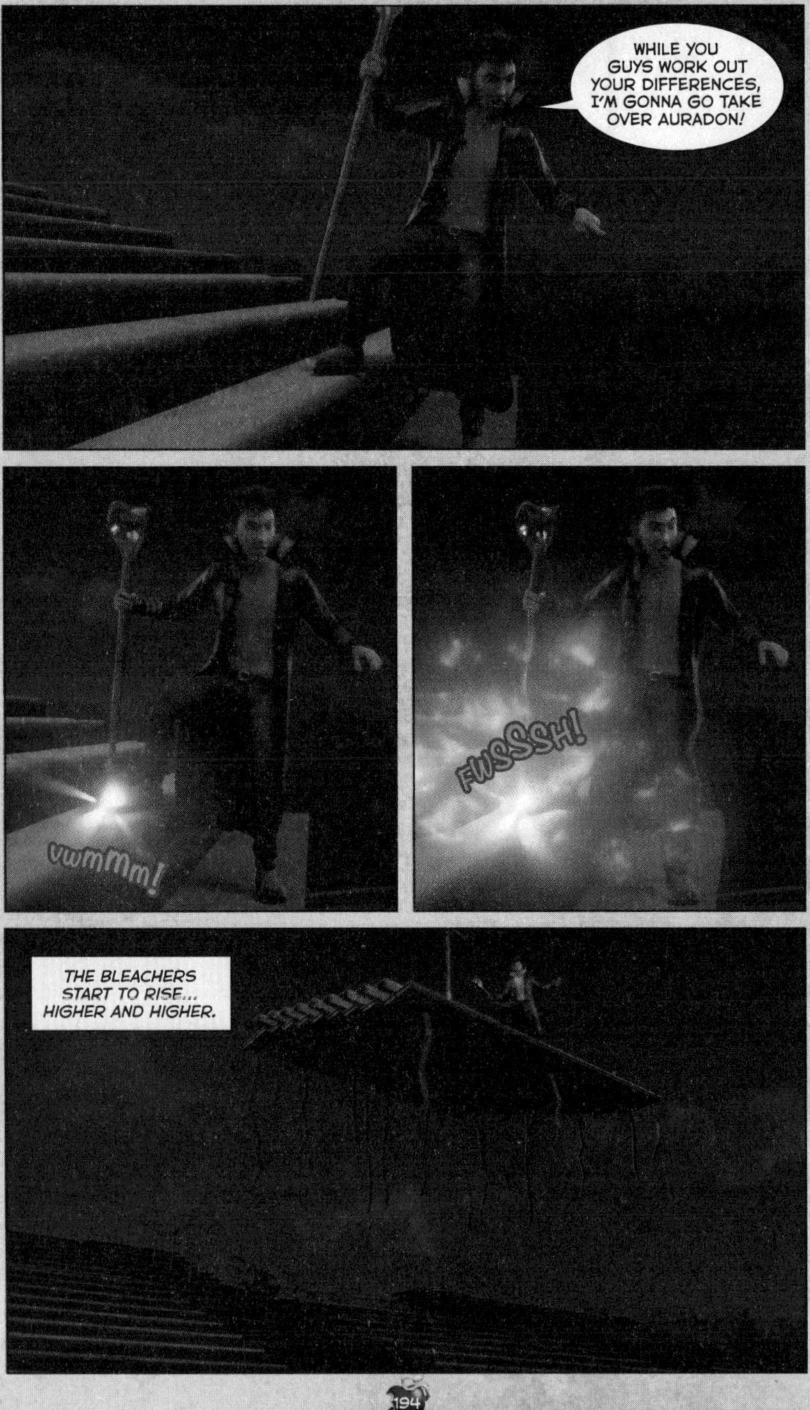
WHILE YOU GUYS WORK OUT YOUR DIFFERENCES, I'M GONNA GO TAKE OVER AURADON!
vwmMm!
FWSSSH!
THE BLEACHERS START TO RISE... HIGHER AND HIGHER.

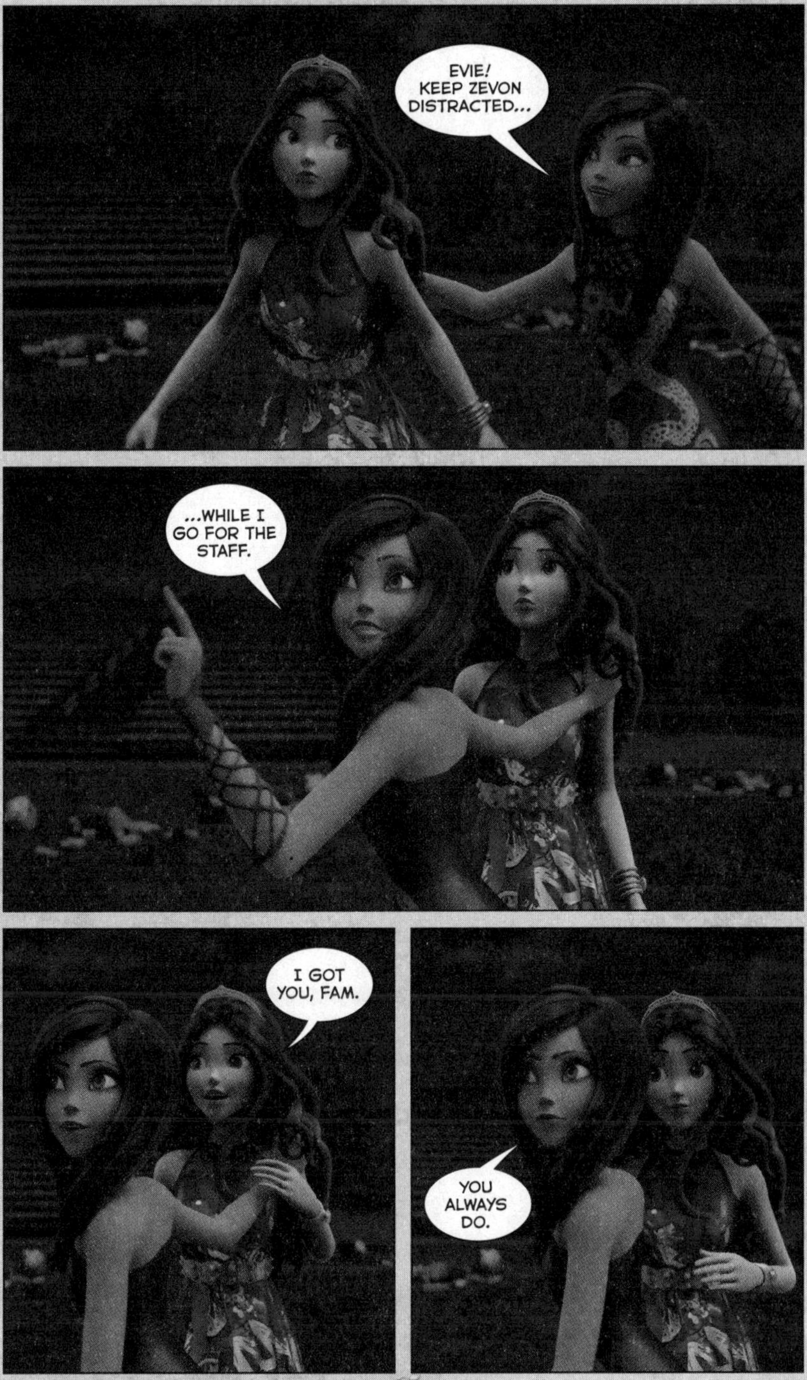
EVIE! KEEP ZEVON DISTRACTED...
...WHILE I GO FOR THE STAFF.
I GOT YOU, FAM.
YOU ALWAYS DO.

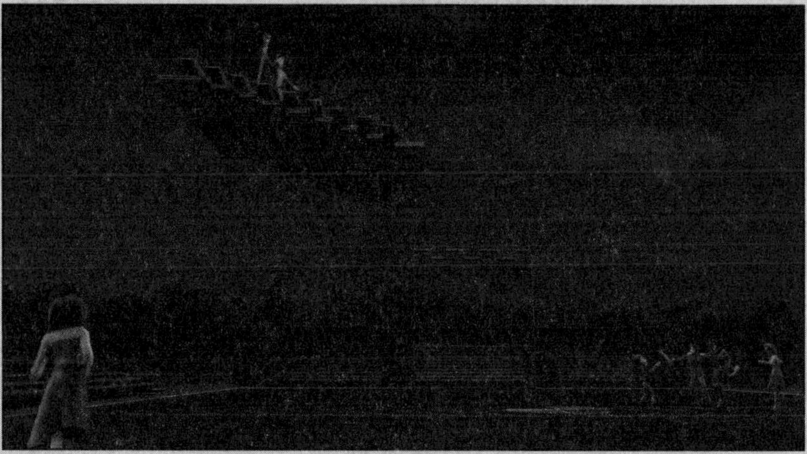

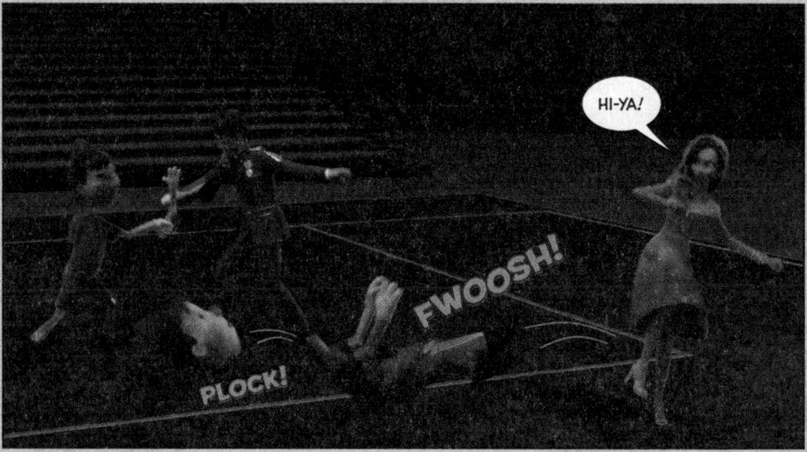
HI-YA!
FWOOSH!
PLOCK!

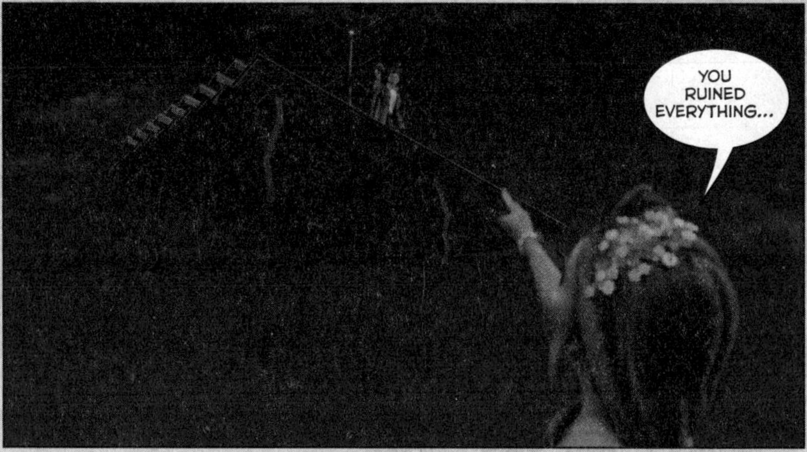
YOU RUINED EVERYTHING...

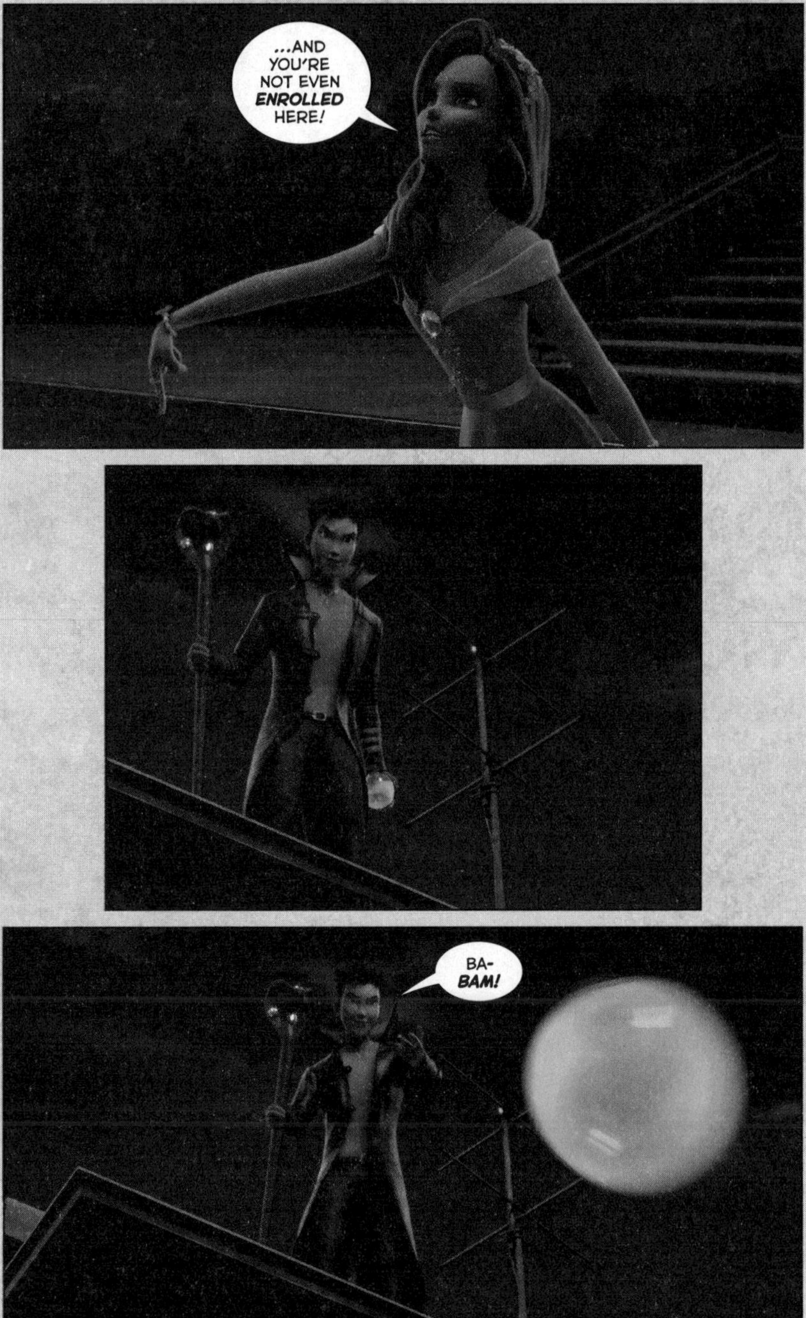
...AND YOU'RE NOT EVEN ENROLLED HERE!
BA-BAM!

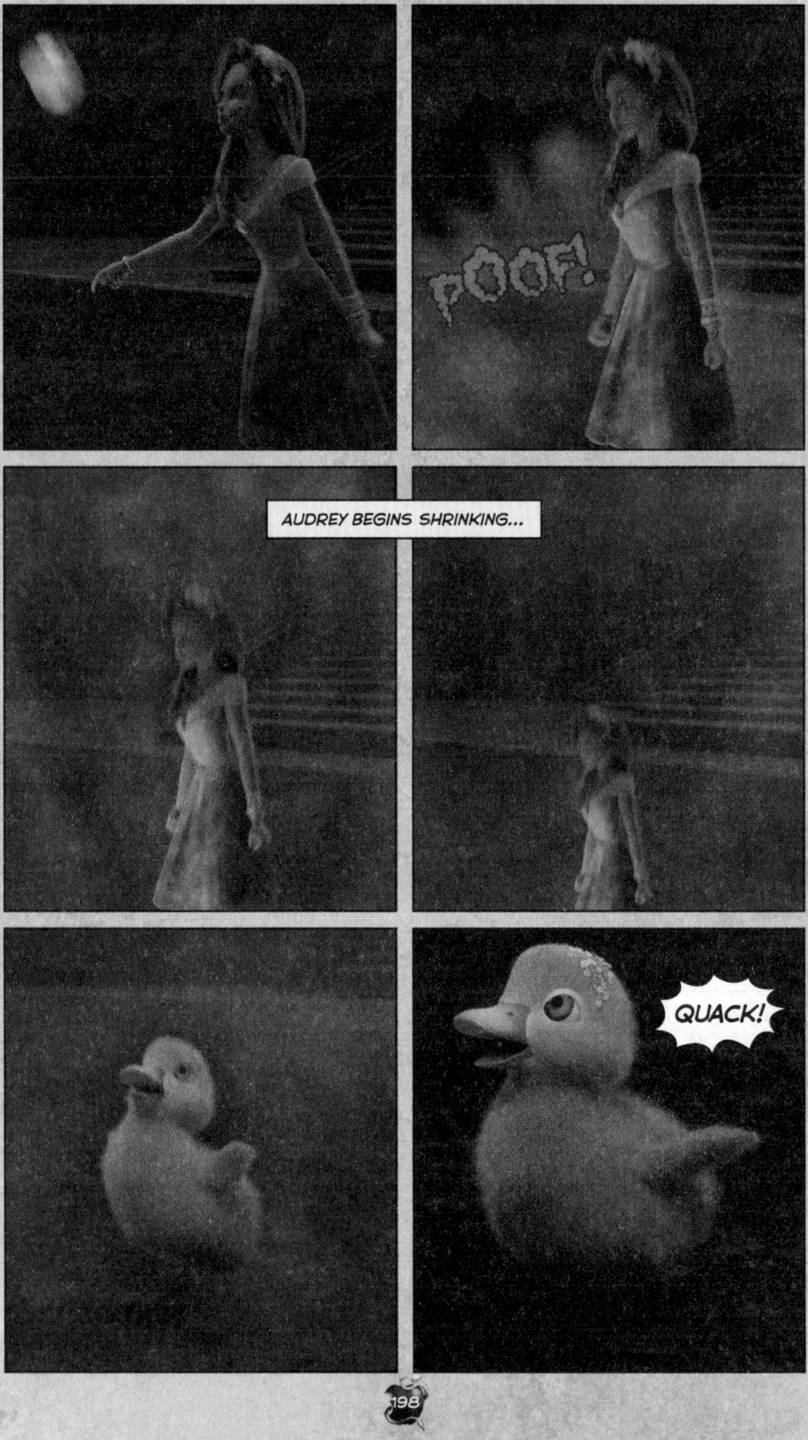
POOF!
AUDREY BEGINS SHRINKING...
QUACK!

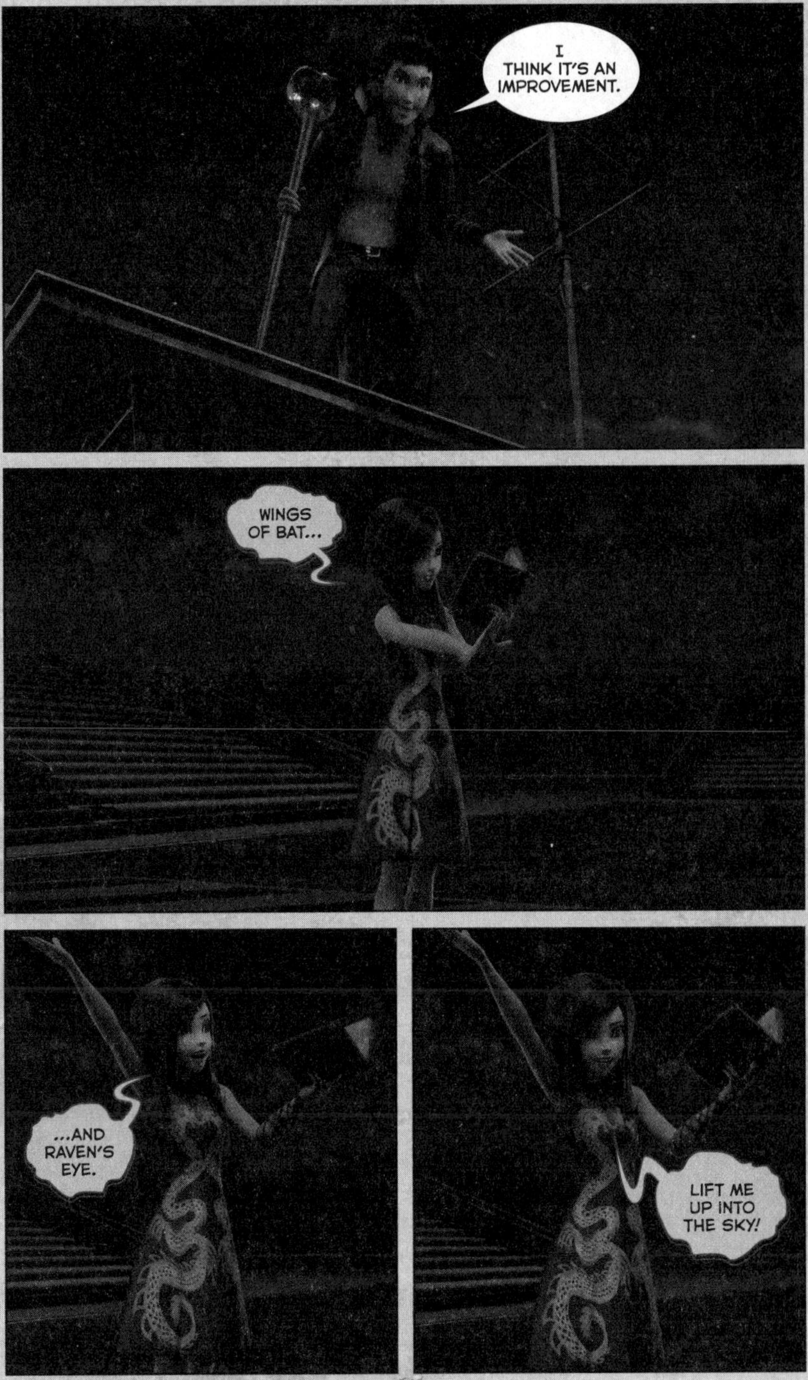
I THINK IT'S AN IMPROVEMENT.
WINGS OF BAT...
...AND RAVEN'S EYE.
LIFT ME UP INTO THE SKY!

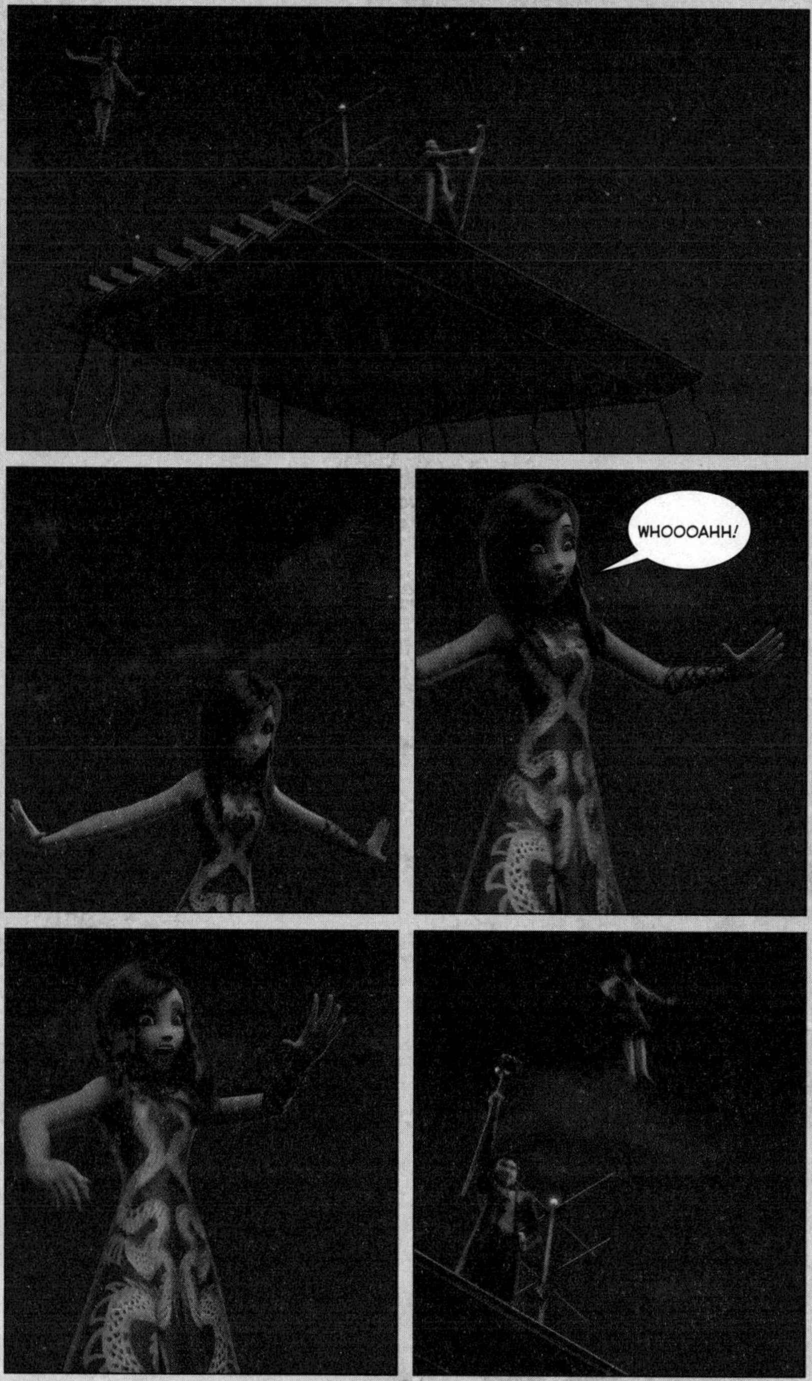
WHOOOAHH!

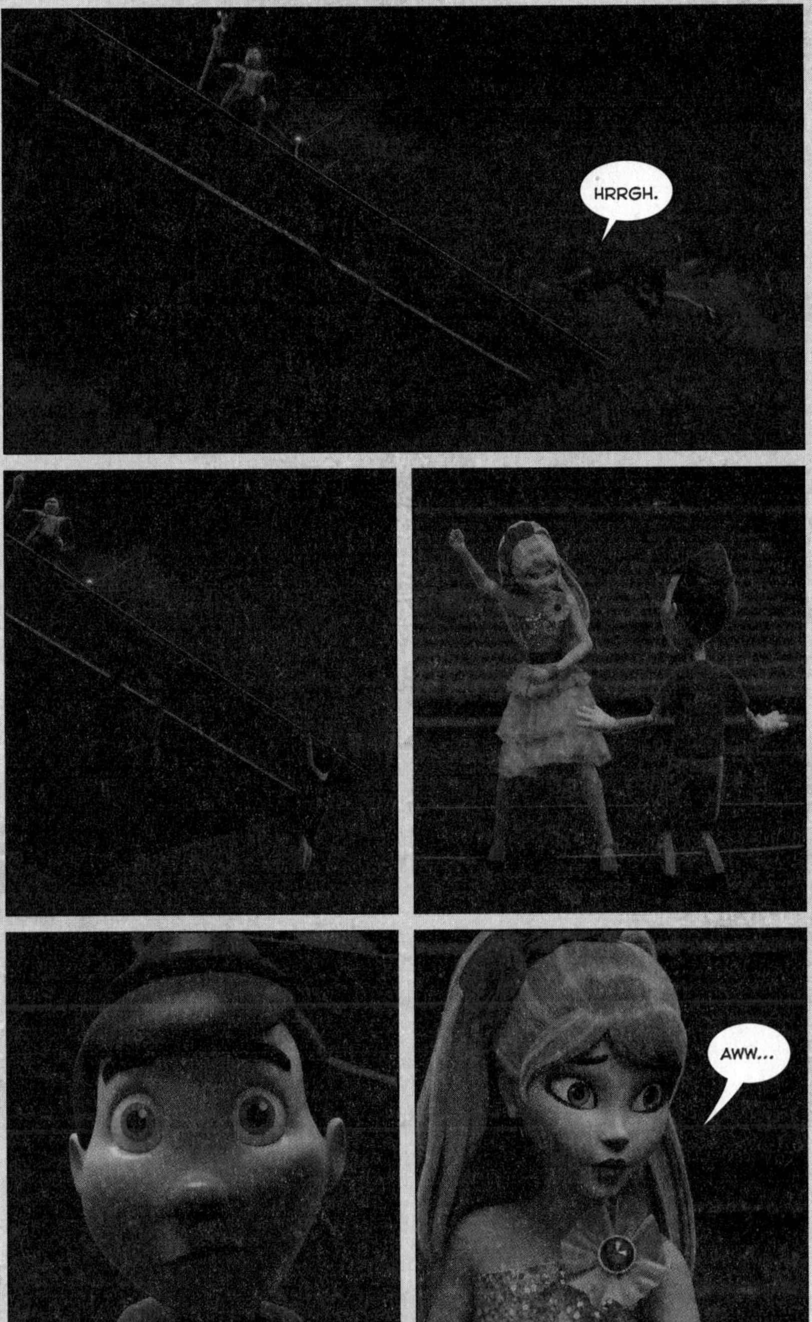
HRRGH.
AWW...

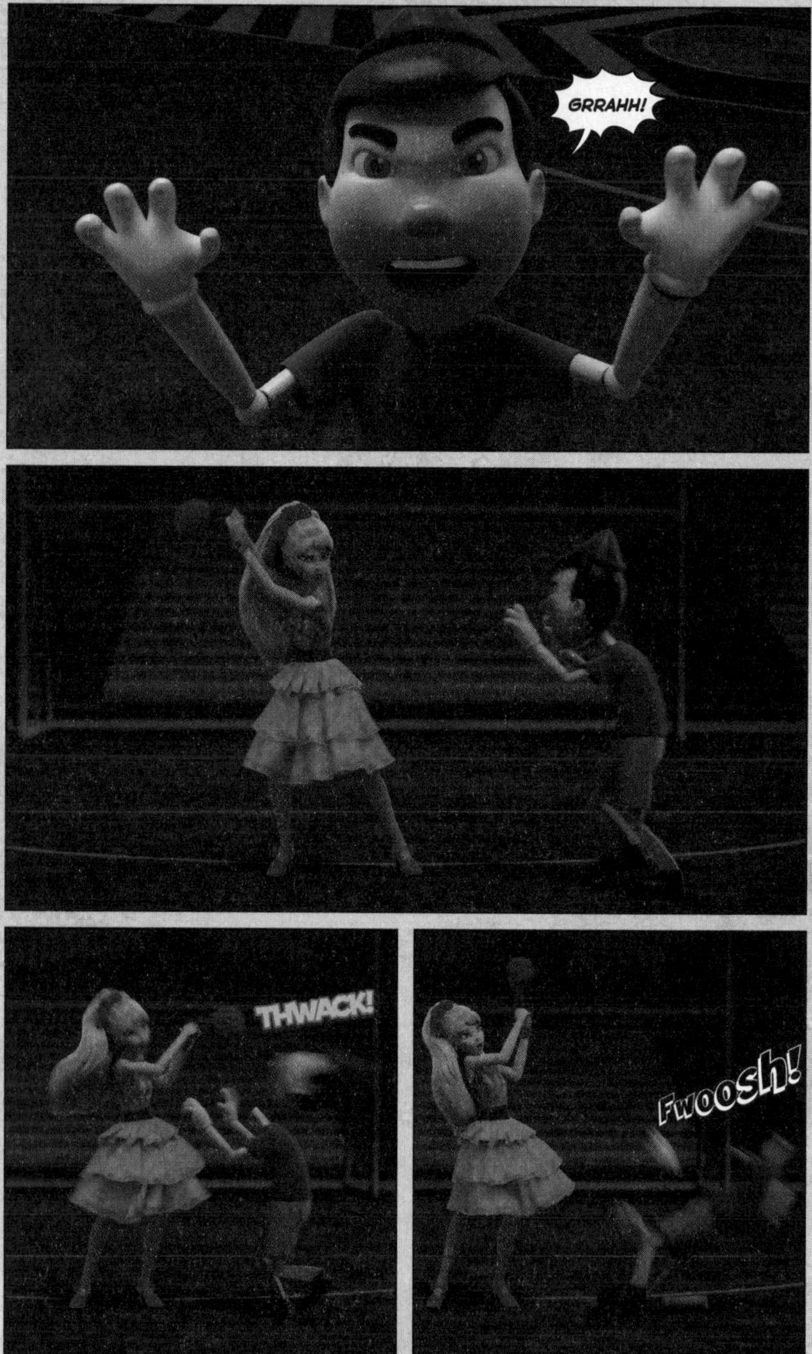
GRRAHH!
THWACK!
Fwoosh!

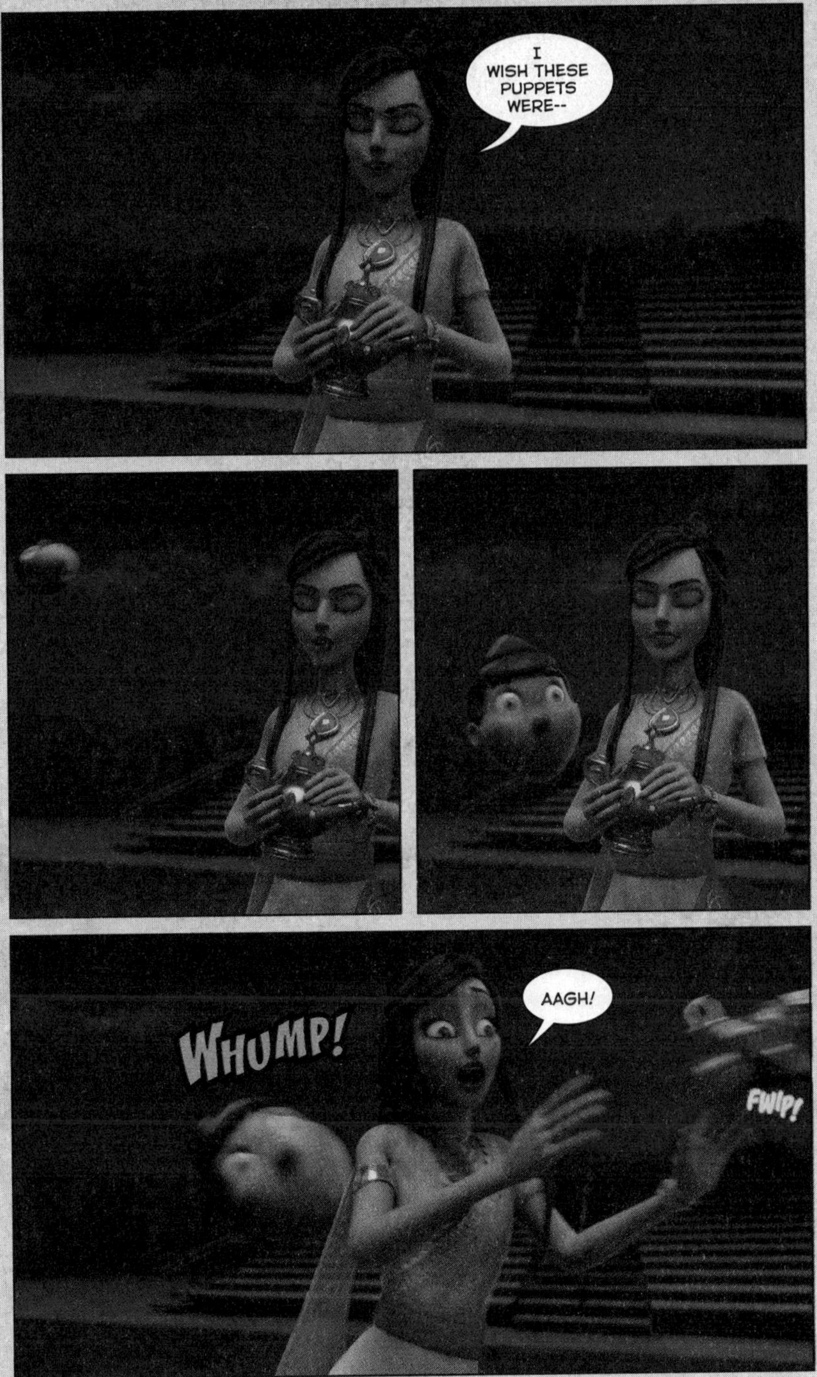
I WISH THESE PUPPETS WERE--
WHUMP!
AAGH!
FWIP!

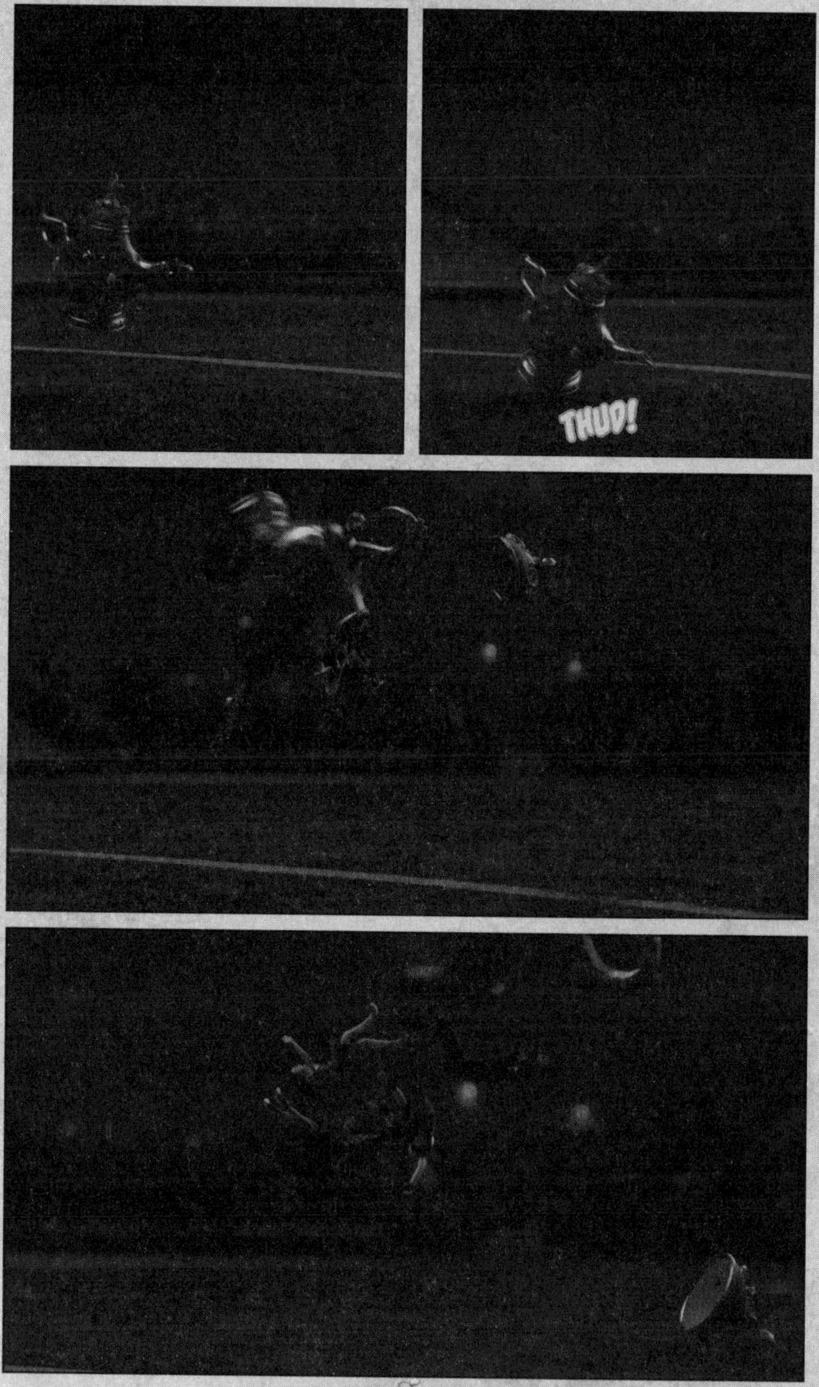
THUD!

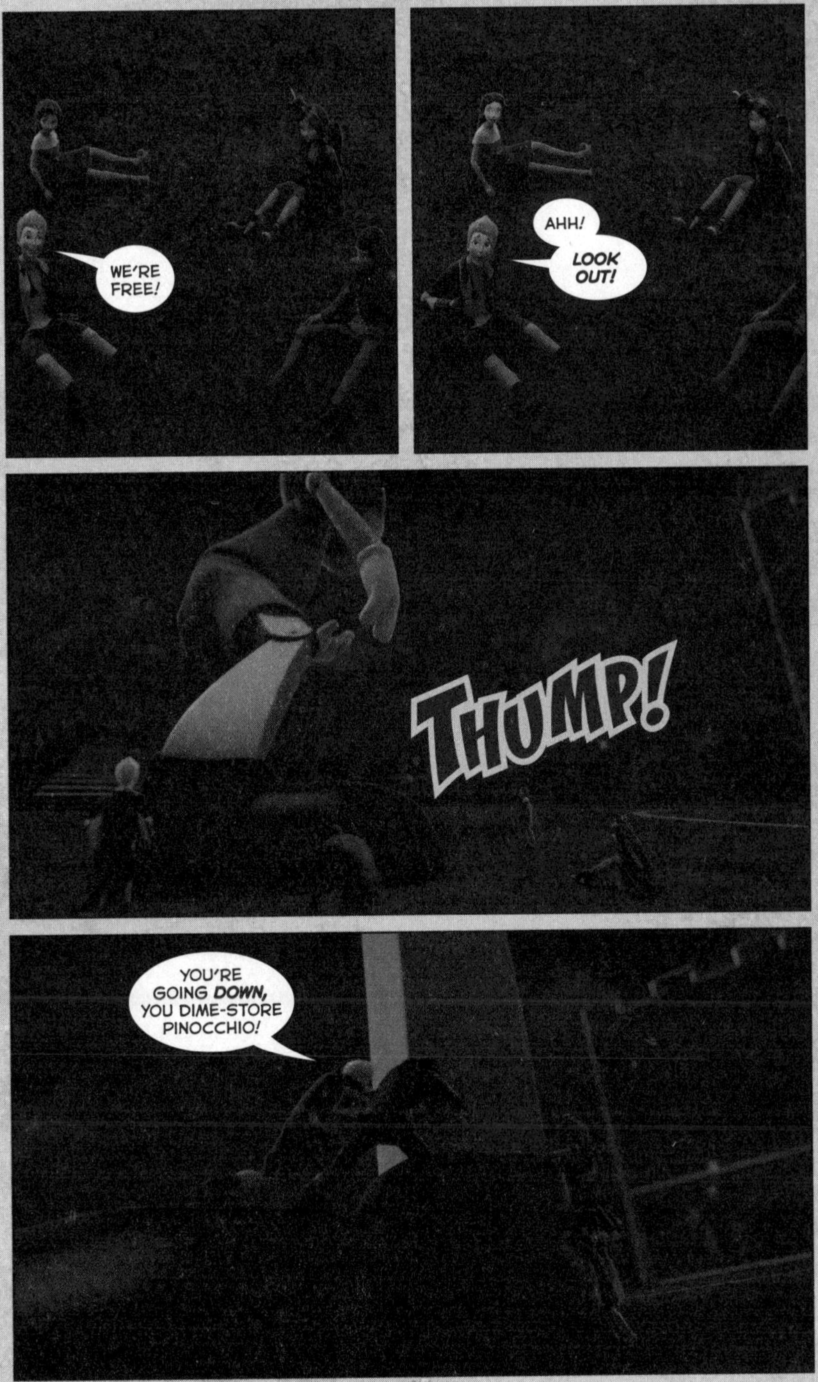
WE'RE FREE!
AHH!
LOOK OUT!
THUMP!
YOU'RE GOING DOWN, YOU DIME-STORE PINOCCHIO!

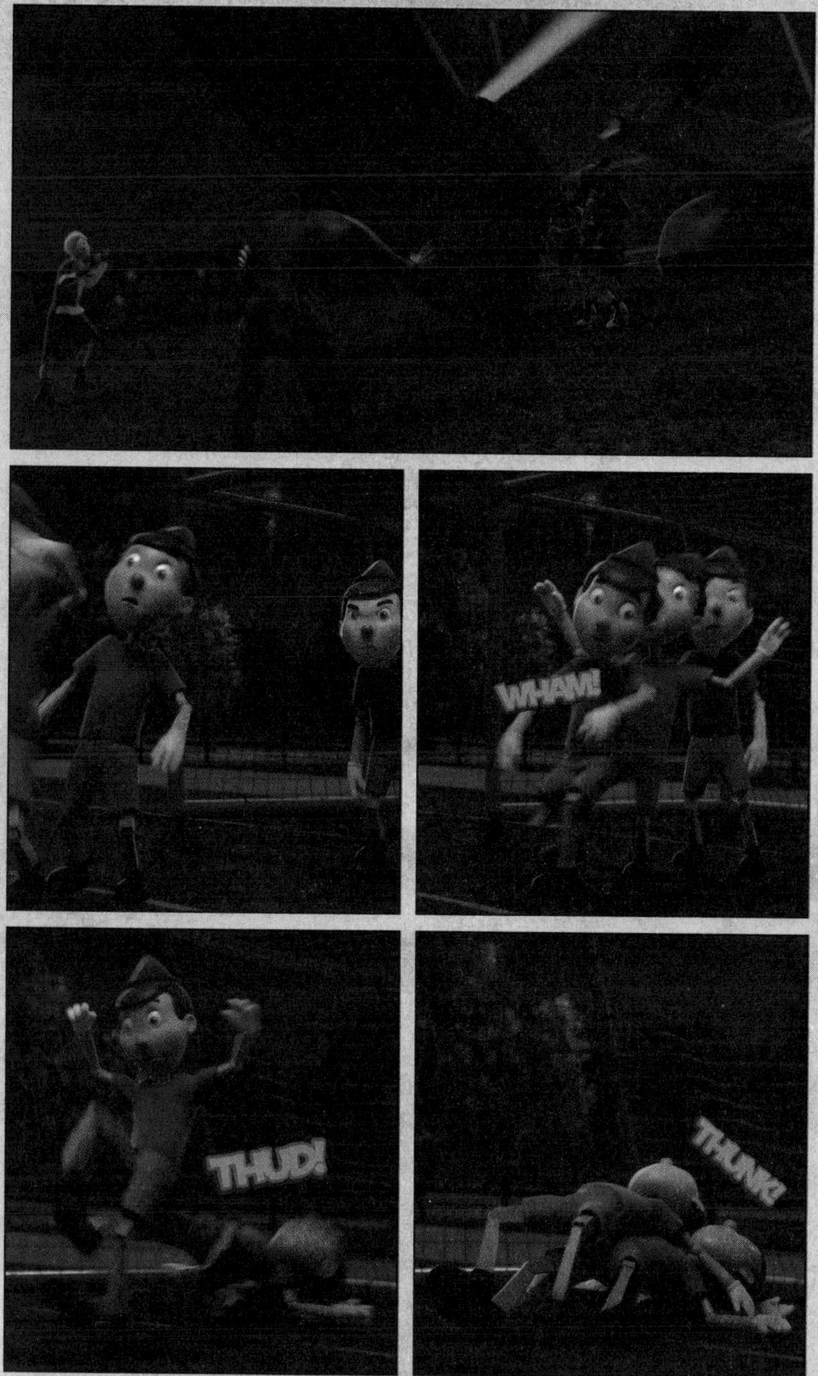
WHAM!
THUD!
THUNK!

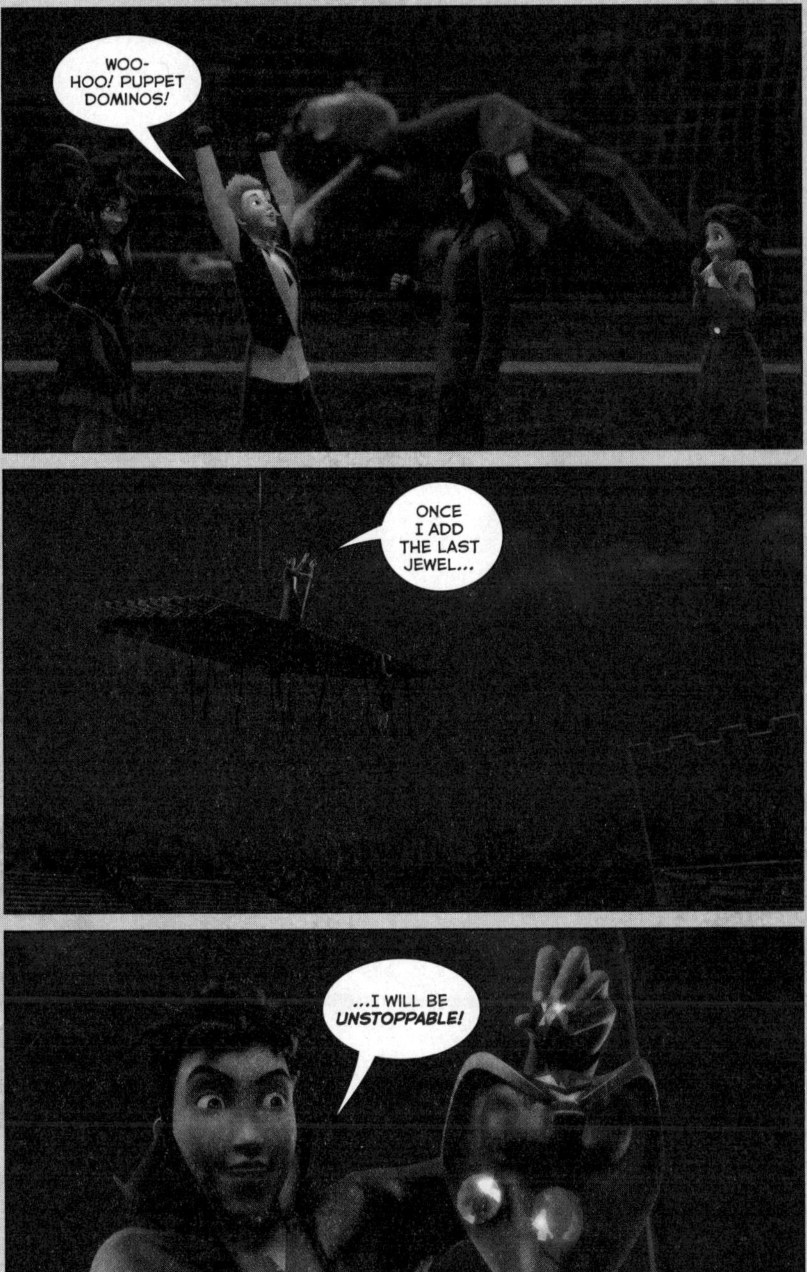
WOO-HOO! PUPPET DOMINOS!
ONCE I ADD THE LAST JEWEL...
...I WILL BE UNSTOPPABLE!

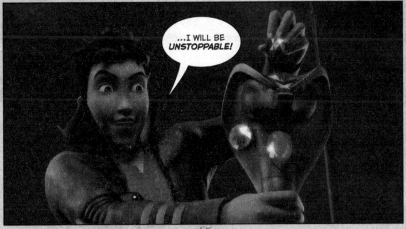

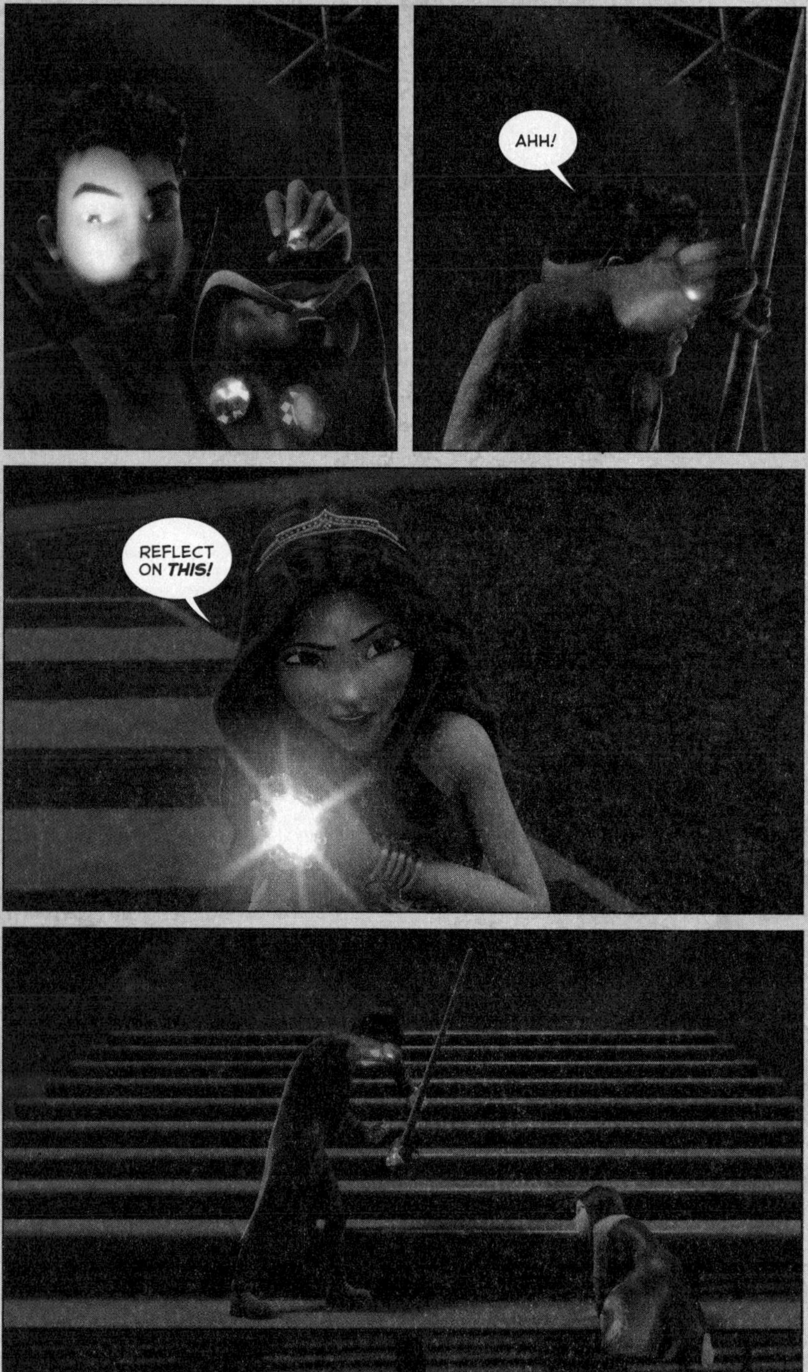
AHH!
REFLECT ON THIS!

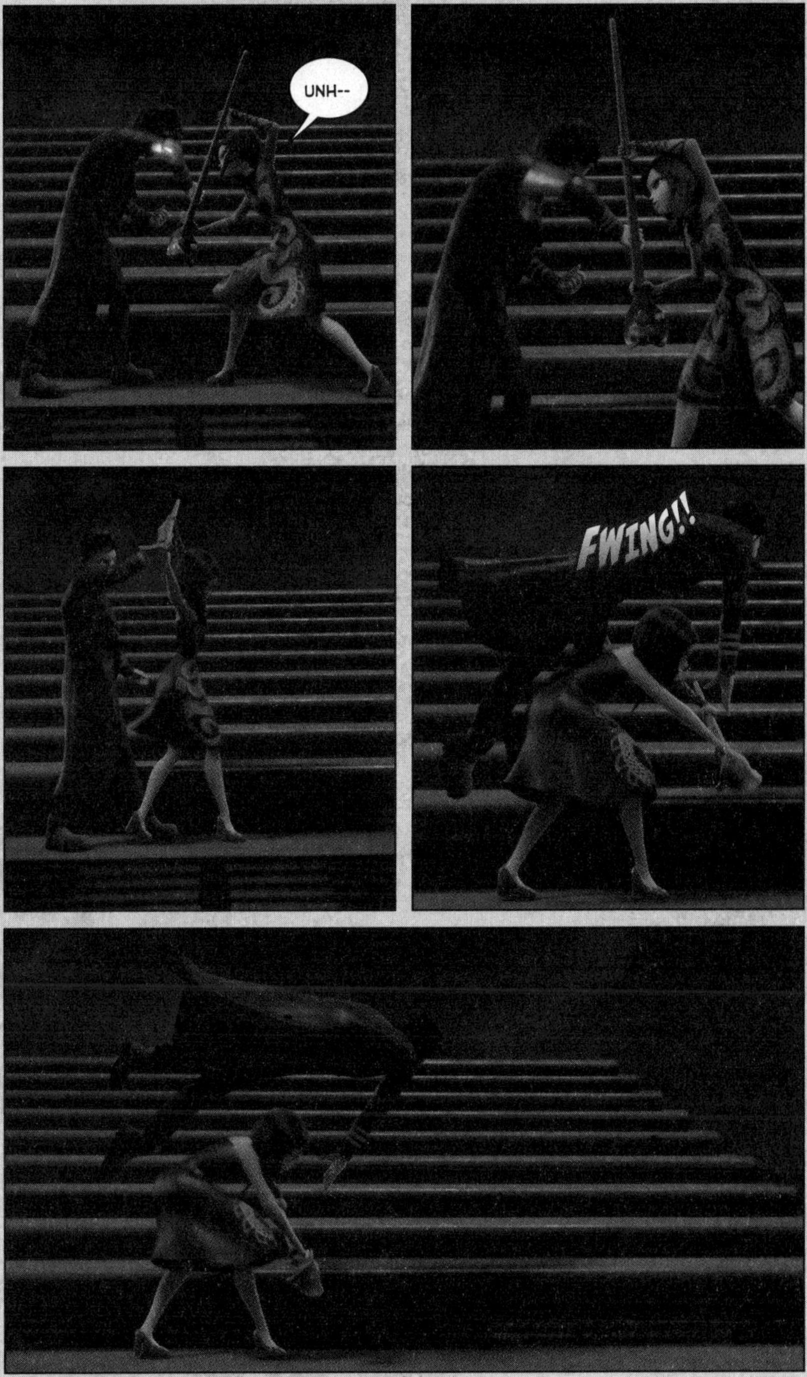
UNH--
FWING!!

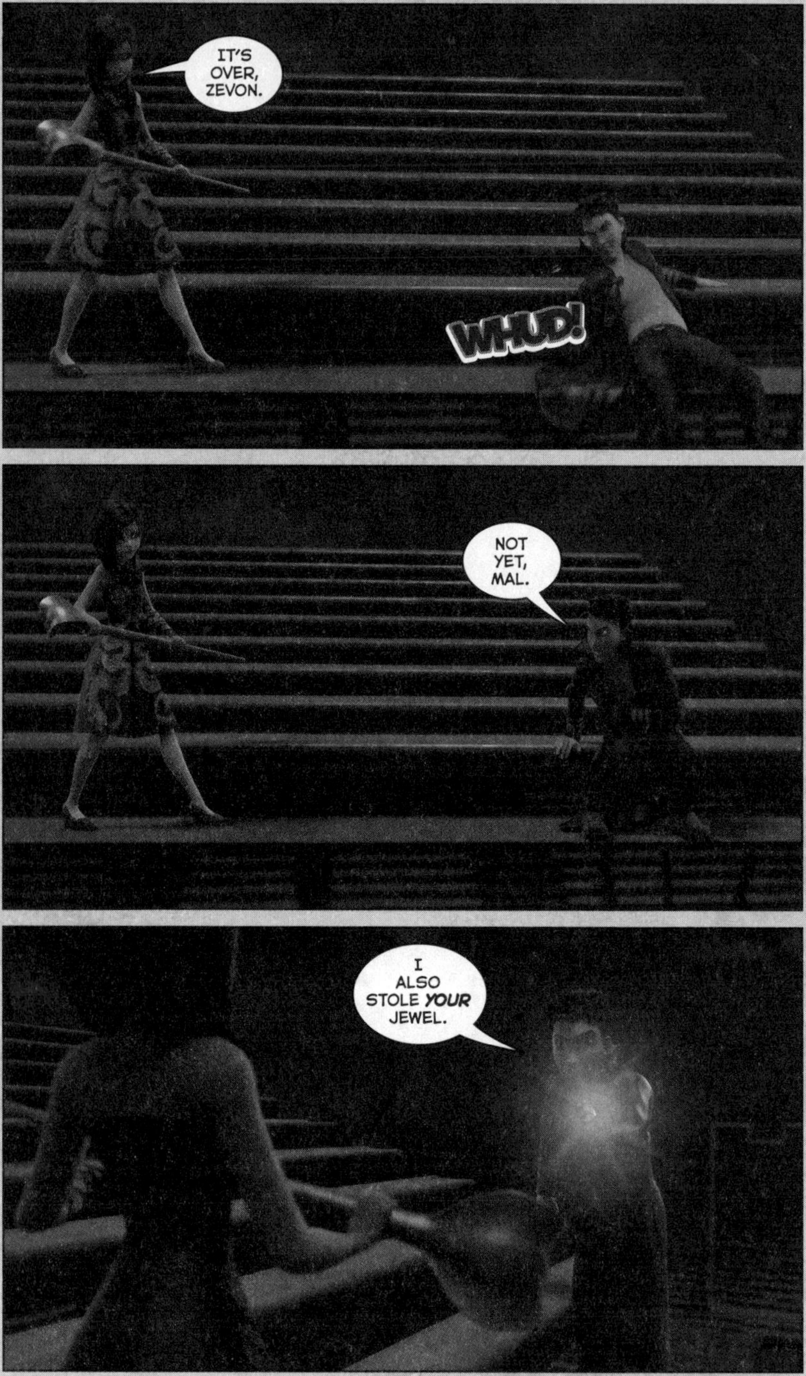
IT'S OVER, ZEVON.
WHUD!
NOT YET, MAL.
I ALSO STOLE *YOUR* JEWEL.

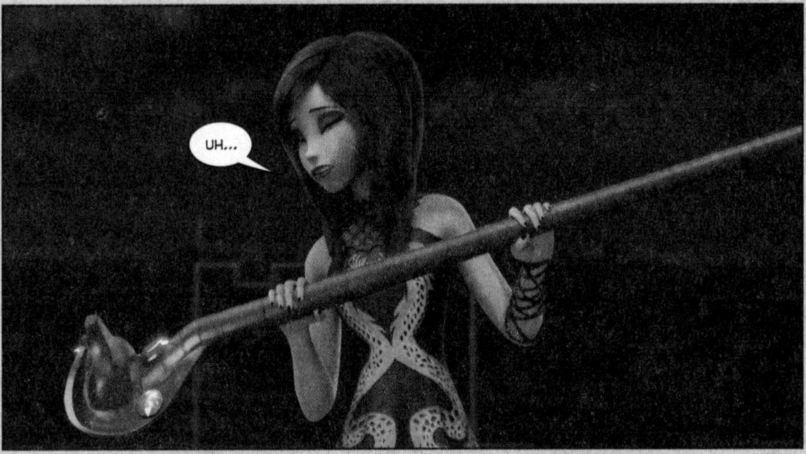
UH...

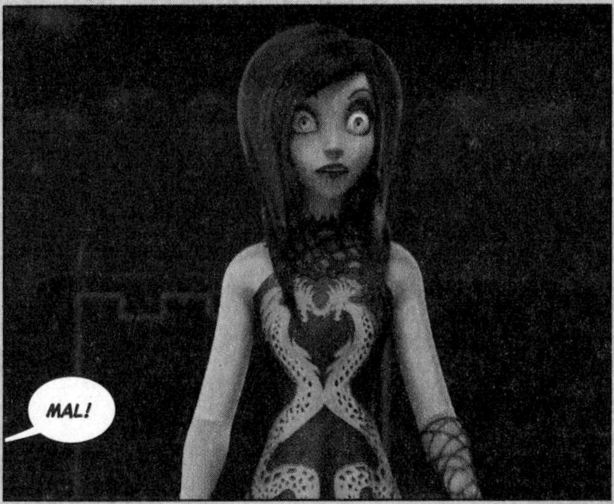
MAL!

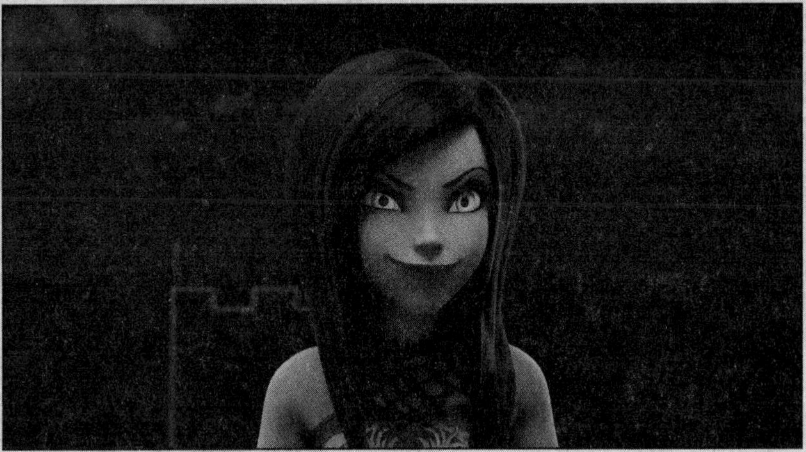

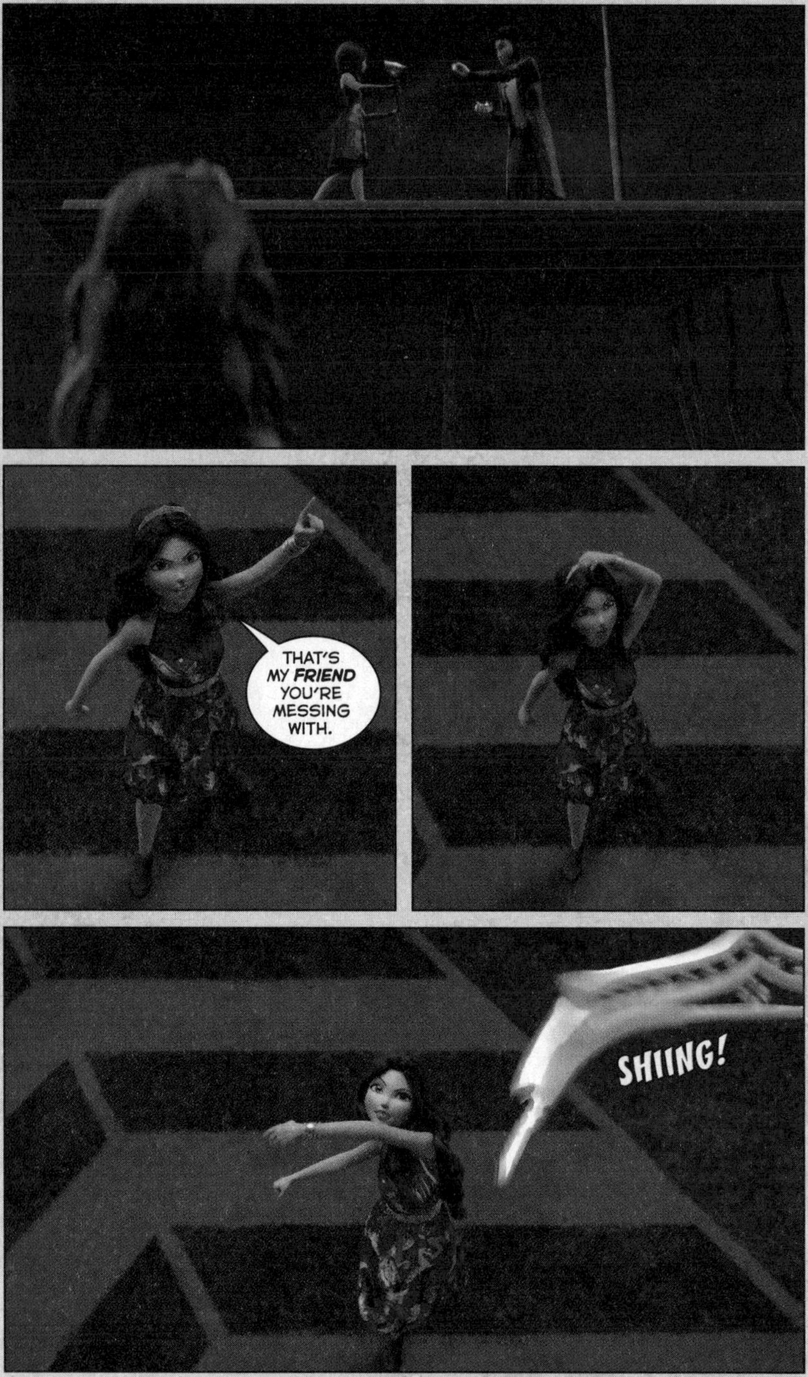
THAT'S MY *FRIEND* YOU'RE MESSING WITH.
SHIING!

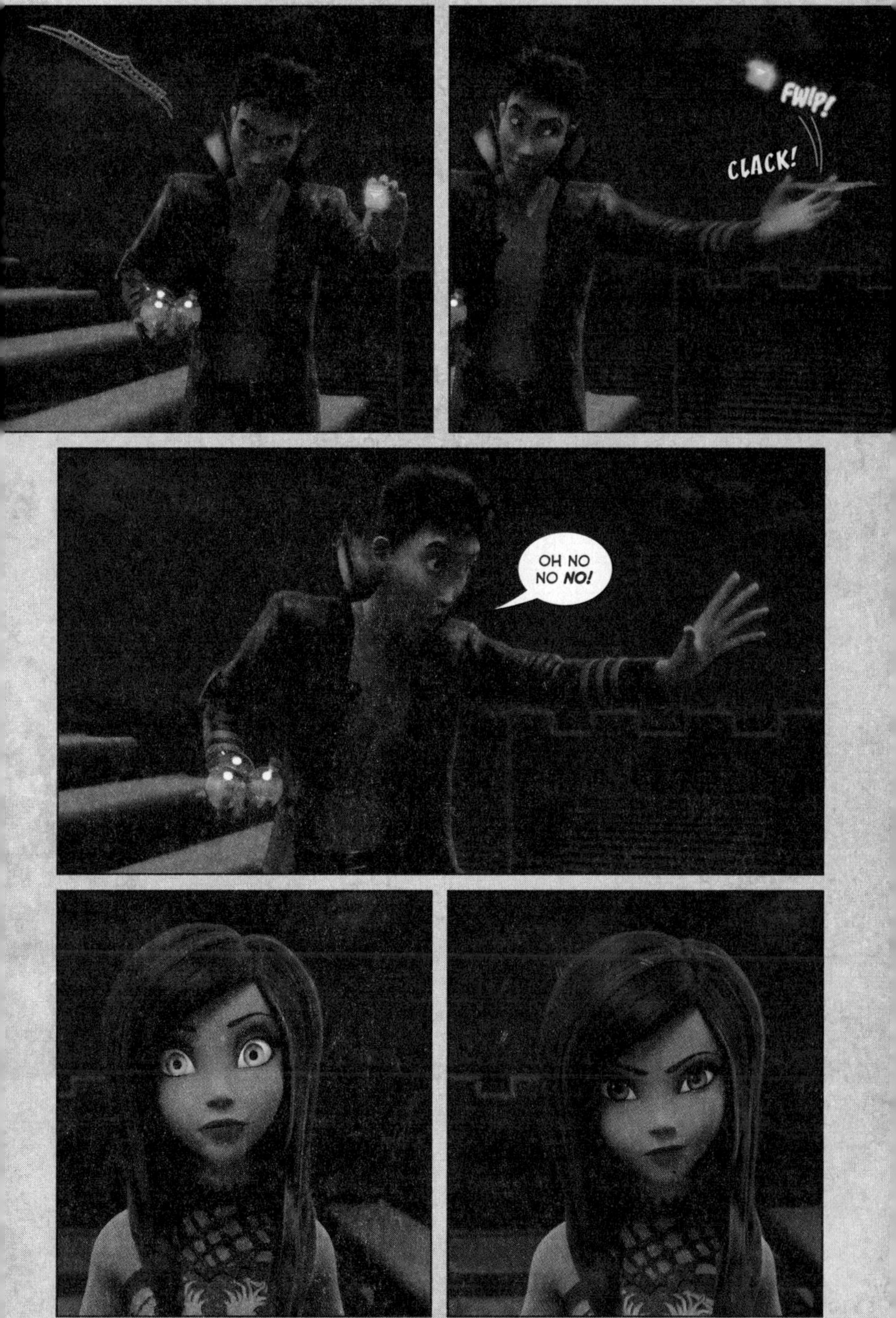
FWIP!
CLACK!
OH NO NO **NO!**

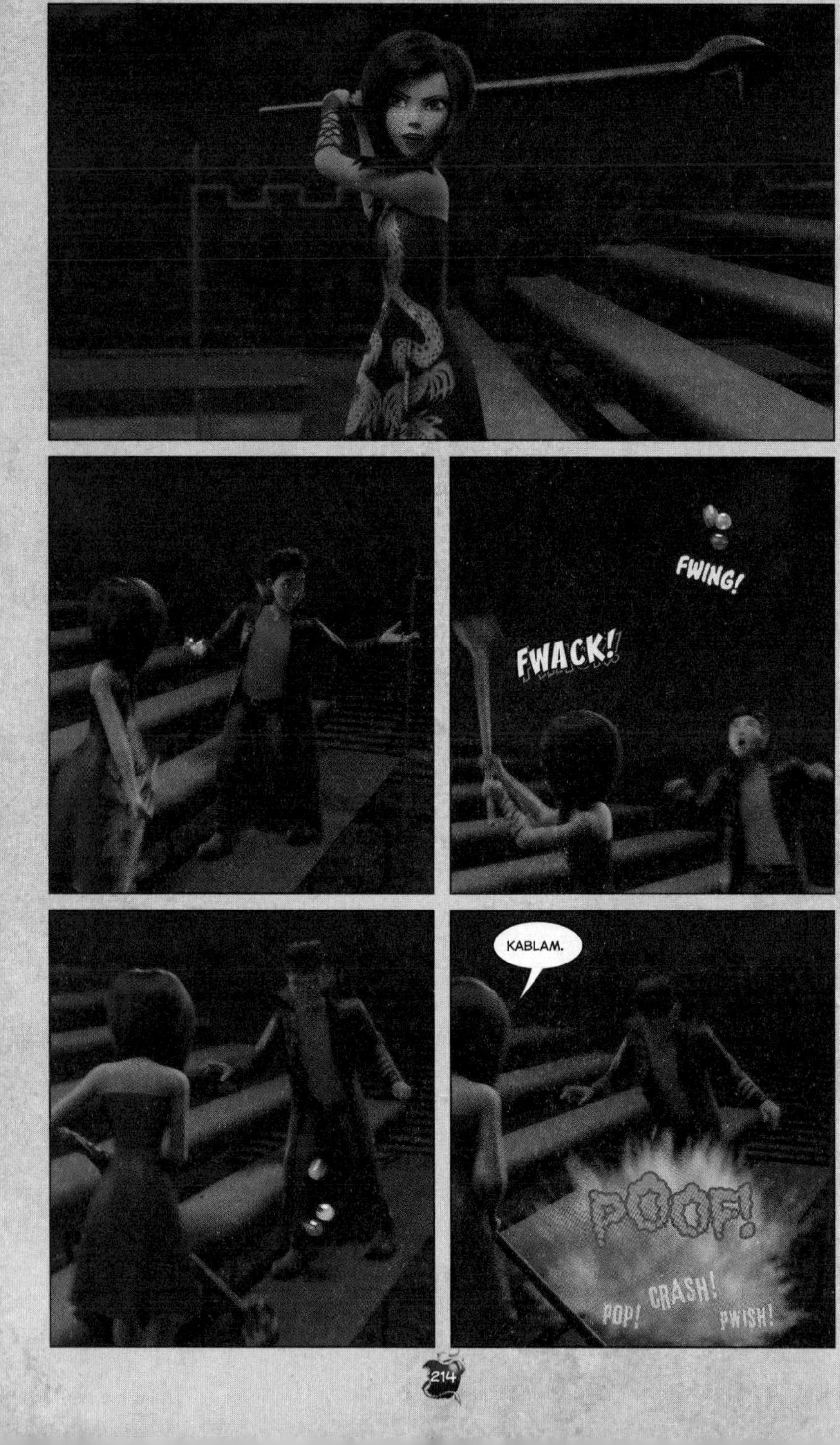
FWING!
FWACK!
KABLAM.
POOF!
POP!
CRASH!
PWISH!

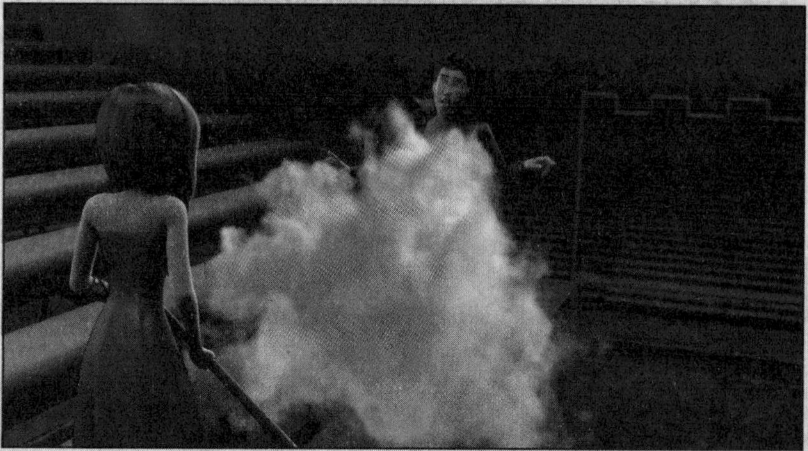

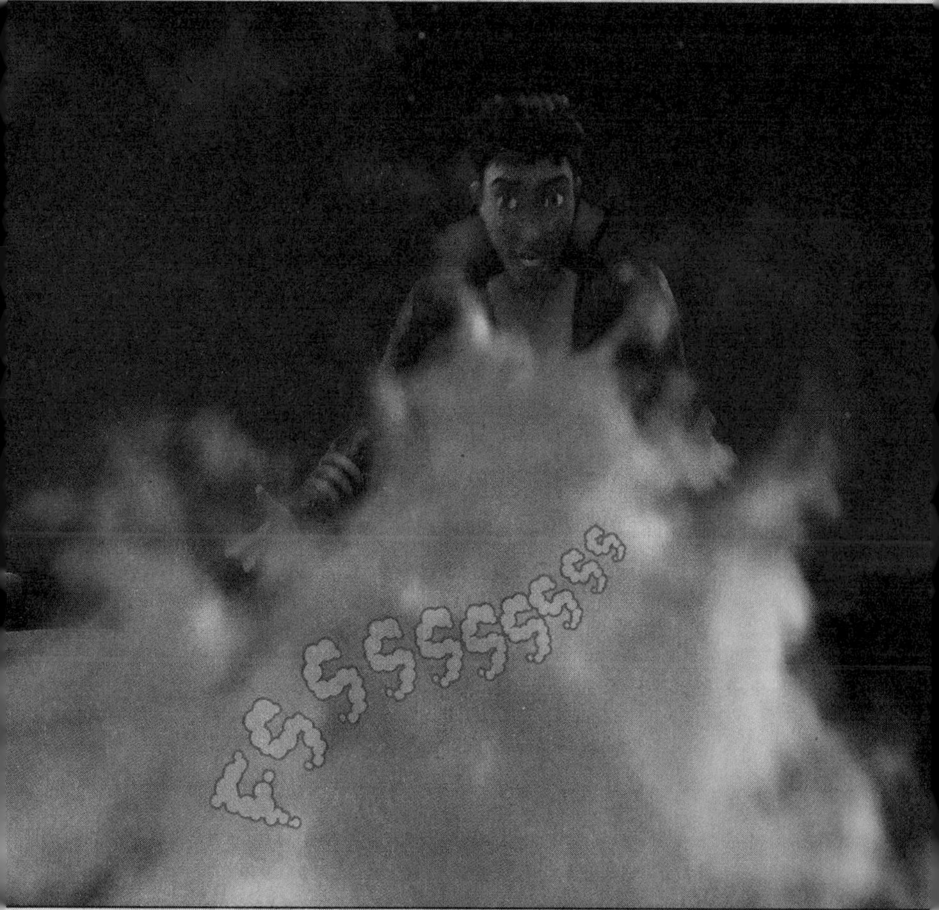
SSSSSSSSS

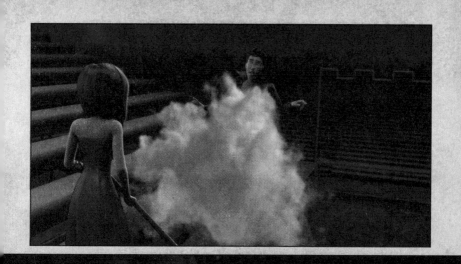

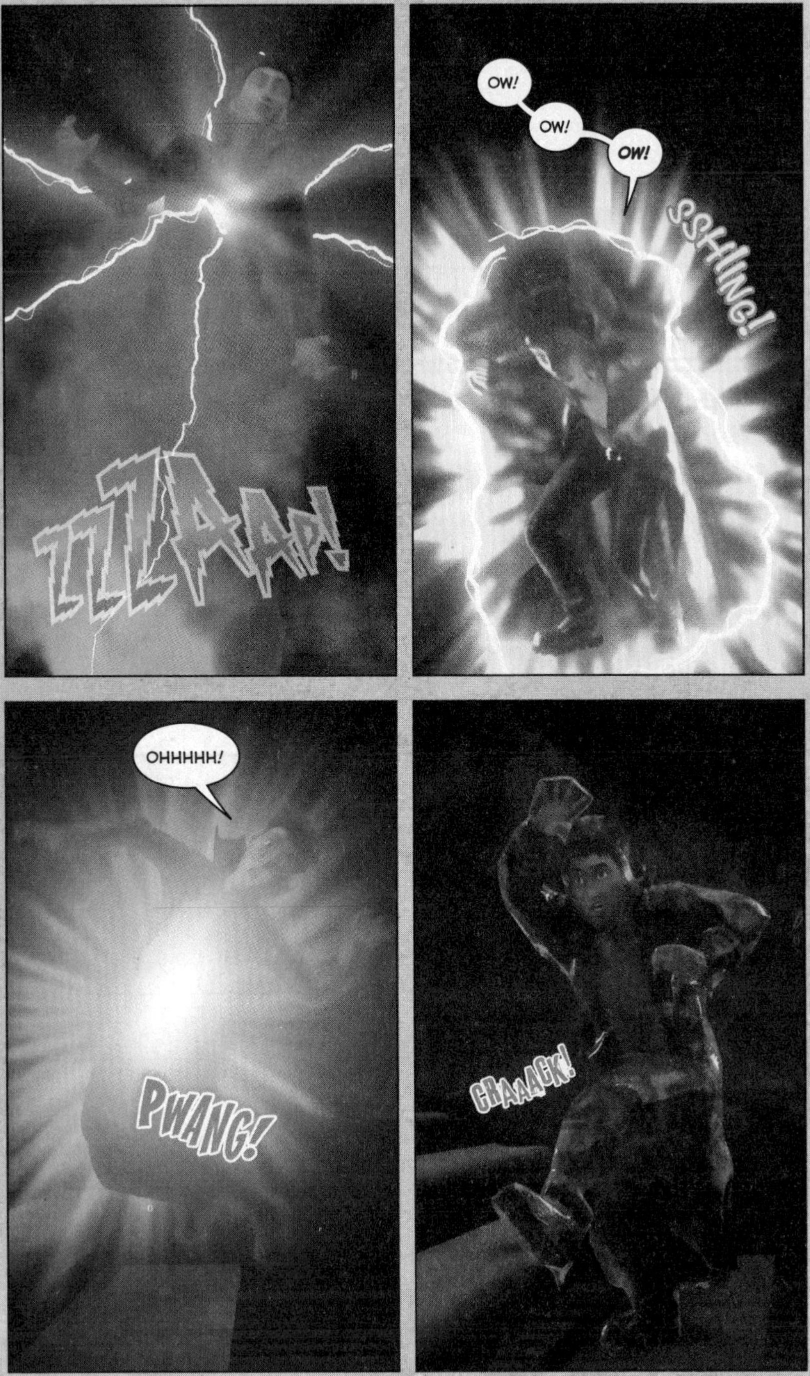
ZZZAAP!
OW!
OW!
OW!
SSHIING!
OHHHHH!
PWANG!
CRAAACK!

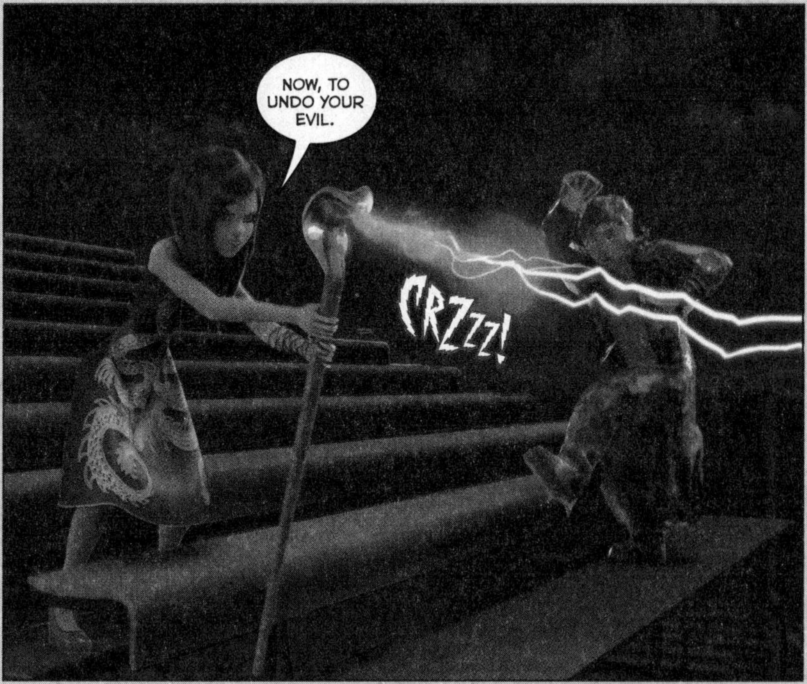
NOW, TO UNDO YOUR EVIL.
CRZzzz!

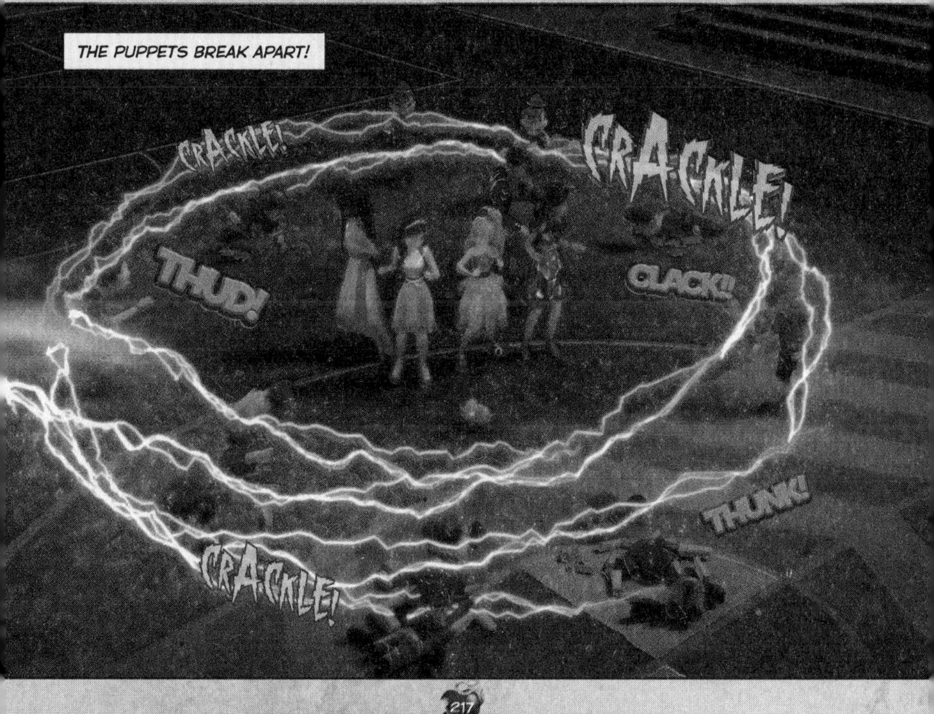
THE PUPPETS BREAK APART!
CRACKLE!
CRACKLE!
THUD!
CLACK!!
THUNK!
CRACKLE!

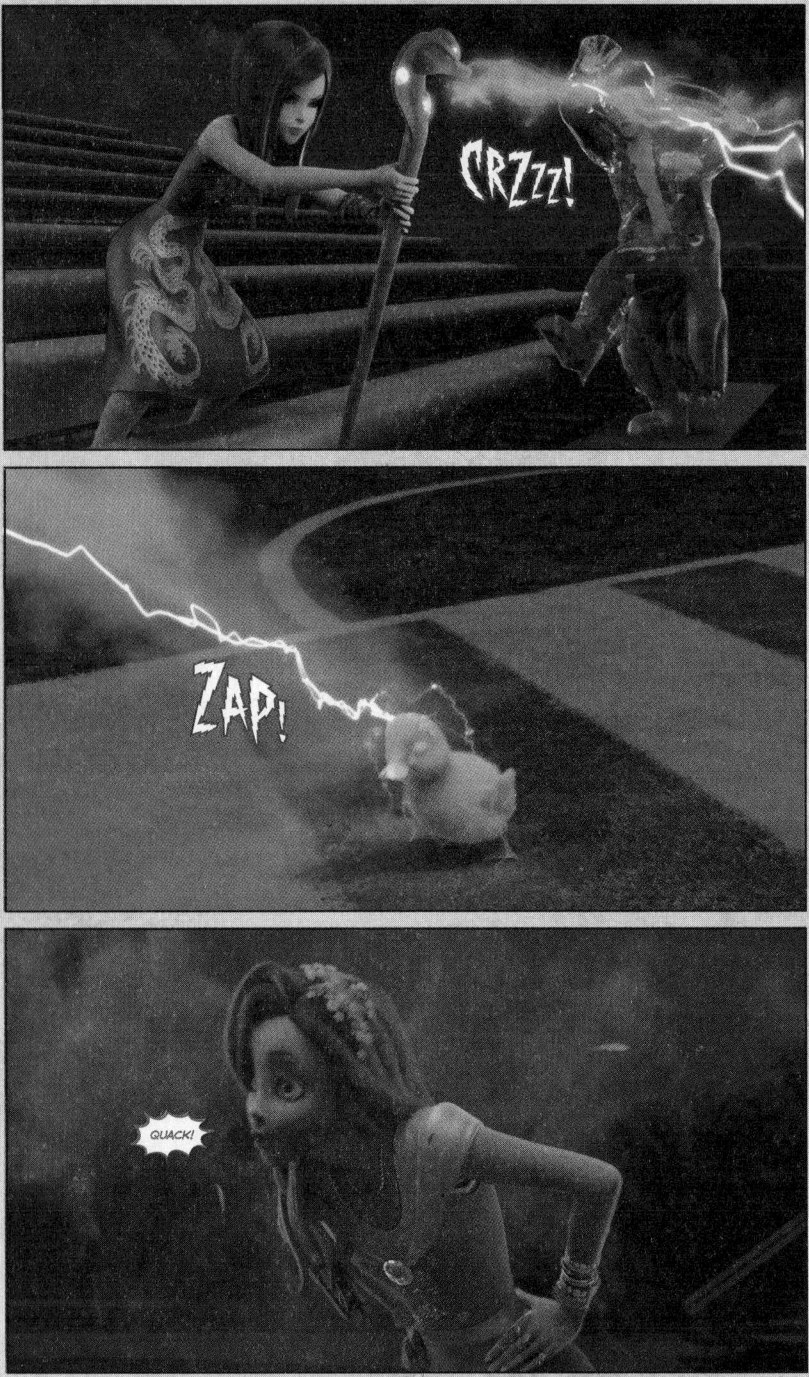
CRZzz!
ZAP!
QUACK!

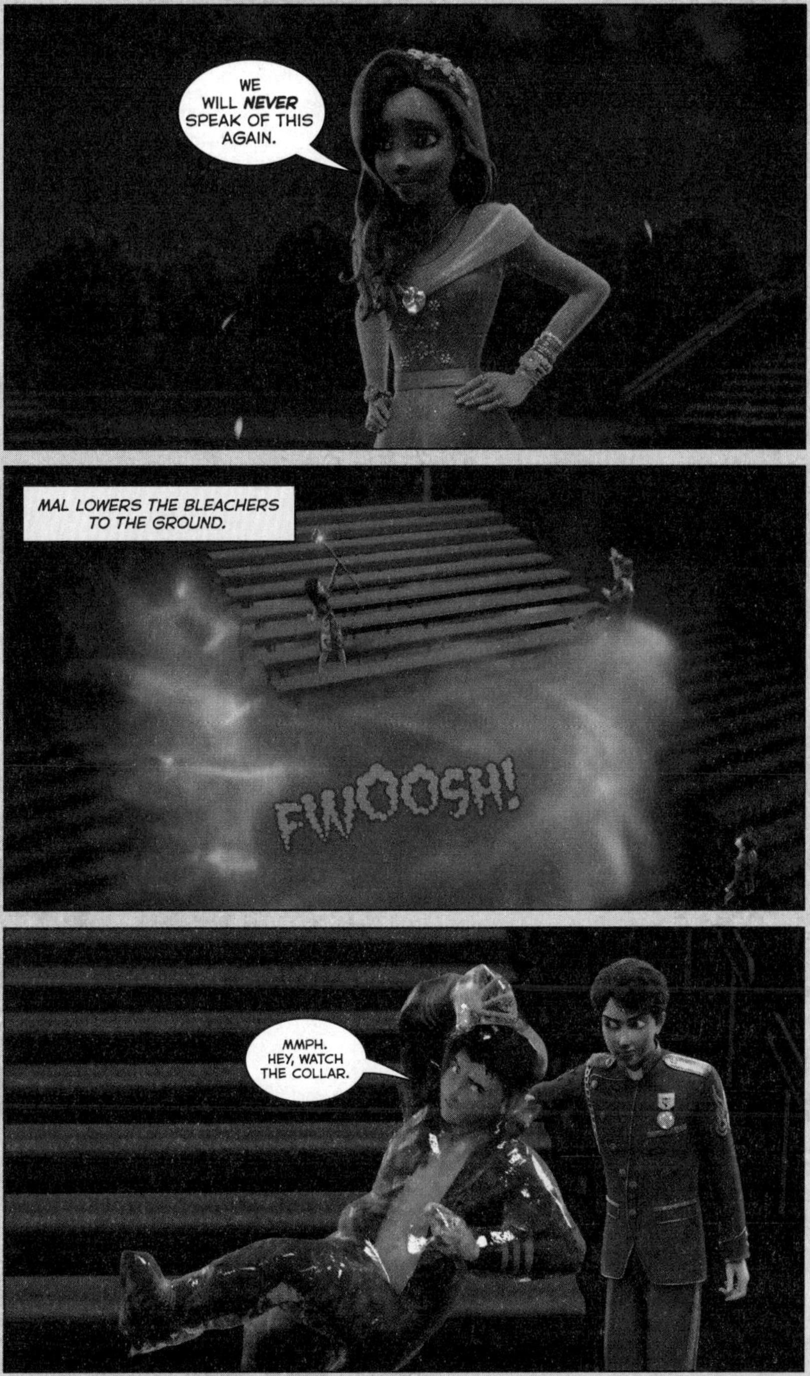
WE WILL NEVER SPEAK OF THIS AGAIN.
MAL LOWERS THE BLEACHERS TO THE GROUND.
FWOOSH!
MMPH. HEY, WATCH THE COLLAR.

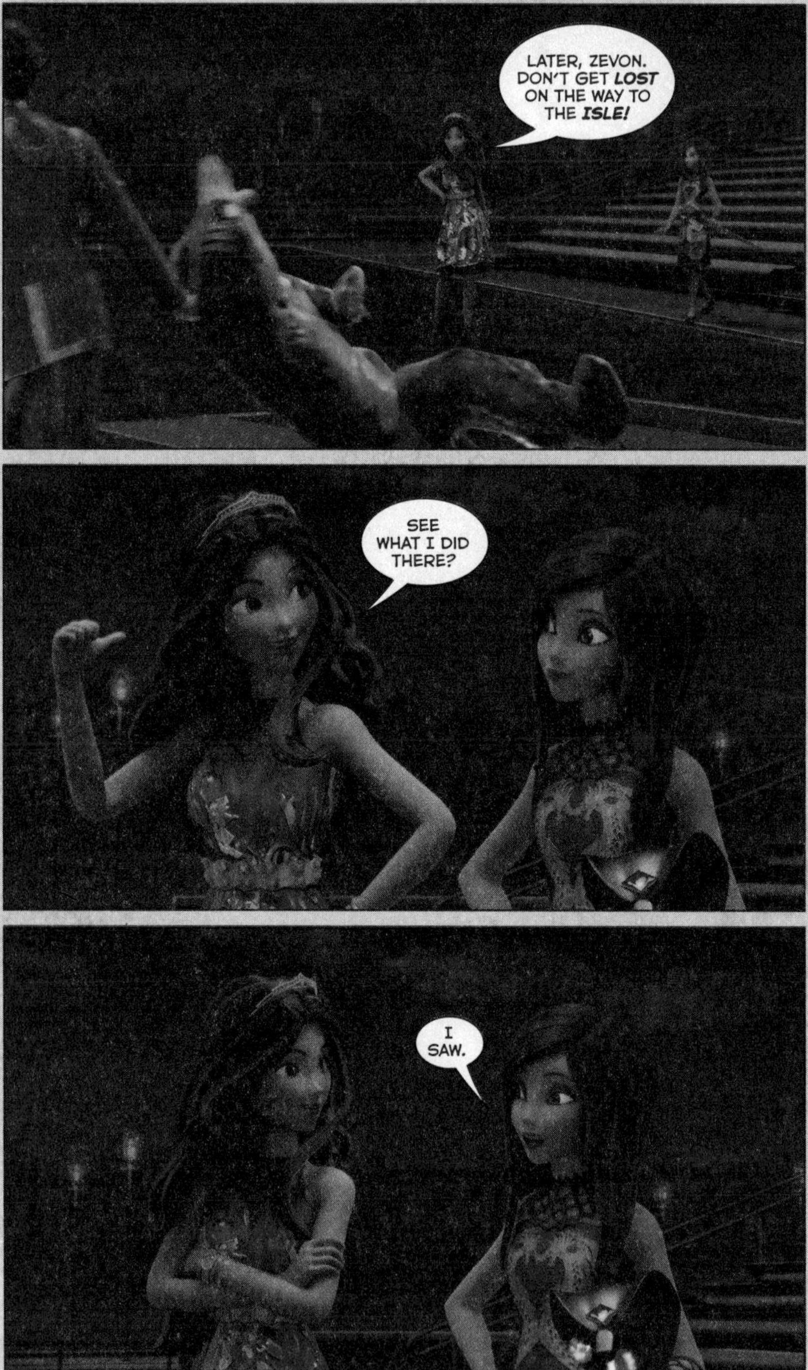
LATER, ZEVON. DON'T GET **LOST** ON THE WAY TO THE ***ISLE!***
SEE WHAT I DID THERE?
I SAW.

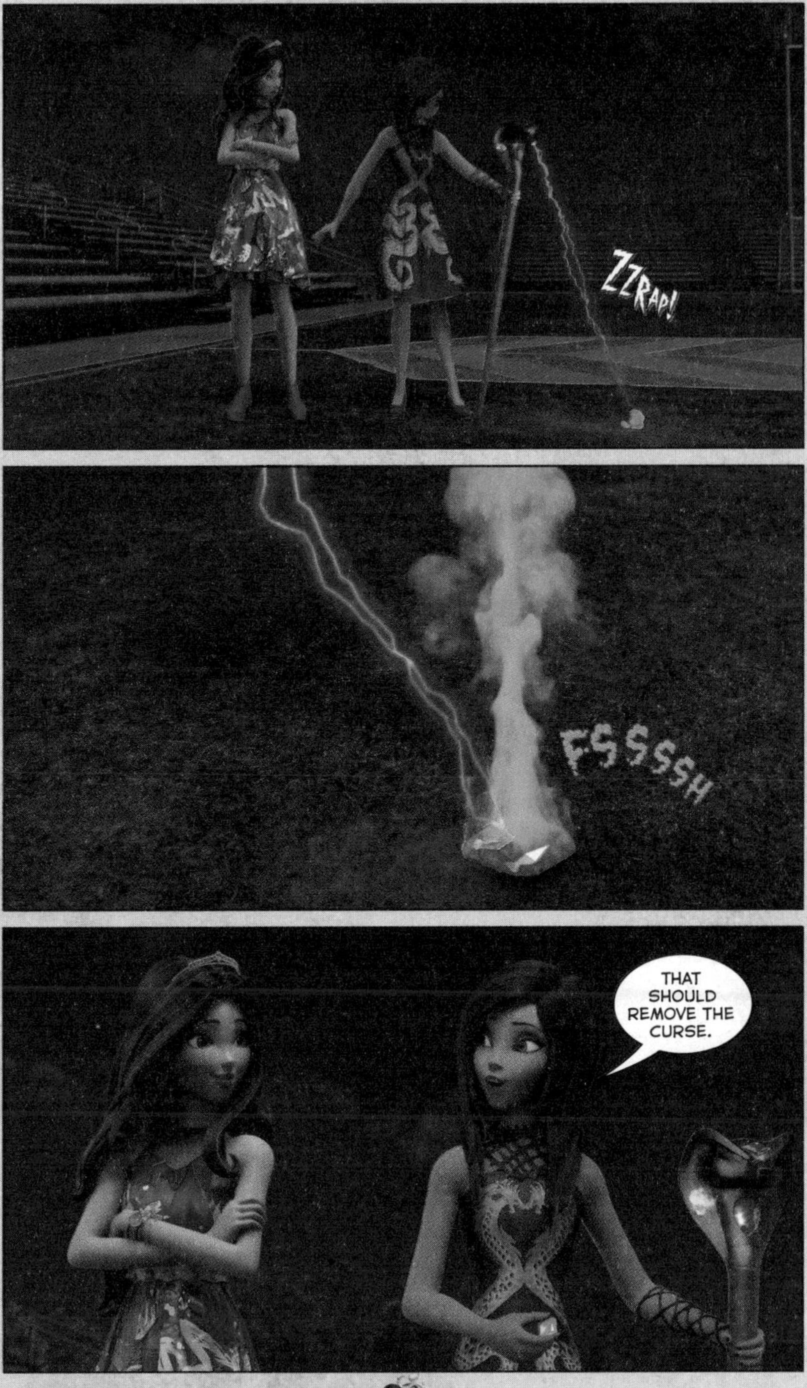
ZZRAP!
FSSSSH
THAT SHOULD REMOVE THE CURSE.

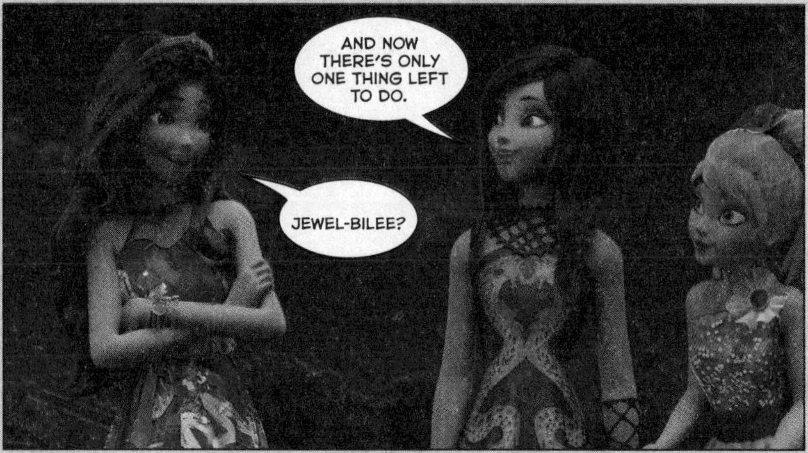
AND NOW THERE'S ONLY ONE THING LEFT TO DO.
JEWEL-BILEE?

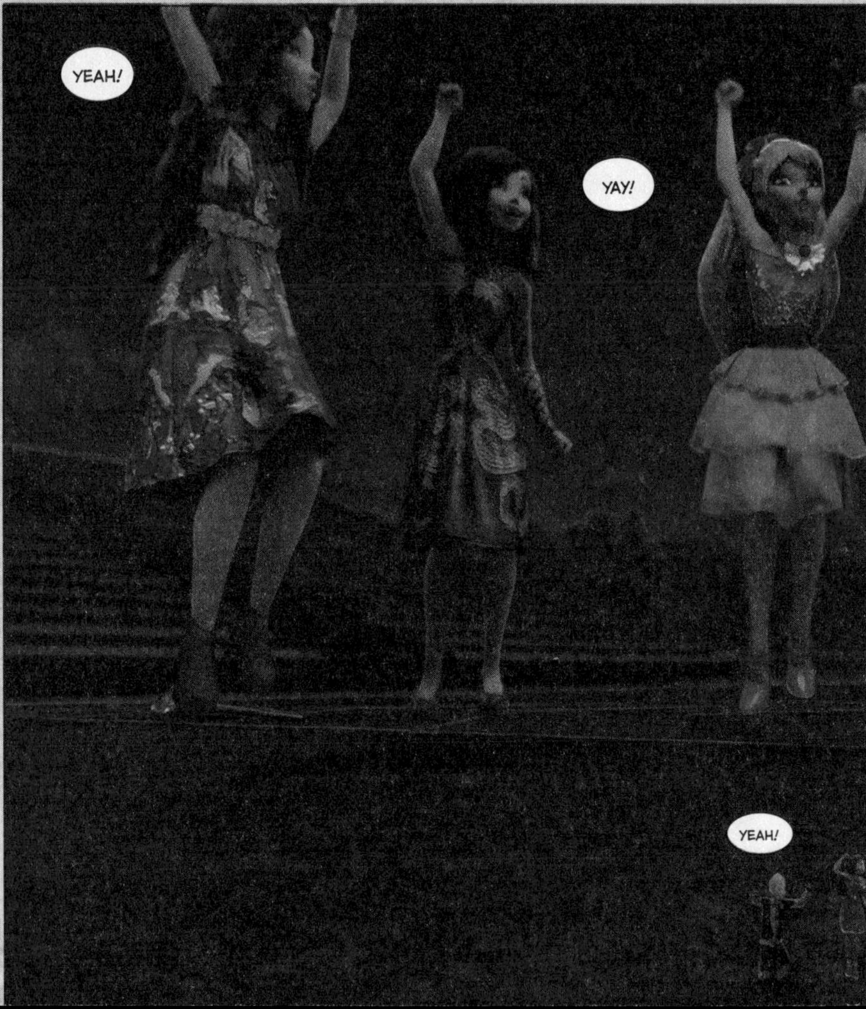
YEAH!
YAY!
YEAH!

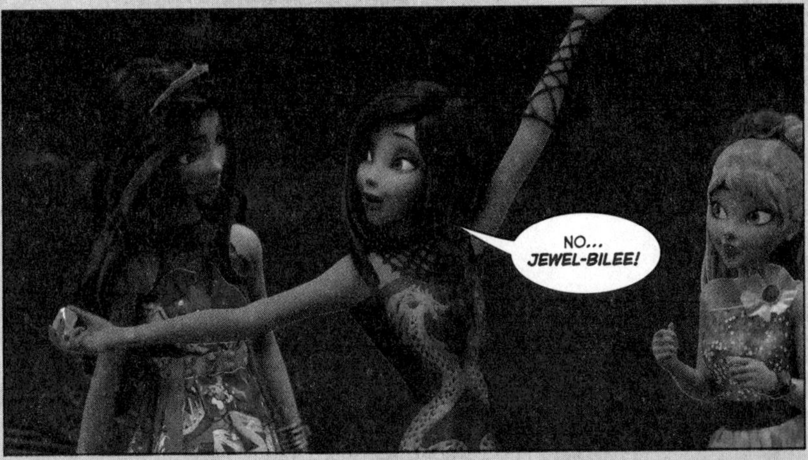
NO...
JEWEL-BILEE!

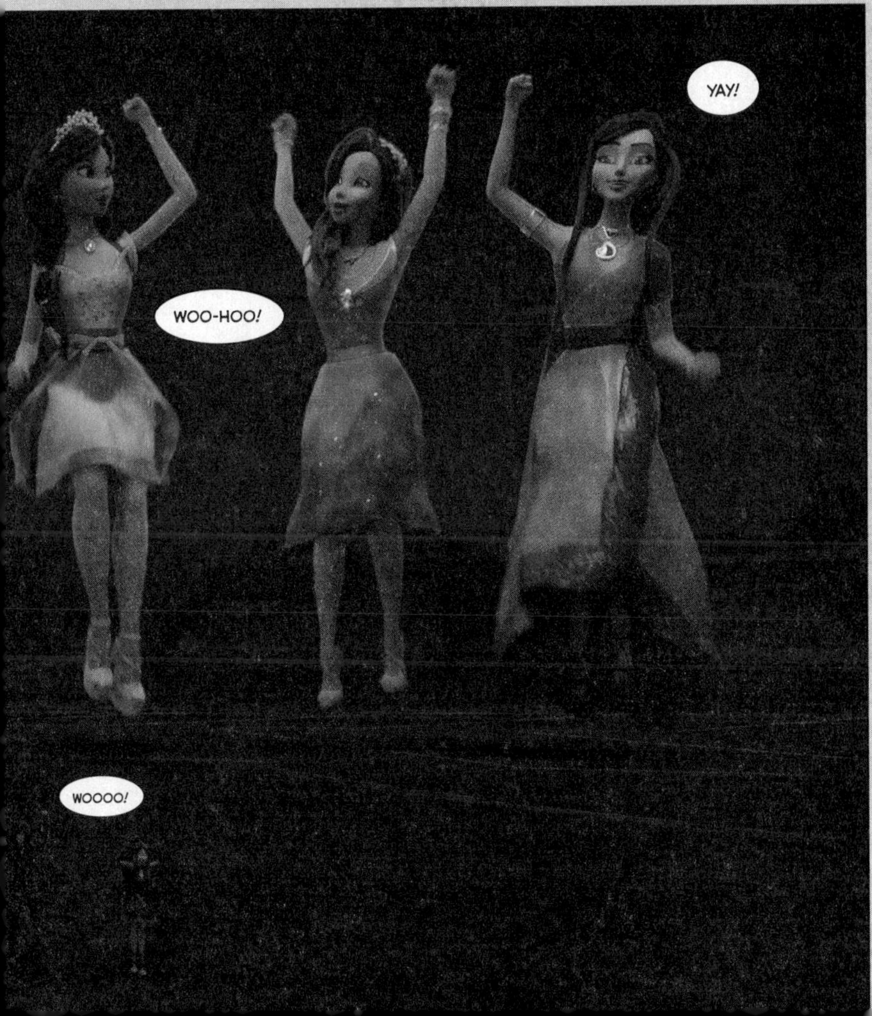
YAY!
WOO-HOO!
WOOOO!

Chapter 33: Celebration

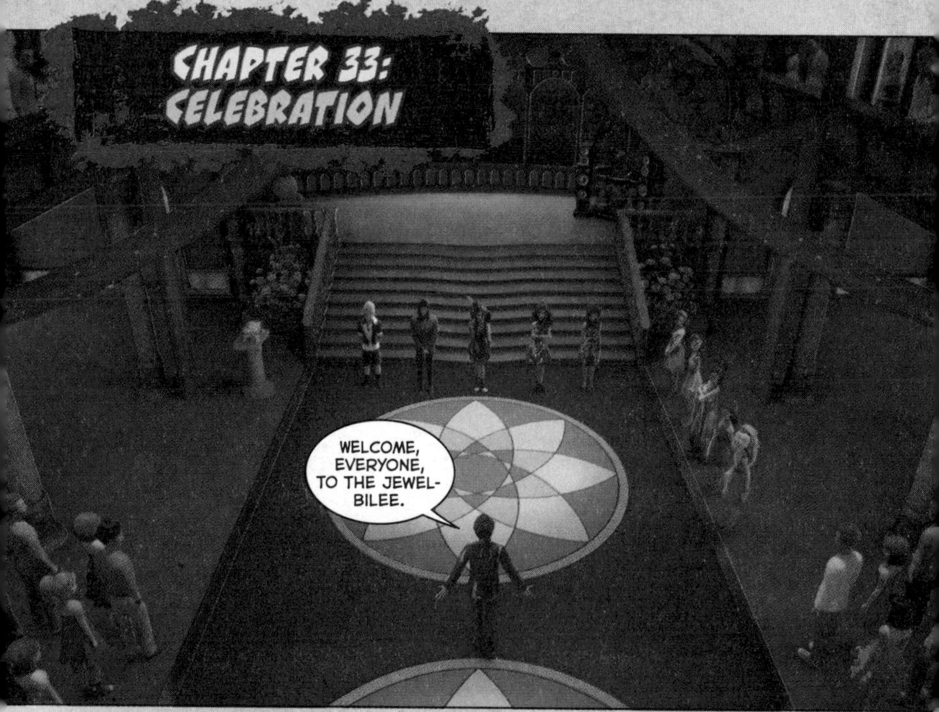
WELCOME, EVERYONE, TO THE JEWEL-BILEE.

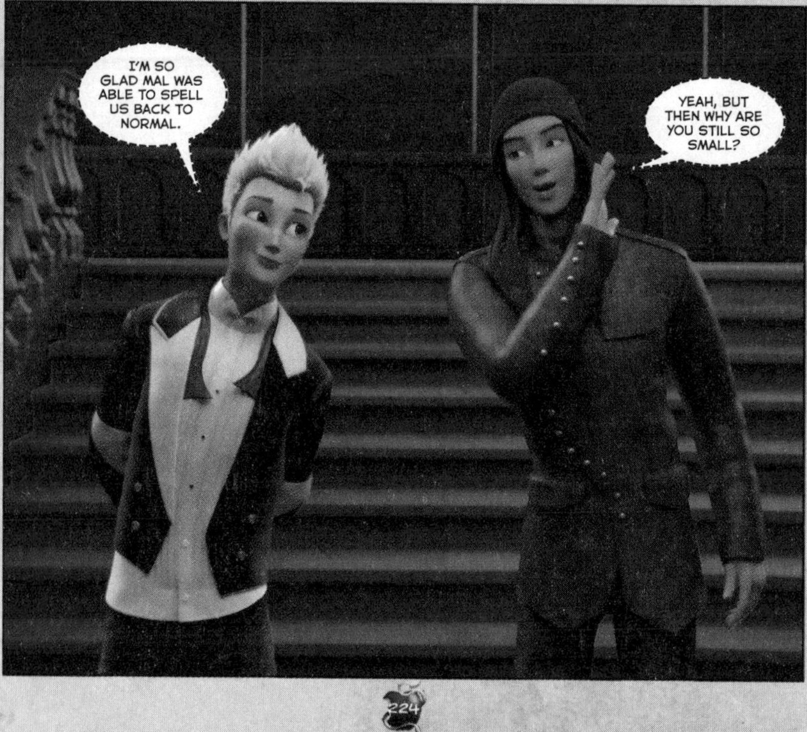
I'M SO GLAD MAL WAS ABLE TO SPELL US BACK TO NORMAL.
YEAH, BUT THEN WHY ARE YOU STILL SO SMALL?

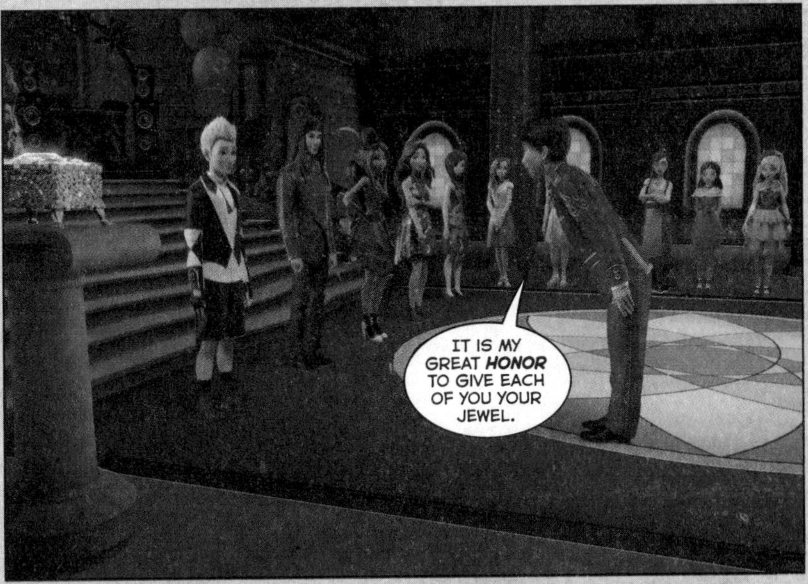
IT IS MY GREAT **HONOR** TO GIVE EACH OF YOU YOUR JEWEL.

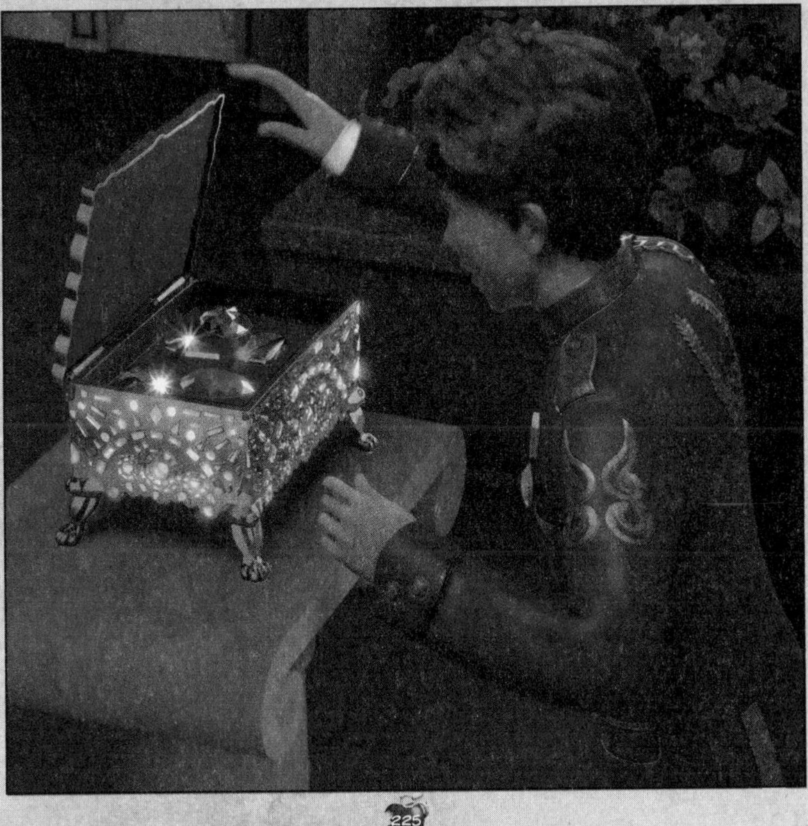

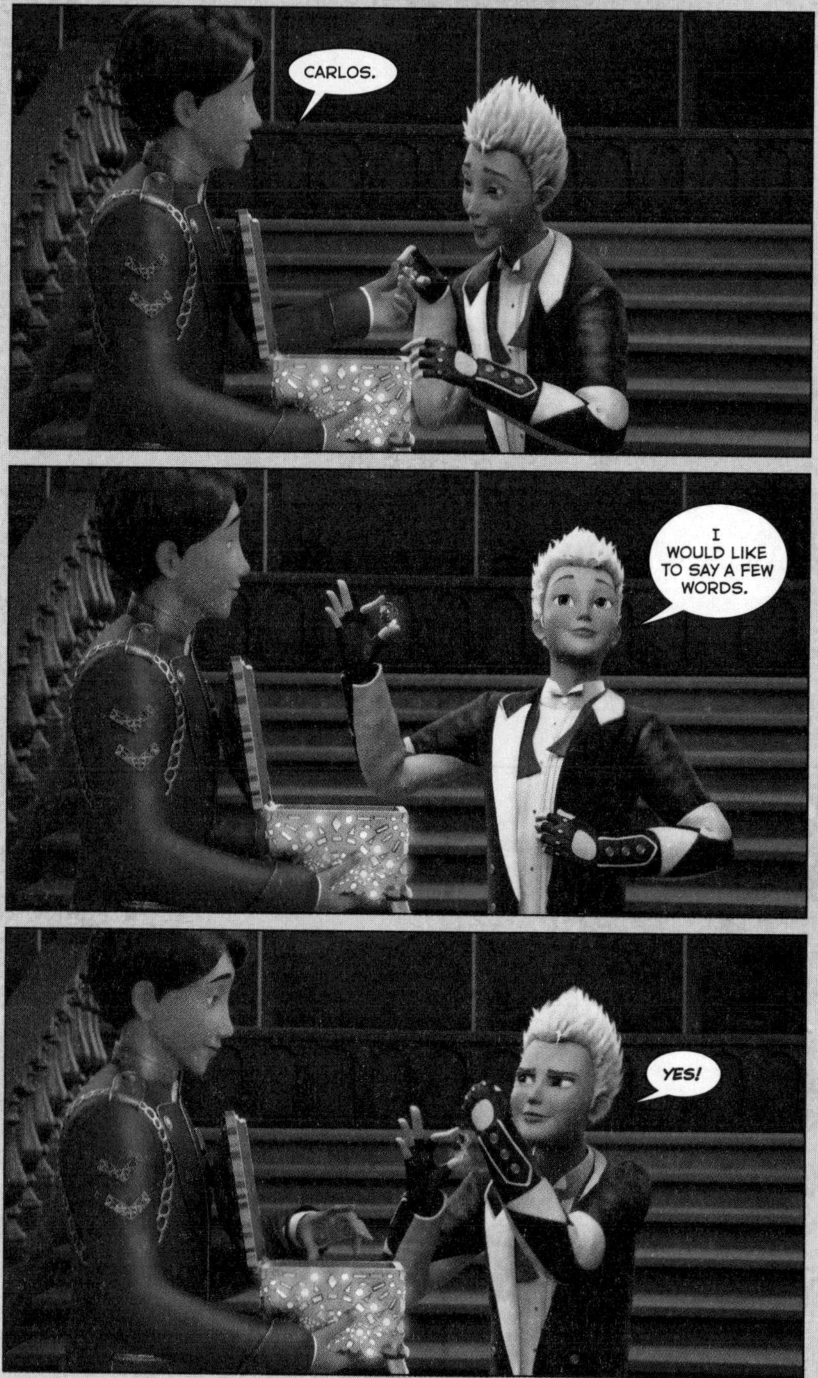
CARLOS.
I WOULD LIKE TO SAY A FEW WORDS.
YES!

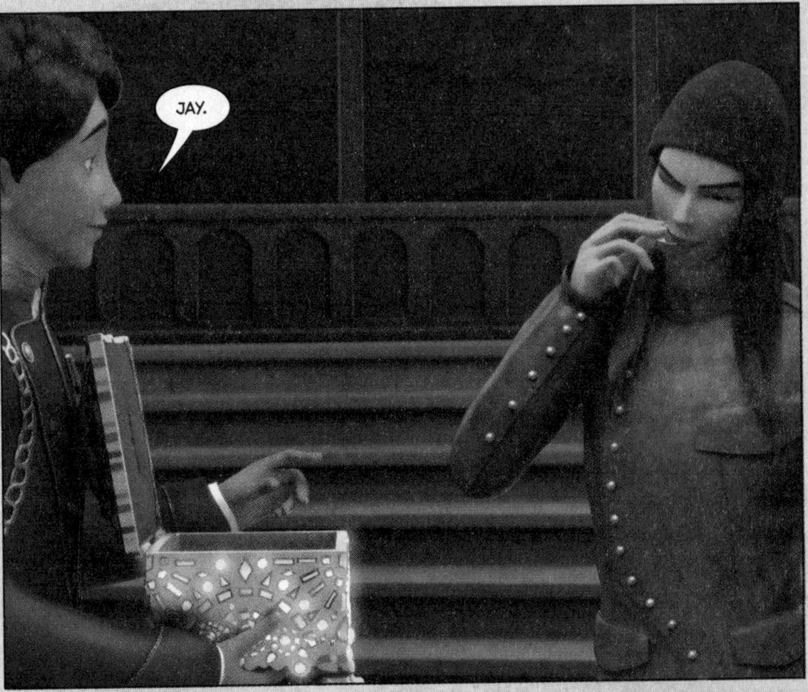
JAY.

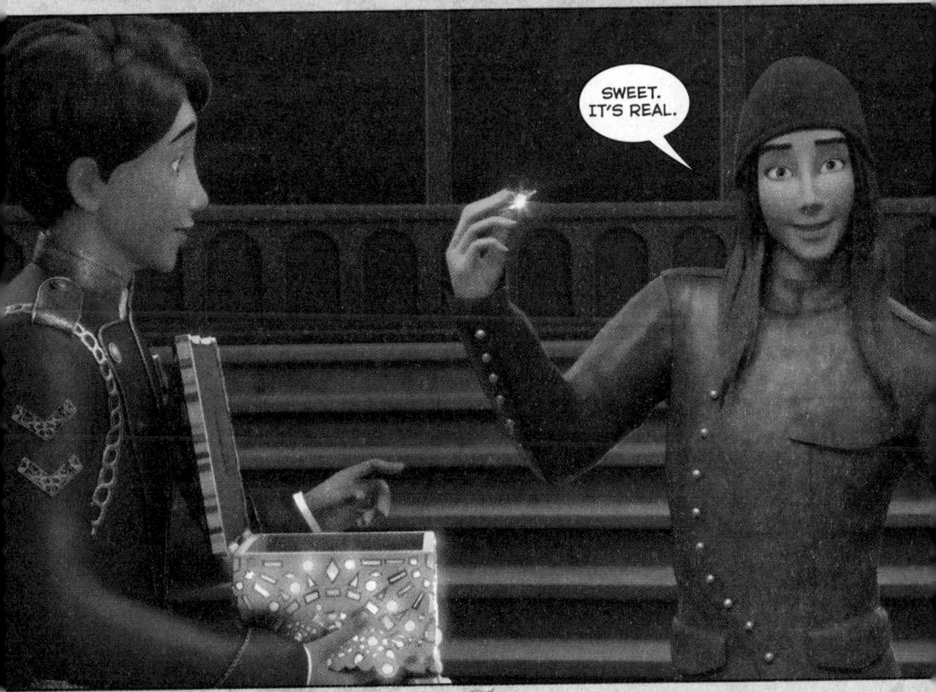
SWEET.
IT'S REAL.

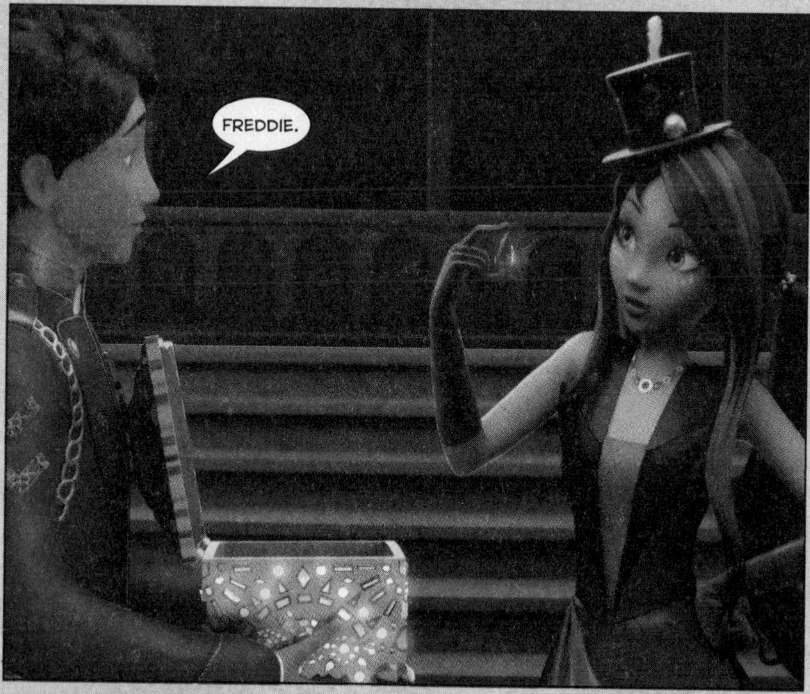
FREDDIE.

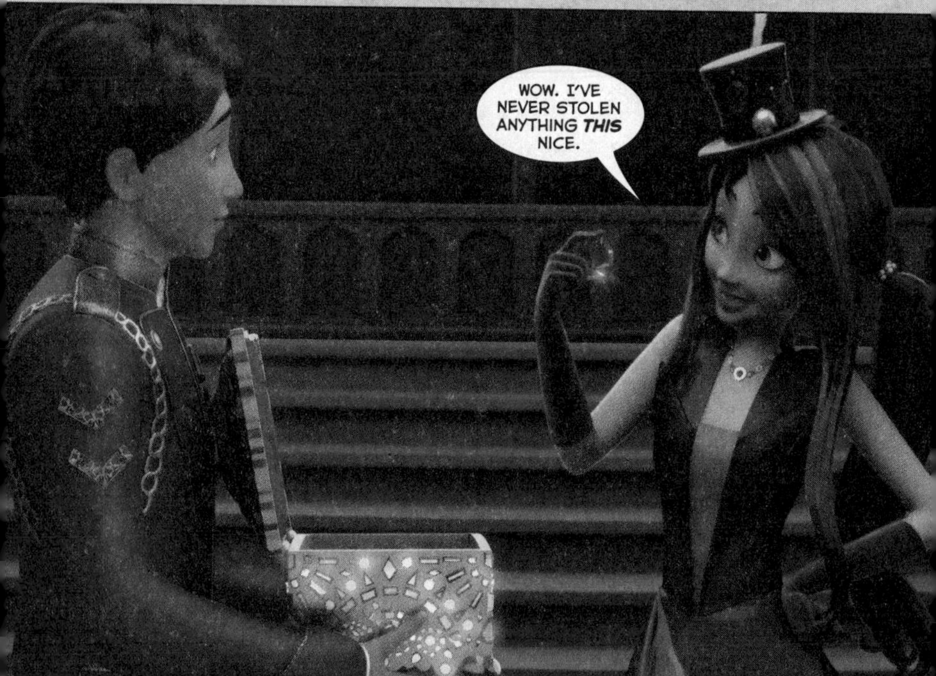
WOW. I'VE NEVER STOLEN ANYTHING *THIS* NICE.

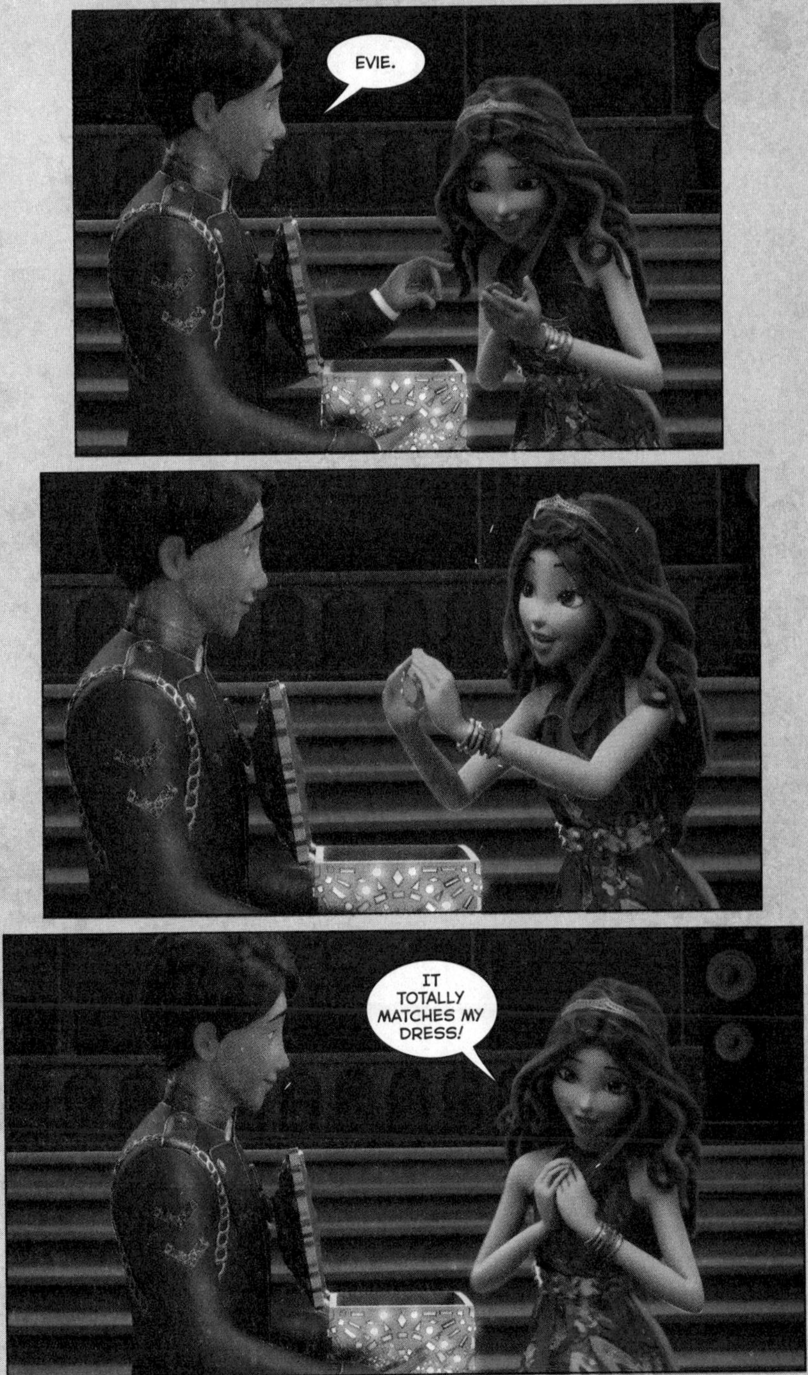
EVIE.
IT TOTALLY MATCHES MY DRESS!

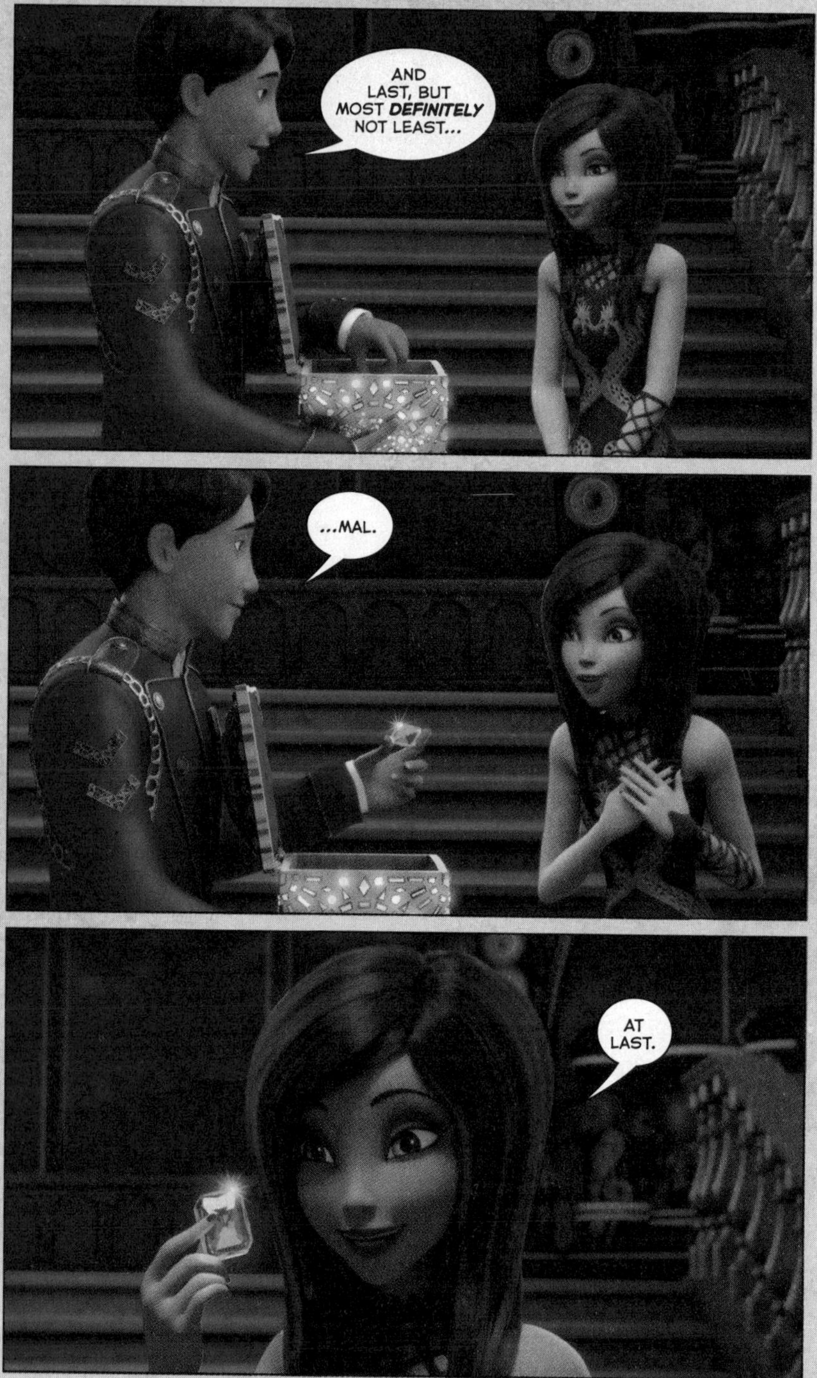
AND LAST, BUT MOST DEFINITELY NOT LEAST...
...MAL.
AT LAST.

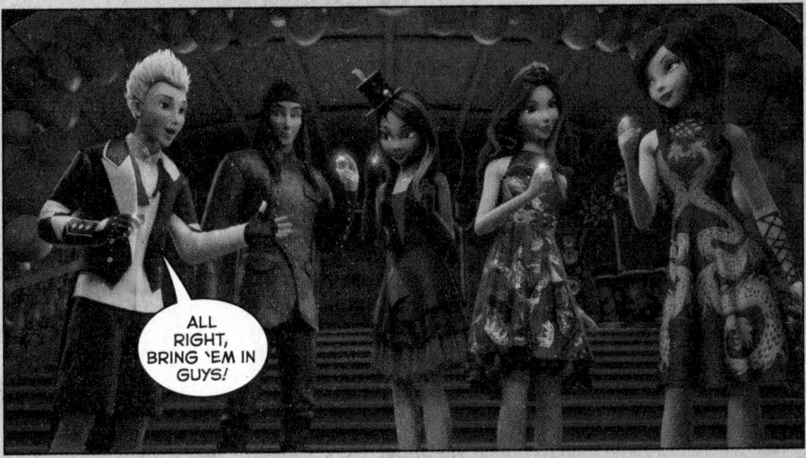
ALL RIGHT, BRING 'EM IN GUYS!

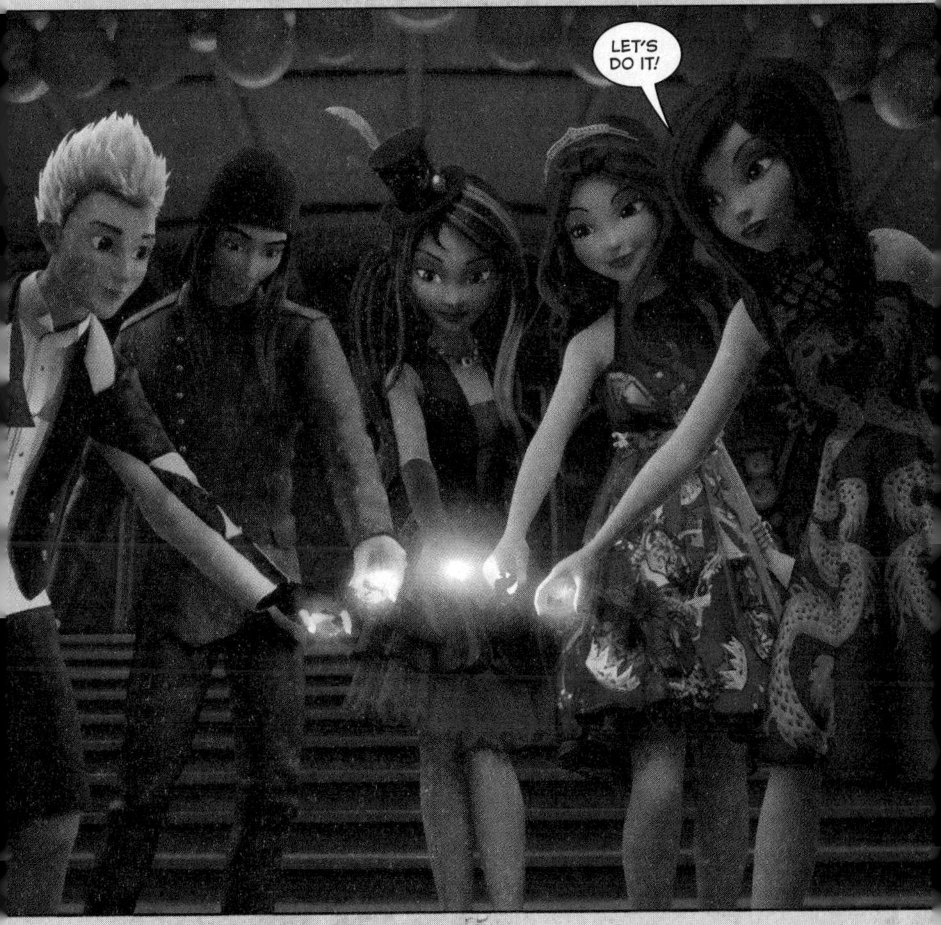
LET'S DO IT!

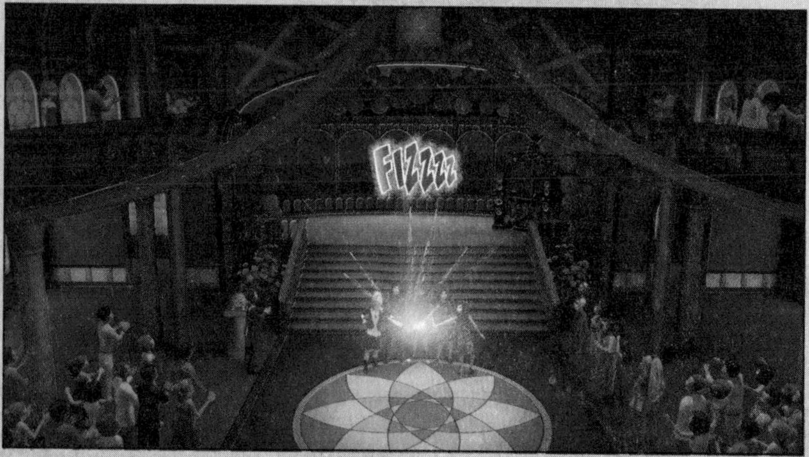
FIZZZZ

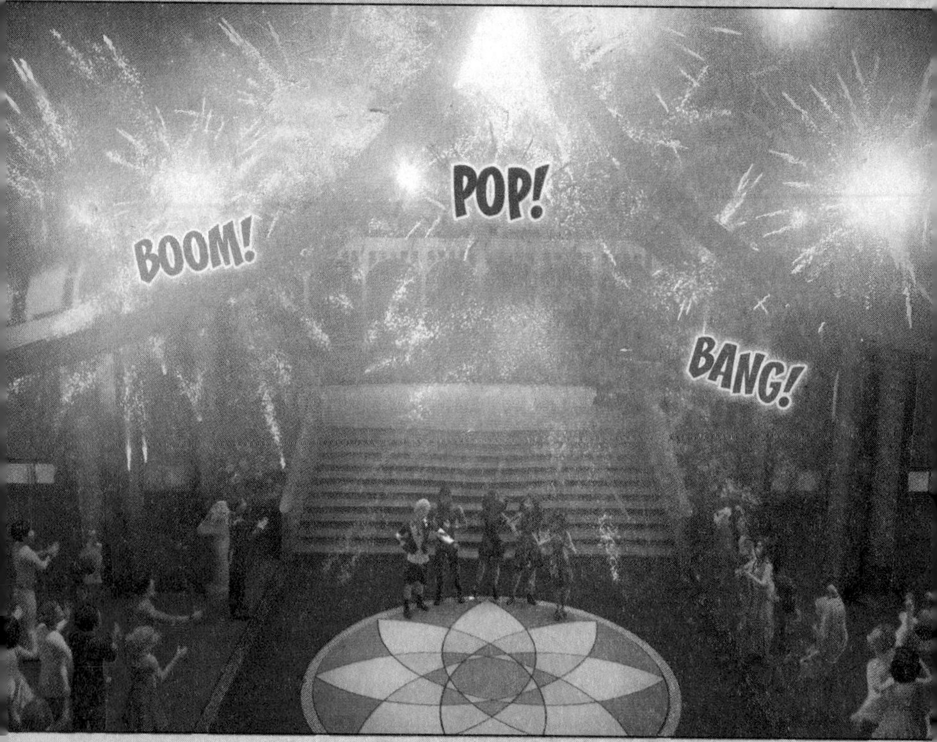
POP!
BOOM!
BANG!

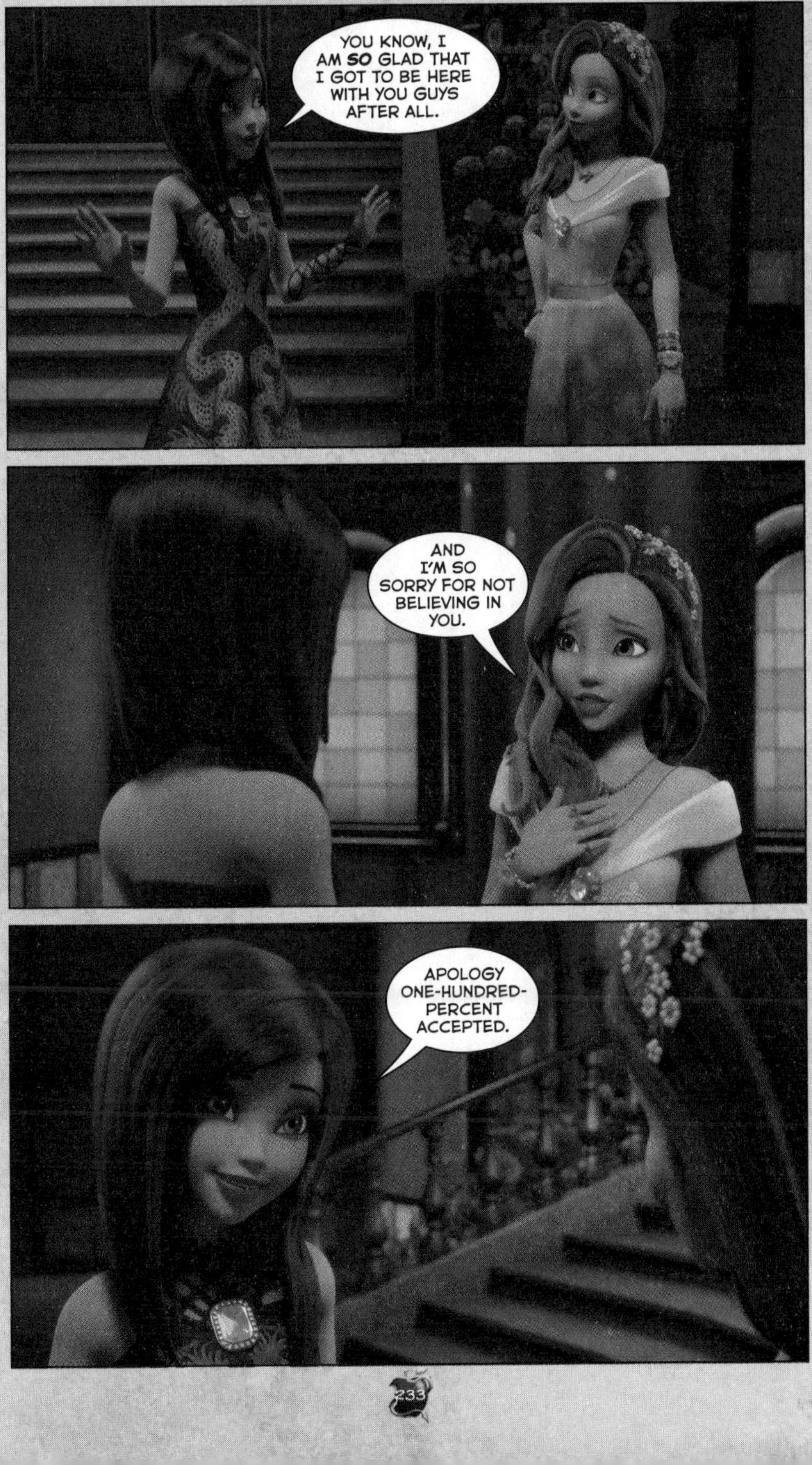
YOU KNOW, I AM **SO** GLAD THAT I GOT TO BE HERE WITH YOU GUYS AFTER ALL.
AND I'M SO SORRY FOR NOT BELIEVING IN YOU.
APOLOGY ONE-HUNDRED-PERCENT ACCEPTED.

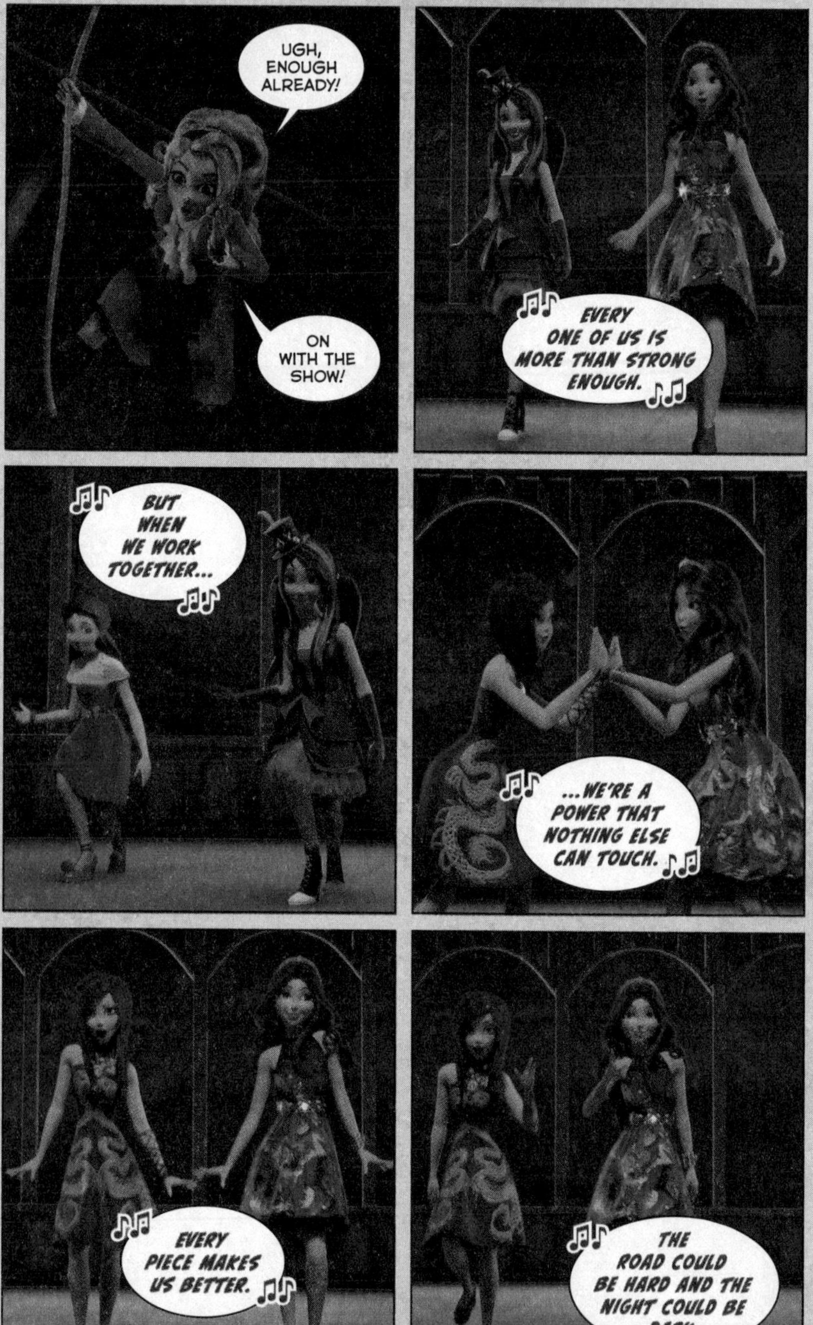
UGH, ENOUGH ALREADY!
ON WITH THE SHOW!
EVERY ONE OF US IS MORE THAN STRONG ENOUGH.
BUT WHEN WE WORK TOGETHER...
...WE'RE A POWER THAT NOTHING ELSE CAN TOUCH.
EVERY PIECE MAKES US BETTER.
THE ROAD COULD BE HARD AND THE NIGHT COULD BE DARK.

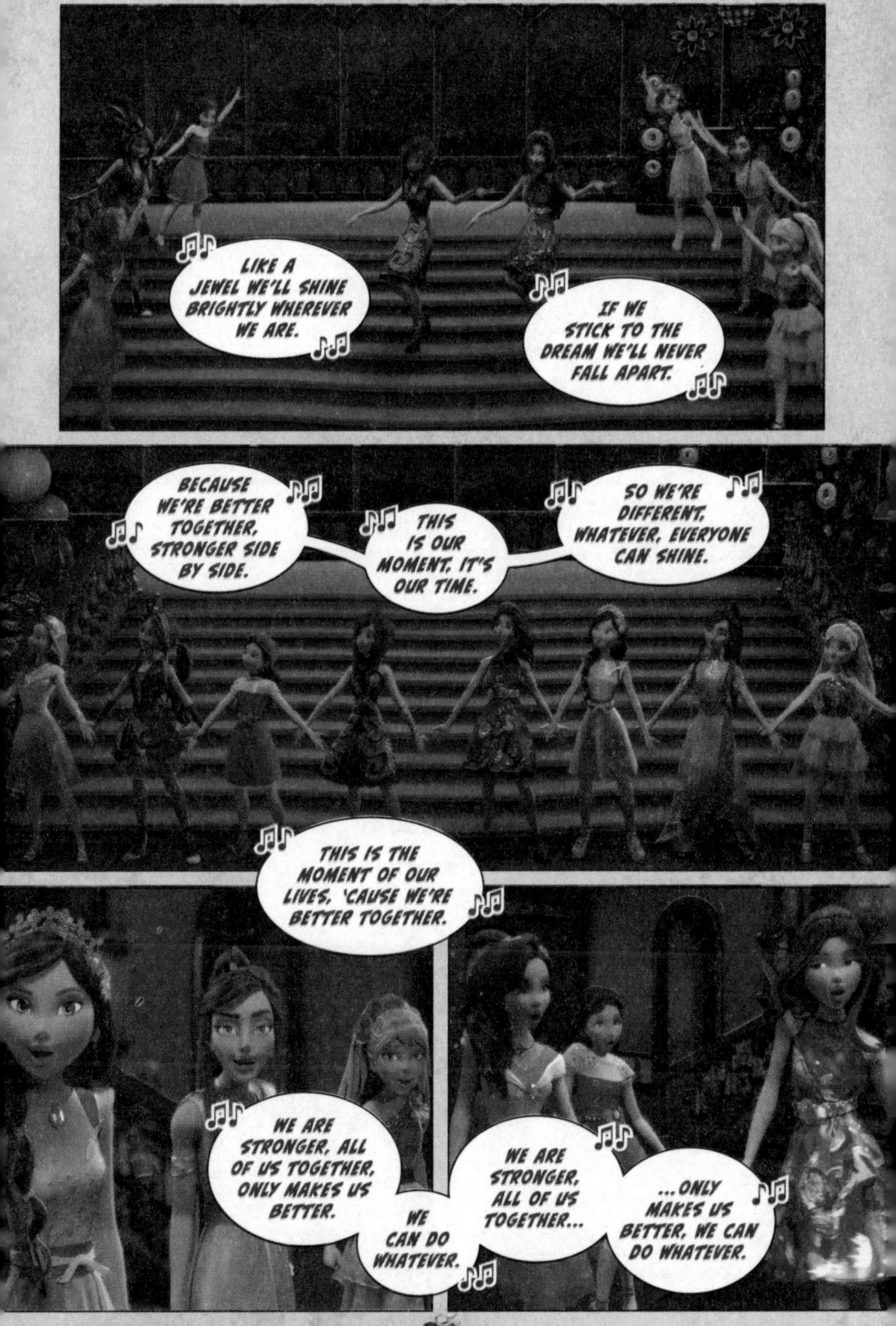
LIKE A JEWEL WE'LL SHINE BRIGHTLY WHEREVER WE ARE.
IF WE STICK TO THE DREAM WE'LL NEVER FALL APART.
BECAUSE WE'RE BETTER TOGETHER, STRONGER SIDE BY SIDE.
THIS IS OUR MOMENT, IT'S OUR TIME.
SO WE'RE DIFFERENT, WHATEVER, EVERYONE CAN SHINE.
THIS IS THE MOMENT OF OUR LIVES, 'CAUSE WE'RE BETTER TOGETHER.
WE ARE STRONGER, ALL OF US TOGETHER, ONLY MAKES US BETTER.
WE CAN DO WHATEVER.
WE ARE STRONGER, ALL OF US TOGETHER...
...ONLY MAKES US BETTER, WE CAN DO WHATEVER.

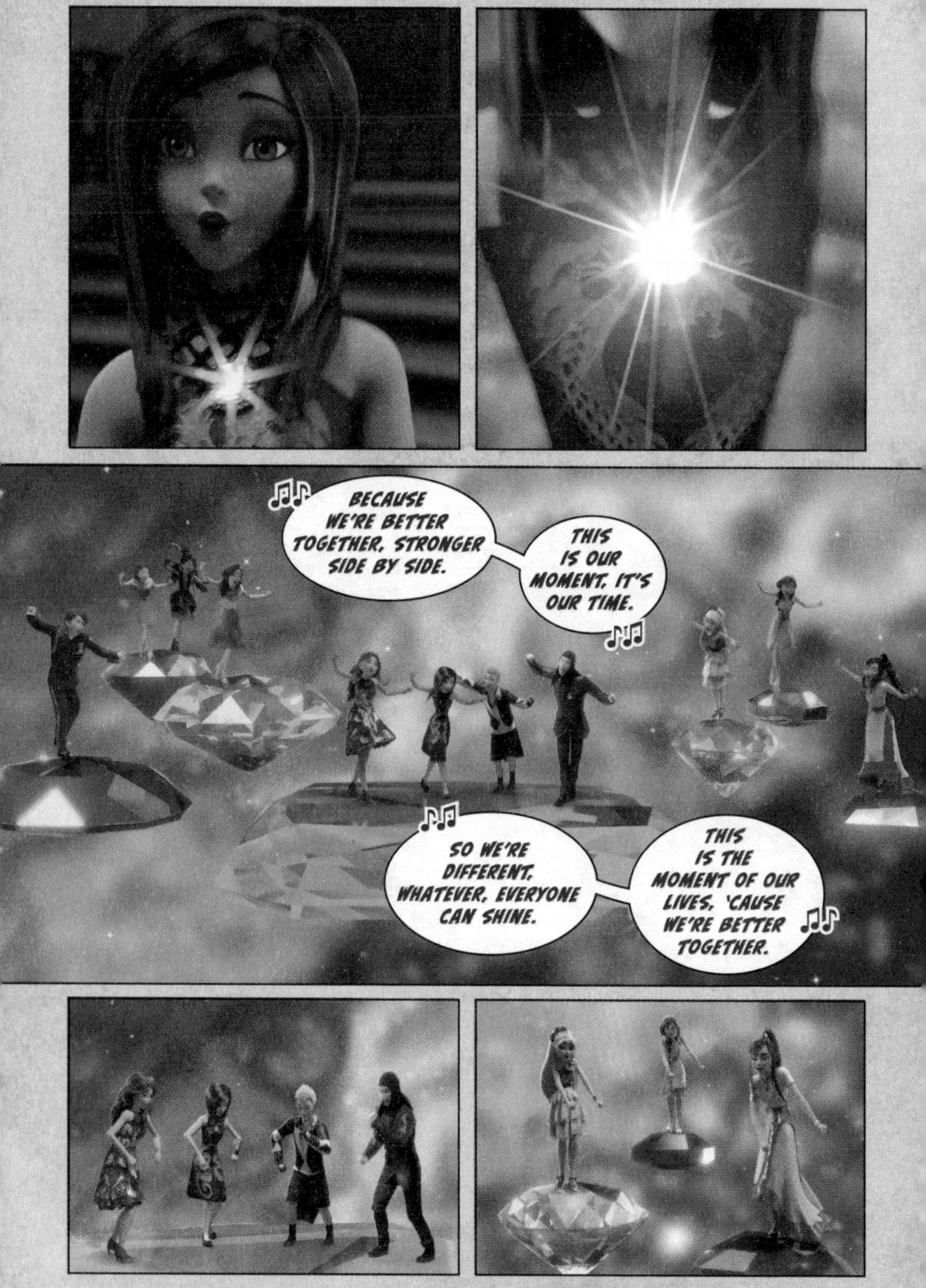
BECAUSE WE'RE BETTER TOGETHER, STRONGER SIDE BY SIDE.
THIS IS OUR MOMENT, IT'S OUR TIME.
SO WE'RE DIFFERENT, WHATEVER, EVERYONE CAN SHINE.
THIS IS THE MOMENT OF OUR LIVES, 'CAUSE WE'RE BETTER TOGETHER.

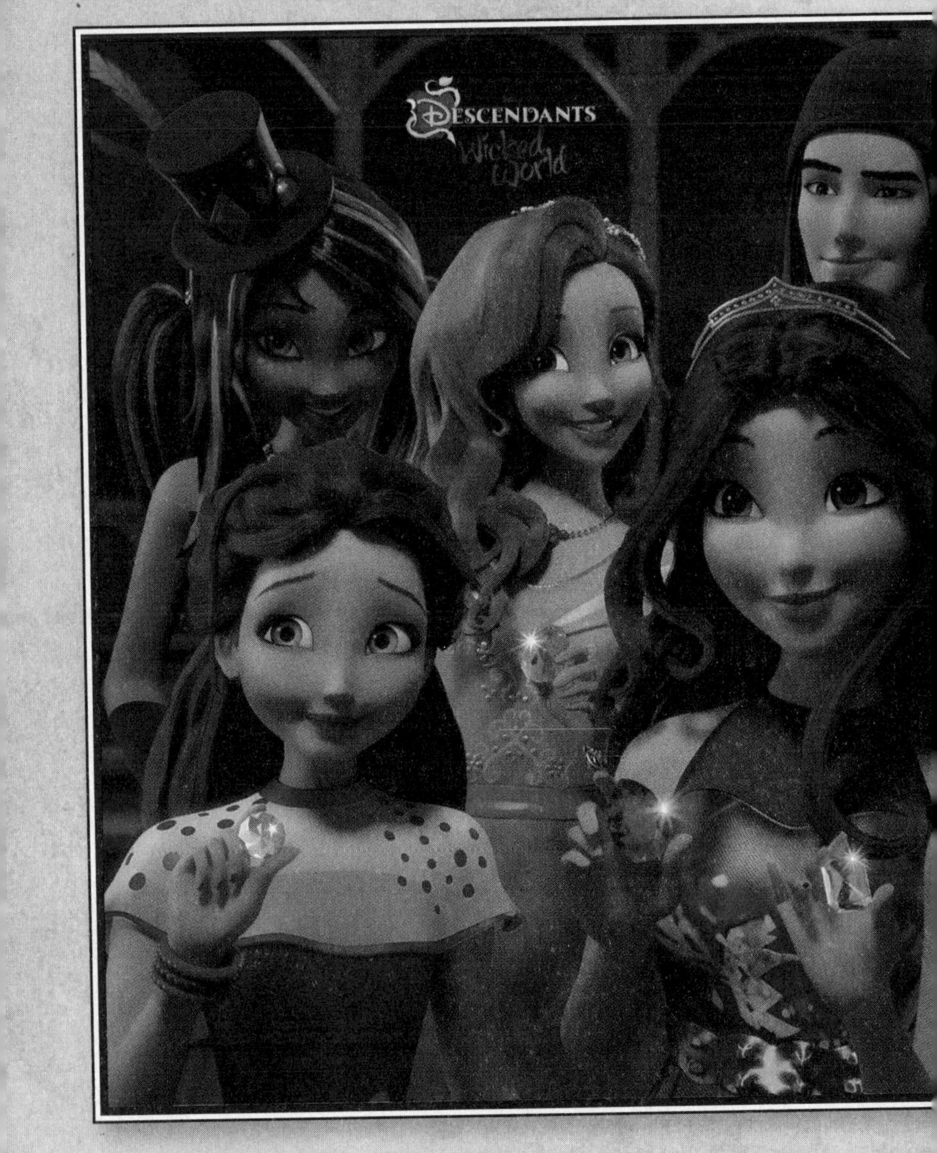
DESCENDANTS
Wicked World

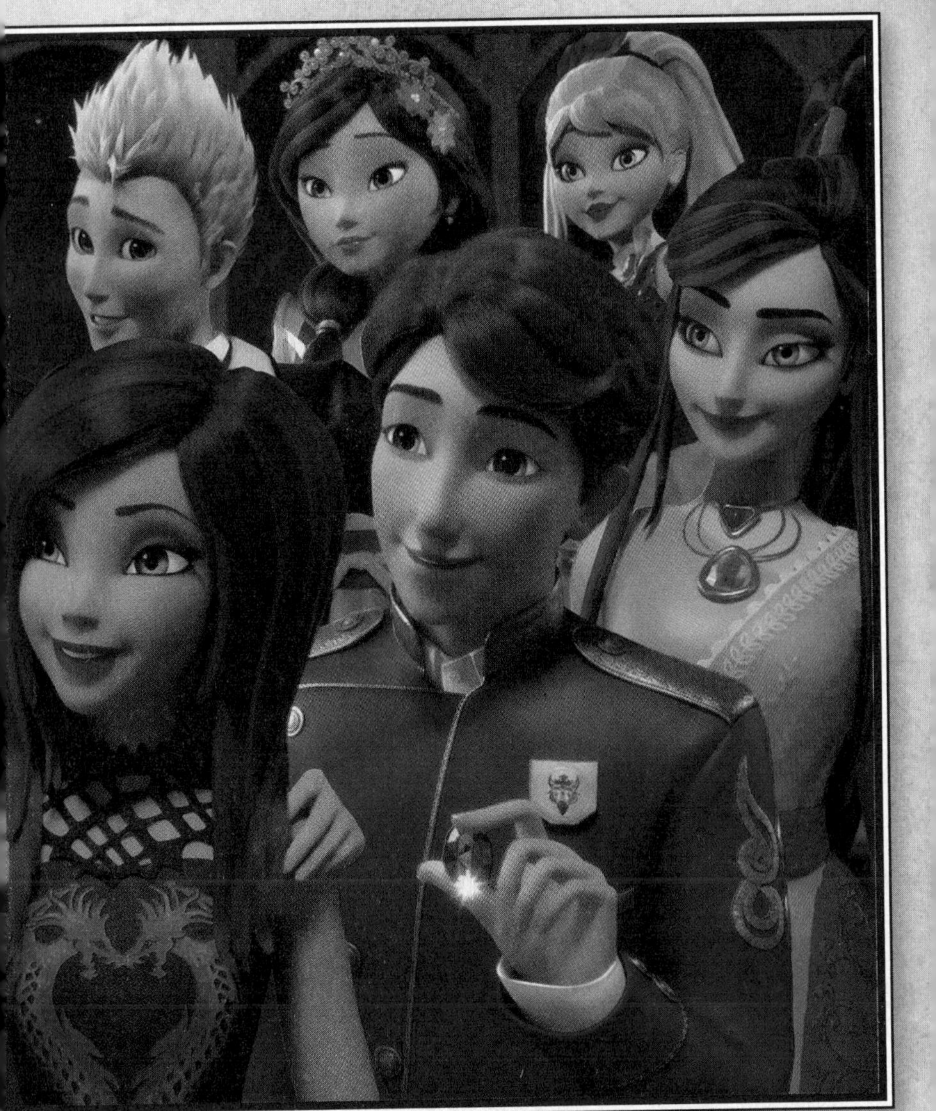

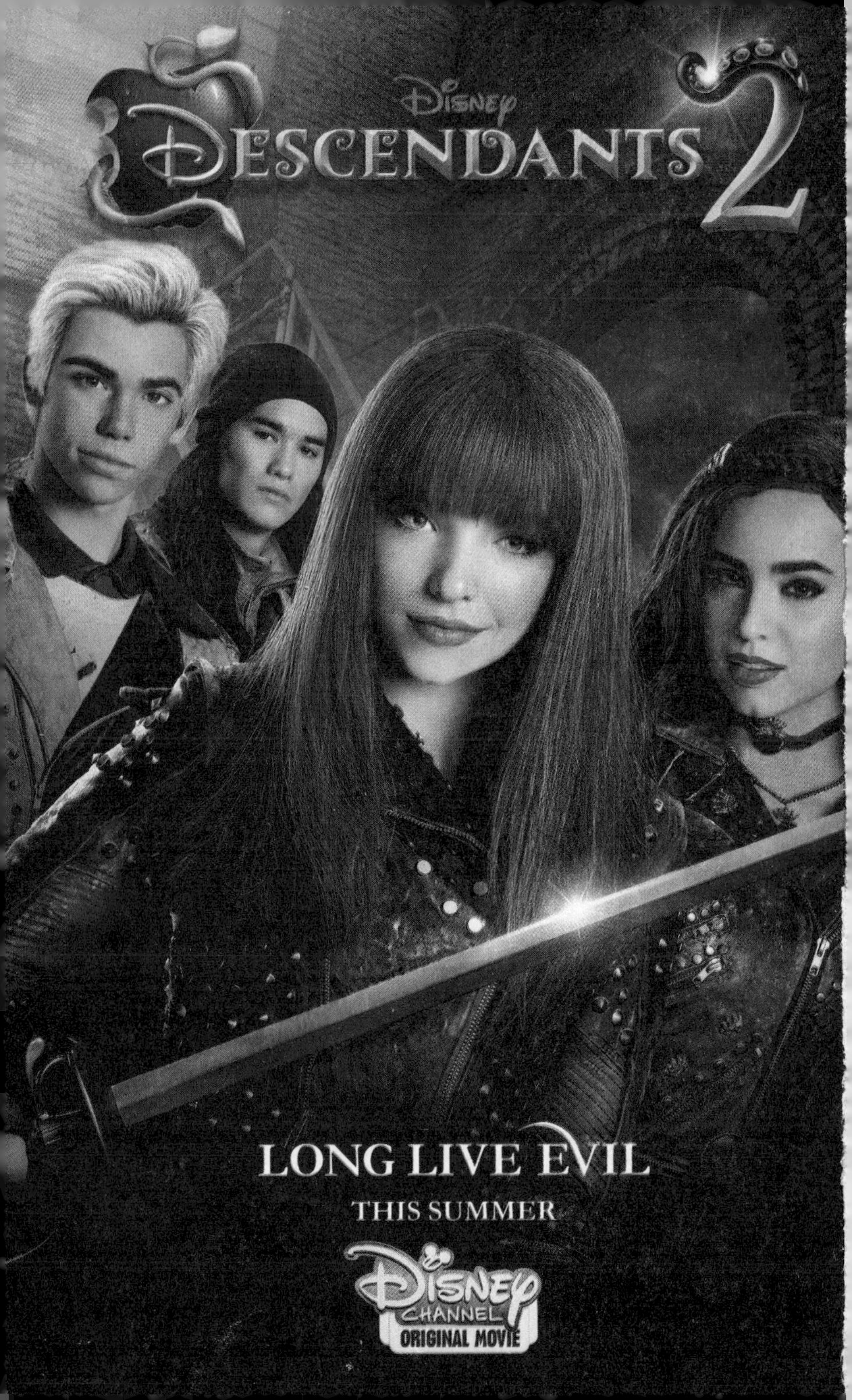

Disney
DESCENDANTS 2
LONG LIVE EVIL
THIS SUMMER
Disney CHANNEL
ORIGINAL MOVIE